J.M. FREY

THE SKYLARK'S SACRIFICE

For Grannie -
whose love and patience were always larger than I sometimes
thought I deserved, but who always made sure we all had more
than enough.

The Skylark's Song

(To the tune of the Klonn traditional drinking song
"The Seven Great Arts"; new lyrics unattributed.)

Upon the cold wind, can you hear that sweet note?
Clear, unafraid, and cyclical keening!
Look up, friends, look up, in the sky how she floats!
The Skylark, the Skylark, with white hair a-streaming!

A hero, a villain, a spy, and a knave!
Behind feathered mask, oh who can she be?
Who does she fight for, and who will she save?
Oh, look how she flies, proud and free!

Her pack hides six blades, her mask hides her face,
Her jacket hides a heart large as Frankin.
Her mind it is cunning, her skill it is ace,
And all used for peace, unless I be mistaken.

So be wary, brave soldiers; chin up men of Klonn!
Fight any and all, but the Skylark!
Our king's pointless war may yet soon be won!
And then he too shall fall prey to her mark.

For the Skylark is Sealie, and Benne, and Klonn,
And Frankin and Telniem and free.
She fights not for glory, nor wealth, nor for one,
No, she fights for us all, you and me.

Do not, oh, do not hear the king's accusation,
Instead, hear the Skylark's sweet song.
Look up, friends, look up, to peace's one champion.
The Skylark, with white hair, shall stay strong!

CHAPTER
ONE

The wind on her face was exhilarating, and Robin was intensely thankful for the amber lenses of Al's goggles. Grit from the streets below blew up into her face, and she had to keep reminding herself not to smile, or she'd be eating the rudding stuff. It tasted awful.

My belly might be full for once, though, she thought briefly, and then rolled her eyes at the ridiculous notion. *Right. And maybe you need to sleep more, too, Captain.*

The wind whipped her fringe into view, and Robin spared a quick second to adjust the scarf wound around the bottom of her face. Made from the remains of her sapphire gown, it kept her ghostly braid bound back, with the Coyote's hairpin to hold it closed. Yet tendrils kept escaping out the sides, and every time a lock of white hair flickered across the lenses of her goggles, she had to remember that it was her own, and to not be surprised. It had begun to grow back, at least—short, scrubby hair now covered the bald patches left by the shock of the accident that had claimed Al's life—but it was all coming in white.

She was still a ghost, but thanks to the Coyote's "generosity," she was at least a warm one.

Just one of the sapphire earrings she'd escaped with had yielded enough coin, when she traded it to a back-alley jeweler, to rent Robin a room above a tavern. She had nothing else to her name, not *even* her name, so she hoarded the money carefully, and never shopped for supplies. Proprietors could identify their customers, especially one with Sealie-dark skin and honey-brown eyes, even if they never saw her ghost hair.

Instead, she stole from laundry lines all over the city—a pair of dark leather trousers, warm socks, leather pilot's gloves, a thick woolen shirt, a felt vest, a tight double-breasted black jacket, and a pair of plain, serviceable woolen men's pajamas—and left a flat gold coin pinned to the lines in their place. She didn't dare venture to the markets for food, so she pilfered what she could from the bins behind the tavern and made due without when she couldn't find anything edible to eat that day.

She was used to going without. WINGS, however, could not. The rocket pack needed fuel if she wanted to stay aloft, and, well, there were plenty of ways to glide into an aeroship base when one was nothing more than a small black speck on a moonless night. She could get the fuel she needed.

She could do this. She could . . . she could do this.

Stay in Lylon, and sneak, and scrabble, and sabotage. She could use the rocket pack she had stolen right out from under the Klonnish king to disrupt his supply lines, destroy his aeroships, scare his soldiers. She could use it exactly the way . . . the way he . . .

No, Robin scolded herself. *No. He's dead. He helped you. And you killed him. You left him to burn. He's gone!*

She had to stop thinking about those final moments in the woods, about the way his eyes had glittered with fear, and despair, and pride. About the way his kiss—his last kiss, her first real kiss—had felt pressed against her mouth. How she missed his constant presence *(Ridiculous! Didn't you used to find it stifling?)*, and how lonely it made her feel to be without it.

How homesick she was for her parents, the Air Patrol, Al.

Gods, shut up! Pay attention, Captain! she snarled at her reeling mind and aching heart.

You can get back home, she promised herself. *But only if you stop spinning your thoughts like a drunk honeybee and pay attention!*

Robin forced her gaze to the horizon. She was flying high enough above the sliver of countryside that separated the outer slums of Lylon and the first of the tall wire fences that encircled the munitions factory to the south of the city that she should be utterly invisible to the watchmen. She let herself glide in a circle on the updraft, breathing deep to clear her mind. She had to squint to see the refinery through the hazy night sky, the smog from the stacks leading off the smelting gallery thick in the air. But she'd drifted over this same handful of buildings nightly for at least a week. She had the guards' routes memorized, knew the buildings and what they each were housing, and had sussed out the best approach, even in the dark.

Tonight was the new moon. The sky was as lightless as it was going to get. And the talk she had gleaned from between the floorboards of the soldier-favored tavern below her little garret room had made it clear that there was a large shipment of aeroship fuel amassed here, ready for deployment to the front. It was literally now or never. The only thing holding her back was her.

A light frosting of snow made the footing slippery, and the landing precarious. Robin skidded a little as WINGS cut out, the weight of the pack tipping her onto her heels without the thrust to counter it. She wheeled her arms once before her feet skidded out from under her in opposite directions and she landed flat on her arse.

A giggle bubbled out of Robin's mouth, and she clamped her hand down on it quickly. *Omens, I wasn't this nervous on my first day as a mid-flight!* she scolded herself.

Robin held her palms skyward, praying briefly for luck, and for someone to watch her back. And then, pressing the buttons on the control box carefully, she powered down WINGS. The pack purred itself into silence. This roof was the last place anyone expected to find a Saskwyan pilot, so naturally, it was empty. Good thing, too, with that little topple. Would have been embarrassing to die just because she'd slipped. Picking herself up, Robin moved toward what appeared to be an access hatch in the corner.

She wasn't entirely sure what she was going to do once she was down inside the building—she had no blueprints, no keys, no idea what was really going on. But "blow it all up" wasn't exactly the kind of sophisticated plan that needed a lot of forethought. And what she did know was that, in the two months since she had resolved to use the Klonn king's prize against his own military, she had promised both herself and the gods one thing: she would only aim at machines. She refused to be responsible for the tears of any more Klonn widows and orphans. She had seen enough of that kind of agony. She'd lived it.

Robin had spent those first few weeks—or nights, rather—up in the air, getting the feel of WINGS and spying on the bases and munitions factories within a few hours' flying distance. Never going so close to the front lines, of course, that the spotlights and anti-aircraft weaponry would find her in their crosshairs. She had no doubt that even as small—and as clothed in dark colors—as she was, the attentive soldiers and snipers would be her doom. Klonn defense or Saskwyan—both would be as likely to shoot her out of the sky as they were to ask questions about how she was up there without a glider in the first place.

No. No. Staying here, staying hidden, finding a way to make all the pain and the anger and the fighting stop, that was her mission now. The gods had brought WINGS to her. And one did not reject gifts from gods. It was unlucky. Not to mention rude.

So she had crouched on many a roof, eavesdropping,

watching, and learning much about how the Klonn organized their forces. She had sat in the corners of taverns, let her bottom get pinched in her efforts to get close to drunken soldiers with loose lips and a desire to impress any shapely thing willing to thank them for their service. She said little, understanding more and more Klonnish each day, as braggarts drenched her brain with their beer-fumed words. She had clung to the sides of buildings, and rifled through offices at night, searching for maps and diagrams, anything she could easily read, feeling grateful for that horrific, long ago primer in the Klonnish alphabet that he had given her to read in the . . . at the . . .

Focus.

She had picked this munitions factory as her target specifically because she had observed it was a primary source of the fuel supplied to the monstrous Klonn aeroships. Great truckloads of it left here every day for the base, and Robin was well aware that WINGS couldn't run for much longer without more fuel.

She'd had good fortune stealing what she needed in dribs and drabs from the canisters in the backs of transportation vehicles, but what she really needed was a secret stash of her own. *Before* that stash was shipped en masse to the front and the tanks here were left empty for the time it took to refine more.

Robin crossed her fingers and brushed away any lingering gods of ill-luck, just to be sure. Then she scuttled toward the hatch. The ivory hairpin, along with her small screwdriver, proved useful in picking the lock. She climbed down the ladder, careful not to bang WINGS against anything on the way in.

Omens, she thought, when she was a few steps down the ladder. *This place is way bigger than I thought. At least twice the size of the canteen back home. How many aeroships do the Klonn actually have?*

She ended up on a grating high above the factory

floor, on a catwalk that ran the expanse of the large building. On either end, a set of rungs had been cemented into the walls, but to her left there was a small observatory, its walls cut out to allow golden lamplight to spill across the roof. Robin ducked, and when she was sure she hadn't been seen, she crept in the opposite direction.

Below her, on the smooth gray floor, rows upon rows of giant copper vats were lined up, filled with fuel just waiting to be decanted into travel canisters. Most had massive, bullet-top lids clamped across the wide top of the tub, circular valves holding them shut. There were rows of portholes, though, all at eye-height—if one was standing on the ground—and behind those portholes lay beautiful amber liquid, bubbling and oh so very explosive. Two stories up, around the upper edges, they were accessible by more spindly metal grating and ladders.

Two of the vats had their tops open, workers in greasy coveralls peering over the side with dipsticks and clipboards—easy enough to toss some little bit of flame into the fuel. And Robin had brought something a little more significant than "a little bit of flame" with her.

At the end of the catwalk, she found a large brass bell hanging from a thick leather rope. While her Klonnish wasn't great, she did recognize the word for "fire."

"Perfect," she said.

Then she picked it up and rang the demons out of it.

The reaction on the floor below was instantaneous. Workers frothed like sea foam to the exits, and the catwalk shook with the pounding beat of a soldier running to see who had rung the bell. By the time he got there, Robin had used a controlled fall and WINGS to get down to the factory floor, and was huddled in the shadows of some sort of hideously noisy machine that seemed to be used to push fuel from one vat to another. She watched the soldier peer around the catwalk and, when he found no one, glare suspiciously at the bell. Eventually, he returned to the ground, following the last of the workers out. When it sounded as if the place was mostly empty, Robin stood and looked around.

Shelves of massive, round fuel storage cylinders lined the walls by the loading bay doors. Keeping to the shadows, but moving as swiftly as she was able, Robin went over to study them. There was no way, even with WINGS, that she would be able to take a whole cylinder. It was twice her height, and the same width. The pack would never have enough thrust for her to lift with it, and she wouldn't be strong enough to hold on, even if it did.

These are a lot bigger close up. I can't just grab one and go like I thought.

The first shout came from the front of the factory just as Robin spotted the cheap metal pot, resting on a thin metal tripod. The lid was held on with clamps that gave when Robin pried at the levers, and it was just big enough that Robin could have curled up and hidden inside—if she didn't have WINGS on. Filled with water, it had a spigot at the bottom that told Robin it was probably used as a refreshment station for the folks who worked back here, where there was little fresh air. Carefully turning over the pot, she poured out the water, dried the inside with the ends of her scarf, made sure the spigot was tightly closed, and then turned to the giant fuel cylinder. Like the fuel vats, the top of the transportation cylinder tapered into a point with a circular valve. From what she had seen, peering through the fence of the Klonn Air Base, there was some sort of hose that was supposed to connect to the valve, and the cylinder was tipped upside down to glug, like a wine bottle tipped on its end, into the tanks in the aeroships.

Robin had no hose, nor the rigging contraption to safely tip over the cylinders.

The shouting and the sounds of footsteps were getting closer—a man on one side of the factory shouted,

"*Nema!*" He was answered by another in the middle, and another on the far side.

They were doing a sweep for fire, Robin realized. And all too soon, they would find something else.

With no other quieter alternative, Robin whispered, "Gods protect me," and gave the nearest cylinder a shove with her shoulder. It wobbled, and then fell. Robin skittered back, fearing the thing might explode. Instead, it merely rolled, knocking into its compatriots and sending them toppling like dominoes. The noise attracted the attention of the Klonn. She was running out of time. She dragged the metal pot over to the cylinder, opened the valve, and jumped back just in time to avoid getting soaked in aircraft fuel. On its side, the majority of the fuel remained in the cylinder, gravity keeping it from being able to flow away—but enough did escape that it filled the metal pot and overflowed into an amber river. The air filled with fumes. Gingerly, Robin picked her way around the puddles, clamped the lid onto the pot, and then ripped the end of her scarf off and used it to wipe the sides clean.

"*Loa!*" someone shouted in Klonnish, and Robin turned, dipping the end of the swatch of fabric into an amber puddle. A man stood behind a complex machine, pointing at her through the workings. It would take him a few seconds to scramble under it to reach her, and Robin used that time to pull the metal pot well away from the fuel on the floor. Then she bent down and started the burn on WINGS's exhaust.

"Get out of here!" she shouted at the man, then added, "*Nema, nema!*" In her clumsy Klonnish, she said: "I am make fire!"

The man froze, eyes going wide, face going white when he caught sight of the fuel all over the floor, and the gently smoking exhaust of WINGS.

"*Nema!*" he cried too, but by then, it was too late.

Robin dangled the end of her fuel-soaked scarf scrap under WINGS, and it flared into hot, noxious flames. They licked at her gloves, and she quickly threw it at the nearest puddle.

It ignited with a soft *fwoosh*.

Fire crawled across the floor. The man screamed and fled. Robin slammed her hand down on the ignition, and, clutching the pot tightly, shot into the air. She ducked around the catwalk and burst out of the roof hatch just as the first warning rumble echoed through the factory. Robin slapped the button on the control box for the stabilizing blades with her chin, and they sprang outward with their signature whistle. The musical chord was followed mere seconds later by a resounding *boom* that shook the sky and threw Robin off course.

The space between the factory and the slums was barren. But it also wasn't that wide. Especially when someone had the force of an entire factory exploding behind them, radiating out in ripples as the fire consumed each vat in turn, pushing them along like carefully timed detonations of a blasting stick. As the shockwave she was surfing reached the first row of houses, Robin was absurdly glad that none of them seemed to have glass in their windows—no unfortunate bystander would be blinded tonight, at least. That was something.

She tumbled through the air until, swinging the pot around as a counterbalance, she managed to find her equilibrium—and not a second too late. She pulled up and just barely kept from smashing into the ledge of a roof. Kicking out, she used her toes to push forward over the lip of the gutter, missing a collision with a crumbled window gable.

What she didn't manage to avoid, however, were the laundry lines.

WINGS caught on the thick cording, and Robin was unceremoniously whipped around. She dropped the metal pot and frantically swiped at the control box, cutting the thrust and detracting the blades so they wouldn't bend if she fell on them. The pot rolled across the flat roof, but the clamps on the lid held. It came to a stop against the lip of the gable. Robin's prize was safe.

Robin herself, though . . . she was tangled upside down, one foot thrust up in the air like a bird in a net. The ragged end of her braid tickled her nose. The rest of her hair was trapped in the line, tugging painfully at her scalp, and she could feel the end of the ivory hairpin poking against her nape where the fabric covering her hair had come free. Cording clinched around her ankle—the bad one, godsdammit—and pinned the arm with the control box behind the small of her back, her other wrist aloft and her elbow turned painfully. She'd lost one of her gloves somewhere along the way, and the night air nipped at her exposed fingers.

She felt, all told, utterly ridiculous.

"Omens," she snarled. "Rudding, frozen *coal-bags*—"

She tried wriggling, but it only seemed to make the tangle squeeze tighter, pinning her more thoroughly. In the distance, the factory belched great fireballs into the air, lighting up the night like a Gods' Day celebration and spewing great clouds of smoke and ash. Her worry was temporarily muted by a surge of fierce joy at the sight.

I did it! she thought. Robin Arianhod had successfully flown WINGS and sabotaged a whole munitions factory, destroying a stockpile of fuel, and yet stealing enough for herself at the same time. Her first mission was a complete and perfect success. *Except for the part where I'm stuck like a pheasant in a snare.*

Robin sighed, craning her head around, trying to figure out how to get out of this ignoble predicament. She was about to try to jam the control box against her own arse in the hopes of activating the switch that deployed the wing blades when a voice in the darkness said, "Impressive."

In Saskwyan.

Robin craned her neck, squinting at the shadows in the many corners and gutters of the roof.

"Who's there?" she asked.

A swath of darkness detached itself from the others, and resolved into a woman. She wore skin-tight, black leather trousers with a thick dark jacket, and had a black scarf wrapped around her hair and the lower half of her face, much like Robin did.

"Who are you?" Robin asked. Her face flushed with the blood running into her head, and the knowledge that she must look pretty ridiculous tangled in the laundry line, skinny legs waving in the air like an overturned chicken. Thank the gods for her trousers. She didn't want to think about what her predicament would be like if she'd still been in that sapphire dress of months' past.

"You do not need to know just yet," the woman said, and her voice betrayed her breeding. Whoever she was, she spoke with the same calm, precise tone as the Coyote. The same lack of contractions. Klonn, definitely, despite the language she presently spoke. "I, however, know who you are."

She pulled a small square of paper from a pouch strapped to her thigh and unfolded it, holding it upside down so Robin could read it. Printed in three alphabets—Klonnish, Saskwyan, and Frankinese; though aggressively neutral as a country, she supposed there was nothing saying Frankin's individual citizens couldn't be opportunistic—there was no mistaking the meaning.

WANTED ALIVE

Saskwyan Air Patrol Officer; Female,
approx. 17-20 years old. Sealie.
Suspected to be hiding among the rebels
of Lylon.
Consider extremely dangerous.

Robin's fear flowed away in a rush of rage as she stared at the bounty notice. The poster was accompanied by a fairly accurate sketch of her face, and a quote for an obscene amount of money. Though her name was nowhere on it, nor was the current color of her hair, Robin knew without a doubt that this would be enough information for anyone looking to line their pockets with honey. It was all she could do to keep from screaming in frustration right there.

The woman crouched and reached forward to brush Robin's braid out of her face, presumably to get a better look at her features. Then she shook her head and clicked her tongue.

"Hold still," she instructed. She folded away the poster, stowing it once more in the pouch on her thigh, and pulled a knife from her boot.

Wild panic surged through Robin's chest, and she thrashed against the lines holding her in place. "No, *nema*, no!" she cried. "It said alive. I need to be alive for you to get your reward! It's a lot of money!"

The woman laughed. "Ai. Good for you I have no need for a reward, then. Now hold still before you throttle yourself."

The woman grabbed Robin's hand—the bare one—attempting to still her, and then stopped, staring at the crisscross of puffed white scar tissue lining her palm. "A pilot," she said. "But it names you Sealie. And your hair . . ." The woman reached out again and turned over a lock. "Interesting," she said, and then she lifted her knife.

"No," Robin whimpered. She squeezed her eyes shut. If this was to be her death, she didn't want to see it. Sure, she was brave—behind the controls of a glider. But now? She had no desire to watch the blade plunge toward her breast, to anticipate its bite slipping between her ribs to pierce her heart. She waited for a breathless second for the blade to slam home, but nothing happened. Carefully, she pried open one eye.

The woman in black stood there, laughing silently at her, as if Robin were a rudding puppet dancing for her amusement.

"What's so godsdamned funny?" Robin snarled.

The woman lifted the knife again, and Robin cringed. One of the woman's delicate eyebrows arched meaningfully, and then, slowly, she set the blade against the laundry line and began to saw.

"Oh," Robin said, sagging against the lines.

Neither spoke as the woman cut Robin free, helping her land gently—and upright—on the rooftop. Then she stepped back and resheathed the knife in her boot. Crossing her arms over her chest, she regarded Robin with a cool, assessing gaze that made Robin's heart constrict with the bitter ache of familiar memory—she'd seen that look before, in a different pair of light-colored eyes. Still, the message in the woman's body language was clear.

"You're letting me go?" Robin asked, mentally cataloging each of her limbs and joints, shaking them out to banish the pins and needles, and making sure that nothing was sprained or broken.

The woman nodded. "There are those, even amongst the Klonn, who believe this war has gone on long enough."

Robin nodded, too—there was no arguing with that

logic. All the same, she took a step back, out of grabbing range, and toward the metal pot. "Good, 'cause I kinda agree."

"You certainly speak like a Sealie. How refreshing!" The woman smiled. "Rest assured, Sealie pilot of the Air Patrol, you have a friend in me, and my people."

"Your people?" Robin asked, scooping up the pot, checking that the seal had held.

The woman spread her hands. "*Ai*. Others. Like me."

Robin smiled faintly. "People who dress in black and cut Saskwyans from nets?"

The woman laughed out loud this time, and it was a pretty, studied sort of sound. "Among other things."

Robin knew that there were Saskwyan operatives in Klonn, had heard all about their exploits—exaggerated or not—at many a canteen table. Now, for the first time, Robin wondered if they ever truly acted alone. If there wasn't someone else out there who had been aiding them all along. And if those same people would be willing to aid her.

After a brief moment of consideration, she shook her head. She couldn't hand over her own safety to that, with neither proof nor trust. She couldn't afford to invest in such a hope, not without backing. It would be foolish. And she'd had enough of being foolish.

"Thank you for the offer, but I can take care of myself."

"Can you?" the woman asked, eyes cutting to the shredded remains of the laundry lines. "I wonder."

Robin bristled. "I've been doing fine until now."

"You are too open," the woman said. "You are clumsy. I found you tonight easily. And if I can find you, the bounty hunters will have little problem doing the same."

Robin scowled. "No," she said. "This is my fight, my people I protect, my people I honor. I won't be a pawn in whatever scheme a dissatisfied Klonn noble dabbling in some half-baked, underground resistance might have."

The woman barked another laugh; this one sounded more genuine. "You call me noble! How quaint! But let me assure you, we do more than dabble. I offer a warm place to sleep, so you might rest before a mission. Good food, so you are not distracted by hunger. And current intelligence, to plot your excursions with more precision and effectiveness."

Robin mulled this over, that previous hope flickering to life like an ember stoked in a predawn hearth. As much as she wanted to stay a solo operative, as loath as she was to place her trust in an ally wearing the skin of her enemy, she was cold, and lonely. She couldn't deny the appeal of camaraderie and real logistical support. But she also wasn't willing to sell her autonomy for shelter and food of uncertain quality and reliability. No, until she knew who these people were, what they could really offer, and, more than that, what they could actually do to help her, she was better off on her own.

"I'm good," Robin said at length.

"Do not mistake ego for strength," the woman warned. "War is a desolate thing."

"Oh," Robin laughed, "that, I know. But let's say that I do decide to take you up on your offer—and that's a really big *if*—how would I find you?" It wasn't a promise. She wasn't ready to trust the first proclamation of affiliated ideals, not yet. And she wasn't about to go from being an agent of the scrubbed-up Benne nobility to just another soldier in someone else's army—if said army even existed. Still, it couldn't hurt to save the possibility of connection, could it?

The woman reached behind her head and withdrew a hairpin from her black scarf. On the end was a delicate rose, crafted out of fine, thin glass. Even in the harsh half-light of the distant factory fire, it sparked with jewel-like beauty. She held it out to Robin. "With this."

Okay, so hairpins must have more meaning than I thought, Robin realized. She'd never thought to analyze or catalog the accessories in someone's hair. What clues, what messages had she missed by not paying attention to people's pins? Had she been missing a huge cultural thing all this time, or was she reading too much into something innocuous?

"I see," Robin said, not really seeing at all. She reached forward and accepted the proffered pin. Then she reached back and used it to secure her own braid in a firm coil against her nape, crossed against the ivory one from–from *him*–like sheathed daggers.

Robin's fingers lingered on the ivory cameo of the wolf's head. She tugged at the fabric of the scarf, making sure the wolf pin was covered, feeling stupidly protective of the only real gift the Coyote had ever given her, the only thing of his she still had to call her own. Whatever secret message was in his pin, she didn't want to share it with this stranger, even if she didn't yet understand it for herself.

This is for me. Just for me.

The woman sighed heavily and shook her head. "Be careful. And be secretive."

Robin bristled at the chiding. "Yeah. Thanks. I got it."

"See that you do," the woman said, her eyes narrowing with a shrewd glance of warning. "I believe you will need us sooner than you think. What do I call you?"

Robin thought of the funny little bird she had seen in the woods outside her prison-palace, how it was brown and plain, how its cry had been plaintive as it sought its partner. She remembered how it dove from the sky, fell upon its mate with a fierce cry of joy; how they had danced together. She thought of how she had dropped down upon the factory, and of the duet she and the Coyote had cut through the clouds over the front lines, the same tense and stalking dance that had played out in his dining room and salon. She thought about dancing in the air with Al, about dancing through dinners and chess games and verbal sparring with the Coyote. It was the name she had given *him* to call her, just *him*.

But he wasn't here anymore.

"The Skylark," Robin said. "I'm the Skylark."

The corners of the woman's green eyes crinkled in amusement. "Very well, *Skylark*," she said. "You are free to fly."

When she got back to her lodgings above the tavern, a second red glass, rose-shaped hairpin, a perfect match to the one in her braid, rested on Robin's pillow—an ill portent if ever the gods had given her one.

"Omens!" she swore. It was now painfully clear that the woman, or her people, had been following Robin the way Robin had been stalking her own prey. She would have to find somewhere else to stay, and immediately. Fear stabbed briefly at her as she realized that, regardless of anything else she'd said that night, the mysterious woman was right—if she could find Robin so easily, who else could?

Much as she didn't want to admit it, it had been clumsy of Robin to hide so openly; renting a room and hanging around the taps, eavesdropping visibly, had been, in retrospect, completely foolish. Though she had always made a point of covering her head with a scarf, though she had always flown out of her bedroom window to avoid the stairs, though she'd spoken as little as possible, Robin had been, admittedly, naive.

She chafed at the scolding, echoing through her thoughts in the strange woman's voice. She thought she had been careful.

Clever.

Clearly not.

Hissing at herself, a litany of *godsdamned, stubborn, you never learn, Robin, you just bull ahead, oh, a genius in the sky, but tactics were never your strong suit, stupid, stupid* ran through her mind as Robin packed everything she called her own into a pillowcase. Her plan was to refuel WINGS, shove some food in her face, and go. But just as she unclipped the lid on the metal pot holding WINGS's fuel, the telltale pound of heavy boots—and a shouted, *"Loa, deh!"*— thudded up the creaky stairs.

Hastily, Robin recapped the pot. Then, hefting everything as best she could, she swung the window wide and launched herself into the night. Behind her, the bedroom door slammed against the wall, kicked open with force enough to shake it in its frame. A single popping whir echoed behind her as she sprang from the sill, followed by the whiz of a bullet passing beside her ear.

Too close.

Robin pointed herself upward, preferring height over distance for now. WINGS snarled and chugged, annoyed by the extra weight of the fuel and clothes, and Robin's own belly rumbled in harmony.

"Soon," Robin told the ornery pack. "Dinner for us both soon, my friend." She glanced down at the fuel gauge—maybe twenty minutes of flight time left; thirty if she used the blades to glide for a bit, which would be difficult with the extra baggage, but no more. She peered down past her legs. Lylon had shrunk to a safe distance, the people below no more than a child's toys on the street, the houses safe and quaint-looking, with their glowing windows, their smoking chimneys dusted with snow.

Safety, Robin thought. *Quiet. Somewhere far enough from the center, but not so isolated that I'll be an oddity* . . . Even Klonn cities had slums, places where people kept their eyes on their own business, where survival often required tight lips and blind gazes, places where a ghost could be just that—invisible and forgotten. Robin turned her gaze northward. Behind her, the munitions factory to the south of the city still glowed cherry red, thick black smoke billowing up to form an ominous halo around the moon, blotting out the stars. But ahead of her, the sky over the deep forests that separated Lylon from the wreckage of the front was clear.

If Robin squinted, she fancied she could make out the tiny red and white flashes that marked the place where the anti-aircraft weaponry sat ready to bring down anything larger than a bird of prey.

Could go around it, Robin thought, hefting the pot of fuel higher on her hip. *Fly out to the Malfi coast, skim up the cliffs, sneak back into Saskwya from the north, and then . . . and then . . . then what, Captain Arianhod? Sit down behind the yoke of another glider, let another Benne cow tell you what to do, get yourself killed, or kill someone else? No. Cut off the blood supply, and the body goes into death throes; destroy the Klonnish supplies, and their army will have to surrender.*

Stay, she reminded herself. *You promised to stay. You promised the gods. You promised WINGS. You promised . . . well, no.* She had never made that promise to him. Hadn't even come up with the plan until after he'd already . . . after the pistol had . . . but it didn't matter. She'd promised it to him, too, in her heart of hearts. Promised him the end of the war, the way he'd wanted.

Having finally caught her breath, and knowing that she didn't have the fuel to linger in the sky for much longer, Robin angled herself down and began skimming the northern buildings, searching for some indication of a safe place to roost. Landing on a crumbling clock tower to scout the grounds of what appeared to be an abandoned community pleasure complex—an overrun garden, bandstands falling to ruin, and small pens she supposed once held exotic animals—she found a roof that gaped open to the elements. When Robin slipped down through the hole, she found the attic empty of all but some cob-webs, a layer of thick gray dust, and boxes of some sort of garish holiday decoration. There was no sound of life below her, except for the soft scratch of rodents.

Perfect.

Satisfied with her newfound "home," Robin took the time to refuel WINGS, and then herself, though she was a bit more stingy with parceling out the meager rations she'd managed to steal away from the tavern kitchens and back-alley bins. Then, both of their bellies full, Robin decided there was no harm in building a barricade against the wind with the boxes; she used them to surround a pallet she made out of swags of moth-eaten fabric from flags and pennants, like those found on castle walls. There was no place in the attic to lay a fire, though, and she didn't dare waste the precious fuel she had to keep herself warm.

Shivering, Robin shook her hair free of the pins and plait, hoping it would at least keep her neck warm as she laid herself down on the miserable little bed and cuddled WINGS—and its strange, ever-warm casing—close. If she wept a little in frigid, self-pitying misery, well, that was between her and the gods.

She certainly didn't dream of the rose woman's offer. Warm beds, plenty of food, and the promise of up-to-date information wasn't worth throwing herself back into Klonnish captivity, no matter how enticing the trappings. She'd had enough of that the last time.

She might be miserable, alone, and cold. But at least she was free.

CHAPTER THREE

Aside from the tangle with the laundry line, the mission had gone pretty well, Robin decided the next morning. A shaft of sunlight through the crumbled opening of the roof warmed the room slightly, and she had managed enough sleep to feel cautiously optimistic about the whole relocation thing. She'd roughed it in training camp before. She could handle this. Absolutely. And if she was honest, if she allowed herself to think about it, this was still a far sight better than the night she'd spent locked away in the Coyote's cold pantry, or the weeks she'd spent in the ostentatious, gilded cage of the bedchamber he'd convinced their "hosts" to afford her. At least here, she was free.

Breakfast consisted of the last of the dried fruit and old bread she'd pillaged, and she debated the merits of bundling up in one of the old fabric swags and using some of her hoarded coin to buy more. She longed for sharp green vegetables, fruit that was crisp and juicy, bread that was warm and soft.

I wonder what Klonn officers break their fast on, Robin thought as she suited up and strapped WINGS in place, using both the wolf and the rose hairpin to secure her braid under her scarf. She was still missing a glove, though. Rudding hells. She'd need to steal one, or procure another pair somewhere. *I could go find out. The train depot's not too far from here.*

The thing about supply trains is that they need tracks. And train tracks, luckily, were very easy to spot from the air. The day was thick with low-hanging fog and ominous clouds, the perfect weather for staying hidden while scouting low. Robin knew where the depot was from previous excursions, but today, she decided, she would actually set foot on the cobbles. See if she couldn't find some new gloves, perhaps an actual aviator's hat with soft fur lining and ear-flaps. And, of course, whatever front-line rations she could snag.

Fresh vegetables, and fruit, and bread were a nice fantasy. But they wouldn't keep, not in her attic-fort. What she needed was hardtack, jerky, and a water skin.

WINGS's haunting chord was hushed as Robin used the blades to steady her descent into the train yard. She landed near the back of a train that was pointed north, toward the front and Saskwya. Workers were closing up the box cars a few carriages up, and Robin ducked under a massive cart filled with coal and covered with an oiled-canvas tarpaulin to see if she could figure out what they'd loaded into the covered transportation. The doors on either side of the box cars were locked, but a quick burst of power from WINGS had her on the roof, where there were loading hatches. These too had locks, but they were smaller, and nearly identical to the ones Robin had picked in the factory fields outside of Pyria.

One by one, car by car, Robin made her slow, soft, silent way up the train. Most of the cars were filled with bullets and rifles, blankets and camp cots, medical supplies and lanterns. In one, Robin found a big carpet bag filled with carefully rolled gauze. After a split second of hesitation, she flipped it open and dumped it out. She then put only the barest of necessities back inside—a small medic's field kit, a pair of woolen socks (probably knit by someone's mother) from a crate full of them, candles and matches, two bundles of blasting sticks, a single thick blanket, a new pair of mechanic's gloves (which she promptly put on), and packs upon packs of rations bundled in waxed paper and tied with string. The guns, she left. She had vowed that she would do every-thing in her power to avoid killing. No more lives. Just an end to the conflict.

When she reached the front of the train, she realized she had a decision to make. If she left it intact, she could keep coming back to this yard to pilfer what she needed. But she knew from the direction it faced that it would be used to resupply the soldiers on the front line—Klonn soldiers. If she sabotaged it, they would move the depot; she would never be able to "shop" here again. But it also meant that this whole train full of supplies would not be used against her countrymen.

Choice clear, Robin scrambled into the engine house. There would be other means of procuring supplies later, at another time. For today, now, she had made up her mind.

She cranked the hand brake to make sure the train wasn't going anywhere, and then closed the boiler as tightly as she could, trapping the water—and the steam it would soon create—inside. It was quick work from there to stoke the fire to life, shovel on as much coal as she could without smothering the quickly growing flame, and then, bag of supplies ungainly balanced, cross back across the tops of the box cars to wedge a blasting stick into the seam of each subsequent carriage. She risked snatching replacements from the munitions boxes she'd discovered, zipping in and out of the roof hatch she'd left open, and then ducked around behind the watching guards to alight on the roof of the watchtower, flattening herself to the shingles so her silhouette didn't stand out against the cloud-dappled sunlight.

The only warning was a deep, throaty, gulping rum-ble from the steam engine. Metal groaned, followed by the almighty shriek of it tearing and a horrible bang as the reservoir superheated and burst open like foil. Rivets shot out into the fog and pinged off the sides of brick buildings. A great shout and the clang of a warning bell followed, startling Robin as it echoed out from directly below her perch. She grinned at her own fright, heart thumping with adrenaline, and watched as the rush of air from the explosion fanned the flames in the stoking house, which set alight the fuse of the first blasting stick conveniently left in just the right place. A second explosion tore the engine in half, sending gouts of flame and chunks of hot metal flying, and Robin covered her mouth with her new glove to keep from laughing aloud as, one by one, the other blasting sticks caught fire and exploded, the cars passing the flame back toward the caboose in a rushing wave.

Workers poured out of the nearby buildings, a water truck screeched up beside the engine, and Robin decided it was time to go. She pushed off to the rear, sliding into the sky, using the billowing funnels of smoke as a screen and the heat of the updraft to glide up, up above the clouds, to where the sun shone fierce and bright.

Only then did Robin let herself whoop in triumph. *See?* she told herself. She could do this. She had *done* it.

And she had done it *alone*.

Robin laid low for the next few days.

WINGS got a tune-up, the ignition tweaked and adjusted until the pack flared to life with a rumbling, satisfied purr. Robin caught up on her sleep during the day, and spent the evenings monitoring the aftermath of the two explosions she had caused on either end of the city. No deaths were reported among any of the workers—so far as she could tell with her limited ability to understand Klonnish, at least—and while they were rebuilding quickly, the guards at each location had also doubled, which meant fewer bodies on the front as a result.

For her third strike, Robin saw no point in changing

the game. After a bit of sneaking reconnaissance, she decided that the aeroship hangars on the northwest side of the city would be her next target. Tonight, four days after her last raid, she would steal more fuel and set fire to the assembly line the same way she had to the fuel refinery. Only this time, she would be smart enough to gain significant altitude when she fled, to avoid any shockwaves that might ricochet outward.

The moon was just beginning to wane, and the air was so cold that frost climbed up all the windows. Robin's breath puffed in front of her face as she landed behind the fuel storage hangar in the aeroship construction yard. Despite the new pair of thick leather gloves (with conveniently wide welder's cuffs), her fingers were still freezing. Gloves meant for forge-work weren't, it turned out, the best at keeping heat inside their linings. She fumbled through a pouch she had secured to her belt, searching for her lock picks. Her fingers brushed the glass rose of the second hairpin, and she scowled.

She didn't need the rose woman, or her leash.

Once inside, Robin took the time to remove and refuel WINGS on the factory floor, and then put the pack back on. She filled two great water sacks with fuel, *then* knocked over a cylinder, and *then* rang the fire bell. Feeling smug about her success, Robin had already begun to climb to the roof hatch when she realized that not all of the workers had abandoned their posts.

Ten stayed behind, ranging themselves along the walls and walking inward to lay a net for their intruder. Thankfully, none of them thought to look up. Robin wedged herself behind one of the great metal roof beams and hid in the shadows cast by the searching lanterns below. She wondered if she should shout down a warning. She hadn't yet dropped the flaming match. They still had time to get out.

She hesitated.

I won't commit outright, willful murder, she reminded herself. *Not anymore.*

Shoving the still dormant match back into her pocket, Robin decided to cut her losses. She could torch the aerodrome another night. The Klonn were getting smarter, but she still had the ability to outrun them—for now. And retreat was the best option tonight.

While the men continued to inspect the storage cylinders, Robin used WINGS to slip up the wall of the hangar to the roof hatch. She stopped on a nearby rooftop, putting the heavy sacks down for a moment to rest her shoulders.

Right, okay. Now what, Captain?

She couldn't blow the fuel hangar just yet, but maybe if she used one of the fuel sacks as a propellant in one of the other buildings—surely there was something flammable enough in the manufacturing building to set off the assembly line—the searchers would abandon the fuel house and she could double back to firebomb it, as well?

While she contemplated her options, a low-level, familiar buzz filled the air. Turning swiftly, Robin was startled to see that one of the Klonn aeroships had emerged from the aerodrome and managed to take flight.

Hells.

It was already making an about-face, bearing down in her direction. She wondered for a moment how the blasted pilot could even see her in the dark. Then she remembered that even with the flames banked, WINGS emitted a soft glow from the tailpipes that reflected on the copper and brass of the pack's wires and gears. She was glittering in the night like a flickering beacon.

Idiot.

From the ground, when she was far up in the air, it looked like a particularly bright star. But standing still on an otherwise dark roof? It was a rudding target.

"Omens," she cursed and dove for the shadows of

a chimney stack, turning her back into the corner so the light was muffled by her legs. She pulled the fuel sacks in swiftly after her, and waited as the aeroship buzzed by overhead. It turned in midair, the stupidly steep banking technique and speed as horrifyingly familiar as the decoration now visible on the aircraft's tail.

Snarling out at her from the tailpipes was the furious visage of a wolf.

Robin's entire *self* exploded with chaotic confusion. Her whole body seized up with shock, fingers stiff on the fuel sacks, eyes wide and aching as she dared not blink, breath jammed in an uncomfortable lump at the root of her tongue. Fear warred with guilt, with panic, with horror. And below that, a stupid, small, fierce little ball of joy at the possibility that he had survived rolled through her guts.

Alive? her heart screamed. *He's supposed to be . . . he was . . . you never checked. You never went back. You left him there, left him burning, and—*

The aeroship came around and panic surged up, blotting out all other thoughts. Despite the hope her heart wanted to feel, her brain knew that there was no guarantee the person she longed for was the one in the pilot's seat. It was his 'ship—of that, she was sure—but wasn't it possible that, upon his death, someone else had stepped in to keep the myth of the hobgob alive? His flying style was signature, but not entirely unique. It could, with practice, be duplicated, couldn't it?

Couldn't it?

Robin found her hand on the control box, her internal debate devolving into a single stricken mantra of *escape, escape, escape,* before she came to her senses and yanked it away. The moment she took to the air, the Coyote, or whoever it was pretending to be him, would be on her. She would have to wait for him to give up. She couldn't risk the possibility that it wasn't really him. Or worse, whispered a small voice at the back of her heart, that it was him, and she no longer knew whose side he was on.

She simultaneously hated him for putting her in this position, for all the hurt he had caused, all the potentially needless worry and grief, and at the same time feared him, feared what would have befallen him when her escape was made known to their captors, feared what they might have done to the man she'd left behind in the forest. She grieved so powerfully for the loss of his comfort that she could not move.

Indecision left her stuck in the shadows, prey trapped in the gaze of a snake, while her insides writhed with confusion.

Just do . . . something! she chided herself. *Don't just stand here like a lump!*

It was clear that he knew which rooftop she was on by the way the aeroship circled back again and again to keep it in view. Was it an invitation? A warning? A threat?

Robin wondered if she could wait him out—eventually, he would have to land to refuel, if nothing else. If she just stayed where she was, she could conserve her own fuel, wait until she was certain she could get away, even if that meant giving up the opportunity to unravel the mystery. It was a good plan, a safe plan, and she hunkered back in the shadows, grateful again for the warmth of WINGS, especially since it looked like she was going to be stuck out of doors for a while.

Stay, wait, watch, she told herself. *And don't cry. Don't cry. You need your vision clear. Don't fog up your goggles.*

It was too late, though. She could already feel the burn behind her eyes, the lump in her throat dissolving into emotions so powerful, into relief and fear and guilt so palpable, that the only escape route was through her eyes.

A shout from a nearby rooftop, and the menacing

bark of a dog, put an end to all thoughts of being able to outwait the Coyote.

"*Ai! Loa!*" someone shouted, and Robin poked her head out from behind the chimney long enough to recognize the smoke-gray uniforms of the Lylon Night Watch. What were they doing on the Aeroforce base?

The reward, Robin realized. *They're poaching.*

"Rudding turds," she said to herself. Settling the fuel sacks so they hung down in front of her chest, and would act as further counterbalance, she slammed her hand down on the control box and shot up into the sky.

The Coyote was in the midst of a turn that would bring him back toward her. She flew straight at him, buzzing under his belly and off in the opposite direction. It wouldn't take her anywhere near the section of town where her new lodgings lay, but it was more prudent to lose him in the alleys of the slums than to inadvertently lead him back to her shelter. She'd already relocated once; she was loath to do it again. Behind her, the buzz of the aeroship grew louder; the Coyote had banked again.

She looked down her own body at the aircraft, and realized that he was gaining quickly. The propeller looked ominous from this angle, yet she didn't dare go much faster for fear of losing control, or ripping one of the fuel sacks. A single stream of fuel could get blown back by the wind and ignite her contrail, which would, in turn, engulf WINGS.

Having no desire to go down like a shooting star, she dove at the canyon of the streets below, shouting, "Out of my way, out of my way!" as she wove around horse carts and early morning pedestrians. The Coyote followed, but the wingspan of his craft wouldn't allow him to get between the buildings like she could. Desperate, Robin zigzagged through alleys and around blind corners, but the Coyote managed to keep her in his sights, cutting sharply whenever she turned and tried to double back.

"Godsdammit!" she snarled into the wind, the words snatched from her lips by her sheer speed. "Would you just leave off already?"

Robin's mouth went dry from the wind. Her shoulders ached fiercely, both with the weight of the fuel sacks and the amount of force she had to pile on to keep each turn quick and clean. If she ever made it back to her attic, she was certain that her waist and shoulders would be a bright patchwork of purpling bruises.

And then, the pack began to splutter. "Omens, no. No, no!" she cursed, angry at both herself, for not keeping a closer eye on the fuel gauge, and at the Coyote for forcing her to waste an entire, fresh tank of fuel in this ridiculous, juvenile chase.

She was already slowing down, she could feel it, and soon there wouldn't be enough thrust to keep her in the air. She glanced around, desperate, and spotted a park. It was small, practically black in the early morning light, but it was exactly what she needed. She tucked her legs up under her and pumped them in the open air, preparing to run when she touched down so she could maintain her forward momentum. She hit the grass with her boot soles, dashing to keep up. She cut the power on the box, tripped when the thrust cut out much more quickly than she had anticipated, and rolled into a dense copse of bushes.

"Ow," she said, fetching up against the trunk of a young, but nonetheless hard, tree. Then she went still, waiting. A bird overhead chattered at her, scolding her for making so much noise. Robin made a rude gesture at it and turned over slowly, peering up out of the foliage at the sky. The Coyote's 'ship circled the park several times before finally moving off toward northern Lylon—back in the direction of his country palace.

"Why would you go back?" Robin asked, watching the wolf's snarl vanish into the night sky. She hefted the fuel sacks, readjusted how they lay, and stood. Her bad ankle was complaining from the tumble, but it wasn't bad enough to keep her from walking on it—her banged-up elbow hurt worse. "Why would you ever choose to go back there? I don't understand."

It did, however, speak to the possibility that he had, indeed, survived—though it also meant that he'd likely been re-indoctrinated into aiding his captors' cause. If that were the case, then he'd likely also suffered for her escape. Robin's heart constricted at the thought, and she pushed the guilt that threatened to consume her away fiercely.

And then, of course, it started to snow.

"Oh, you've got to be rudding *kidding* me," she hissed.

There was nothing she could do about it, though, not if she wanted to avoid the Night Watch, so she bit the inside of her cheek, lifted her chin, and limped toward the edge of the park. She had never been to this section of Lylon before. It was filled with respectable houses with watchful servants, and therefore held few places to squat during the day. As it was, she felt terribly conspicuous traipsing through the empty, predawn streets in a pack and flying leathers, even if she was sticking to the shadows. But nobody came out of the houses to chase her. The great and the good of Lylon were all still asleep, apparently. For that, at least, she was thankful.

Robin kept her head and spirits as high as she could, which, by this time, wasn't much higher than her own nose. She was tired, hurt, cold, and hungry. The fuel sacks cut into her shoulders, and the belt of WINGS was rubbing after so many hours in the pack. She missed Mama and Papa, fiercely. She missed Wade. She missed Al.

She missed the Coyote. Or rather, she missed what the Coyote could have been. What he had *told* her they could have been.

But despite the pretty words he'd said to her, he—or at least, his ghost—had just chased her across the sky, downed her in a park, and left her for the bounty hunters to find. It made her feel isolated in a way nothing else quite had. If she was honest with herself, she could admit that she'd held those final moments in the forest with him close, had found solace in carrying the Coyote's memory in her heart, purpose in avenging him by enacting his own plan for WINGS, and now . . . perhaps it was childish and overly romantic, but it had been the fuel to her fire. And now even that had been stripped away. For a moment, a pervasive, desperate despair touched Robin's soul.

She wanted this to be over. She wanted to go home.

Of course, the closest thing she could hope for was a freezing attic, open to the elements, and what food she might be able to bribe out of a traveler with her velvet purse. Feeling more miserable than she had in weeks, she slumped back toward the dilapidated building she now called home, with its unknowing and absentee landlords, brushing snow off of her shoulders.

As she crossed before one of the straight, clean houses that lined the street beside the park, a curvaceous woman stepped out of the shadows. She was dressed in little besides a low-cut coat, and Robin wondered if she was looking at Klonn's version of a prostitute. The woman didn't look cowed, or ill-treated, or starving, though. She just looked beautiful and shrewd.

"Take it, Skylark," the woman said, thrusting a bundle into Robin's hands, and then she turned back to the shadows and disappeared into the house from which she'd come, using the servants' entrance to escape the cold. She was gone before Robin could argue, or respond with her surprised thanks. So instead, she merely accepted the bundle and, not daring to go after the woman, made her hurried return to her own hideaway. When she got there, she managed a careful sort of spluttered flying up the side of the building, digging her toes into the brickwork. Inside at last—such as it was—Robin gratefully set down the fuel sacks, unclipped and removed WINGS, and then untied the bundle.

It was filled with bread and cheese, cured meats and winter apples, a bottle of milk, and a small glass rose. Robin was too hungry to curse, and too grateful to resent the people stalking her. She shoved this new hairpin into her pouch to join the other one, the original still in place at the back of her head.

Deciding to refuel herself before her pack this time, Robin shook the snow off her clothing and devoured everything. It was good, and fresh, and Robin felt significantly more human when it was all gone. She cleaned off her knife with one end of her scarf and replaced it in her boot. The only thing more she could wish for was a hot bath, and something to clean her hair with, and maybe a soft, fuzzy robe that had been warmed by a grate.

Indulgent, she scolded herself. *Selfish.*

And yet, she wondered . . . what was *he* doing tonight?

Had he truly gone back to the palace? If he had survived, had the seneschal? Was he being beaten for failing to capture her? Was his brother? Or was he gloating, boasting about how he had made the Skylark feel something for him, used her for . . . for . . . what *had* he gotten out of it, if he was a liar? What had been the *point* of it all?

Instead of letting her thoughts spin her in circles, tangling her in a web of paranoid *what* ifs and unfounded acceptance of facts she did not have, she saw to WINGS.

Someone else still needs their dinner.

She was just siphoning one of the sacks, holding the cap in her mouth as she steadied the hose over the pack's glass fuel canister, when the roof creaked. Robin froze, the adrenaline which had just started to subside pumping back through her body, and listened. The roof creaked again, and this time, it sounded closer to the hole. Someone less paranoid might have put it down to the building shifting as the sun rose and warmed its timbers, or to a particularly fat pigeon seeking a roost.

Robin, however, had a wanted poster with her face on it. She couldn't afford to not be paranoid.

She considered calling out, to see if it was the woman with the glass rose, or one of her contacts, but then thought better of it. As quickly as she was able, she re-corked the fuel sack and set it aside. She screwed the fuel canister into place, and then put on WINGS. She'd only gotten a few fingers of fuel into the canister—barely enough to keep her in the air for more than a few minutes—but it was enough to get away. The pack chugged regretfully when she turned it on. Whether she should use WINGS to escape or as a weapon, Robin wasn't yet sure.

And then, suddenly, she was.

Because the person who dropped down into the attic, wreathed in blowing tendrils of snowflakes, was gut-wrenchingly, heart-achingly familiar. Like a specter looming out of her past, he lowered himself to the floorboards, head obscured by a lupine countenance she never thought she'd see again. The ice-blue uniform was gone, replaced by rough black trousers and a long dark coat, serviceable and plain, but that mask, the wolf-nosed helmet, was unmistakable.

"*You*," Robin breathed, before her lungs clenched in shock.

The Coyote straightened, silver nose lifting until she could see his eyes. Emotions warred in Robin's chest as she stared into that pale gray gaze, indiscernible as ever. Fear collided with relief, and hope, and yes, even joy. But she never had been able to tell which of his many faces, his many versions, she was facing off with when he sealed himself away behind the mask. So she stood, pinned in place like a butterfly on a board, and waited.

It wasn't until a lazy, triumphant smile curled into the sides of his mouth that she noticed the pistol in his hand, the one aimed squarely at her chest.

"Hello again, my dear Skylark," he growled, voice low and husky. Robin noted, absurdly, that his lips were chapped. "Have you not missed me?"

CHAPTER
FOUR

R obin couldn't move. She had hoped—of course she
had hoped—that he had . . . that he was still . . . she
hadn't really *thought*, though, had not honestly believed
that . . . there had been so much fire, and anyone can wear
a helmet or fly a plane, but his voice, his eyes through the
eye slits of the helmet—her stomach lurched like she was
doing barrel rolls, throat tight and hot. Shock atrophied
her limbs, even as her blood whooshed in her ears and
adrenaline surged in her veins. She wobbled a little, and
lied to herself and said it was because she had rocked
back on her heels and WINGS was tugging at her. Not
because her knees were jelly, her breath stopping up in
her lungs, black twinkling at the edges of her vision.

He was *alive*.

He was alive. He was *here*.

And she had left him to die.

Oh, gods, Robin thought, sucking in the frigid night air.
From this angle, the barrel of his pistol looked as wide as
a cannonball. And the worst part was, she couldn't blame
him, not really. If their positions had been reversed, she
might well be the one pointing a gun at him right now.

He's gone back to them, then, she thought, spreading her
hands out and to the sides, uncertain as to what to do
now. *Is he a pawn on his king's chessboard again? Is he here to
collect the bounty on my head? To return me to that gilded prison?
Or to exact revenge for leaving him to burn?*

"No," she whispered, the word strangled by the
knot of emotion bunched up inside her throat. "No, I—

don't—I can't—" But she wasn't sure how that sentence would end. Can't believe he was still alive? Didn't want it to be true that he had become the enemy? That this wasn't another godsforsaken act he was putting on.

Touch him, her heart cried in anguish. *Run*, her brain screamed.

Robin thought she might just be sick, and swallowed her recently eaten rations back down, hard.

"No?" he repeated, voice crackling, and Robin remembered that he'd asked her a question. Asked her if she'd missed him. She hadn't really been trying to answer, but then again, what she'd said wasn't wrong, either. Not really. How can you miss someone if you secretly, deep, deep down, knew you were fooling yourself, *lying* to yourself when you thought he might still be alive?

How can you miss someone who was supposed to be dead?

"Well, now," the Coyote said, lowering the pistol. "That is not quite the reception I had hoped to receive."

He set it back in the holster at his hip, and Robin felt all the air rush back into her lungs, her seized muscles loosening with a relieved burn. She took a step back, catching her weight, unsure of what she should do or say. What he *wanted* her to do or say.

"Not what *you* wanted?" she asked, voice shaking. "You had a gun aimed at me!"

"I could not be certain you would be alone." Then he reached up to pull off his helmet. His face was gaunt, eyes rimmed with red and nose flush from the cold. His shoulders hunched, and he had a worrying scratch across one pale cheek. His hair was floppy with dirt and too much length, his artful scruff near on a full beard now. He looked rougher than she thought he would, and it filled her all at once with a fearsome joy—*he didn't go back!*—and deep pity.

He was vain enough, she knew, that if he had gone

back, if he had betrayed her, then he would have washed and shaved. His misery wasn't artifice. He was on the run, just as she was.

A long, wracking shiver made his whole frame tremble, and he clenched his teeth. He was nowhere near dressed warm enough for life on the winter streets. The helmet—scuffed and tarnished, she could now see—slipped from his fingers to clatter against the floorboards with a loud clonk. His clothes may be those of any other middle class workman, but his gloves were the same— that soft, supple black leather—and his uniform boots, when her gaze dropped to the floor, were shiny beneath a layer of recent grime, betraying his lingering vanity.

His realness.

But his eyes, *oh*, his beautiful, silver-gray eyes looked at Robin and danced.

Joy, she saw in them. And relief. And something like the feel of putting down a heavy weight for the first time all day, the exhausted reprieve that immediately becomes a desire to just curl into comfort and warmth, to revel in the pride of the ache the burden pressed on you without your quite being aware of it until you put it down. "It is a shame that you say no. Because I," he said, eyes hooded as he gazed at her across the snow-dusted attic, "have most certainly missed you."

And then he strode forward, across the creaking floorboards, heedless of the loose nails and uneven footing, wrapped his gloved hands around the sides of Robin's face, and kissed her with such force that she stumbled a few steps back. She grabbed his elbows as much to stay upright as to try to get some sort of control over what was happening. Whether to push him away or haul him closer, though, she wasn't sure. It didn't matter, either, as all rational thought fled her brain like a swarming hive, scattering to the winds as his tongue—hot, wet, pleading—licked across her bottom lip. The tip of his nose was freezing against her cheek, and when she opened up to him, he tasted not like the apple liquor she remembered, but like the same sort of dried jerky that Robin had been surviving on. His beard was soft against her chin, and his fingers dug in behind her ears just perfectly. Not hard enough to hurt, but definitely holding on.

Robin jerked back when he parted for breath, her fingers flying to her lips as though to confirm the sensation had been real. She placed her other hand against his chest, holding him in place when he tilted his head in the other direction and tried to bend down for another go.

"Wait," Robin pleaded. "Just . . . let me get my bearings here."

"Skylark," he murmured, kissing her temple, sliding his lips through her hair, beard catching as she pressed close. "Please . . ."

"You're . . . *dead*." Robin heaved the words. They were hot, slimy and sour in her throat. "You're supposed to be dead."

He made a gesture with one shoulder that might have been a shrug, or might have been a chuckle, and that cocky, boyish grin lifted one corner of his lips. "Not so, it would seem."

"But I . . ." Robin looked up at him, standing so close, breath mingling in the air between them, white puffs building like clouds, her face held captive in his palms. Her eyes prickled as heat surged behind them, and with a blink, the tears she hadn't even known she'd been building were rolling down her face. She reached out to hold him again, curled her fists into his biceps—shrunken, she realized. He had gotten so skinny, almost dangerously so. What happened? Where had he been? How had he *survived?* "I didn't come back for you."

"Better you had not," the Coyote whispered, arms dropping to encircle her waist, fingers worming beneath the awkward shape of the rocket pack as he pressed his chilled face into her neck, seeking the warmth of her skin and her scarf, hiding his face in her horrible hair. He was shivering. Robin closed her eyes for a moment, sagged slightly into the embrace, into the feel of him against her, and circled her own arms around his neck.

Hadn't this been exactly what she'd imagined? What she'd longed for in the secret parts of her heart?

He kissed her again, and this time, Robin met him half-way, stretching up on her toes, letting him cradle her skull as she obligingly tilted her head back. When it became too uncomfortable a position to sustain, Robin pulled back for breath and was smugly pleased to see that the Coyote's face was warm and pink now, instead of pale with cold.

"Do *they* know you're alive?" Robin whispered, petting down the back of his head. His hair was mussed, filthy, wrong, but he was here, gods, *here*, and *alive, alive, alive*.

"Mmmf," the Coyote said, which was no answer at all.

Omens, he's still shivering, Robin realized, and tucked him in closer to her body. She didn't have a lot of heat of her own to spare, though, and she wasn't sure how much good it would do. Eventually, he lifted his head from where she'd pressed his cheek against her own, and then slowly, gently dropped another, sweeter kiss against her mouth. Robin started to think less about the kisses, fine as they were, and more about the little nook she had in the corner, blocked from the wind, with pennants to bundle them both up together.

"What happened to you . . . after?" she asked when he was done. She searched his eyes for . . . for something, for rage, or hate, or betrayal. Anything that would give away how he really felt. He was calm, yes, but was this the mask? Or the real him? "Did they—I mean, were you . . . ? Did you go back?"

He shook his head slowly. "I made it into the forest, away from the dogs. There was a, hmm, a place I used to play as a child. A little house in the woods that the nanny used to use for her, ah, assignations. Storage for shooting things, you see, but there hasn't been a shooting party at the estate in a decade, and none of the officers would ever have known about it."

"It's been months," Robin said. "You stayed there the whole time? Alone?" She stepped back, sliding her hands down his arms to take his palms in hers. The Coyote grimaced and pulled away.

Ah, there it was—the anger she'd been anticipating.

"I did not say it was easy," he said with an affronted little sneer. "I ran for you, Skylark. You were right. After all I had done for you, all the ways I had kept you safe, I could not return to the house. So I ran. For *you*."

"I would have found you, if I'd thought you—" Robin started, but now that he'd let the anger surface, the Coyote wasn't listening. Instead of gesturing in frustration, sawing at the air like he sometimes had back at the palace, he had his hands tucked up against his chest, protective and odd.

"I had to throw myself into a stream to survive," he continued, and Robin quickly cut off the noise of dismay that was crawling up her throat. "Since then, I have been trying to find you. I have slept in the streets. I have *starved* for you. I have never in my life ever had to . . ." He trailed off, growling in the back of his throat.

Robin swallowed heavily. Was he trying to make her feel bad, to make her feel responsible for his suffering? She wouldn't let him. He had made his own choices. He was master of his own fate. He had already planned to run—what did he think was going to happen? And he had given her his blessing. He had known, at least somewhat, what she intended to do, and he had approved. Without saying the words, he had told her to go, to take WINGS and fly. She couldn't be blamed for the mistakes he'd made for himself.

"I'm sorry, but I—"

"It was worth it," he added softly, seeming to realize that his anger—likely aimed more at himself than at her, she realized—wasn't doing either of them any good right now. That it was putting her on the defensive. "It was hard, Skylark. But I am here now. With you. With the pack. We can make this right, now."

"Wait, if you've been hiding, then who was flying your aeroship?"

"I have no idea, my dear," he said. "But it was an effective ruse, all the same. They wanted to flush you out, and flushed you were. It is well that I found you first." He reached out and ran his thumb across her cheek, gentle, possessive, and oh so familiar. "Oh, how I have *missed* you, Skylark."

Reflexively, Robin grabbed his hand, holding it against her skin, but as her fingers wrapped around his, he winced and flinched back. He curled his fingers into a loose fist and looked away, face down, expression . . . ashamed?

Concern flashed bright in Robin's heart.

"What . . . what's wrong?" Robin asked softly. "Are you . . . ?"

"They are still, ah, tender," the Coyote answered, just as softly, gaze averted. For a moment, Robin thought he wasn't going to show her, and she would have been okay with that. She wouldn't have pressed it. But then he slowly uncurled his fingers and held out his hands, palm up, like he was praying.

Watching him carefully, silently asking his permission, Robin reached out and gently peeled off his gloves.

"Omens," she breathed as the wreckage of his palms was revealed. She cupped the backs of his hands. "These are . . . these are bad. How . . . ?"

"I was protecting my face," the Coyote said, and she noticed he'd tried to dredge up some of that confident charm that had seemed both desperately fake and comfortably honest while they had been trapped in the palace together.

"Burns," Robin said, peering carefully at each of the puffed masses of white skin. "They look a bit like, well"—Robin let go with one hand and turned her own palm up, where he could see it—"mine."

The Coyote leaned down and pressed a kiss to her palm. "So it does," he said, before trailing his fingers around to the control box on her wrist.

Before she realized what he was doing, he had cut the power to WINGS and spun her around, making her world whirl and blur, hands tugging at the shoulder straps of her harness.

"What . . . what are you doing?" she cried, confusion slamming into her. She jerked out from under his reach, turning to face him even as she backed further away, putting space between them. She wrapped one hand tight around the shoulder strap he hadn't managed to slip down her arm.

The softness in his expression was gone, replaced with the cool mask of indifference he'd always worn when "performing" for their "hosts".

No, she thought. *Please, no. Don't do this to me. Not now that I know you're alive. You can't.*

Needles of betrayal tapped against Robin's heart. She had seen how mercurial he could be, knew that he was a master at concealing his emotions, at presenting what he wanted her to see. She knew she couldn't trust that the expression was genuine, but that didn't stop her heart from racing with sudden fear. Why couldn't he just be honest with her? And why did she have to fall for it every stupid time, like some scrubbed-up cow being led around by the nose?

"Come now," he said, voice dropping into that intentional husky rasp he'd first used on her in the forest, the day they first came face to face. "Enough, my dear. We both know that I cannot allow you to continue with these amateurish attempts at terrorism. You escaped and won free the pack, as we had planned, but this? This is not what we discussed. It puts you in too great a danger."

"So, you're . . . you're not trying to . . . ?" Robin asked, inching a bit further back, desperate for clarity.

"My dear, I am cold, and I am tired, and I do not feel like dancing with you tonight. The only thing I plan to do is to make you see the error in how you have gone about this. So please, do me the courtesy of surrendering the pack, and we will devise our next moves. Together."

He held his hand out—an imperious gesture that demanded compliance, that couldn't fathom the possibility that Robin wouldn't just immediately see the "sense" of his plan and surrender herself fully to his control, and Robin laughed. It was a harsh, bitter sound, filled with all the disbelief and shock that had welled up high within her.

Oh, Captain, she scolded herself. *You've forgotten how changeable he was. How you never really knew which lie was the truth and which the fancy. What a bossy little snob he was.*

"You expect me to . . . to just give you . . . no," Robin said, backing up and turning to the left. The Coyote advanced, and she backed up more, turned to the left a bit further. "No. We can talk, but I'll hold on to WINGS, if you don't mind."

"You are clever, Skylark. Please, continue to be so," the Coyote warned. His eyes seemed to be locked on her face, his steely gaze cold and assessing, and Robin decided to take advantage of his distraction.

"I won't just blindly follow your orders, either, for that matter." Robin retreated another turning step, and again, the Coyote matched her pace for pace.

Good, she thought, *pay attention to me and not my feet. That's it, a few more steps . . .* "I'm not your prisoner anymore, and I don't have to do whatever you tell me."

"We can work as a team, my dear," the Coyote pressed. "End the war, just as we said."

"With Klonn the victor?" she challenged.

Some unknown emotion flickered along the edges of his gaze, but his features remained a blank mask.

"Well, yes," he said simply, as if there was no other possible outcome, and Robin felt her heart scream in anguish. Here, then, was the crux of their relationship. No matter what else was said, they were, at their core, enemy soldiers on opposite sides of the war. They might agree over the fact that the war needed to end, but they would never agree as to which side the victory should fall. They had fought this battle time and time again. Why, now, did she expect it to end differently?

"Why would I ever let that happen?" Robin ground out. "Why can't your side be the loser?"

Frustration pinched his lips into a thin line, tightened the skin around his eyes. He took a step toward her. "Obstinate as ever, I see. Very well. There are other lands, other courts. We can—"

"No." Robin shook her head, tightened her grip on WINGS's shoulder strap. "I won't just run away. It has to *stop*. We both know that! Why are you—?"

The Coyote snarled and closed the distance between them. He gripped her by the shoulders, and Robin wondered just how much restraint it took for him to not shake her. "I have just found you again, made my thoughts and feelings clear, and yet still you resist me, Skylark, still you brush me aside. You say you worried, you ask how I am, but you will not listen."

"No, you listen!" Robin hissed. "I'm not one of your little minions. I have made a choice to be here, and I'm going to finish this, with or without your plans and your permissions, and you need to rudding well respect that!"

"You have no idea what waits for you if you continue to—"

"Then help me!" Robin snapped, breaking free of his grip and stepping back. "Instead of standing there, waggling like a useless drone with one wing, support the hive a little! I *need* to do this."

"Everyone says they *need*," the Coyote spat, a rage in his voice that was so unexpected that Robin nearly stumbled. "The king! That general! But nobody knows what *needing* something really is."

His hand hovered over the butt of his pistol, anguish and rage battling across his face as he hesitated. Then he drew the gun, aimed it at her, and cocked the hammer.

"You don't mean that," Robin said, quailing. "You wouldn't . . ."

"I am a good enough shot. I could shoot you straight through the chest and hit nothing vital. I could take the pack by force, leave you to bleed the way you left me. It would take a long time, Skylark. It would be an agony. And a fitting revenge, I think. A heart for a heart."

Blood rushed into her ears so quickly, she thought for a second that she might faint. She sucked air in hard and tried to keep her face schooled and blank. This was not a side she'd ever seen so plainly in him. She'd suspected it was there, of course, had seen glimpses of it when he was nothing more than a ruthless enemy pilot chasing her across the sky, when he ran his sword through Al's chest and called it mercy, but he had never levied it at her with such naked, unrefined fury. Gone was the calm, collected nobleman.

Here, now, was the version who'd inspired his hobgob infamy, the version he'd claimed was reserved solely for the benefit of their captors—captors who were no longer present.

Rage. Fury. Entitlement.

Like a child throwing a tantrum.

He can't have the toy he wants, and no one is playing the game the way he thinks it should go, Robin realized. *A child with a gun pointed at me, all the same.*

"And this is what you call admiration?" Robin sneered back. "This is that same affection you were so adamant about?"

"Affection!" he snarled. "You left me behind, Skylark. And then you set me on *fire*. Your thoughts on my affection have been made quite clear, indeed! I suspect, my dear, that you would have preferred I stayed dead." He drew himself up, imperious and red-faced. "Now, hand over the pack like a good little Sealie. Do not make me do something I cannot take back."

"If that's what this is, then you better just shoot me," she challenged, bravado swelling up to protect her from the confused sting his words had caused.

His head shifted, and she thought he might actually be calculating the odds of the bullet piercing WINGS, like he'd said. Finally, he seemed to come to a decision. Pain lanced through his gaze, sorrow carving into the planes of his face. The Coyote blinked, and in that moment, she knew. She knew what he had chosen.

"Something's different about you," Robin said softly. *It's my fault, she wanted to add. And I don't blame you. No one could, really, when someone you wanted to trust had instead left you to die.* "I'm sorry."

Distress pinched at the fine lines on the outside of his eyes. "How do you—?" he started, and then cut himself off with a yell of surprise.

With each turning step back and away, Robin had managed to get herself directly under the hole in the roof, and now, before he could say any more, she slammed her hand down on the control box and shot upward. WINGS chugged and spluttered at the abrupt ignition, the dearth of fuel, and Robin tumbled through a barely controlled fall to the ground. The cobbles outside were slick with ice. She hit hard, and her stupid weak ankle turned sharply under her, screaming its protest. She toppled to the side and bit back a yelp. A loud, metallic *crunch* filled the air, far worse than her own cry of agony, but Robin didn't have time to check.

Behind her, she could hear crashes from inside the building as the Coyote dashed down the stairs to the street. She didn't wait to check that her ankle wasn't broken, or that WINGS was unharmed. She just rolled up onto her feet and ran, gritting her teeth against the hot agony.

WINGS jostled awkwardly as she loped, jamming into the small of her back with each burning footfall, but Robin didn't dare stop to adjust the straps or remove the pack. She had left her fuel behind. She wasn't going to leave WINGS behind, as well.

Breath loud in her own ears, Robin took as many random turns as she could find. The sun was rising, and tenants were starting to pour out from the houses, heading toward the markets of the city, the homes of their employers, or the various factories and industrial areas, the bases of the Klonn Aeroforce. Robin couldn't risk getting trapped in the throng—or worse, recognized by a would-be bounty hunter—so she turned and ducked down a narrow alley.

Behind her, the thud of heavy boot falls told her that the Coyote was following close. Robin ran, eyes peeled for anything she could use to escape—but there was nothing.

Day was coming, and there was no way she would be able to navigate either the skies or the streets without being seen. With her wanted poster plastered all over the kingdom, she couldn't trust anyone to hide her, either.

There *was*, though, she remembered sharply. There was a place where she had been offered sanctuary.

"Skylark!" the Coyote barked into the dawn, his voice hollow-sounding in that telltale way that meant he'd donned that godsdamned helmet again. He was closer than he probably realized, too, just around the corner from the alley in which Robin was huddling.

She was out of time.

The rose it is, she decided. *I'll risk WINGS this one time.* She slapped her hand onto the booster button and shot up into the sky. *Yes! Okay, not so bad then. I can fix—*

Then, just as suddenly as she was airborne, Robin was falling.

CHAPTER FIVE

Heavy rope cut into her face, and Robin realized that someone had thrown a godsdamned *net* over her, plucking her down out of the sky like a fish out of the ocean.

The weight of the net prevented her from being able to raise her arms enough to get at the control box to boost WINGS's thrust, and as soon as she had been hauled down enough for her boot heels to brush the top of a roof, several pairs of heavily gloved hands snatched at her shoulders and arms.

Someone slapped a hand down on the control box, shutting off the engine. Robin wriggled and writhed, snarling like a feral beast. She managed to twist down and around enough to free her knife, and then it was flashing forward, dancing in the lamplight toward the gray-clad, uniformed bodies pressing in around her. Blood sprayed in an arc from where she landed a slice on an arm, and a man cried out and fell away, giving her enough room, at last, to slash at the net. Swiftly, she took it to pieces around her.

For a precious few seconds, her arms were free of both rope and hands, but a quick glance up revealed a second group of watchmen coming up over the ledge of the roof, a net made of chain in their hands. If they got that thing over her, that would be it. She wouldn't get away a second time.

She pounded on the ignition button. WINGS whined and spluttered in protest at the rough treatment, but started up. It was dangerous to ignite the cylinders when she was surrounded by highly flammable rope, and the moment she realized what she had done, the watchmen seemed to do the same. They each backed away, shielding their eyes from the sudden flare of burning hemp that crawled across the pack and made for Robin's legs, where her ankles were still entwined.

"Rudding hells!" she snarled and, with the butt of her knife, tapped hard at the next button, blasting into the air, hoping that the rush of wind would snuff the blazing ropes. The burning sections fell away, blown back by the sudden inertia, but something tugged hard at her foot. The trailing net had caught on something below—or was caught by someone. Momentum interrupted, Robin swung in a wide arc that sent her hurtling at a chimney stack.

Unable to do anything to dodge, Robin covered her face with her arms and braced for impact. She crashed hard into the bricks, hard enough that the chimney cracked. Thankfully for her bones—but badly for the pack—WINGS took the brunt of the blow. The pack crunched distressingly.

She landed with a resounding thud on the roof and watched in a daze as the soldiers of the Night Watch scrambled down the fire escape of the opposite roof to swarm up her own building. The net tangled on her leg was still taut, spread across the open street like a tight-rope, and after a moment, enough sense returned to her knocked head that she thought to reach out and cut it away from her boot.

It fell onto the men below, halting their progress, and Robin took advantage of those precious few seconds to regain her feet and assess WINGS. The glass fuel canister had cracked, and was leaking all over Robin's back. There was no way she could start it up now; even if it would light, it was far too dangerous to even attempt it.

"Omens," she snarled again. "Frozen, turd-covered, rudding *omens!*"

Limping, she made her way to the fire escape on the opposite side of the building. She had just managed to make it down to the street, jumping the last few feet and wincing her way through the pain that flared up her leg, when the first of the Night Watch who had made it to the roof reversed direction and began to flow down after her.

She ran into the deepest section of shadows she could find, scanning the street for the Coyote, but he had vanished. She knew him far too well to assume she had lost him for good, though. Wherever he now was, she was sure that he would find her again.

The question was, did she *want* him to?

Shuffling hurriedly, she wound her way through narrow alleys until she came out at the market square. The stalls were still closed for the night, shuttered and surrounded by barrels, blankets, boxes, and baskets, the sun not quite high enough to signal morning preparations. Knowing that time was short, and that the market wouldn't stay empty for long, Robin cut across the square and dove behind a spice seller's stall, hoping that the scent of saffron and ginger would disguise the reek of fuel from her clothing.

Making herself as small as possible, and covering herself with a blanket that was obviously the owner's answer for chilly afternoons, Robin went still and waited. The Night Watch cut through the square, racing for the far exit. Robin remained hidden. The clock tower in the corner struck the hour, but still, she didn't leave. It wasn't until the clock struck the half that Robin dared to move again. Slipping out from under the fuel-soaked blanket, she took a deep breath of fresh air. The fumes had started to make her dizzy, and Robin was grateful for the breeze that carried the smell downwind.

Free—for the moment—from pursuing parties, Robin fished one of the rose-shaped hairpins from the pouch on her belt. She inspected it carefully, turning it this way and that in the growing light. It was beautiful, delicately formed with obvious skill, but gave no other indication she could use to locate the rose woman's operation.

"Give me a pin like it's a godsdamned map, like I have any rudding clue what I'm doing here . . ." she muttered bitterly into the wind. Frustrated, she placed the pin back in her pouch. She couldn't go back to the attic—not unless she wanted to risk another run-in with the Coyote, and she wasn't yet ready to continue that conversation. Her emotions were too tangled, his actions too confusing. She didn't know which version of the man she could trust—the respectful nobleman intent on courting her, or the enemy soldier who couldn't bear to see his side lose.

Robin sighed and scrubbed at her face, pinching the bridge of her nose to relieve the pressure of a mounting headache. She couldn't stand around in the open, either. So that left only one option—the rose woman's offer. But how in the hells was she supposed to beg for sanctuary from a place she couldn't even find?

Offering a small prayer up to any gods who were listening, she hopped from shadow to shadow, taking the long route of ducking from stall to stall. The freezing dawn air burned in her lungs as she tried to find a sewer to disappear into, some covered bridge to duck under. The surrounding streets were all wide, though, meant to accommodate the market wagons, and too well lit. With no other option, she pressed close to the sides of the buildings and hoped the slanted shadows cast by the sunrise would obscure her.

Every street she dashed down, every corner she turned, she kept her eyes peeled for a rose. A garden, a sign, a decoration—she found none. She saw lilies, lavender, daisies, but no roses.

Godsdammit, she cursed to herself. *Do the Klonn not like the flower, or something?*

The day was lightening steadily, ruining her chances at further skulking. She was running out of time. Returning to the attic was out of the question, but if she couldn't find the rose, what was left?

Abruptly, she came to an open green space. Ah, yes, the park she had crash landed in just hours ago. The ringing scuffle of boots on cobbled streets rang in her straining ears, and a shrill watchman's whistle shattered the quiet morning.

"Bloody hells, they're persistent," Robin snarled to herself, dashing for the closest copse of trees. There was just enough leftover foliage on the branches to give her adequate cover to hide in. She crouched under a hedge and waited, listening for the sounds of pursuit.

After a few long, quiet moments, curious balls of light appeared around the edges of the park. It took Robin a moment to realize that they were lamps held by the Night Watch. The random, bobbing stream of lights soon became a grid, spaced evenly around the perimeter and advancing slowly inward. Robin cursed. The bastards were getting too well organized. There was no godsdamned way she would be able to escape now, not without being seen, especially since she couldn't fly. Her only chance was to lie still and hope that they missed her.

"Skylark," the Coyote hissed beside her ear, and Robin stifled a yelp, spinning around on the balls of her feet. The knife from her boot seemed to leap into her hand of its own accord.

"Stay back," she snarled, glaring at the dull glint of his helmet.

"Silence!" he whispered. "Or they will find us."

"Shove off, you turd!"

"Me or them, Skylark," he said. His voice was soft, but it carried across the slight distance between them like a slow roll of thunder.

Her heart jammed up in her throat.

"Do not be stupid, my heart," he pressed.

"Don't call me that."

"But you insist on being stupid." The Coyote chuckled. He reached out, and she weaved back, brandishing the knife in warning.

"No, the 'heart' part. You don't really mean it."

"Of course I—"

"You threatened to put a bullet in my chest," she hissed, scuttling back a bit further. He'd made his intentions for the pack clear—it was WINGS he wanted, not her—and she wasn't sure she trusted him to not turn her in, to not use the Night Watch as a means to gain what he was after. She needed to be ready to run.

The Coyote grimaced and looked almost . . . chagrined?

He ducked his head again, lupine nose bobbing down. "Forgive me, my dear. I was . . . overcome. I did not mean it. I could never bear to harm you. If nothing else, please trust in that."

"Trust?" She barked out a bitter laugh. "Trust is the last thing I feel right now. And we don't have time for a heart-to-heart."

"I will be very cross if you run, Skylark," the Coyote warned.

"Gods*damn* you," Robin snarled in return, voice low, her face hot with rage.

"Your gods most certainly will, my dear, if you do not shut up and stay still!"

Robin was certain that he was only saying so to give the Night Watch time to get close.

She was out of time.

She thrust forward with her blade, and the Coyote ducked to the side just barely in time to keep the tip of the knife from slamming into his shoulder. The blade was deflected with a low clang, skittering along the side of his helmet.

The screech it produced didn't seem that loud to Robin, but apparently, it was enough to carry. A watchman shouted the alarm, and then there were dozens of boots closing in on them, rabbits in a snare.

"Get out of here!" the Coyote growled, shoving past her and rising to his feet. He stood, deliberately drawing the attention of the approaching watchmen. They paused as they caught sight of him, confused murmurs hissing through their ranks like wind through autumn leaves.

"Go, you foolish girl!" the Coyote snarled, quiet enough that his voice wouldn't carry to the assembled crowd. Without looking, he shoved her hard with his knee. Robin tumbled back onto her arse, the ruined weight of WINGS pulling on her shoulders.

One of the watchmen said something in Klonnish, too rapid for Robin to catch, advancing slowly, the pistol in his hands clutched with a grip she was sure would leave his knuckles white. He was . . . afraid, she realized.

"Surrender," the watchman said in Klonnish—she knew that word—and it was an order. Then she remembered: the Coyote was a fugitive, too. He'd abandoned his post, turned his back on his king—for her? Or for WINGS? He was protecting them, sacrificing himself, but to what end?

"*Nema*," the Coyote answered, his own pistol now trained on the grim-faced watchman.

The watchman paused, eyes narrowed. He barked a guttural order to the others and, reluctantly, they dispersed, falling back to the perimeter of the park. The meaning of what he'd said eluded her—the words not yet part of her limited understanding of the language, it seemed—but she couldn't help feeling impressed by the power the Coyote still had. Or the doubt that he was indeed the fugitive he claimed.

Pistol still trained on the watchman, the Coyote

reached down and hauled Robin to her feet. He pulled her close to his own body, blocking her from view. "Take the pack and go," he said into her ear.

Robin dared to take her eyes from the watchman for a second and wished she could read the Coyote's face. She was caught flat-footed by his sudden show of solidarity, when he had just spent hours trying to part her from WINGS. Would she ever truly understand him, or would his intentions always be a confusing mash of mixed signals? Why did everything always have to be so rudding complicated with him?

She flicked her eyes back to the watchman, then up to the Coyote, hesitating, the knife still clenched in her fist.

The Coyote snorted. "Do not worry, my dear. I found you once, I will find you again. And then, you will listen to what I have to say."

"We *will* finish this," she snarled.

The Coyote made a choking sound, which might have been a laugh if the mask hadn't been in the way. "Go." Then he shoved her back, further into the shadows, and turned the nose of his lupine helmet toward the watchman he still had trained in his pistol's sights.

She was about to do just that when Robin caught the glint of something in the early morning sunlight. On the other side of the copse, the barrel of a watchman's rifle was aimed directly between her eyes. And neither she nor the Coyote had noticed.

Darkness swam at the sides of her vision, and her head felt too heavy, her lungs too small. Her gut burned. The world went still, as if every god around her held their breath. Robin's hand hovered over the control box. She was covered in fuel. Igniting WINGS now, if there was even enough fuel left in the damaged fuel canister to spark the ignition, would be a death sentence.

But it would destroy WINGS, which meant that even if she was killed here, now, no one else would be able to get their hands on the pack.

"She is here!" the watchman behind the rifle cried, giving away his position to expose hers. "The Sealie! She is here!"

Instantly, the soldiers waiting on the edges of the park surged forward.

The Coyote swore, voice crackling. He skittered back, away from the oncoming watchmen and the man with the rifle both, pulling Robin with him, pistol firing. Bullet after bullet, one after another, he fired into each man's foot, dropping them groaning and screaming into the grass. He could have easily taken the head shots, Robin knew, but she attributed his deliberate compassion to the fact that these were his countrymen. He could no more kill them than she could have killed hers.

Robin stumbled, trying to keep up with the Coyote as he pulled her toward the edge of the park, ankle screaming and mind whirling. When only the man who'd discovered her remained, she was spun unceremoniously behind the Coyote's back and shoved off to the side. But she tripped and fell to her knees, breathing hard, hating that she could be so easily manhandled when she was without the confines of a glider.

The watchman got around the Coyote and stopped with his back to a tree, his gun aimed again between her eyes. When she looked up at him, she saw that his face was pale but determined, sweat beading around his hairline. Not close enough to grab at his gun, too far away to stab. Robin knelt there and seethed.

"Try to run, Sealie, and I will blow off your head," the watchman said in far better Saskwyan than she would have expected.

"Do not be foolish," the Coyote countered, leveling his own pistol at the man's head. "You pull that trigger, and I will pull mine. The rocket pack is not to be harmed."

"I am prepared to die for the Art of War," the watch-man said, and with no further warning, squeezed.

Robin was pretty sure that she was dead. Not even she could dodge a bullet. There was a set of cracking shots so close together, Robin wasn't sure if they were the sound of one gunshot or two.

Something heavy slammed into her side, knocking her flat over onto WINGS. The Coyote's helmet ricocheted against her shoulder, and she let out a yelp that turned into a whuff as the weight of him drove her stomach against her spine. Robin held still, waiting for the sound of another shot, or a shout, but the night had gone disturbingly silent.

Warmth oozed along her neck and shoulder, and Robin winced, but felt no pain beside that of her ankle and growing bruises. The Coyote was face down on top of her, and Robin grunted as she flipped him over onto his own back. A raw red wound pierced his chest, right above his heart.

Gods no, Robin thought, whipping off her scarf and balling it up into the wound. *Not again. Wade, and Al . . . not him, too. Please. Don't do this to me. Not again.*

CHAPTER
SIX

"**R**udding hells," the Coyote burbled, and Robin, startled by the Saskwyan oath and his sudden full-body twitch, actually laughed. It burst out of her like a flock of startled birds, and she clapped her hand over her mouth to muffle it. His own mouth, already pinched tight with agony and turned down at the corners, morphed into a teeth-bearing grimace. He glared out at her from the slits in his helmet. "I am in pain, my dear. Do not find pleasure in it."

"Oh, but I do," Robin teased with a smirk, and patted him once, lightly, on the stomach. "Means you're alive."

"Eyes on the enemy, Skylark," the Coyote scolded. He flopped one hand over the fuel-damp scarf, pressing down so she wouldn't have to.

She thought about making a glib remark that she was already doing exactly that, but instead sprang up to find out what had happened to the watchman with the rifle. She needn't have bothered, though. The Coyote had been serious when he claimed he was a good shot. He'd hit his target perfectly, despite having been thrown back and around by the momentum of the watchman's bullet as it slammed into his torso. The watchman was dead, a single bullet hole between his eyes. And the rest of them were either unconscious, or too preoccupied with crawling away on their bellies to try to shoot them again.

Relieved, and reminded of how bullets can travel, Robin grabbed at her own shoulder, but the only wetness there was from the Coyote. Wherever the bullet that had hit him now was, it hadn't gone through him and into her. The Coyote groaned again, and Robin dropped back down onto her knees beside him. There was no blood on his lips, so the bullet couldn't have gone too deep, or pierced a lung. But that didn't mean that he was out of danger, that he would yet survive the wound. The last person she'd seen hit like this had lost his arm, and she had no idea where she could find a medic with the caliber of skill required to patch him up—or who would be willing to use it on a fugitive. She reached forward to get a better look, praying that it wouldn't look as horrible as the wound he'd punched into Wade's shoulder all those months ago.

"Whatever possessed the gods to make you do that?" she asked as she peered under the scarf. There was definitely a puncture through his leather jacket, and the woolen vest and shirt under that, and a perfectly round, burned and gory hole had been bored into the flesh of his chest. How deep it went, Robin had no idea, and she had a sudden fear that moving him would send the bullet rattling around inside his ribcage.

The Coyote's face was still covered, but Robin had the distinct impression that he was sneering. "Was I not clear when I said that I admired you?"

Robin thought of the kisses in the attic and felt her cheeks flush.

"Yes, but you're also a fool," she said, albeit softly.

He *had* been clear. He'd said it repeatedly. And he'd protected her—or so it had seemed—time and again. But there was also the fact that he seemed to harbor a continued desperation to get his hands on WINGS, and the lengths he was willing to go to indulge his obsession: downing mid-flights, keeping her prisoner, trying to wrench the pack off her, threatening to shoot her for it. And what he'd said to the watchman, the emphasis on protecting not Robin, but WINGS, had left her won-

dering just how much of his action really had been out
of admiration. She couldn't forget how quickly he had
turned on her when she'd refused him. That he had made
excuses for it did not erase the fact that it had occurred,
or that it very well could again.

She couldn't trust him.

That was the scope of it. As much as he may "ad-
mire" her, as much as he might have actually fallen in love
with her—as he claimed—he wanted the pack just as badly. And Robin couldn't afford to let herself be a casualty
in his inner war.

She wavered, watching the pool of dark liquid creeping out from beneath the scarf, spreading along his chest
to drip into the hungry soil. She had feelings for him, too;
she couldn't deny that. Underneath his rage and confusion, his angry desperation, she'd seen glimpses of a good
heart and a good man. He'd been tortured and beaten and
scarred by the violence he'd grown up in, just as much as
she had. And he was doing all he could to end the war,
just like she was—only, he wasn't used to being told no,
to being told that he was wrong, to not getting what he
wanted.

She could make him see, though, could make him
understand, couldn't she? He could change. She could, for
lack of a *better* way to phrase it, save him from the turmoil
the war had caused in him. He could do better. Robin,
with the pack, or no Robin, and no pack either. When she
made that clear to him, he'd understand what she needed
from him, wouldn't he?

But not if he was dead of a gunshot wound.

"We can't stay here," Robin said at length.

He nodded slowly in agreement, something akin to
surprise, or maybe hope, flaring beneath the pain in his
eyes. Had he been worried that she meant to leave him
here for dead?

Though it was a messy, painful struggle for both of

them, she got him to his feet, and he was mostly able to propel himself forward.

Robin wondered again if this was really the best idea. He could endanger the people of the rose. He could return her to the hands of her enemies, absolve himself in the eyes of his superiors, his king.

But he was wounded. Badly. He needed help, and leaving him to go find it now would certainly mean his death. Someone would have reported the gunshots. More of the Night Watch was undoubtedly on its way. And despite the lingering misgivings she may have about his trustworthiness, Robin was better than that. She would not do to the Coyote what he had done to Al. Though this was war, she still believed it was right to save those lives you could.

Guiding him carefully out of the park, and away from the posh neighborhood that lined it, Robin led him to the back entrance of a half-decent, disreputable-looking tavern. By the slump of the Coyote's shoulders, and the way his head bobbed as she got him settled against the wall behind some bins, she guessed that he was nearly unconscious. Robin sat him down against the wall of the tavern, and then carefully unwound his scarf from around his neck. Her own scarf was still jammed against his wound, and she needed to hide her hair. She settled the scarf in place, using the ivory hairpin to secure it. Then she pushed her goggles up onto her head, under the fabric, and left WINGS behind the metal garbage bins, tucked carefully beside the Coyote and hidden under her coat.

It was cold without it, but she wasn't going to be away for long.

A moment of uncertainty washed over her as she turned away, but she dismissed it just as fast—the Coyote was in no condition to run away with the pack. He was sunk so far into his pain that he probably wasn't even aware of his surroundings.

Decision made, Robin headed inside, being careful to not look at the wanted poster with her own face pinned to the outside of the door, and walked over to the bar. The place was dark enough, and filled with enough other folk who had their heads down and hats pulled low that Robin wasn't entirely out of place. The barman took his sweet time coming to serve her, his face flushed with alcohol and probably the heat of a cook fire. When he did, Robin held up both the rose-shaped hairpin, and a shiny gold coin.

"*I look for the woman,*" she said, careful to pick out her words in her admittedly limited Klonnish.

The barman's eyes got piggy and wide, and then skipped around her face. They caught on the wolf cameo peeking out from behind her head on the pin, and then snapped even wider. "*Ai, deh!*" he said crisply, and then rattled off a jumble of something Robin assumed was directions. His hand pointed left, then left again, and there was something that required three fingers, and the motion of going up stairs. She caught some of the words, but not all of them.

Robin narrowed her eyes, suspicious of his helpful deference, and hoped that it was because of the money, or perhaps because of the rose, and not because she was about to walk herself into a trap. She held up the coin, and then touched her finger to her lips warningly. The man nodded, eyes on the wolf, then back to her, and only then to the money. If he recognized her from the posters, he didn't show it. He was also her only lead, so she had to hope that he wouldn't go running for the Night Watch the moment she left. She placed the coin carefully on the bar and turned away, not even waiting for him to scoop it up.

Back outside, she put poor, battered WINGS back on, and got the Coyote to his feet. His head was lolling, the weight of his helmet probably no help, but she didn't dare take it off of him in public. Robin had her own secret identity; she would let him keep his.

She followed the barman's instructions—or at least, what she thought they might be—and eventually came to an ornate stone staircase that led to a much more refined and discrete part of town.

"Of course," Robin groused, slumping under the Coyote's weight. She wished WINGS was in any condition to turn on. A few quick thrusts would have gotten them both up the stairs in no time. Instead, it seemed to take forever, and made her legs burn, tears of pain and frustration building against her lashes. The Coyote was now out cold, and she couldn't keep dragging him along on his toes. For one, he was heavy, and her grip under his arms couldn't be doing anything good for his wound. For another, her ankle, forgotten in the rush of adrenaline, was killing her.

At the top of the stairs, she found herself on a tidy little street populated with close-crowded, whitewashed homes with black crossbeams and peaked roofs. Each had a riotous flower garden out front, where, in the lower town, those fortunate enough to have any garden space at all had given theirs over to vegetables. But above one of the dozens of similar doors, three blocks away, Robin spotted the sign she'd been looking for—a single rose carved into a lintel.

It could be just a coincidence, but so far, everything else in this venture had smacked of the tinkering of gods. She wasn't going to place faith in the chance she might be wrong. Gritting her teeth against the pain in her ankle, Robin humped them down the street as quickly as possible. Leaning back against the door, bracing the Coyote against her chest to free one hand, she tried the door handle. It was locked tight, and must have been reinforced on the inside with metal bands, as not even the subtle shove she gave it made it give even an inch.

Shifting the Coyote so she could step back and knock, the door suddenly swung inward. Utterly unprepared for the door she was leaning on to just suddenly not be there, the weight of both the Coyote and WINGS pulled her down to sprawl in an undignified heap on a lush, dark red carpet, legs akimbo and bottom bruised.

Once more trapped under the weight of the Coyote, she heard the swish of long skirts and strained to see a figure out of the corner of her eyes. The figure moved to stand over Robin, and leaned down until she filled Robin's view.

"Welcome, Skylark," the woman said. Her hair was an intensely dark red, not at all a shade found in nature, and hung in regimented ringlets. It framed a pair of shrewd, up-turned and calculating green eyes, set against darkly olive skin. Robin recognized those eyes as belonging to the woman who had cut her from the laundry line. She'd found the rose woman at last, it seemed. "*Ai, ai*, I knew you would see sense eventually."

"I'm not here for me," Robin said quickly, gesturing vaguely at the Coyote's body, face down over her own. "He needs a medic, and I didn't know where else to go."

The woman crouched down and turned the Coyote over on the floor, freeing Robin. He moaned and tried to curl in on himself. The woman's eyebrows bounced up her forehead. "This is . . . the Wolf. You are saving the life of your enemy?"

Robin pushed up into a sitting position and gave the woman a wry smile. "It's kinda a long story. But yes," Robin said, blowing out a sigh. "He started it."

"I see," the woman said. The scarf had come away from the Coyote's wound, and she jammed it back under his jacket before she rose and turned away. She took a few steps to what Robin thought was a red wall, but which turned out to be a ring of thick curtains around the entrance. Pulling them aside, she called into the interior of the house: "Thorne! A patient for you!"

A few young men and women, seemingly summoned by the rose woman's call and wearing shockingly little, entered the antechamber from another unseen slit in the curtain and gasped collectively when their eyes landed on the Coyote. It was a pretty, studied sound that matched their pretty, studied looks.

"Take our guest into the room at the back, please," the rose woman said.

The half-nude people crowded around at her command. They each took a limb, and lifted the prone Coyote with expert ease. It appeared as though they'd had a lot of practice hauling unconscious men around, and Robin couldn't help but feel trepidation about the nature of the establishment she'd literally fallen into. The Coyote moaned softly at the jostling.

"Be careful!" Robin warned as they slipped out of view with their charge.

"Peace, Skylark. He will be well cared for," the woman admonished. "It is you who must remain hidden. Come, to the kitchen. Up you get. It seems you have a story to tell me." She held out a hand, and Robin took it, letting the woman help lever her to her feet.

"Probably more than you think," Robin said softly, shifting to get the weight off her ankle.

Just a few more steps, she lied to herself. *Come on, Captain. You can tough it out.*

The rose woman let out a startlingly honest-sounding laugh, and offered Robin an arm to lean on. Now that the adrenaline was used up, the pain was excruciating. Grateful for the assistance, Robin took the offered support and let the woman lead her through the curtain, paying careful attention to where they were going in case the day had to end in another dash out a door. There was no telling just how far in over her head Robin might have landed herself, after all.

Together, they moved from the curtained-off foyer to a rich, opulent salon. Where the Coyote's salon had been formal and imposing, this one was warm, and slightly chaotic—all overstuffed pillows and vases of feathers. Drapes of fabric created playful nooks for secret whisperings out of the otherwise large room, and there was a fire in the massive hearth opposite the door, cones of incense smoking gently beside the grate to perfume the air with a sort of heavy, exotic spice that irritated the back of Robin's throat. Where a portrait should have been, over the mantle, was instead the largest mirror Robin had ever seen. The surface was etched with a dense, smoky pattern of curling, climbing roses, and lent the room a bit of extra reflected light, while at the same time obscuring the reflection to keep it from being too clear. Viewers would be offered a tantalizing glimpse into the darkened corners of the salon without betraying anyone's face. Clever.

The rose woman herself matched the house—she wore a tight black jacket with one of those choking Klonn collars, smart and snug. It topped a skirt so filled with fabric billows along the bustle that Robin wondered how the woman didn't blow away in a stiff breeze. Embroidered roses grew up the train of the dress, as if climbing a trellis, and light sparked in metallic thread as she moved.

She even smelled nice. The scent of roses pursued her like a shadow. It reminded Robin of summers spent playing in the neighbor's back garden, when she was very small and the rose bushes had been almost the height of the garden wall. That wall was gone now . . . as were the roses, the garden, their hive—and the neighbors.

The portrait hung on the left wall caught Robin's eye. The man was noble-looking to the point of absurdity. His nose was strong and straight, his eyes a piercing blue under scowling, intelligent eyebrows. His cheeks were sharp, his chin strong, and dimpled in the middle so perfectly that Robin doubted any man could actually have had such an attractive little indent. His uniform was the ice-blue affair that Robin remembered well from the Coyote's dinner suits, but the front was so bedecked with medals and silver frogging that the man in the picture might have tipped forward if he ever tried to stand.

Still, the thick black hair and the structure of his cheeks was familiar. The man was unmistakably related to the Coyote. Robin supposed that a lot of the Klonn nobility probably looked alike; if they were anything like the Benne, there was enough intermarriage between the families that cousins often appeared to be twins.

The woman noticed her interest and snorted. "Our magnificent King Eloy, in all his heroic glory."

"Exaggerated?" Robin asked.

"Extremely."

She led Robin through a door to the side of the ridiculous portrait that led to a surprisingly humble kitchen. A massive harvest table sat in the middle of the room, age-whitened and scarred with the reminders of a thousand communal meals. The walls were lined with long white countertops, and dozens of cupboards. It was tiled with white ceramic and porcelain, and the rose motif she'd noticed permeating all of the rest of the home's decor was noticeably absent. Instead, a cheeky ceramic rooster presided over the window ledge.

Limping over to the table, Robin chose the seat that afforded her the best view of the door. She unbuckled WINGS and lay the pack against her own legs. The warm metal against her shins soothed the throb of her ankle. Then she stripped off her gloves and unbuttoned her jacket, letting the warm air buffet pleasantly against the skin of her frigid hands and throat.

"Tea?" the woman asked, but the question was clearly rhetorical as she bustled about, pulling down a teapot and filling up a kettle. Robin said nothing as she watched, trying to study both woman and room without looking like she was terribly interested in either.

"So," the woman said, when the teapot was on the table and the cups had been laid at each of their elbows, "the Skylark has come to us at last."

"Well, you did ask ever so politely," Robin said. She'd meant it to be light, but bitterness crept in. She hated having to trust someone she didn't know, and a Klonn, to boot.

Instead of being insulted, the woman just laughed that genuine, heartfelt laugh again. Her eyes crinkled at the corners, betraying the fact that she was a bit older than her artful appearance made her look. She reached out to pour the tea, flashing the delicate skin of her wrist as she did so, like a courtesan.

The tea itself was pale beige, anemic from not having been steeped long enough before being served, and disgusting. It swirled with a generous daub of milk that was already waiting in the cup.

Ugh, Robin thought. *Why pollute tea with milk? What's wrong with perfectly good honey from perfectly good bees?* In that exact moment, filthy, reeking of fuel, hungry, and hurting, cold, and far from home, Robin would have given anything to have honeyed tea again.

"*Ai*, I did ask politely," the woman said, folding her elaborate skirts to the side so she could sit in the simple kitchen chair opposite Robin. "But you declined."

"I didn't need the help," Robin said, sipping at the tasteless tea. It may not have been made the way she preferred, but she couldn't deny that the warmth of its steam felt nice on her face, in her belly, and against her palms.

"And yet you clearly need it now," the woman scolded with an arched brow and a tut that sounded like it belonged on the tongue of a worn-down mother, and not on that of a woman blessed with the sort of ageless beauty that could have put her anywhere between twenty-five and forty. She was pillowy, with curvy hips, ample bosom, and the sort of naturally pouty lower lip that Robin had seen other women try to paint into existence. She looked pointedly at Robin's ankle and gave an imperious little hand wave so like the Coyote's dismissive superiority that Robin bristled. "You might as well accept that here is where you will be staying, at least for the near future. There is no need to be stubborn for the mere sake of stubbornness. Even I can see that your marvelous little gadget is broken, and so you will be neither flying nor running anywhere."

"Gadget?" Robin echoed, insulted on behalf of her poor rocket pack. She glanced down to where WINGS leaned forlornly against her shins. Whatever other damage had been done to it, she hoped it hadn't ruined too much of the internals. On top of the cracked canister, one side of the casing had been visibly and severely dented, and Robin doubted she could still deploy the blades, if they were even still straight enough to do so. She needed some time alone with her tool kit to fully take stock of the damage. She might even need a forge.

The enormity of what might be required to make WINGS fly again hit Robin hard. She stripped off her stinking coat with frustration, scrubbing at the back of her neck where the leather collar hadn't been tall enough to keep her skin from getting splashed.

The woman was right. There was, at least for now, nowhere else she could go. Every bolt-hole she'd created, every hiding spot, had been found by this woman, or the Coyote, or the Night Watch. And none of them would give her what she needed to fix WINGS.

"Fine," Robin conceded, hoping that she wasn't making a terrible mistake and brushing her crossed fingers over her shoulder just to be safe. "But I'll need the stuff I left behind. The fuel, my tool wallet. If it's still there."

"It will be done later tonight, after the commotion

with the Night Watch dies down," the woman said with a self-assured little nod. She rang a small bell that sat in the middle of the table and a young person with luxurious dark hair and eyes came in. Their skin—and Robin could see a *lot* of it—was like burnished gold, glowing with the fine pale hue of yellow porcelain. Robin blushed at their ensemble. Whatever it was they were wearing, there wasn't much of it.

"Bandages, Grier," the rose woman said. "A bowl of ice, some hot water, and that balm for inflammations. The attic room, I think. Our songbird might appreciate being away from the, ah, action of the house, and in a room with a window wide enough for taking flight."

She looked to Robin, and Robin realized what she was being offered—a room that was clearly not a prison cell.

Grier nodded and left, showing off a fair bit more of their nicely shaped rump than Robin was sure she'd ever seen on another person before.

"Omens," Robin breathed. "Where the hells am I?"

"*Ai*, of course," the woman said with a little smile. "You would not know, would you? I am remiss. You do not have them in Saskwya, so I am unsure if you have heard of them, but this is a *zentapi*."

"I don't speak much Klonnish," Robin said stiffly.

"You would call it a brothel, I believe," the woman said, wrinkling her pert little nose with obvious disdain for the lack of complexity in the translation. "That word is crude, though. There are too many negative connotations, and I do not like it, but it is the closest to accurate as I can conjure."

"You run your rebellion from a common bawdy house?" Robin asked, aghast.

"There is nothing common about my establishment." The woman bristled. "Madam Rosa's is all class."

"And that's you, is it then? Madam Rosa?"

"*Ai*. Madera Rosa—to the public, at least. Just 'Rosa'

is acceptable between us." Rosa shot her a fond look. Then she gently tapped the knuckle of her first finger against her lips, studying Robin's face carefully. Robin wondered what she saw there, beyond her exhaustion and wariness. "You will join our rebellion."

"No," Robin said quickly, firm with the need to reiterate her stance. "I really won't. I thank you for your help with . . . with him. But I'm not submitting to anyone's authority. And I'm getting sick of people telling me what to do, just so you know. Doesn't make me want to cooperate."

"My dear Miss Skylark," Rosa said, folding her hands primly on the well-worn tabletop. "Let me put it to you like this: you have a very powerful weapon, and a very powerful enemy in defying our king as you do. The Night Watch has made hunting you down a vital mission, and the people of this town have no reason to protect you and every reason to turn you in. You need a place to hide, and people to keep your secrets. We are those people, and this is that place. Our aims mesh. We both want to see this war ended, do we not?"

Robin nodded, wary. Where was this leading?

"Then this is what I propose: stay here, with us, and let us guide you. You are like an errant bomb—destructive and noisome. You have no aim. Let us be your spotting scope. You may retain your independence, but let us point you to where you can be most effective."

It sounded like a good idea, but Robin hesitated. She was tired—tired of being anxious, tired of being vigilant, tired of being cold, tired of being tired. She wanted to sleep. She wanted to trust someone, but wasn't sure it was wise. She'd once thought she could trust the Coyote, and that had obviously been a mistake. She didn't know how to play the manipulative mind games the Klonn seemed to favor, and she couldn't be sure that agreeing to Rosa's proposition would not also be agreeing to yet another dance she wasn't ready for.

"I don't know," Robin admitted.

"Think on it, then, as you convalesce," Rosa urged. She looked meaningfully at Robin's ankle. "Heal first, and then, when you have had the chance to know us better, I am sure you will make the right choice."

Robin bristled again. Could none of the Klonn ever respect the fact that she might be able to decide something for herself? "Fine. Yes, okay. But only for as long as it takes for me and WINGS to get healthy."

"WINGS?" Rosa repeated. "You named it? How quaint."

Robin drew herself up. Not with affront, but with pride. "She named herself."

CHAPTER SEVEN

Sometime later, when conversation had dwindled, and exhaustion had set in, Grier arrived to announce that the upstairs room was ready. Robin was half dozing in her chair, chin on her palm, the warmth and the small sandwiches Rosa had provided going a long way toward reminding her body that it needed real rest. Rosa immediately stood and began collecting up the tea supplies. The sound of clinking porcelain knocked Robin back into wakefulness, and was a clear signal that their conversation was over.

"Come, I will escort you to your room," Rosa said, offering her arm once more. Robin pushed herself wearily to her feet, then leaned over to pick up WINGS. As she shouldered the rocket pack, her throbbing ankle and bruises reminded her sharply that they existed, and she wondered how the Coyote was faring.

They haven't told me anything about him, Robin realized, sudden fear gripping at her heart. *How tired was I? What have they done with him? Is he okay?*

She didn't know Thorne, didn't know what their qualifications might be. What if they hadn't helped him? Rosa had assured her he would be well cared for, but what proof did she have that these people were capable of handling a wound like the one he'd sustained? What if they had deliberately left him to die? He was their enemy, after all; they had no proof but her own word that he wasn't. What if they'd locked him away somewhere, left him to suffer and die alone? What if she never saw him again?

"Can I . . . can I talk to him?" Robin said, seized by the sudden, fierce need to make sure he was all right, to check him over with her own eyes, hear that his heart still beat with her own ears. "Before we go up?"

"The Wolf?" Surprise colored Rosa's features, but her eyes took on a knowing gleam. Robin felt her cheeks heat at the implications that glance contained, especially since they weren't . . . well, *wrong*. "I do not know if Thorne is done."

"Please," Robin said. "Even if he's not, I just want to see. I just . . . I need to check."

Evaluating silence met Robin's request, and she did her best not to fidget. She poured her sudden nervousness into flexing her fist a few times, discreetly, behind her back. She knew what it sounded like, how it made it clear that she didn't trust the *zentapi* madam's people (and she didn't). But after everything she'd been through, everyone she'd lost, she knew she wouldn't be able to rest until she'd confirmed for herself that the Coyote would live. Despite everything, he was still the closest thing she had to an ally—and a friend—and she didn't wish to see him dead. Quite the contrary, in fact. The thought that she might lose him again, for good this time, made it hard to breathe.

"Of course," Rosa said at last. She turned and sent Grier to fetch news of the Coyote from the mysterious Thorne. Then she turned back to Robin and raised a carefully painted eyebrow, asking a question Robin didn't know how to answer just yet; she didn't know what that answer was.

"Don't . . . don't read too much into that, okay?" Robin hedged. "The Coyote—the Wolf, I mean, we have a . . . complicated history. To be honest, I don't even know what I'm doing about this whole rudding mess."

She plopped herself back into her seat, WINGS held tight against her chest. "He's still an enemy soldier."

"I have no illusions about my countryman, Skylark," Rosa agreed. "I am certain he has taken hundreds of Saskwyan lives."

"And I've taken hundreds of Klonn ones," Robin said, shame curling into her core, but chin lifted in defiance as she forced herself to admit this awful truth without looking away. She hugged WINGS tighter as Rosa retook her own seat opposite Robin.

"You are defending him, then?"

"I'm not defending him. I just think that . . . we all need to remember that soldiers do as they're told. Sealies, more so," Robin added bitterly. "That's just the way it is. Doesn't mean I like it."

Rosa tapped her bottom lip with a knuckle. "What I am asking, Skylark, is if you would place any faith in his apparent choice to defect from his position. Though we do not know his identity, we do know that the Wolf is very highly placed. And that he vanished. Gone from the eyes of the Aeroforce for months, and now, suddenly, you bring him to my door and profess him to be allied with you. You ask *much* of me to place my trust in him."

"I know that," Robin said softly. "I do. I just . . . he was a prisoner, too. At least, that's what he said. And we escaped together. Sort of." Robin didn't blame Rosa for her hesitation. She couldn't ask someone to trust the Coyote when she wasn't sure that she fully trusted him herself. Compassion was more what she had in mind, acknowledgment that he was a human being and deserved empathy, despite what he'd done in the name of his king.

"I see," Rosa said, eyes narrowed and assessing once more. There was a lot in her mannerisms and demeanor that reminded Robin of the Coyote. He, too, liked to play things close to the vest. The comparison made her shift uncomfortably.

Worried that she wasn't making her case clear, Robin took a deep breath and added: "He told me he flew under duress, that he'd tried to defect and that he had a brother they used as leverage against him." It felt like a betrayal, in some ways. This was the Coyote's confession to make, and Robin had no place sharing it. But right now, she needed to make sure Rosa understood, and she would do whatever it took to make sure the Coyote was safe at the hands of their erstwhile saviors.

"And where is this brother now?"

"Dead, I think," Robin said softly. "I didn't ask. He hasn't said, and I . . . there's a sadness in him that wasn't there before. If that makes sense?" Robin's voice crackled, blinking back frustrated, exhausted tears. "And I . . . I don't know, okay? I just . . . he's put himself at risk to help me over and over again. I wasn't going to let him just bleed to death for it. He's . . . well, he's hard to read. I get that. But he ran away for me. That has to mean something, right?"

"Something, indeed," Rosa said, cryptic. Then she sighed and tugged on the hem of her jacket, smoothed her hair back from her face, deliberately took the time to compose herself.

Robin flexed her fist again, and wondered if all these pauses were supposed to unnerve her.

Grier returned then, and Robin looked up expectantly.

"I have had a chance to speak with Thorne about your companion," Grier said. "His wound will heal, and he may even be able to pilot an aeroship again. Though, his hands are in quite a state. Some of the scarring may need to be cut away. Thorne suspects that some of the wounds have gone putrid under the skin, but even that should not keep him from the yoke."

"Oh," Robin said, sagging as the worry that had held her upright faded. "I guess that's . . . good?"

Don't think about Wade, Robin chastised herself. Aeroships are not gliders. It takes less strength. It's not fair, but that's the way things are.

"Is it?" Rosa asked, and Robin tried not to squirm under the scrutiny of her gaze. The woman was far too shrewd. It felt like she could see straight to the depths of Robin's soul. No wonder she'd organized this little rebellion; she was a born spy.

"He is awake, and has been asking for you, Miss Skylark," Grier said softly. "He wants to know that you are well."

Robin blinked. "He's worried about *me?*"

Grier nodded. "He is refusing to take the willow bark tea until he has spoken with you."

Robin rolled her eyes. Of course he was. Stubborn, overdramatic arse.

"Well, then," Rosa said, getting to her feet. "It seems you two are of like temperament. I shall take you to see our other guest, if only so he will rest."

"Thank you," Robin said, gritting her teeth against the pain of standing again. "I think."

"You have a good heart, and I cannot fault you for that," Rosa said after another long, deliberately silent moment. "But your stubbornness needs tempering." She sighed, and then tossed her hand in the air as if literally throwing away her caution. "Very well. We have removed anything from his room that may identify us, and there are no windows. Hopefully, he will not know where he is. Until we are absolutely certain of his loyalty, he must remain unknowing."

"You mean, he's your prisoner?"

Rosa nodded firmly, as if saying the words aloud made her uncomfortable. The irony of the situation was not lost on Robin. Now, he was the one locked away, and she was the one with the freedom of the house—she hoped; there was no telling whether they'd ever let her *out* of the upstairs room they'd prepared for her. Neither did it escape her notice that responsibility for his captivity sat squarely on her shoulders. She'd done what she needed to save his life, though. She wouldn't feel guilty for that.

"Okay. I understand. I won't tell him."

Satisfied, Rosa led Robin to the base of the grand staircase, and then, with a little smirk, pushed the center of one of the roses carved into the decorative framework. A seam in the wainscoting opened and resolved itself into a door.

"Clever," Robin said.

"It used to be the lumber room—storage for the downstairs fireplaces. But with the gas installed, we have converted the room for other uses." Rosa led Robin through a low, dark passage and into a small space that still smelled strongly of sawdust and earth.

The little room was dark, with only the light of an old-fashioned oil lamp set upon shelving bolted to the wall to provide illumination. It created a pool of orange light, casting sharp shadows amongst the jumble of fabric on a narrow camp cot low to the unfinished timber floor. There was no fireplace, and the air was significantly chillier than it had been out in the salon. Extra blankets were piled on the foot of the bed, and the handle of a warming pan stuck out the side of the mattress. The air smelled of iodine and metal, the tang of blood, old wood, and the vaguely stale smell of unwashed man.

Unlike the Coyote's pantry, this room had not been meant to be used as a torture chamber, but rather as a secret bolt-hole. It had been made as comfortable as such an inconvenient little room could be, and Robin wondered if any Saskwyan operatives had stayed here, or if it was only known to Klonn resisters. How far, exactly, did Rosa's network run? How deep? Were they known to her own superiors in the Air Patrol? Was it possible to use it to get a message back to her family, to let them know she was still alive?

No, she thought immediately. *That's not safe. Not for them. Nobody can know who I am, not yet.*

The Coyote was buried amid the hodgepodge of blankets on the cot. His back was to the door, his form just a series of lumps hidden by quilts and throws, but the buffet of warm air made him stir and roll onto his back. The blanket fell aside, revealing a tight wad of bandages wrapped around his otherwise naked chest and arm. A sharp sense of déjà vu strangled Robin, and she had to take a few deep breaths to remind herself that he was not Wade.

He maneuvered carefully until he was sitting up against the wall, the pillows scrunched up behind his back.

"He's still wearing his helmet," Robin blurted.

"He insisted," Rosa said softly.

The Coyote gave them a grave nod that looked ridiculously solemn with the lupine mask covering his face. Robin supposed it was meant to be one of gratitude. She couldn't see his expression, but she caught the full-body flinch as the courtesy twinged his injury.

"There is willow bark tea in the pot by the bed," Rosa instructed. "When you are finished, knock, and I will let you out."

She nodded to the Coyote, then formally to Robin, and was gone in a rustle of silk before Robin could figure out if she was expected to nod back. Or maybe curtsy? She wasn't wearing a skirt, though. She gave it up as a ridiculous bit of Klonn frippery, as Rosa was already gone, and turned to the Coyote.

His eye slits were trained on her. But if she was going to talk frankly with him, she wanted to see his actual eyes, and not just their shadow.

"If I close the door, will you take that off?" she asked.

"I would appreciate the opportunity to do so, yes,"

the Coyote agreed.

Robin pulled the trick door closed, watching carefully to see how the secret latch worked. Rosa had been right—she would have to knock to be released. There was no knob on this side, just a small ring of metal screwed into the back of the door's paneling that was used to pull it closed. Shoving down the small fear that Rosa might change her mind and decide it was best to keep them both locked away in here, indefinitely, she turned back to the Coyote and assessed him. He looked weak, vulnerable. His chest was as pale as the rest of him, sprinkled only slightly with black hair. He had no need for the ridiculous upper body strength of a glider pilot to fly his aeroship, but his shoulders were still defined. Perhaps not quite as strong-looking as Robin's own arms, but what he lacked in strength, he had always made up for in leverage and reach in their scuffles. The bandages made his skin look sallow, and his breaths were rapid with obvious pain.

"I am afraid I cannot reach the tea," the Coyote said after her long pause, the sour look on his face suggesting that he detested having to request help. "Nor can I lift off my helmet alone." His eyes drifted meaningfully toward her hands, still clutching WINGS to her chest like a child clinging to their favorite toy.

"No, no, of course . . ." Robin crossed the room, feeling foolish for thinking he could. She tried to limp as little as possible, and rested WINGS against the wall before sitting on the side of the bed.

The Coyote bowed his head, submitting to her aid. She trailed a finger along a deep scratch in the metal, along his cheek, that she'd never noticed before. Had it been there in the attic? Or had it happened as he pursued her through the streets? From the fight in the park? Or maybe in the forest, after the explosion, when he'd fled his own prison-home?

She reached under his chin to release the strap. The

soft flesh of his throat was warm against her fingertips, and she swallowed hard, trying not to think of how intimate a place it was, the underside of a chin. How effective a place to slip in a knife. How it said much about the trust he placed in her that he allowed her this access.

The gentle *click* as she undid the buckle was the only sound in the room, and, for reasons Robin didn't quite understand, it made her breath come a little fast. The soft bristle of his beard tickled her knuckles as she pulled the helmet carefully off his head. She set it on the foot of the bed, and bit back a laugh at the way it had left his normally slicked-back hair standing up at odd angles. Instead, she slowly and gently smoothed it down for him. He was sweaty, his hair filled with grit, but warm.

Alive.

His good hand came up, suddenly, and circled her wrist. She expected him to dig in, to shove her away, to bristle. Instead, his fingers fluttered against the underside, tickling against the sensitive skin. Gently, he tugged her arm down until her palm rested against his cheek.

Robin didn't pull away. He seemed to be measuring her pulse with his thumb. His hands were bandaged as well, only the tips of his fingers left unwrapped, just as hers had been when she'd first become a pilot. He turned his face into her hand and nuzzled it, kissing the swell of her thumb.

His skin was hot, his face slightly flushed. The pinkish tone made him look more human. Sweat beaded around his hairline—was he feverish? Grier had said his hand wounds might have attracted an infection, and she imagined that the pain from his wound was intense.

"Tea now?" Robin asked, unable to make her voice much louder than a whisper.

"Yes, of course." The Coyote let go, and used his good arm to prop himself against the wall, leaning his elbow on one of the shelves to keep his balance without straining his back.

Willow bark tea, an effective painkiller and disease prevention technique, was another thing she had been denied in her own captivity. She felt it would be petty to ask why, now, so instead, she just fetched the cup from the shelf. She moved to hand it to him, and they both realized at the same time that he couldn't hold himself up and accept the cup.

"I just . . . let me . . ." Robin said awkwardly, leaning slightly over his hips to steady the cup against his bottom lip. His eyelashes, spiked with moisture that Robin told herself was the product of pain and not shame at his own helplessness, fluttered as she tilted the cup up.

He took measured sips, wincing with each swallow. It didn't feel too hot against her hands, so it couldn't be scalding him. It was likely the taste. Robin had always found willow bark tea to be a little bitter, unless her mother had put a spoonful of honey in it.

When the cup was empty, she put it back on the shelf among the medical detritus that littered the surface. Then she helped him scuffle back down the bed, bodily lifting his hips so he wouldn't have to press with his arms and settling him back again into the pillows, shoulders propped up and comfortable. She tried very hard not to think about the way her strong fingers spanned his naked waist, and pulled them back to hang at her sides before they lingered past the point of necessity. Some of the tension drained from his posture as the tea began to take effect. "Better?" she asked.

"It will be soon," he acquiesced. He wiped the slight sheen of sweat from his forehead with the back of his hand.

"Why did you refuse the tea before?"

A familiar smirk curled into the corner of his mouth as he brought his eyes back to hers, but it was strained with pain, a ghost of its usual cocky self. "Would you have come if I had not?"

Robin huffed, sitting back on the side of the bed, arms crossed. "And what if I hadn't? Would you have spent the night suffering on purpose?"

He gave that one-shouldered, boyish shrug that was so at odds with his otherwise careful and calculated persona.

"I wanted to be lucid," he said. "Until I was certain that I was—we were safe." He looked pointedly down at WINGS.

At the pack. Not at her. Not at . . .

Rudding omens, Robin swore. *So he does mean to . . . ah, hells, I don't understand, I don't . . . why is he—how could he—?*

Robin felt tears build behind her lashes, slipping over her cheeks. She was exhausted, and confused, and relieved, and now that she was warm and fed, she was *angry*.

She had spent months grieving him, only for him to barrel back into her life, caring not about her, as he had so often claimed, but seemingly only about reacquiring WINGS. He had threatened to shoot her, and then been shot protecting her, or WINGS, or hells, maybe even them both, and . . . and . . . and she just didn't *know*. Was it Robin Arianhod, WINGS, or the Skylark that he loved? If he honestly even loved anyone at all.

"Skylark?" he asked, soft and hesitant, full of concern, and Robin let out a bitter laugh. Everything she'd been holding in rushed forward, obliterating the dam she'd stoppered it up behind, and she shoved to her feet, turning away from him so he wouldn't see her fall apart.

"I thought . . . omens, I thought you were dead," she said, hiccupping as the tears came harder. She shoved the heels of her hands against her eyes, but it didn't stop them. "I thought he had shot you, and you were *dead*, and I couldn't . . . I couldn't do that again, and I'm so mad at you, and I'm so relieved, and I just . . . I just . . . I *couldn't* have it happen again. Not to someone that I . . . that I . . ." But she couldn't say the word. Not now. Not like this. Not knowing whether or not he felt the same. Or if she really felt it at all, and it wasn't just the relief and confusion swirling and buzzing together like a shaken hive in her heart.

He heard it, anyway. "Ah, at last, you admit it," the Coyote murmured.

"Don't be smug," Robin said. She wiped sullenly at her face, huffing hard to try to get her stupid emotions under control.

"I do not mean to offend," he said quickly, but even without looking at him, she could tell that he was smirking.

"You're such a prick!" Robin countered. She whirled on him, and the smirk died on his lips. "You never mean what you say, and I don't know if I can trust anything out of your mouth!"

"You can," the Coyote protested. "Of course you can—"

"Can what? Trust you, believe you, just because you said I should? Uerrg!" Robin snarled, running her hands through her hair in frustration. "I just . . . I can't do this anymore. I don't know what you *want*."

"You, Skylark," he said, and his voice had that gravel-filled cadence to it that always made her insides shiver. "I want you. Have I not made that obvious?"

"No!" she cried, throwing up her hands and barking them ridiculously on the low ceiling of the lumber room. "No, you bloody well haven't. Hells, for all I know, this is yet another of your stupid rudding games, meant to lull me into complacency so you can steal away with WINGS and put a bullet in my head."

"Put a bullet . . ." Shock made his features go lax, and he stared at her with wide, honest horror. It was perhaps the most naked expression he'd ever shown her, and it twisted like a knife in her heart. He scrambled at the sheets, trying to swing his legs around, to reach out to her.

"Skylark, no. I would never—"

"Oh, so that isn't *exactly* what you threatened to do just a few hours ago?" She cut him off, and felt a small surge of victory when hurt and realization replaced the horror.

"No, I—" he started, and then stopped himself. The blank mask he always wore crashed back into place. It meant he was off-kilter, that he was feeling some emotion so strongly that he couldn't cope with it. She just wished she knew which one.

When he said nothing else, didn't move more or try to reach out, or even try to deny it, she bent down and scooped up WINGS. She had confirmed that he would live, had fulfilled the obligation to her guilt. If he wanted to suffer, then she'd leave him to do it alone, in peace. "I'm tired," she said softly. "I can't do this."

"Skylark, wait."

Robin ignored him, hefting the pack to her shoulder and turning toward the door.

"My dear, please," the Coyote said behind her, and there was a note of desperation she'd never heard from him before. Robin paused, hesitating, until a loud growl-groan pulled her back around.

"Oh, for the love of the gods," she said. "What in all the hells are you doing?"

The Coyote had levered himself up off the bed, swaying where he stood, his good hand braced against the ceiling. He looked as though he would pass out at any moment, eyes glossy with pain and desperation and something else Robin couldn't quite define. "Please, do not go," he whispered, teeth grit together against the pain.

"You're a fool," Robin said. Then she sighed and, placing WINGS carefully beside the room's door, returned to his side. His skin was burning hot as she chivvied him back to the bed, propping him up against the wall when he refused to lie down. She turned to pour him more of the willow bark tea, but his hand wrapped around her wrist, holding her in place again.

"I am sorry, Skylark," he said, plain and sincere. Beneath the sheen of fever in his gaze, she saw an incomprehensible sadness that he quickly shut down, blinked away, closed off. When he looked back up at her, there was moisture dotting his lashes, sticking them together in dark spikes. "I made a mistake, earlier, in the attic. I would *never* harm you. Forgive me, Skylark. Let me stay by your side. Let me help you."

"I can take care of myself," Robin bristled.

"Have I intimated that I believe you cannot?" the Coyote said, cocking his head to the side and tracing Robin's arm lightly with his fingertips. It was intimate, and grounding. Tender.

"I want this war over with the same fervor you do. I want stability. Please believe me, my dear. I am sorry."

"Are you, though?" Robin said, pulling away, firming her resolve, distancing herself from his desperately grasping fingers with each step backward to the door. "See, that's the problem. I can't tell. I have no idea what you're thinking. And I can't bet my life, and the outcome of this war, on your word alone. I'm sorry."

She rapped on the door with her knuckles, and it opened. She ducked out with WINGS, ignoring the Coyote's final, anguished-sounding, "Wait, please—!"

She was glad he was alive. But he had nothing to say that she wanted to hear.

CHAPTER EIGHT

Robin lay in the warm, soft, clean bed for hours, fuming. As exhausted as she was, she couldn't stop replaying the moment she'd realized the Coyote had a gun trained on her heart, and the way that he'd appeared, for all the honey in the world, as if he was ready to pull the trigger. No matter how many promises he made, or kisses he pressed into her thumb (the place on her hand she absolutely was not pressing to her own mouth, not at all), no matter how many pretty words and pleas for trust he warbled at her, his *actions* always spoke the truth.

And he had aimed a gun at her heart.

Twice.

The sun was well and truly down by the time Robin had dropped off. Her sleep was fitful, filled with angry dreams, and she jolted awake every time she knocked her ankle. Having forgotten to draw the drapes, Robin woke the next morning with the sun in her eyes, sweaty and upset, and feeling like she hadn't caught a wink.

And then a mountain brought her breakfast.

He was nearly as wide as the door frame, brawny and dark-skinned, and his sudden appearance on the threshold startled Robin. His smile was wide and honest, though, and Robin couldn't help but smile back as she shuffled up to sit against the headboard. He set the tray he carried on the bedside table, and then introduced himself as Taddeus Thorne.

"Oh, you're the medic," Robin said, and the man nodded.

He explained, in as few heavily accented Saskwyan words as possible, that he was ostensibly the *zentapi's* security enforcer, handyman, and, as in the case of the patient downstairs and her own ankle, its sawbones. He, like most of the people who worked there, lived in the house and shared in the domestic chores it took to keep the establishment running smoothly. He then checked her ankle, making noises to himself as he asked her to push her foot against his warm palm, or to rotate it this way or that, and declared it simply strained. She was to walk as little as possible for the next few days, and never without support.

Breakfast after that should have been awkward, but was not. Thorne was silent, except for some encouraging noises when Robin spoke, and was the sort of man who managed to make you say more than you meant to by means of the simple act of listening. It made sense that he worked with Rosa, spying on their own people by smiling pleasantly, letting them condemn themselves with their own bragging and rambles.

After the breakfast tray was removed, Robin discovered that he was also a tinkerer of the first degree.

He helped her lay WINGS on the foot of the bed, and puzzled over the writing as Robin had, though he admitted that he didn't know the other alphabets used alongside the Klonn and Saskwyan letters. Together, they assessed the structural damage—thankfully, nothing that a few good bangs of a hammer couldn't pop back into shape, and some time with a forge wouldn't create replacements for—measured the fuel canister so they could commission a replacement from a glassblower, and took stock of what tools and materials would be needed to repair the damage done by the crash against the chimney. Afterward, Thorne left with a shopping list and instructions that Rosa expected Robin downstairs when she was dressed.

Grier came in as Thorne departed, sleepy-eyed and

blowsy, a satisfied smile curling against flushed cheeks. Robin felt herself blushing at the thought of what Grier might have done while at work last night to earn that expression, and tamped down hard on the curiosity that flared up, trailing memories of the Coyote's kisses through her mind. Grier carried a wash basin, a bundle of clothing, a pair of scissors, and a cane.

"Oh," Robin said, accepting the cane and running her hands along the gleaming black handle. The Coyote had never offered her one during her days of captivity. She had, instead, been forced to lean on him, to take his—or the seneschal's—arm every time she'd had to walk anywhere.

Stale resentment flared up under her skin.

"Thank you," Robin said, forcing herself to unclench her fists and jaw. All the anger, all the hurt that she'd been too busy running for her life to process came crashing down on her, leaving her curled up and shaking on the edge of the bed with WINGS spread out like a gruesome autopsy at her feet.

"Miss Skylark?" Grier asked, setting their burden down on a small vanity against the wall opposite the door. "Did breakfast not agree with you?"

"It was fine," Robin said, pressing the heels of her hands against her eyes, willing her heart to stop jumping and racing under her ribs. The tips of her fingers tingled, and she felt, suddenly, like someone was trying to crush her windpipe. She swallowed hard against the sensation, willing her stomach to stop roiling. "I'm just . . . I don't know. I just . . ."

Grier laid a soothing, warm hand on Robin's shoulder. "You have experienced much recently. It is quite normal to suffer an attack of nerves, or to feel panic once you are safe."

Robin looked up at Grier, ashamed that a few tears had squeezed out of the corners of her eyes and were rolling down her cheeks. "Am I safe?" she asked softly.

"Yes," they assured her. "My family supports the king and his war. I therefore could not, in good conscience, remain at home doing nothing. One of our servants had a brother who sometimes, for reasons that were never asked by my parents, slept in our cellar."

"He was part of the spy network?" Robin guessed, breath still shaking, but grateful for the distraction. She wiped her face with the cuffs of the blowsy—and thankfully opaque—sleeping gown that had been provided for her.

"Hmm, yes," Grier said, moving their hand to begin carding it gently through Robin's tangled hair. Their fingernails were delicate against Robin's scalp and neck, and gave her a small attack of the shivers. They pulled the braid loose and, confused, Robin sat still and let them pet her. It felt nice, but was also bizarrely intimate for someone Robin had only met yesterday. "So I joined the *zentapi* and the rebellion. Though my family does not understand why I elected to enter a trade when I could have lived on the family wealth, they have left me to my choice. And I have been able to funnel that wealth into making sure that people like you, like Rosa, have what they need in the fight for peace. And I am not the only one. We have power, Skylark, though it is unseen. You are safe."

"Okay," Robin said. "Thanks."

"It does not hurt that I rather enjoy the work of the *zentapi*, too," Grier added with a saucy wink.

It put her in mind of gentle caresses and passionate kisses in the forest. She caught herself stroking her bottom lip with a finger and scowled, dropping it back down to her lap. Robin sighed. It was a pretty story, and oh, how she hoped it was true.

"He is asking about you," Grier said at length, once Robin's hair was smoothed down her back and her breathing had returned to normal.

"He can ask all he wants," Robin snapped.

Grier raised an amused eyebrow. "Lovers' tiff?"

"We're not lovers," Robin answered honestly. She was tempted to add more, to say, *maybe we might have been, before he threatened to shoot me*, but instead, she stood.

Grier passed her the cane, and shook out the clothing they'd brought. Robin was immeasurably relieved to see that the pile of fabric resolved itself into a pair of plain brown woolen pants, a matching waistcoat, and a dark orange shirt. They looked like something a young man would wear into town, and Robin wondered if they had been left behind by some client or another after a drunken, happy night at the *zentapi*.

Robin washed up quickly, making a point to get the engine grease out from underneath her fingernails, and then sat at the basin at Grier's request. They had all manner of potions and bottles in a little satchel they'd brought with them, and Robin realized that they meant to wash and style Robin's hair.

"I'm not some grand lady. You don't have to do this for me—" Robin began, but Grier tsked at her.

"It is my job," they interrupted. "I am going to trim it, too, if that is acceptable."

Robin nodded, not really having a preference one way or another.

"Will you color it?" Grier asked as she ran a comb through Robin's hair.

Robin paused. It wasn't the first time she had considered the option, but it was the first time she was in a position to make good on it. She looked in the mirror and ran her fingers through the scraggly fringe.

"Have you heard of the nowhere folk?" Robin asked softly.

Grier thought for a moment, and then shook their head.

"The Coy—I mean, the Wolf called them . . . alb—

uh, albinos," she said, struggling for the word. "People with no place. The gods have blessed them with the ability to go anywhere, because they don't look like they're *from* anywhere. I didn't think so before, but I . . . maybe this is supposed to be a gift."

She stared at her reflection in the mirror, at the horrible white hair sprouting from her scalp.

"How so?"

"I'm one of the nowhere folk now. I can go anywhere, do anything, because I look like I could be from anywhere. I'm not a Sealie, or a Benne, or a Klonn. I'm just a . . . person, trying to end the war. Maybe this was supposed to happen."

Robin pursed her lips and let the pronouncement settle on her skin. What if the gods had blessed her? Maybe this was their plan? She was nationless. She could fight everyone. She could fight for everyone. As the Skylark, she could put an end to all the fighting, all the death, and then, as Robin, she could go home.

Grier ran their fingers through Robin's locks, which were oily and filthy from Robin's flight through the forest and rivers, from her nights in an attic and her months on the run. Fingernails scraped against Robin's scalp, scratching gently and rhythmically, soothing. Robin closed her eyes and leaned back into the touch.

It was nice to have someone touching her without the intent to hurt, or control.

Grier dipped the comb in the basin, and ran it through Robin's hair, smoothing out the tangles. It hung in limp, damp strands, but the bald patches had filled in nicely. Then Grier took up a pair of little silver scissors and began to snip. Robin, who'd never had her hair cut by anyone but her own mother, swallowed hard against the sudden lump in her throat and tried very hard not to cry.

Washed, dressed, and feeling decidedly more human, Robin made her careful way down the narrow stairs that curved along the end of the building, using the cane as Thorne instructed. This put her in a hallway that ran the length of the place, four doors along each side, which she had to hobble down to reach the grander staircase that led to the ground floor.

Her room was tucked into the peak of the building, above the fourth floor, and there was an identical hallway along each of the three subsequent landings. She studied each of them as she passed, in case she needed to make a getaway later. Every floor was the same—four solemn doors, with an elaborate and racy image in a stained glass window capping the far wall at the end. It was luxurious, and formal, and still. It reminded her uncomfortably of the Coyote's country manor, until a bright peel of laughter rang out from behind one of the doors, followed swiftly by the echo of giggles and mock-horrified exclamations. The sounds of people enjoying themselves. The sounds of *happiness*.

Robin felt her spine soften a bit as something in her guts unclenched.

She resumed stumping down the stairs, looking forward to sitting when she got to the bottom. It would only be a few days before she no longer needed the cane, Thorne had said, but the forced dependance on it chafed against her patience.

I can't be the Skylark without the ability to run.

"Hmph," she said to the cane. "I'm happy to have you now, but I will also be quite happy to be rid of you. Your days are numbered."

"You are also talking to a stick," Rosa said.

Robin's head snapped up.

The madam was walking toward her from the far end of the hallway she'd paused beside, and Robin had the misfortune of catching herself in an embarrassed blush before she could try to suppress it.

"Morning," Robin said.

"Good morning. Grier has done well."

Robin couldn't help the involuntary pat at the back of her head, where her hair was significantly shorter than it had been in years. It was now a shining, smooth white sheet that hung around her shoulders. It kissed her collarbones, curling in toward her face, as if directing attention to her freckles and her wide, honey-brown eyes. Her fringe was now a straight line that just brushed her eyebrows, which were still incongruously sparrow-brown. "Er, thanks? I sort of . . . decided I should probably embrace a gift of the gods. I've never been touched by a god before."

"You Sealies and your superstitions." Rosa laughed, but it wasn't mocking. It was nothing at all like how Renge would have said it, or even how the Coyote had. Still, Robin felt her spine go stiff at the perceived insult; even if it wasn't meant as one, it was still too much a reminder of all the times it *had* been thrown in her face. She tried to force herself to relax, to stop betraying the sudden surge of emotion that flowed up her throat. Her free hand curled around the shaft of the cane.

"Do you wish to talk about it?" Rosa inquired, taking in her sudden defensive posture.

"No," Robin said.

"Very well. We have much else to discuss. Give me a moment, while I finish up." Each doorway had a little half-moon shaped table beside it, a silver dish etched with roses resting on top. Rosa reached out to the one dish cradling an envelope, beside the door from which laughter still tumbled into the hall. She scooped it up, peered inside, counted the colorful paper bills, and then put it into a pocket hidden under her bustle.

"A regular," Rosa said, when she noticed Robin watching. "She would not be here otherwise. Not in this weather."

Robin turned to peer out the window. The roof of the building adjacent had a layer of snow as thick as a man was tall. She hadn't noticed the storm growing, but the sky was now white with flakes, the daylight blocked almost completely.

"I've taken off in worse," Robin said, truthfully. "But it sure is blowing."

"That is due to the harbor. Though, ai, I suppose that further north, in Saskwya, it does snow more. The south of Klonn, where I am from, hardly sees snow at all. When it does, the populace reacts as if the world is ending—the roads must be shut down, and the children kept home from school."

"I used to build snow forts," Robin said, "and go riding down the high street hill on a piece of old plyboard."

"My mother would never have allowed such improper behavior," Rosa said, laughing slightly, eyes on the distant past. "When you are well, you must show me."

"Sure," Robin agreed, startled by how quickly she seemed to be building rapport with her vibrant hostess.

Rosa smiled, and for a moment, Robin was warmed by the memory of many bright winter days with Al, before they had been sent for their government-mandated apprenticeships. Robin's hands balled into fists of their own accord, and she forced her fingers to flex outward, forced herself to take a deep breath.

It was okay to miss him, even still. It was natural.

"If you please," Rosa said, indicating that Robin should continue her journey, and together, they made their slow way downstairs. Rosa was patient with Robin's speed, watching carefully, but allowing Robin the freedom to move without grabbing to hurry her along. When they reached the bottom, Rosa gestured to a corner of the ground floor salon that was lined with deep red sofas. Plush, dark violet throws adorned the seating area, and a sheer curtain allowed for a semblance of privacy, while revealing the silhouettes of the people within the snug nook to anyone who might be standing across the room.

Robin raised an eyebrow, but followed, trying very hard not to think of how useful that corner might be with a candle to backlight one of the *zentapi's* employees.

Rosa sat primly—her corset and breeding both clearly would never allow for a slouch—and arranged today's bouquet of skirts artfully around her legs. Robin, in direct contrast, fell back into the sofa, relieved to be off her foot. She laid the cane across her lap, shifted so her ankle was elevated on a fancy pouf, and waited. A tea service was already set out on a small table beside Rosa's elbow, and she poured two cups, adding milk to both before Robin could stop her.

Robin took the proffered tea, but didn't sip. The delicate cup was warm against her palms, which was enough. The *zentapi* wasn't chilly, but the snow whistling outside the windows was enough to make a person want to curl up in a blanket beside a roaring fire and stay put for the day.

Once her tea was tasted, Rosa looked up at Robin and said: "I trust your visit with the Wolf yesterday was to your satisfaction?"

"Uh, yeah," Robin hedged, attempting to avoid Rosa's shrewd gaze by bathing her face in the steam rising from her tea.

Does she know? Robin thought. *Did she hear us fighting? Has Grier told her already that I know he's been asking for me again?*

"You stand by your decision to trust him, then?" Rosa pressed.

Turmoil soured Robin's mood, and she set her vile cup of tea aside.

What should be the maneuver here? Admit that she was having trouble trusting the Coyote herself? That he had threatened to shoot her? Or that, maybe, Robin had overreacted, that she hadn't given him the opportunity to explain himself? It was possible, she could now admit, that he had aimed a gun at her heart because they'd been followed, that he had been observed, or they were being overheard. There were a hundred different reasons why he had said he'd never want to hurt her, even while trying to do so.

Rosa waited, patient as Robin chewed on her warring feelings of pity for the Coyote, and anger at what he'd done, the warmth of the intimacies they'd shared, and the chill of that horrible look in his eyes when she'd thought he was going to betray her. The kisses they'd shared. The way her heart had tasted when it leapt into her mouth when she'd realized he'd been shot.

"I want to," Robin said at length. "I really want to. And I really think he wants to, too. I just . . ." She twined her fingers in her lap, nerves jangling. "I don't think he . . . he's conflicted. He's given up everything to be here, and I don't think he knows what that means yet."

"Many here have done the same," Rosa pointed out.

"Yeah," Robin said. She picked at her nails for a second, and then said, "Yeah. Okay. I trust that his heart is in the right place, even if right now, he isn't sure what to do with that. And I want to believe very badly that he'll figure it out."

"Very well," Rosa said after a long, calculating moment. "If you say you vouchsafe for him, then I put his responsibility in your hands. Understand that any misstep on his part will come down upon your head. It is up to you to ensure that his loyalty is true. And trust me when I say that there are others in my network who will not hesitate to remove you both if it appears as though one of you is a danger to us. You understand, do you not?"

Robin swallowed hard and nodded, sitting up a bit straighter. This had suddenly got a lot more serious than she had been expecting. Of course she understood the gravity of what she was trying to do as the Skylark. But that was back when it was just her own safety and life on the line. To agree, in however a roundabout way, to take the Coyote's life into her hands as well, was a much bigger responsibility than she had anticipated facing.

But if I'm responsible for him, and he understands that, Robin mused, then maybe I can finally get a straight answer out of him.

"May we all hope that your decision proves a wise one," Rosa said with heavy finality.

It felt like a benediction, requiring an equally serious response, so Robin lifted her hands, palms up, and replied: "May the bees deliver your wish to the gods' ears." And then she crossed her fingers and brushed her shoulders, just to be sure.

Rosa blinked at her, clearly caught off guard by the response, and her red lips curled into a soft smile. "Well. Thank you, then," she said. "And what now, Skylark?"

"Now, I think I have to have a chat with, um . . ." She hesitated, unsure of how to refer to the man who used to be her archnemesis while around his countrymen.

"Your beau?" Rosa offered.

Robin wanted to squawk and deny it, but in their strange, barrel-loop flip of a relationship, she supposed it was an accurate term.

"My masked turncoat," Robin said instead, meeting Rosa's smile with a smirk of her own, indulging in the ability to have someone to tease with. She missed the simple social banter of the mess hall.

"Now?"

Robin picked up the tea and forced herself to drink some of it. It wasn't so bad, now that it was cooler. It didn't taste so much like hot milk. She settled back further in the settee. "After tea," she said, remembering that there was a lot more to the little rituals around dining and food for the Klonn than there were for Sealies. It meant something that Rosa had offered her tea for this difficult conversation, whether Robin understood it fully or not.

She could tell that she'd made the right move when Rosa relaxed back into the cushions as far as her underpinnings allowed. "Do you miss flying your glider?" Rosa asked, conversational and completely without prompt.

Robin startled so badly that her teacup clattered against the saucer.

Leaning forward slowly, as if not to spook a wild animal, Rosa took Robin's left hand off the cup handle and turned it palm up. She drew one finger along the grid of scar tissue, studying it with the same intent she'd had the night she rescued Robin from the laundry line.

Robin pulled her hand back and curled her fist over her heart. "I have WINGS now. I have all the sky I want."

"Except for that which stretches over Saskwya—which, I believe, is the one you long for most."

Robin blinked. That was a little more insightful than she'd been ready for. "There's no way I could cross the front, though. Even if I avoid the Klonn guns, I might get hit by the Saskwyan anti-aircraft cannons. I'm stuck here." Robin looked around at the decor, taking a good long look at *here*.

"Can I ask?" she said, reluctant to break the companionable hush, but curious for the answer. "Why are you doing all of this? I mean, the shelter, the genuine interest?"

Rosa sighed softly, as a teacher might at a particularly thick question. "Because you are the Skylark—you can be a great symbol for the resistance. Because people already know who you are, and you have only been out three times. Because we need you. As I said on that rooftop, there are those of us who weary of war."

"But why *not* turn me over?" Robin asked. "There's an

awful lot of zeros on that wanted poster. You could use that money to fund your operations."

Rosa gestured with her teacup to the very same decor Robin had been assessing. "I do not need money. I make all I need here. What I do not have is an abundance of *peace*."

Robin scoffed.

Rosa snapped her head up and scowled. "Do not make noises at me, Miss Skylark," she cautioned. "Children I have known since their birth have died like pigs in the mud. I lay with soldiers at night knowing they may never see another morning. I see the actions of my government, my royals, and I am shamed by their intolerance and petty greed. Eloy is a selfish, stupid man who toys with armies. It shames me to be of noble birth, and thus, to share even a little of his rubbish blood. He is a coward who listens to far too many of the poisonous lies that are dropped inside his ear."

Robin, shamed by Rosa's heartfelt words, asked quietly: "How do you know?"

Rosa smirked, relaxing again. She sipped her tea. "People talk to my staff, talk about things they should not. No one expects us to be listening. But we do, and we use that knowledge to incite change where we can. We cannot do it alone, though. Together, we could see an end to this misery."

Robin dropped her gaze to her lap, trailing her eyes over the lines of the cane. Rosa's proposition was sound, but Robin still wasn't sure she was ready to trust it at face value. She'd already had her wings clipped once, and there was much of her situation that reminded her uncomfortably of the one she'd escaped.

There was also so much about it that was different, too. But was it enough? Rosa spoke of freedom, of ending the war, yet had immediately locked the Coyote away. What, really, was her aim?

"You do not need to pledge yourself to us now," Rosa said, standing to collect the tea supplies—a clear signal that their conversation was over. "Rest, heal, as we agreed, and we will discuss when you are well. Perhaps then, you will have seen the potential in allying yourself to our cause."

"Thank you," Robin said, hands wrapped around the cane. "Thanks for helping him, anyway. And thanks, you know, for not locking me up, too."

Rosa smiled, and it was genuine and warm. "Come now, Skylark, even with your marvelous gadget broken, I doubt that we could ever keep you here against your will."

"Funny," Robin said, pulling herself to her feet. "That's the exact lesson the Klonn Aeroforce failed to learn."

CHAPTER
NINE

When Robin let herself into the lumber room under the stairs, the Coyote was asleep. His helmet sat on the floor beside the bed, the covers pulled over his head so only a sweaty tuft of black hair peeked out the top, like the irritable sprout of a carrot. Robin found it adorable, and wondered at herself for thinking anything about him was any kind of cute.

"He's covered," Robin whispered back over her shoulder to Grier, who pushed a small trolley of bathing things behind her. "Just park it there, please," she added, pointing to the only bare spot inside the tiny room, right beside the door. It closed in the entire space, made it impossible for more than one person to be standing at a time, but that was fine. Grier was leaving.

It was colder here than in the main room, just like the day before. Robin passed Grier the cold warming pan, tugging it carefully free from the bedclothes so as not to jostle the sleeping Coyote before they were left alone.

As soon as the door was shut, Robin turned up the lamp. She tugged the trolley as close as it could get, and sat gently on the side of the bed. She set the cane on the ground, screwed up her courage, and touched the Coyote's hip gently through the blankets. Normally, she'd have shaken his shoulder instead of touching somewhere so, ah, intimate. But the only one available to her was covered in bandages, and that wouldn't do.

The Coyote made a rumbling, annoyed sound, and

then sucked in a hissed noise of pain as he rolled onto his back.

"Hey. I have willow bark tea," Robin said softly into the hush of the room.

"Skylark?" he asked, voice crackling, and he pulled the blanket down just enough to crack open a red-rimmed eye at her. He looked awful, face strained with pain and creased with sleep. "You came back?"

"I did," Robin said, a stab of guilt tightening her own voice. *He thought I'd abandoned him. Maybe forever.* "Let's get you up."

It took some maneuvering, but eventually he was propped against the wall, panting and white-faced. As soon as he was upright, Robin pressed the cup of medicine to his lips. His hands were shaking too much to hold it himself. A soft knock at the door brought Grier back with the warming pan, filled with coals and wrapped in a quilted cozy, and Robin made sure to block their view when she retrieved it.

"Ah," the Coyote said as she slid the pan into place at the foot of the bed. "How kind." There was something in the way he said it that made Robin look up sharply.

"Did you think I wouldn't be?" she asked.

He took a moment to shakily lift the teacup and drink. Robin fisted her hands by her sides and watched him, ready to dive in if the cup started to wobble too much. "I believed you thought me undeserving," he finally said, his voice clearer now that he'd wet his throat.

Robin bit back a frustrated growl. "Not undeserving. No prisoner, no matter what their crime, should be treated as anything less than the human being they are. Just . . ."— she grunted, annoyed at her lack of graceful, diplomatic wordsmithery—"really rudding hard to trust."

The Coyote was quiet for a long moment, silver eyes thoughtful, before he at last whispered: "So I am a prisoner, then."

"But still human," Robin insisted. She refilled the cup in his hand with fresh, hot tea, making sure that he could hold it, and prompted him to drink. "And still worthy of compassion. Drink that, and I've brought water to wash with. I've been told I'm not allowed to change your bandages yet, but if we promise not to strain your shoulder, we can get your hair and face cleaned up at least."

The Coyote made a small, irritated sound around the rim of his cup. "I would appreciate it."

Robin didn't let herself dwell on how domestic it was, helping him shuffle to the edge of the bed, bracing his neck gently as she poured the warm water on his head, or wiped down the skin she could access with a damp cloth to chase away the last of the grime and dried blood all over his stomach and back. They were both silent, something about the tasks and the situation not lending itself to chatter, so the only sounds were the water splashing into the bowl, the crackle of the lamp wick, and their syncopated breathing.

When he was as clean as he was going to get without being able to actually get into a tub, and settled back in the now warmed bed, Robin sat on the edge of the cot and once more screwed up her courage.

"I've vouched for you," she said, the first words that had passed between them in some time. "So, you know, don't get us killed."

"Why?" he asked, his gaze full of soft surprise as he reached out to take one of her hands between his. She let him pull it into his lap, let him brush his bandaged fingers across her knuckles.

"Because you asked me to trust you," Robin said simply.

"And you walked out of the room." He lifted her hand and kissed the back of it, and though his beard pricked a bit, she found she didn't mind the gallantry of the gesture, however Benne-ridiculous it was.

"You would align yourself with these rebels so quickly?"

Robin started. "How do you know who they are?"

"I was an officer in the king's own Aeroforce. I know of the rebels. I even expected that you may eventually fall in with them, when I realized you had fled without me." Robin kept her features carefully schooled, jamming her frustration and distrust down. He already knew. Of course he did. "What I did not expect was how swiftly you would choose to side with them."

"Well, the enemy of my enemy is my friend, as they say." Robin narrowed her eyes, trying to figure out what he was getting at. It was almost as if he was trying to ruin the peace she was struggling to build between them.

"Hmph," the Coyote grumbled. "I am not your enemy, my dear. I have chosen a side, and it is not the one my superiors hoped for. If you will not forgive me for my foolish outburst in the attic, then allow me to prove my allegiance. You owe me that, at least."

"I owe you nothing," Robin said, carefully, wanting it to be very clear. "And we're even, you and I. A life for a life."

The Coyote lowered her hand, gaze careful and guarded. "Am I not forgiven for a misstep made in desperation?"

Robin regarded him in silence. Should she forgive him for the moment in the attic? Could she trust that it was just another of his melodramatic fits, brought on by exhaustion and the frustration of being forced to live on the run, that it was not an omen of the man he truly was? Was she a fool for even wanting to believe what he'd said? He was confusing, certainly, but could she stomach the thought of not forgiving him? Of going out there and telling Rosa she'd changed her mind, that she never wanted to see him again? Were her feelings blinding her, or was *this* the truth, this calm regret?

She had a sudden, overwhelming desire to fit her mouth over his own, to kiss away the worry and the guilt that played around his eyes, to soothe the tense way his shoulders curled up from the pillows. To feel how warm the fever had made him against her own palms, to make the stain on his cheeks spread all the way down his neck. To just stop rudding caring about right, or wrong, or *why*.

Robin shook her head, trying to shake the confusing, circular thoughts into some form of order. "This is crazy. You realize that, right? That we're both totally crazy? I don't even know what to call you. You're not in an aeroship anymore. I can hardly continue calling you the Coyote."

A lazy, triumphant smile appeared on his face. She hadn't said the words, but he'd heard her willingness to try all the same. Smug jerk.

"I suppose, if it must be something, you may call me Velph."

"Velph," Robin repeated. "I heard the general call you that. When we were . . ." *standing over Al's corpse*, she thought. "In the forest."

"It is the Klonnish word for 'wolf.' Wolves are my family icon."

Robin nodded and stood. "Very well, Velph. I'm still not certain I can trust you"—the Coyote grimaced, though he chose not to argue—"but I've decided that I'll at least give you the opportunity to prove me wrong. The gods only know if I'm being an idiot for doing it, but we're both equally at a disadvantage here, so I'm willing to give you one last chance. You say you want to help, so let's start again, a fresh slate, a clean chapter."

Velph lifted her hand again, pulled it up to his mouth, and dropped a chaste kiss in the middle of her scarred palm. It sent weird tingles racing up her spine.

"Good evening," he said, flicking a look up through his lashes that made the tingle stronger. "My name is

Velph, and I sincerely appreciate that you saved my life yesterday."

It was all Robin could do to stamp down on the stupid, surprised giggle that threatened to jump out of her throat at his unexpected and ridiculous charade. "Pleased to meet you, Velph. I'm Skylark, and I sincerely appreciate you saving mine."

The Coyote released her hand and sat back, studying her face carefully. "I may not call you by your given name?" he asked, expression falling only slightly.

Robin shook her head. "No, not here. You get to hide your face. I get to hide my name. I have a family to protect, and I'm not ready to give Rosa and her people everything."

The Coyote grinned at her, a sideways, conspiratorial smile. "But you will tell me."

"Eventually," Robin hedged.

The smile softened. "And so each will be a secret only for the other."

Robin felt something warm spread through her stomach at the thought, stirring in with the tingles. A truce, it seemed, had been brokered.

Gods, she thought. Don't let me regret this choice.

She stood, adjusting the sheets around his naked waist, and so was caught off guard when he leaned up and pressed his mouth against hers. The kiss was swift, but strong, and filled with a meaning that Robin didn't quite catch.

"Thank you," Velph said, flicking another look up at her, voice full of that wonderful gravelly rumble, and Robin felt her face flush up.

"Rest now," she squeaked, and was still blushing when Grier let her out.

"Shut up," Robin grumbled as she passed Grier's knowing smile, and she limped up the stairs to die of embarrassment, alone.

For the next two weeks, Robin remained as sedentary as possible, just as Thorne ordered. And, at the same time, tried not to go utterly stir crazy. When the Night Watch continually failed to appear at the zentapi to haul her away, she relaxed and began to believe that Rosa really was who she claimed to be: a woman who genuinely wanted to see the end of the war, for whatever personal reasons she might have, and who was willing to do whatever she could to make that happen.

Thorne brought Robin her breakfast most mornings, and helped as she laid bare the innards of WINGS, greasing gears and tightening joints in preparation for a time when Robin would again be well enough to fly. Together, they tapped out the dents in the crunched casing, marveling at how seamlessly the mysterious metal popped back into shape, and replaced the worn leather straps of the harness with new padded ones. Robin had been right, and had indeed been lividly purple with bruises for days and days after her wild flight from Velph's aeroship and their scuffle in the attic.

At first, she wasn't sure how comfortable she was in sharing the secrets of WINGS with this helpful stranger. It felt oddly like a betrayal—to the pack itself, which she had sworn to keep safe, and secondly, to Velph, who had a greater claim to the pack than anyone besides herself simply because of the way in which he'd acquired it—not to mention, all the blood he'd shed for it. But she was a fool to think she could get the replacement parts she needed without Thorne—she had no forge, no raw material, no experience in glassblowing, and no connections to get what she needed in the middle of Lylon. She couldn't very well silence every person she engaged in trade with with a gold coin. And so, just as she had when she'd first repaired the ornery rocket pack, she was once again reliant upon her benefactors to provide the resources she needed. This time, at least, it was a less onerous task, as she had only to fix it, rather than sabotage it under the guise of repair.

Beyond that, the *zentapi* was a cheerful place. People sang as they went through their chores, and strains of music wafted up from downstairs in the evening, along with the scent of roses, incense, and fragrant cigar smoke. The happy hum of conversation, wild laughter, and breathless exhalations permeated the air. The Klonn, it seemed, took their Arts very seriously, and both the Art of Love and its subsidiary, the Art of Pleasure, were practiced joyfully, openly, and without recrimination. Only those who wished to worship did, and no one was master of anyone else's body or desire—for lack of a better way to describe it, everyone's castle was their own. And the only fee Rosa seemed to take from a worshiper's monetary tribute was that which was then used to cover their room and board.

The fussy, prudish Saskwyan part of Robin curdled in protest at the thought of all these people indulging in carnal pleasure out of wedlock, but she had to admit that there was something wonderful in the happy energy of the house. People loving one another just because they could . . . a society where marriage didn't have to be the only goal to intimacy—it all held a sort of undeniable appeal. And, if she was honest, when she indulged in the memory of that kiss in the forest, or the one she'd received in the attic (before Velph had ruined it), all the malarkey about being a patron of the Arts started to make brilliant, sparkling sense.

Robin was, she realized, queen of her own domain, and what she sought to do with her land was no one's business but her own. Which is why she found herself visiting Velph with ever increasing regularity.

Tension still rippled between them when she would

stump her way down to the hidden room for a visit. But for his part, he did genuinely seem to care about earning back her regard.

And it was easier to think of him as Velph than as the Coyote. It helped to separate the man from what he'd been forced to do, from the people he'd killed, from the way he'd treated her when their captors had been watching, or when he'd been hidden away under that fearsome lupine countenance. He still wore the helmet when not in her presence, but was eager to remove it once the door to his secret cell sealed shut and they were alone.

Late afternoons were often spent over a cup of tea with Madam Rosa. The *zentapi's* mistress brought the tea up to Robin's bedroom herself, just before the brothel opened for the evening's trade, but Robin couldn't bring herself to ask the woman for honey. She already owed Rosa much for sheltering her and Velph while they both recovered, and she didn't want to impose further on their gracious hostess, even if she did long for just a tiny bit of home. She wasn't even sure the Klonn kept honey in their kitchens. She'd never tasted it in any of their food.

Instead, over vile, milky tea that Robin was certain she would never get used to, she indulged her hostess, answering questions about Saskwya and the little Sealie traditions that were so exotic and fascinating to her. Robin was happy for the opportunity to explain, hoping that it might turn even one more Klonnish head to the plight of the poor, who were, in Robin's eyes, the true victims in this war. In return, Rosa provided companionship and friendship. She was not a replacement for Al, but she was the first woman Robin had formed an acquaintance with one who wasn't also a rival in some way. It felt nice.

Slowly, Rosa began to tell Robin about her own nights. She glossed over the work of the *zentapi*, calling it unimportant, and instead focused on what she did outside of it.

"I went out," she would often say, which Robin eventually decided was code for "I pranced around the city in tight black clothing, spying." Rosa wasn't particularly athletic, and didn't seem to do any fighting or attacking, but she was very good at climbing and creeping. Everyone else creaked the stairs when they came to visit Robin. Rosa never did. And, like Thorne, she was very good at listening.

One afternoon, Rosa said, "The wanted posters have come down," and the next, she added, "I heard that the munitions factory in Lylon has tripled its guard. Did you know, there is one in Habbas that supplies most of the troops on the northern line, and that their guard rotation is half that?" Another day she said, "The repairs on your funny little machine seem to be coming along well." In this way, day after day, Robin realized that Rosa was not so much dropping hints as slamming down cannonballs. Subtlety, it seemed, was not the flamboyant madam's style.

Soon, Robin thought, she might be able to do something with all the hints. Her ankle was healing quickly, and it wouldn't be much longer before she returned to the sky. The question was, how much did she trust the intel Rosa dropped so plainly at her feet?

Just because I haven't been arrested and hauled off yet doesn't mean I won't be if I become an inconvenience, or the reward money becomes too tempting. And what would happen to WINGS, to Velph, then?

CHAPTER
TEN

"Well now," Velph said, when Robin set the chessboard and small table she'd begged from Rosa in front of him. He looked up at her through his lashes, smirking with amusement. "These are certainly quite . . . suggestive. Wherever did you find a set like this, my dear?"

It being Rosa's set, the pawns were all bosom wenches, and the soldier pieces were all drunkenly lusty, grinning and clutching their phallic swords like tiny woodland gods. Robin just rolled her eyes. She'd never been good at small talk, and Velph seemed to fall back on annoying courtly inanities whenever the silence got too long. Flirty banter was, she supposed, preferable to the awkward formality of the alternative, if not altogether unexpected.

"It belongs to the lady of the house," she said. Rosa had retained her request that Robin not give away information which might identify their surroundings, and though she was no longer convinced of the necessity of such measures, she complied out of respect for Rosa's hospitality.

"Ah, yes. And what, pray tell, does my enigmatic hostess have in the books for me, I wonder." The humor faded from his gaze as he watched her over the heads of the tiny soldiers. "Am I to be locked away in here forever?"

Robin trailed her fingers over the chess pieces, and shrugged. "She doesn't trust you."

Velph grumbled, readjusting his position on the bed, and grimaced when the movement pulled at his injury. His wound was stitching together well. The shot had been far, far cleaner than Wade's injury, and the bullet hadn't shattered, lodging instead in the bone of Velph's sternum, which had made it easier for Thorne to dig it out and for the wound to heal. Velph may not have believed in them, but Robin had sent the gods a prayer of thanks that the watchman hadn't been standing closer, and that his aim had not been true.

"Surely you can't blame her," Robin said, taking in the sullen expression that colored the lines of Velph's face. She dropped her gaze pointedly to the wolf-nosed helmet resting on the pile of blankets beside him, at the foot of the bed. "It's been two weeks . . . you could take it off around them, you know. I can't imagine it's comfortable to sleep in."

He followed her gaze with his own, one corner of his lips lifting in a wry smile. "It is not, and I do not, as you well know. But I have my reasons for concealing my identity, much as you do for protecting yours, my dear." The mask of practiced indifference was back, but Robin caught a flicker of something else in the stiff way he held himself, in the small twitch of the muscle in his jaw. Then he leaned forward and nudged the black king piece with one long finger. "Shall we make a bargain?"

It was a deliberate reminder of their first wager, but held significantly less threat this time around. Robin cocked her head to the side and regarded the chessboard with what she hoped was a studied expression. She had a suspicion, based on the way he was looking at her across the board, that she already knew what his terms would be, and her breath came faster at the thought. "What did you have in mind?"

"A kiss for every win," he said, and the grin that spread across his face was boyish and full of mischief. It reminded her of just how young he truly was.

"And if I win?"

"Whatever my lady doth wish," he answered, eyes hooded and voice soft, and it was so put upon, so affected, so foppishly calculated, that Robin laughed. A mock-wounded expression flashed across his face, and Robin forced herself to swallow her remaining giggles.

"Deal," she said, and she pushed her pawn forward.

Velph said nothing, concentration puckering his lips as he countered her move with his own. They fell into a comfortable sort of silence then, the soft *tock* of the pieces against the board at once comforting and familiar.

"Does it hurt?" Robin asked sometime later, when one of Velph's hands drifted up, absentmindedly, to press against the bandages tucked away beneath his shirt.

"Some," he said, eyes flicking up to meet hers over the board.

"I can ask for more tea . . ."

Velph shook his head, leaning forward to move his rook closer to her knight. "Thank you, my dear, but that will not be necessary. It is a dull ache only. And the itch of new skin."

Robin studied him, studied the way his torso listed to the side, curling around the wound, studied the tightness of the skin around his eyes, the sallow, grayish tint to his flesh. Robin sighed and moved her piece on the chessboard. "Why are you always so rudding proud? You're obviously in pain. Why not let me help you?"

"Would it assuage your guilt, my dear, to afford such kindness to your prisoner?" His tone was light, but the unexpected words were sharp and laced with such bitterness that they hit Robin with the effectiveness of a slap.

"My . . . *my* prisoner?" she gasped, looking up at him in shock. *Where is this coming from?*

"Am I not? Was it not you who brought me here, who—"

"I was saving your life, you rudding ass!" Robin interrupted.

"And yet you have left me here to rot," Velph snarled

back. "I am a captive, locked away with nothing but these four walls to occupy my time. I am going *mad*."

"Don't snap at me just because you have cabin fever!" Fury bubbled up beneath Robin's skin, and she stood, glaring down at him. "*I was captured! I was locked up!*"

"And it could have been far worse," he growled. "Do not forget, my dear, that it was only my knowledge of you—my admiration for you—that saved you from my superiors."

Robin scoffed, throwing her hands up in frustration. "So you keep saying."

"You do not believe me? After everything, you still believe my affection a farce?"

Robin leaned forward over the board, gaze down-turned, hands fisting against the tabletop, and bit her lower lip to keep it from shaking. Things had been going so well for so long, she had forgotten how quick his moods could turn, how sharp his words could cut when she wasn't ready for them.

"I don't know," she said finally, turning away. "I don't know what to believe."

Behind her, Velph snarled and pushed to his feet. "You foolish, stubborn girl," he growled, stepping around the side of the small table to reach her. The fingers of his good hand wrapped around her wrist, and he spun her back to face him, moving his hand up to cup her cheek. "What more must I do to convince you that I am genuine? You do not call me prisoner, and yet you allow them to keep me caged as if I am one. I have given up my home, Skylark, my family, my nation. I have bled for you, protected you, professed myself your ally, and yet still you doubt me? Still you allow them to keep me locked in here, instead of allowing me to be by your side. We both know that one word from you would end it."

Do I know that? Robin wondered. *Maybe, somewhere in the back of my mind. Maybe I did want him here, where I could predict him, for once. Where I always knew where he was, what he was doing, where he couldn't plot or betray. Does that make me any better than him, though? Omens.*

Strained silence stretched between them as he waited for her answer, searching her gaze as though he could parse the details of her soul. But Robin didn't know how to respond. They had done this dance so many times, and yet, the pattern never became any clearer. His actions confused her, his words confounded her . . . he asked for kisses and cursed her in practically the same breath. He demanded cooperative trust and mindless obedience together.

It was like even he didn't know what he wanted.

He was supposed to be her enemy. He was supposed to be the Coyote, the monster who had shot down her compatriots, the hobgob mothers used to keep their children from picking the Air Patrol for their apprenticeships.

And yet, Robin wanted him. She wanted what he said to be true, wanted to believe the evidence before her—that he was nationless. He had no allegiances. No master. Nobody.

Everything has been taken away from him, just like me.

"Just like me," she said aloud, the realization striking in such a startling rush, it felt like some god had reached into her brain and flicked on a propeller.

"In what way am I—?" Velph began, but then Robin was there, fingers buried in the shock of black hair behind his ears, scarred palms on his sharp cheekbones, nose smooshed inelegantly against his, stealing the rest of the sentence with her lips.

"I'm sorry," she whispered into his mouth, dropping kisses between words, trailing them along the underside of his jaw to his ear. "I'm sorry. I didn't understand it before. I didn't know."

Velph threaded his own scarred fingers into her hair, cradling her scalp with intimate insistence. Something in

Robin's chest cracked open, and she was kissing his lips again, had to be kissing him, couldn't *not* be kissing him. He stumbled back, bumping into the bed and sitting with a grunt that was lost into her mouth.

"Skylark, Skylark," Velph said, and it was a laugh muffled by the way she kept mashing kisses against his lips, crawling into his lap to get as close as possible. "My goodness, your enthusiasm. Understand what?"

"That we're the same, you and I," she said, leaning back so she could meet his beautiful, but confused, gray eyes. "That this isn't something you wanted either. That we've both been at the mercy of those above us. That we've done things that neither of us wanted to do, and that it's cost us dearly. That we've both had everything taken from us."

Something flickered through his gaze, incomprehensible and complex. He dropped his eyes away from her, expression closed.

"I see," he said, and his voice was ragged, torn and small and scared. "Yes."

"I've been, as you said, foolish," she said, pushing her forehead against his and closing her eyes. She tried not to chuckle at the image of their heads pressed together, at the way her white hair mingled with his black like ink on paper. "You've said it time and time again, but you're right, I didn't believe. I didn't *understand*. Worse, despite everything I said about being a human deserving of respect and compassion, I've hated you for it, for the things you were forced to do."

Velph made a strangled, choking sort of sound. "Do I deserve no pity of my own?"

Robin opened her eyes, stared earnestly into his guarded gaze. "You do. That's my point. I've judged you unfairly, and I'm sorry. I will speak to our hostess about letting you out of this box, if you swear you'll not repay our hard work saving your life by betraying us."

Hurt flashed across his face, but the expression was brief. "On my honor, Skylark—what little of it I may have left."

He used the grip on the back of her head to pull her back down for another kiss, one she was quite willing to give up. They kissed until the position made Robin's shoulders cramp up and her ankle throb, and she flopped back to sit beside him on the bed.

"What now, my dear?" Velph whispered softly.

Robin ran a finger over her kiss-swollen lips and glanced at the chessboard. A mischievous smile curled into the corner of her mouth as she saw just how close they'd been to finishing the game. Then, eyes locked on Velph's, she slowly reached out and knocked her own king over.

"Checkmate," she said with a raised eyebrow. "You win."

"Do you have honey?" Robin asked Thorne a few days later. Snowflakes piled up on the outer sill of the window, crowding against the glass as though eager to peer inside. Robin was crouched on her bedroom floor in the gray morning light, hovering over WINGS, wrist deep in the engine's guts as she replaced a corroding segment of fuel line.

She had reached for the cup of tea on the bedside table and frowned when she realized that Thorne had ruined it with milk again. Robin sighed and left it on the table.

"Whatever for?" Thorne asked, and Robin grumbled and shook her head.

"Never mind."

"Tad, darling," Rosa said, coming into the room, arms laden with a bundle of fabric that Robin feared was intended for her, "the weather has driven all of our customers indoors, and not through ours. We will be getting no work again today."

"Hmf," Thorne said, pouring his own tea.

"I trust that the repairs of this funny little pack are well underway?" Rosa asked, moving to lay the bundle of fabric on Robin's bed. Robin waved a greasy hand in the air, mumbling her agreement.

"*Ai*, good," Rosa said, turning away from the bed and smiling down at Robin. "I thought perhaps you would like to join us for a walk, Skylark, regain some of the strength in your legs now that your ankle has recovered well enough. Grier has found a dress we think might fit your . . . unique musculature." She eyed Robin's shoulders not with distaste, as Robin had feared she might, but with undisguised appreciation. *Well,* she thought, t*hat's certainly new, and weirdly flattering.* "Out, Taddeus."

Thorne smiled adoringly at Rosa and set aside his tea. He tossed Robin a sympathetic look over his shoulder as he crossed the room. Then he dropped a sweet kiss on Rosa's mouth, and went.

"Come, love," Rosa said, holding out her hand to help Robin up. "Let us get you fitted with suitable attire." She brushed at the hair stuck to Robin's cheek, where the white strands clung to a spot of engine oil.

"Surely Klonn women wear *pants*," Robin protested as Rosa pulled her over to inspect the pile of fabric gleaming dully in the hazy gray light.

"Not unless they work in the trades," Rosa said with a dismissive wave of her hand, "and Madam Rosa would never be seen promenading with a bit of rough."

"Ugh. Fine," Robin said, trying hard not to rankle at the superiority in Rosa's tone. The madam never really meant to talk over her head; Robin was learning that it was just the way the Klonn phrased things. "Let's get this over with, then."

"The air will do you good, no matter how you are

dressed. Your color is back—there are, forgive the reference, roses in your cheeks." Rosa looked rather pointedly at Robin's palms, clutched now between her own, and added, "It is a good thing ladies are expected to wear gloves in all weather, no? To do otherwise would be to hang a sign over your head, declaring: 'Arrest me, please.'"

Robin caught herself laughing at Rosa's dry wit, and marveled at how quickly she had become comfortable here, after only a few short weeks with the people of the rose. The conversation with Velph rattled through her thoughts, reminding her of her promise, and she hoped that when she asked them to offer Velph the same courtesy, it wouldn't put a strain on the relationships she'd been building. She needed everyone to get along, if they were really going to work together.

"Rosa," she said as she held her arms out, letting herself get stuffed into the dress like sausage into a casing. "I have a request . . ."

The first breath of open air on Robin's face was an absolute delight. She paused on the cobbles outside of the brothel, raised her face to the sun, and enjoyed the cold bite of the breeze, the kiss of the light. The day was sharp and cold, and Robin had to admit that she'd missed the crisp air of the outdoors. It had been a long time since she had put on WINGS and flown—a fact that was driving her mad with boredom. Robin hated being inactive, hated being superfluous.

She felt a small twinge of guilt that she was here, outside, while Velph was still stuck under the stairs, but it wasn't like he could have joined them, even with his helmet on.

After much coercion and many promises on Robin's part—plus a reminder on Rosa's that both their lives would be forfeited if he betrayed them—Rosa had agreed to grant Velph at least some of his liberty, allowing him the freedom to move about the *zentapi* as he saw fit. He'd been asleep when Robin went in to check on him, though, before the walk, and she had opted to let him rest rather than to wake him. She was also perfectly happy for him to never know that someone had wheedled her back into one of these terrible Klonnish dresses he'd seemed to like on her so much.

She'd give him the good news later, when she returned.

The snow had stopped falling, and the sun turned the streets and nearby roofs into glittering mounds of crystal, beautiful enough that Robin and Rosa—and more than half of Rosa's staff, filled with the same fretful, sunshine-created restlessness as Robin—had decided to make their way to the market. Dressed in finery that was stiff and shiny and had a ridiculous amount of layers, in bonnets and scarves, they strode in pairs and trios, gossiping and holding hands through dainty leather gloves. It was the most flagrant display of wasted money Robin had ever seen in her life, and she tried not to let resentment curdle her enjoyment.

Robin herself had on a wide-brimmed hat, a frothy confection of green flowers, yellow silk, and oodles of the scratchiest lace she'd ever been subjected to. Her white hair was hidden away, bound up in a black scarf beneath it. She wore a matching dress and felt exactly like an overdressed show dog.

She looked nothing like the Skylark, though, and that was the point.

Rosa had insisted on a light corset, and when Robin had protested that she had nothing to suck in, and little to support with it, Rosa had glowered at her and said, "The dress was made to go over a corset. I do not care how indomitably skinny you are, you must wear one. You will ruin the lines." Robin had rolled her eyes and given in. When it came to clothing and food, there seemed to be little else to do around Rosa. The woman knew her job, and her job was to create perfect fantasies out of her charges.

Over half the vendors were closed or absent when they reached the open-aired square. The profuse amount of snow had impacted more than just Rosa's profits, it seemed, but there were still a good many patrons browsing through the wares of those merchants who'd been brave or desperate enough to remain open. The sun seemed to have brought out every Klonnish citizen as tired as Robin of the gray and cold en masse. Robin and Rosa perused the stalls, while the rest of their entourage peeled off to find a cafe to gossip together away from their employer.

Robin had her velvet bag of coins, and had been seriously considering if it would be a danger to her disguise as a Klonnish woman to purchase a new knife, when they came across the beeswax stall. She stopped at the glorious, nostalgic scent wafting from the wax candles, and inhaled deeply. Beside her, Rosa had also stopped, and watched with intent as Robin approached the stall. "Do you sell honey?" she asked in careful Klonnish.

The man behind the table narrowed light eyes at her, scratched his scruffy chin once, and then nodded, reaching under the stall table to produce a single glass jar of the amber liquid. It glowed like gold in the sunlight, and Robin sucked in a breath between her teeth.

"For preservation," the man said.

"Yes," Robin lied.

She paid quickly, and then secreted the jar into the pocket in her bustle. She caught Rosa's disapproving scowl as she turned, but when she looked up to meet the madam's gaze fully, Rosa had quickly rearranged her expression into one of bland content.

Robin didn't care if Rosa thought buying honey might

endanger the secret of her identity; right now, she was just desperate for this small taste of home. Rosa said nothing on the matter as they resumed their stroll, pausing only to point out that a new poster had appeared on the community announcements board. It had the same line art sketch of the Skylark in WINGS, but this one said that any person found to be harboring or abetting her would be arrested for treason and imprisoned by order of the Night Watch. In thick ink, someone else had dared to draw a caricature of the king, posed in such a way that the flames drawn shooting out of WINGS's tailpipes were roasting his bottom.

King Eloy, as he was illustrated, was revoltingly heroic. He was drawn so out of proportion, chest barrel-shaped and waist slender, that Robin wouldn't have been able to spot the real man, even if he stood right beside the poster. She suppressed a pleased grin as Rosa pulled her away to the next stall.

When the sun began to set and the air grew steadily colder, they turned down a side street to head back to the *zentapi*. One last, lonely table marked the end of the market, and Robin let her gaze drift over its wares as they passed.

A portly man sat behind the display of strange and jumbled items that at first confused Robin, and then shocked her. As she stared at the pile of bric-a-brac, it resolved itself into familiar trinkets: pieces of gliders, Benne rank pins, Air Patrol medals, and Sealie good luck charms.

It was a table of war prizes.

Fury washed over Robin in an instant. The talismans and artifacts of her culture should not be for sale as though they were exotic treats for the common, curious buffoon. She folded her hands behind her back to keep from following through with the urge to tip over the table and send the offending items scattering into the sewage gutter.

Beside her, Rosa's eyes went tight and her lips pressed together hard, and Robin followed suit to keep her livid tirade in check.

"Caught your eye, there, girl?" the vendor asked, mistaking Robin's clench-toothed glare for interest. Robin immediately stepped back. She lowered her head slightly, making sure that the wide brim of the hat obscured her eyes. A sketch of Robin's face had saturated the empire. She would take no chances with a man who clearly liked to collect Sealie things.

"Saskwyan," the vendor said, national pride evident in his puffed chest and tone. Robin did not wince. He pointed to a pair of mid-flight goggles, lens-less and bent. "Stupid bugger got himself shot out of the sky like a goose."

Robin felt her hands ball into fists, so she jammed them deep into the pockets of her skirts. "Oh?" she said, knowing that she shouldn't engage, but unable to help it. She tried to at least sound as disaffected as possible. "Where?"

The vendor jerked an oil- and dirt-encrusted thumb behind him. "Forest outside of Lylon. There is the wreckage of a few around there. The Wolf likes to pop them down in that area, and the trees make sure there are no survivors."

There was one, Robin thought fiercely. *And the Klonn still haven't succeeded in snuffing out that spark.*

Carefully, Robin let herself reach out and stroke the rim of the nearest trinket—an angled Air Patrol captain's rank pin. It was scuffed and battered, and Robin wondered if this scrounger had taken it off her own ruined capelet in the forest. She caressed it gently, just once. Then she put her hand back into her pocket to stymie the temptation to scoop up everything on the table and walk away with it. Whatever the vendor wanted for his wares, Robin couldn't afford. Nor could she ever wear them, even if she did buy them—it would be disrespectful to those who had died in these things, and far too easy for the bounty hunters to identify her.

Robin took in a breath and steeled herself to turn away from all that she might ever have again of Alistair or Wade, or whoever it was who had been in that crash; of the one small object that she might have to treasure, the one bit of home she could ever keep on this side of the front lines. Just as she began to move, Madam Rosa's graceful hand slipped into her field of view and deposited one small round coin on the table. Robin was still learning the values of Klonnish currency, and how they matched with Saskwyan, but even she knew that it was an extravagant offer for the pin. The vendor nodded once, firmly, and then handed the rank pin to Robin. Equally quiet, though unsure of what secret transaction had actually just occurred—had Rosa bought his silence?—Robin accepted the pin and slipped it into her pocket with a matching solemn nod.

CHAPTER
ELEVEN

The next afternoon, Robin was called down to the kitchen by Grier, and told to wait for Rosa and Thorne. She sat at the table, turning the rank pin over and over again, watching the light of an early afternoon sunbeam make patterns on the walls and ceiling where it bounced off the beaten-up metal. She wasn't sure what she planned to do with it yet, wasn't sure how to feel about the fact that the rank pins she'd once worn were nothing but exotic trinkets, war prizes, and conversation pieces to the Klonn. She'd known, of course, that the Klonn viewed the cultures of their neighboring countries with disdain, but she hadn't fathomed the outright disrespect that would lead to merchants trivializing their symbols in such a dehumanizing way, hadn't fathomed just how personal an affront like that would feel; how infuriating it would be to see something so personally significant on display like it was cheap and the spirit of the person whose corpse it was stolen from didn't matter.

It made her angry, but more, it made the itch to strap on WINGS, to fly, all the more difficult to ignore. She'd been idle here too long. She needed to be out there, doing something. The sooner she finished her mission, the sooner she could go home—the sooner there would be no more Benne or Sealie bodies for the Klonn to pick over like vultures. Or coyotes.

As if reading her thoughts, the gods saw fit to send Velph into the kitchen next. Led there by Grier, he entered the room cautiously, eyes narrowed and assessing through the slits of his helmet.

Robin had informed him of his newly granted freedom just as soon as they'd been back from their walk and she was free of her skirts. Rosa had agreed—for the time being, at least—to allow him to be a part of the *zentapi's* daily life, and to know the identities of his hostess and her employees. It had led to another round of enthusiastic kissing, and Robin had floated off to bed with a sudden understanding of what her mama had meant when she'd complained of "beard burn."

A comfortable red chair was tucked up against the hearth, and, at Grier's direction, he lowered himself down into it with slightly more ease than he had previously shown. He still had one palm pressed against the wad of bandages as he used the other hand to lower himself, though. As if he feared something as simple as sitting would send a fount of blood gushing out of the mostly closed wound. Robin wondered for a moment just how much of it was an act geared toward garnering sympathy, and then admonished herself for being uncharitable.

"Want help?" she asked when Grier had left them alone, deciding for the time being to play along.

"Mm, if you come here, there is indeed something you can do for me," Velph said softly. His voice had that husky growl that always made her heart stutter funnily, and his eyes were filled with mischief.

Robin pocketed the rank pin and stood, walking slowly until she was by his side. "Yes?"

"Lean down," Velph said, tilting his chin up and smirking through his scruffy facial hair.

Robin huffed a laugh, rolled her eyes, and dropped the kiss he was so obviously angling for upon his mouth.

"You can't still be that hurt," Robin chided him gently.

"It is always best to be underestimated," Velph said, airy and dismissive.

"Is it?" Robin countered. "Even if it means they

make a mistake with your care because you're faking something?"

"What do you imagine they do to me at this stage of healing?"

"I don't know. It just seems . . ."

"What, my dear?"

"Dishonest," Robin said at length.

"It is not," Velph replied.

"Don't dismiss my worries so easily—"

"My, but you are feeling combative today," he interrupted.

"Am not," Robin said mutinously, petulant for being caught out. She turned to go back to her own chair.

"Perhaps it is a different kind of dance you wish for, instead," Velph said when she pulled back, and though she couldn't see his eyebrow, she could easily picture the way it arched. The sardonic smile took on a measure of impishness. He held out a hand, inviting, and Robin took it. "Are we in battle again, my dear?"

"Don't try to distract me with flirting," Robin said, but felt an answering smile curl along her lips, as well. Velph tugged her into his lap. She landed gracelessly, twisting to keep from elbowing him in the chest. "Watch it!"

"Shall I chase you all across the sky, my dearest?" he asked, pressing the nose of his helmet against the back of her head, breath an intimate tease against her ear.

"Maybe this time, you'll be less of a jerk and actually turn to face me," Robin teased back, and then his free hand was cupping her jaw, turning her face to his for a biting kiss that was just as exhilarating as any aerial maneuver.

"Well now." The door swung open unceremoniously, an incongruous flurry of snowflakes trailing Rosa as she bustled in, shaking her head to disperse the snow that clung to her hair and bonnet like an elemental goddess.

Thorne was tight on her heels, a heavy-looking cardboard box cradled under one arm, the brim of his own hat piled high with white powder. Puddles formed instantly in their wake. "Perhaps someone is a patron of the Art of Love, after all?" She smirked at them, but it was not unkind.

Robin scrambled to her feet, cheeks flaming, and straightened her collar, patted down her mussed hair.

"Do not tease, madam," Velph said from behind her. "She does not yet know what that means."

Rosa paused, giving them both an appraising look. Robin decided to sidestep the innuendos, and the fact that Rosa had caught them in a private moment, and pointed to the box instead.

"What's that?" Robin asked as Thorne deposited his burden on the kitchen table.

Rosa smiled and reached into the box, eyes sparkling with delight, painted lips stretched into a bright smile. "This," she said, "is for you, Skylark!" She withdrew one of the wanted posters. Robin glanced at it, not really wanting to look at something she despised so much, and then paused to take a second glance. It looked like the wanted posters, printed in the same mechanical way, on paper of a similar weight and color, but instead of the text about Robin, it had instead a sketch of the Skylark, and said:

WANTED

An end to the tyranny of war, to the
penalties and restrictions the Crown has
forced upon his people.
Freedom of religion for our neighbors
and respect for human lives lost, Saskwyan and Klonn alike.
A hero of the people.
A hero for ALL people.
Support the SKYLARK.

Robin blinked, her eyes feeling dangerously dry, her mouth sticky with shock.

She reached out with shaking fingers and took the poster, studying it closely. The Skylark looked heroic—her hair was bobbed and colorless, her face obscured with a scarf and feathered goggles, her clothing exotic and festooned with braid and buttons that vaguely smacked of the Saskwyan Air Patrol, but also of the elaborate needlework of Frankin, the lush fabrics of Telniem, the crisp lines of Klonn. Her body was drawn slim, lacking in curves, sexless.

In short, it looked nothing at all like Robin, but everything like what she hoped to achieve.

Velph reached up, sitting forward in his chair, and angled the poster down to study it for himself. He made a strange sort of exhaled snarl as his eyes scanned the text, his mouth a thin frown under the nose of his helmet. "Are they made public already?" he asked, turning to Rosa.

"They will go up today, if our little vigilante approves."

"I do not think—" Velph started, and Rosa silenced him with a swift glare.

"Then it is good it is not up to you to decide, is it not?"

Velph tipped his head back, so his eye slits could meet Robin's gaze. He placed a soft hand on her wrist. "Skylark—"

"Just . . . give me a moment, okay?" Robin said, studying the poster. This would be a commitment. A promise to follow orders again. A loss, at least in some small part, of her extremely hard won freedom. And yet, she had been protected here. She had been given exactly what Rosa had promised—warmth, safety, a place to heal and recover. And Rosa had asked for nothing in return save for Robin's help to accomplish a task that Robin was already trying to accomplish, anyway.

"It is perhaps not wise to advertise so openly—" Velph said softly, and the note of concern, of fear, in his voice brought her gaze to his.

"Why not?" Robin interrupted. "The people of Klonn are already speaking out against their king. You should have seen the graffiti someone left on the wanted poster in the market. They're discontent, chafing under the burden of war just as the Saskwyans are. Why not give them someone to follow? A symbol to rally them to our cause?"

Velph said nothing in response, but she noticed his posture had stiffened.

"There's only one pack, right? You always said whoever had it would win—you felt sure it would be the deciding factor. Well, why not make it obvious? Make it clear just how much of an advantage we have? Is this not the exact plan you wanted, to use rumor and reputation to put an end to all this rudding fighting?"

"I . . . I do not like that we are confirming your appearance so obviously. There are those who would harm you terribly, if they knew who you were."

"But it *doesn't* look like me. That's the point. The Skylark looks like *everyone*." She turned the poster toward him again, to make her point, but his eye slits were locked on her face. For a moment, she thought she saw a flicker of honest emotion in what little of his eyes she could see, as if he wished to communicate something, but feared to say the words out loud. Then it was gone, locked behind the careful mask he'd always worn in front of an audience, as impossible to read as the helmet he hid behind. Robin turned to Rosa and Thorne and held up the poster. "Whose idea was this?"

Thorne coughed and turned red. Robin laughed, and then flung her arms around his shoulders—or at least, she tried. She had to grab him by his vest lapels and haul him downward for his hug. "You are a smart, smart man!" she laughed. "Tinker, medic, security guard, artist! Is there anything you don't do?"

"Dishes," he deadpanned. And Robin laughed harder as she pulled away.

"Does this mean you approve, Skylark?" Rosa asked, stepping forward to place a sobering hand on Robin's shoulder. "Will you join us in this fight?"

Robin felt the smile die on her face. She flicked her gaze to Velph, but he was the very picture of blank, courtly poise. She could neither tell what he was thinking any more than she could untangle her own chaotic thoughts.

"I do not like this," Velph said, pushing himself to his feet. "I forbid—"

"You what?" Robin asked, turning to face him, hands on her hips. "It's not your choice there, buddy."

"You are mine, Skylark," he said, not possessively, not angrily, but like it was the most obvious bit of common sense. The sky was blue. The rain fell down instead of up. And Robin Arianhod belonged to Velph the Coyote. It was both endearing and irritating. "It is therefore my duty to ensure your safety—"

"Whoa!" Robin said, palm cutting off the flow of his words as he sputtered against her skin. "I thought we were over this." She ever so gently pushed him back into the chair, and he went, grumbling.

"You thought we were over what?" he asked when she'd let him go.

"This you telling me what to do nonsense." Robin tugged the poster out of his hand. "You may outrank me, but I don't report to you. No more orders. We're a partnership now. We discuss. We don't order. Is that clear?"

Velph's mouth curled up into a sardonic smile. "She orders."

Robin huffed and rolled her eyes. "I'm not ordering

you. I'm . . . laying out an opening volley."

"I prefer the other kind of dancing," Velph said sulkily, but when he didn't protest further, Robin handed the poster over to Thorne with a nod.

"Here, you fight to stop the war," Thorne rumbled as he replaced the poster inside the box. "If you had gone home, they would have made you fight to win it."

That was the most intelligent thing anyone had ever said to her. Even Velph. Robin stilled for a moment, contemplating it.

She had been a good little Sealie all her life, but here, she finally had a chance to choose who she would follow. Robin looked down at Rosa's hand, held angled toward her in quiet offer, then up at her warm, open expression. She looked past Rosa's froth of curls to the plea on Thorne's face—they were asking her to stay. Asking her to fight. Not against the Klonn, or against the Saskwyans, but for the people who suffered because of the war. The same people she had already promised the gods she'd end the war for. Decision clear at last, she said:

"Yes. Yes, I'm with you. I'll join this fight, and we'll end this thing together. All of us." She dropped her gaze to Velph's, making it clear that she was including him, too, and wished again that he'd remove the infernal helmet blocking his face from view.

Rosa pulled Robin into a warm embrace, then stepped back and squeezed her shoulders once. "From your lips to the ears of your gods," Rosa said softly. "May we all hope they actually do exist. We are going to need as much luck as we can get."

Robin's first test flight went remarkably well. It was dead midnight when she took off from the roof of the *zentapi* and did a quick tour between the chimneys and peaks of the district to make sure WINGS was back in working order. After the exhilaration of once again feeling the wind on her face and the warmth of WINGS on her back had faded, she paused for a breather on the gutters of a milliner's shop.

Satisfied that her ankle could support her, and that WINGS wasn't making any funny sounds, Robin decided to head back. Before she could take off, though, a bit of brown fluff whirled by on the wind, and Robin reached out to grab it. It was a feather—a plain brown, spotted feather. She looked around for the bird it might have come from, and found instead that a trash bin had been knocked over behind the nearby hat shop. More feathers danced on the breezes that skimmed across the slushy cobbles, and Robin was struck with an idea.

The next afternoon, when Rosa came up to Robin's room for their daily chat, she found Robin carefully adhering the fussy little feathers she'd gathered to the leather padding around the brass rim of Al's goggles. The glue was sticky, and Robin had to stop often to remove feathers from the tips of her fingers, and from the handle of the tweezers she used for the smaller pieces.

"Lark feathers," Robin said at Rosa's unspoken question. She grinned and held the goggles up over her face, peering out of the smudged lenses at Rosa's reflection in the vanity mirror.

"My, you are certainly embracing this notion of a symbol."

"Well, you started it. I guess that poster was just the push I needed, you know? If I'm going to do this, then I'm going to do it right." She paused and stroked the buckle of the goggles, lying bright against the horrid white of her hair.

"Whose goggles were they?" Rosa asked as she placed the tea service she'd brought up on Robin's bedside table.

Robin forced a flat laugh. "What, they can't just be mine?"

"Not with the reverence of that touch."

Robin paused, and took a few deep breaths, trying to keep her shoulders down and away from her ears. Rosa wasn't trying to be confrontational, Robin knew that, nor to poke at the sore spots marring Robin's heart. She just seemed to have a knack of knowing exactly where they lay. Her vision wobbled, and Robin blinked hard to keep the tears at bay.

"Al. Alistair Brigid. He was my . . . my mid-flight."

Rosa nodded, shrewd gaze watching Robin from the mirror's glass, teacup poised against her painted lips as she took a delicate sip. "He crashed with you?"

"Yes."

"And he died in the crash?"

"Eventually."

"I see," Rosa said, understanding, voice low with pity.

"He was a good man. Bit of a coal-bag when he didn't get what he wanted, I'll admit. But still good, underneath. He deserves to be a part of this, you know? To be a part of the Skylark."

Rosa shifted, setting aside her tea to pour a cup for Robin. "Where did you find them all?"

"Behind that milliner's shop at the edge of the market. These are the rejected feathers." She held some up. "Too fluffy, too tattered, too short."

"But not for you." A hint of a smile warmed Rosa's tone. "Nothing is ever too wasted for you to make use of, it seems."

"That's what happens when the nobility decides to play the game of war—the poor are the ones who lose. We learn to ration everything," Robin said, trying to match Rosa's levity as she accepted the offered tea. She picked irritably at a pinfeather that had somehow become stuck to the paper she'd laid down to protect the surface of the vanity.

"From here, it is beautiful. You would not even

know." Rosa sighed as Robin added a small dollop of honey to her cup. She kept the jar in her room, in case a stranger for some reason ended up in the kitchen and spotted it. It made no sense to take it down, anyway, as Robin was the only one who consumed it.

Rosa took another breath, as if she wanted to speak, but instead just let it out again. Robin waited her out. Then Rosa stepped forward and reached out to brush a tentative finger against the feathers adorning Robin's goggles. "This is your magic, Skylark. You can take the most scraggly, desperate things and make a beautiful whole out of them. You can see how things fit together and can make them work, even when the parts are from different machines."

Robin set down her cup and turned to look at Rosa. She might not be as familiar with spying as Rosa, but even she could tell the conversation wasn't about goggles anymore.

"We need that," Rosa said softly. "Your Coyote calls us a 'network,' but the term is generous. We are a beast with many heads, and many opinions, and no rallying point. We need someone to turn our desperate and scraggly thing into a beautiful whole. We need something to follow, a sign. We need your magic. The people have not seen you in weeks, but the posters, Skylark. The stories I am hearing on the streets. There are songs even. You mean something to them."

Robin's ears went hot, and she knew she was blushing. Instead of replying—because what was there to say to such an earnest confession—she said: "I thought the Klonn didn't believe in magic."

Rosa chuckled. "Not until some impertinent Sealie tries to prove us wrong," she said, and then she gathered Robin against her, running her hands through Robin's short, wind-tangled hair, and hugged her fiercely. It was wonderful to be folded in someone's arms, to be squeezed, to know that the other person cared for her; she hadn't had a hug like this since Mama . . .

"I just want to go home," Robin whispered into Rosa's shoulder, the confession ripping from her guts, spilling against her friend's skin with an ugly, choked noise. "Al's dead, and I hate this stupid war, and I just want to go home."

"I know, Skylark. But you have found a home here, for now," Rosa said softly, her voice laden with pity. Both of them knew that though the offer was kind, Rosa's grand zentapi would never replace the tipsy, freezing row house in the Sealie slums of Pyria, with Robin's blown-in window and the small parlor with its threadbare and time-eaten furniture.

It would never replace the soft scratch of Papa's mustache on her cheek as he kissed her goodnight, the humming and gentle clatter of Mama working the loom, the smell of honey pervasive in the kitchen and the soft snick of a knife on the cutting board. It would never replace the boisterous energy of the Air Patrol canteen, the stuffy uprightness of the Benne commanders, the freedom of being at the yoke of a glider, the thrill of the dueling dance. It would never replace what she had lost.

"Brave Skylark," Rosa whispered in her ear. "What amazing things you will do."

She cupped Robin's chin in her hands and leaned her face close. For a second, Robin wondered if Rosa was about to lick her nose, but then she pressed a soft, warm kiss to Robin's lips.

"Um," Robin said, touching her mouth when Rosa pulled back. "You . . . kissed me. Wh-why would you kiss me?"

Rosa laughed. "Why would I not? You are not repellent."

"No, I just . . . um . . . I mean, I have . . . and you, um, you have Thorne, right?"

"Correct. It is just a kiss. I only wanted to convey my affection for you. And my pride in your strength."

"So you kissed me," Robin repeated, flummoxed, sure that she was missing something here.

"*Ai.*" Rosa frowned slightly. "Is this unacceptable?"

"I'm . . . no. I mean, well . . . maybe just weird?"

"Because I am female?"

"Because you're my friend, and we're both, um . . ."

Rosa grinned. "Ah, I see now what the Coyote meant. A novice to the worship, indeed." She shrugged and patted Robin's head like a fond parent. "I will kiss your cheek next time, if that is acceptable."

"Yeah, um . . . sure," Robin said, scrubbing at the lip paint she could feel on her mouth.

Rosa laughed. "Are all Sealies so reserved?"

"I guess?" Robin said. "We just . . . we don't really kiss people we aren't, uh, romantically . . . you know," she finished awkwardly.

"Fear not, dear Skylark. I will respect that," Rosa said, laughter still rolling through her words.

Robin tried to laugh, too, but it came out flat. Rosa had called her brave, called her magic, but if she had to admit the truth of it, Robin didn't feel brave. She was scared, unsure of so much in this foreign country, of what she might have committed herself to, of the customs and traditions and Arts she had no experience with and little desire to learn. She was scared that, in the end, the Skylark might not have the power to change anything—or that, worse, she might make Saskwya lose.

As she watched Rosa disappear back through the threshold, heading downstairs to do gods knew what, Robin took a deep, shuddering breath. Fighting against the burn at the back of her eyes, she turned her palms up in prayer.

Oh gods, she thought. *Guide me. I have no idea what I've gotten myself into.*

CHAPTER TWELVE

On the evening of the winter solstice, the Skylark made her glorious return.

They chose an officers' club for her first target. It was closed for the night, but had that very afternoon played host to some war ministers. There had been some small fanfare as some general or other stood outside and made some sort of formal announcement about redoubling the effort against the Saskwyan Air Patrol, but the only people in attendance had been the officers' wives, some newspaper reporters, and the curious shopkeepers from across the road. Military speeches weren't drawing much of a crowd these days.

Robin had very little doubt, however, that if the Skylark were to appear and make a speech, the people would come in droves—as would the Night Watch.

Robin hummed to herself, feeling light and thrilled to be back out in the open air. She alighted on the roof of the club and unslung the satchel that lay nearly flat across her chest. Inside was a small canister of fuel and five very well fashioned blasting sticks. Velph had seen to that, much to Rosa's concern and chagrin; it turned out that he was a defter hand at explosives than an officer of the Klonn Aeroforce had any right to be. When asked why, he'd smirked and said, "Youthful fancy," and nothing more.

Rosa had pulled together for her an outfit meant to be both instantly recognizable and iconic. Robin wore her own brown, knee-high boots, but now had matching brown leather britches, a heavy belt that kept a knife strapped to her thigh and which housed two snug pouches stuffed with all manner of supplies: matches, a compass, maps, hair fasteners, a roll of lock picks, and anything else Robin might need in any given situation—including hardtack, in case she got hungry, or was isolated in the wilderness again.

Her jacket was of the same brown leather, fronted with two heavy rows of buttons, but had a snug, Klonnish collar that felt like it was strangling her, even as it kept out the wind. She had retained her thick mechanic's gloves to protect her fingers from the chill of the air high above the city, and a scarf, thick and short to keep it out of the exhaust trail, was again wound around her neck and the lower half of her face, tucked into the bottom rim of the feather-bedecked goggles. Robin had fastened the rank pin to the middle of her jacket, right between the rows of buttons. Rosa had also produced a brown aviator's cap—sewn together from a mishmash of leftover patches of brown leather—which had flaps that kept her ears warm and the rushing noise of the wind at a minimum. Her hair only waved free at the back, too short for a woman's, too long for a man's, and too white to belong to anyone in particular.

She looked just like the version of the Skylark Thorne had created for the poster—in silhouette, at least—and yet not at all the same in detail. It was, in all, the perfect disguise.

Breaking in through the roof access hatch of the officers' club was easy, but Robin knew that once their careful campaign of harassment and explosions began, people would start locking, barricading, and possibly even bricking up their upper windows and doors. She felt sorry for the average Klonn citizen, who likely no more wanted to partake in their king's war than Robin had in hers, and who, once the newspapers got hold of the story and the government started crafting articles aimed at changing people's adoration of the Skylark into fear, would begin to feel unsafe in their own homes, and would police their upper entrances rigorously. Robin knew how it was to try to sleep while knowing that something bad might happen to your home, and that there would be no way for you to stop it. And she felt bad that they wouldn't know that the Skylark had no interest in murdering anyone, much less honest citizens in their beds.

Of course, the propaganda machines would make certain that the citizens of Lylon thought the worst of the Skylark soon enough. That was the way of wars—the enemy was always demonized, truth be damned. And the squeeze for a war chest meant the difference between a child going to bed with a full belly, or an empty one. It was never the nobles who paid for their games.

Robin crept down the stairs from the roof into the library on the uppermost floor. She felt a pang of regret for the books, but when she remembered the texts that had been printed by the king, those books on Klonn written in Saskwyan to teach people like her the glories of their conquerors, the regret vanished. She carefully tucked four of the blasting sticks into shelves on the four separate walls, wedging them between the covers of the fattest books she could find, and kept the fifth stick for herself.

She found the windows that faced the street and threw them open as wide as they would go, ensuring that there would be enough fresh oxygen to feed the fire. Then, she exited the way she came, moving slowly and quietly in the still night, and flew down to the front door. She yanked on the doorbell pull viciously, loudly, so there would be no chance that anyone inside—if there was, indeed, anyone inside—could remain asleep. Lamps spluttered to life in the buildings across the road, and Robin was glad that those apartments had cobblestones and concrete to separate them from what was about to become a ball of fire in the middle of a park.

Finally, a cranky-looking butler came to the door, wiping sleep from his eyes.

"*Are you the only one inside?*" Robin asked in Klonnish, voice muffled by the scarf. She'd been practicing the inflection of this particular phrase with Thorne for days now. The butler, still too tired to really understand why this person swathed in leather and goggles might be asking, nodded.

"*Good,*" Robin said. "*Get out.*"

"*Excuse me?*" the man said. He drew himself upright in his nightshirt, but then froze as he got his first good look at her. "Skylark," he breathed, shock flashing across his features.

Robin slapped the thrust button on the control box, rising into the air before his eyes, deliberately showy. She paused when she was level with the library windows, and reached behind her to light the last blasting stick against the fire from the exhaust pipes.

The butler scarpered, heading down the street as fast as his spindly legs could carry him. The wick crackled to life, and Robin tossed it in the window. She turned tail as fast as possible, throwing herself into the sky and landing several blocks away to take cover behind a chimney.

The first blast was followed quickly by four more as the fire ripped through the books. The clang of the Night Watch's alarm bells rang out in the distance and shouting filled the streets. Robin crept out from behind the chimney, pausing to take in the conflagration, angry against the dark night sky. Pride bubbled up under her skin, and she grinned in satisfaction as she launched herself into the sky and turned back toward the *zentapi*.

After that, missions became something of a routine.

They carefully plotted around the various schedules of the Klonn forces, focusing on times when the bases and factories that supplied the Klonnish military would be the least populated. They also plotted the attacks to be seemingly random, so no pattern could ever betray them.

Slowly, with each subsequent success, the tension and mistrust between Rosa and Velph started to fade. While debate and differing opinions still flew back and forth like carefully worded bullets, they did, for the most part, work together as a united team. A comfortable sort of companionship began to form between the four of them—Rosa, Thorne, Velph, and the Skylark—a rhythm that gave Robin a productive sense of momentum that had, just as Rosa said, been lacking from her prior attempts.

For her part, Robin was simply grateful to be flying again. She had desperately missed the wind on her face, the utter silence of the world above the clouds, the way her stomach dropped out from under her when she pulled up steeply from a dive, the slight and comforting vertigo of a barrel roll, the joy of the freefall, and the small upsurge of terror and adventure that pressed into the hollow of her throat when she let herself dip too close to the tops of trees, or the sides of buildings. She felt free.

Threading between the stars, Robin was free to just be Robin.

Tonight's target had been provided, as promised, by Velph. It had also, unbeknownst to him, been confirmed by one of Rosa's many spies in the other *zentapi* scattered across Klonn. It was an air base outside the city limits, to the south. Robin had taken a carriage to the *zentapi* located at the southern edge of town to save fuel, and had taken off from there. The world below her was silent and dark, only the odd crofter's cottage sending up small sparks of light and color from amid the rolling fields.

Then, in the distance, the faint orange haze of the base appeared over the tree line. Her heart thumped faster in anticipation. When the whole of it came into sight, Robin realized that it wasn't nearly as large as the one she had worked at back in Saskwya. But it was a key strategic point—the aircraft housed here were used to patrol the waterways to the south. With it removed, the Saskwyan Navy would have a better chance at winning skirmishes, with no Klonn aeroships to bedevil their ships.

Robin wondered, and not for the first time, if perhaps she should find some way to get word to the Saskwyan military that the Skylark was one of their own, and that she was working on their side. She didn't relish the thought of being shot at if she accidentally strayed too close to a Saskwyan operative or military encampment.

As always, though, she dismissed the urge. The thought of being issued orders, which she would be compelled to follow—but which would probably be less informed and less timely than the decisions made by their quartet of conspirators, informed by Rosa's network— was unappealing. It was just as Thorne had said: any instructions from home would be of strict advantage to the Saskwyans, instead of to the advantage of everyone.

More exciting, more thrilling, and more nerve-racking than all of that, however, was that tonight would mark the first time Robin was to use the W of WINGS. Until now, she had only used WINGS as a means of propulsion— tonight, she was going to try to use it as a weapon.

It was Velph's idea, initially. Could she, he theorized, both fly and fight offensively at the same time? Was Robin trained enough for it? Was WINGS capable? Or were the blades that extended from the pack's sides meant only for close-quarter combat, to protect the wearer when they were vulnerable on the ground? Had they even been meant to be used as a weapon at all, or were they just for stabilization? She had been practicing—with Velph's help—and thought she would now be quite able of using them to slice the wings right off a Klonn aeroship, should she get trapped too close to one in the air.

They had spent hours with paper and pencils spread out before them on the kitchen table, calculating wind speed and turn ratios, arguing angles and trajectory. Rosa, on those few occasions when she had walked through the room, had fondly called them both such utter pilots, but had said it with a small, happy smile.

As Robin angled herself toward the base, a familiar noise found its way to her ears over the rush of the air. It was a low buzzing, and Robin pushed herself up higher to get above the aircraft. Someone was either taking off or landing, and, like her namesake, she intended to circle and drop down upon the aircraft from a height. That would keep her unseen until the last moment. The plan was to debilitate every aircraft she could, and then set fire to the hangars. She would never be able to set fire to each individual aircraft before they scrambled, so the success of the plan lay in her small size, her relative invisibility in the night, and her ability to get in very close and destroy the aeroships themselves before they could be properly manned. Of course, she would only do so when it was close enough to the ground that the pilot might survive the crash. It was a good plan, and, surprisingly—or maybe unsurprisingly, given all that she'd learned about him—it had been Velph's.

Trust him now, do you? she asked herself, angling downward, and couldn't help but smile. She pressed the button on the control box, and the soft ring of steel snapping outward was like music, the blades vibrating in the wind. They sang the familiar, crystalline chord.

Grinning, the Skylark dove.

The problem with over-fanciful flying (like the sort Robin loved to indulge in while unpursued, and had to execute while being shot at) is that it used up an awful lot of fuel.

Grumbling with cold and distantly angry at herself for being such a wastrel, Robin trudged through the snowbanks piled along the side of the country road. Her feet were already numb.

Thank the gods for this scarf, was all she could think as she stole into the small Klonnish town via a back alley. The map she carried in her pouch called the town Recine, and a small red dot beside the name—added by Rosa— indicated that it sported a single *zentapi.*

It wasn't a hard building to find, thankfully enough. The central market square was only surrounded by a few adjacent structures, one of which was the *zentapi.* Robin couldn't read the name of the establishment, but like Rosa's, there was a single long-stemmed rose carved into one of its lintels. She made her way through the shadows cast by the buildings to the servants' entrance, and tapped out the rhythm Rosa had taught her on one of the kitchen windows.

A few agonizingly long moments later, the back door was unlocked, and Robin was being ushered into an alcove at the back of the kitchen, beside the baking fire. She was sure it would be horribly undignified for a vigilante to drape herself across the warm bricks of the bread oven, so Robin contented herself with leaning against it, instead.

As soon as Robin had stripped off her gloves, hot tea was pressed into her hands. Robin tugged down her scarf to take a sip, and then coughed as politely as she could. It was absolutely swimming with whiskey.

"Omens," Robin husked. She couldn't drink this. She'd be plastered. Instead, she just cradled the cup between her hands, happy to roll the warm china along her stiff fingers, and let the steam from the tea warm her face between carefully held breaths. "Thank you . . ." she said, waiting for the woman who'd given her the cup to provide her name.

"Ripka," the woman said. She was voluptuous, comfortable in her own skin, and brimming with matronly care. "Welcome, Skylark. I can have some dinner fetched in for you, if you desire it." She spoke in heavily accented Saskwyan, which Robin only realized once she'd defrosted enough to pay attention.

So, the secret of the Skylark's origins had been passed along, it seemed, with the rest of the information. A frisson of worry crept down her spine, bringing with it whispered echoes of Velph's warnings. If the rebels of this zentapi knew her country of origin, then there was every possibility that it could be leaked to the Klonn Aeroforce, or the Night Watch. And then, how hard would it be for them to infiltrate the Saskwyan Air Patrol records, to figure out her name, her family . . .

Is this what Velph was worried about? That someone could use the poster, the call to arms, to revenge themselves on my family, my people, with knowledge of who I am? Maybe even onto him?

"*Nema*, Ripka," Robin replied, suddenly desperate to be gone. Her lenses had fogged with the sudden shift in temperature, and she wanted the woman to go away so she could take them off and wipe them clean. "I ran out of fuel."

The woman continued in Saskwyan anyway, either certain in her intel or unwilling to catch the hint as Robin had hoped: "We keep spare fuel in the pantry. I will fetch it."

"Er, thank you," Robin called after her retreating back, silently stunned. Rosa's network really did support the Skylark if they all had fuel hoarded away for her.

She sipped at the cooling tea a bit more to pass the time—though not enough that her ability to fly in a straight line would be compromised—and opened her earflaps to take in the ambience of this *zentapi*. It was smaller than Rosa's, less formal, and, from the sound of it, a good deal more rowdy.

From a room that Robin assumed would be the reception parlor, if the layout of this house was anything like Rosa's, a rousing cacophony of voices slammed their unmelodic way through what Robin presumed was a drinking song. She could only make out some of it, until the singers suddenly switched into Saskwyan.

"Upon the cold wind, can you hear that sweet note?" they sang. *"Clear, unafraid, and cyclical keening! Look up, friends, look up, in the sky, how she floats! The Skylark, with white hair a-streaming!"*

Robin was so startled that she nearly dropped the teacup. With shaking fingers, she put it down on a table and edged toward the door, ear cocked at the keyhole.

"A hero, a villain, a spy, and a knave! Behind feathered mask, oh, who can she be? Who does she fight for, and who will she save? Oh, look how she flies, proud and free!" the crowd sang.

Robin felt her breath stopper up behind the collar of her jacket, her heart thumping behind her rank pin in time to the song. I'm a folk hero, Robin thought numbly. I have a drinking song! Omens!

"Do not, oh, do not hear the king's accusation. Instead, hear the Skylark's sweet song. Look up, friends, look up, to peace's one champion. The Skylark, with white hair, shall stay strong!"

"Miss Skylark?" Ripka said from behind, and Robin whirled around, startled back away from the door. She straightened, feeling oddly like a child whose fingers had just been caught in the honey jar before dinner.

"Er, yes. Hi. Sorry."

Ripka laughed at Robin's discomfort, but it was sweet and well-meaning. "Here you are, then." She set a large tin milk jug on the table. But as soon as it was out of her hand, her good mood evaporated. A scowl pulled at her features.

"What's wrong?" Robin asked, concern flaring near as hot as the embarrassed flush burning in her cheeks.

"You . . . you should not stay," Ripka said softly.

"Why? What's happened? Is it that crowd?" She jerked a chin at the door.

Ripka shook her head. "The master. I am sorry. I spoke with him just now, and he does not approve of the network supporting . . . ah . . ."

"Me," Robin finished for her, squashing her disappointment and jamming her earflaps and gloves back into place. "No, that's fine. I'll go. Thank you for this, anyway." She gestured to the milk can. There would be more than enough fuel in it to get Robin safely back to Lylon, if it was full. It was. Carefully, and without removing WINGS, Robin unscrewed the fuel canister and bent to the task of filling it.

"If it is not too bold to say so, Miss Skylark," Ripka ventured, "you should not return here. He will call the Night Watch the next time." She twisted her hands before her, clearly wrestling over a decision of some sort, and then blurted: "But I want to say thank you."

"For what?" Robin asked, startled.

"For trying. The master may not like your methods, but he cannot deny you are having an effect."

Robin finished filling WINGS's canister and looked up. Ripka had her head turned away, staring out the window, but what she was really looking at, Robin could only guess. A lost lover? A dead sibling? Someone at the front that she desperately wanted to see come home?

"You're welcome," Robin replied, instead of the hundreds of other things that sat on the tip of her tongue. "And thank you, too. For . . . all of this." Replacing the cap on the fuel canister, Robin handed the milk tin back to Ripka. Then she offered the woman a sad smile, touched her briefly on the shoulder, and disappeared into the night.

CHAPTER THIRTEEN

Late the next afternoon, Robin decided to take advantage of the wide table in Rosa's kitchen to review a recent set of aerial maps—illicitly obtained—that detailed the new front lines. She couldn't help running her fingers over the place where her own base was located, so far back that it was nearly off the map. She traced, too, the place where she thought Al had died, though that was merely a guess. The palace that had been her prison was marked here as an emergency gravel airstrip in the middle of an otherwise empty forest, and Robin was suddenly glad that Velph was nowhere to be found. Though he had been a prisoner there, as well, the lack of recognition for his estate was sure, she assumed, to offend his noble pride. Unless he was the one who had suggested it remain mismarked, in case someone exactly like Robin had obtained a copy of the map.

The lines of the front had moved in the half-year Robin had spent trapped on the wrong side of the war. Trenches dug on the Saskwyan side were now being used by Klonn soldiers in the east, closer to Lylon, but it was reversed in the west, near Pyria. The fighting was getting further and further from her parents and their home, thank the gods, but ever closer to the Air Patrol supply warehouses. Robin rubbed her forehead, feeling frustrated and impotent.

"Omens, this is endless," she whispered. "We flip, they flop, and then we do it all again." Annoyed with her own melancholy, she hummed the jaunty tune she had learned the night before, trying to bolster herself with the song of the Skylark—the hero, the rebel, the traitor, the freedom fighter. According to Rosa and her spies, it was already making the rounds in the taverns. And when she'd sung what she'd remembered to Velph, he'd said it was a Klonnish folk song that had been given new lyrics.

More wanted posters had appeared that morning, of course. The amount of money on the bottom of the paper was nearly twice that which had been offered up for Robin when she was a simple Sealie and pilot of the Air Patrol. Thorne told her that this one said, "Dead or Alive" along the top, and "Terrorist" at the bottom. It kept Robin from getting too smug. It kept her cautious. There was no telling when a supportive citizen would turn desperate or greedy enough to give up their folk hero to feed their hungry children.

When Rosa sashayed through the kitchen door, shortly before the first of the zentapi's clients were scheduled to arrive, shedding her wide hat and gloves and trailed by one of her employees playing valet, Robin shuffled the map of the front out of view, replacing it with one of Lylon, feeling oddly caught out.

"Ah, Skylark," Rosa said, painted lips curved into a bright, beaming smile. She crossed to where Robin sat perched above her maps and dropped a quick kiss against Robin's cheek. True to her word, Rosa had refrained from any more attempts at Robin's lips, and now offered quick pecks on the cheek when greeting, or bidding goodbye. Robin had still found it a bit odd at first, but now that she'd grown accustomed, she found she quite liked the familial, sister-like gesture of affection. She'd started kissing Rosa's cheek back at the same time, like she saw the other employees around her do to one another. "Last night went splendidly, I hear. And no casualties. Congratulations."

Robin grinned. "Really? No casualties at all? That's good."

"*Ai, ai*, but do not get smug. For you," she said, and pushed an envelope into Robin's hand. "Read it quickly, and then go—there is an operative who requires your aid tonight. He has been sent to do some small bit of pillaging, but he needs your ability to get inside the upper windows."

Robin hastily read the directions, consulted the map that had been contained within, and then excused herself. Rosa gave her a quick, oddly smug smile as Robin disappeared up the stairs to her room. Within moments, she was dressed in her Skylark costume, out the window, and on her way.

She landed a block away from the intended destination, not exactly distrustful of Rosa and her people, but feeling distinctly suspicious about that knowing little smirk she'd seen on her face. Caution had never served her ill in the past, and until she knew what it was Rosa had tucked away up her sleeve, Robin was determined to err in favor of it. She crept through the shadows of the quiet buildings, avoiding the Night Watch sentries that had begun to appear with frustrating regularity, their field glasses pointed futilely at the sky. She peered around as she drew close to the target location, and found the operative waiting, as specified, beside the doorway of a tavern. A long coat obscured his form, and his face was turned away, but Robin thought there was something familiar about the way he stood.

She ducked around the corner, sticking close to the shadows of the darkened alley and, when she was close enough that her voice wouldn't carry, whispered, "Hello?"

The man in the shadows chuckled softly, and growled a husky greeting that never failed to make her blood thrill: "Hello, my dear."

"*You're* the operative?" Robin blurted, and then

clapped her hand over her mouth, chagrined at her out-burst. "Wait, are you even well enough to be out here like this?"

"You are unhappy," Velph said, voice muffled by the metal of his helmet. He turned, the silver lupine mask flashing dully in the lamplight as he slipped around the corner to join her. He pulled her close, the nose of his helmet cool against the nape of her neck as he whispered in her ear. "I thought it would be a pleasant surprise."

"It's a surprise of some kind, that's for godsdamned sure," she huffed, pushing back so she could glare up at him through his eye slits. "Are you strong enough to even squeeze a trigger?"

He smirked in answer, and crooked his finger at her saucily.

"I'm being serious," Robin hissed. "This isn't a game."

"And yet, for the last week, you have been unbearably cocky."

"I'm the Skylark," Robin said, voice low, but teasing now. "Haven't you heard? I have a drinking song and everything. I'm a godsdamned symbol." She poked him in the arm.

Velph made a disbelieving sound in the back of his throat, half chuckle, half scoff—entirely infuriating. Robin scowled. Velph grinned. Then he gently tugged on the edge of her scarf, slipping it down so it was no longer covering her mouth and nose. "What are you—?"

Cupping her cheek with one hand and lifting up his helmet, just a bit, with the other, he leaned down and swallowed the rest of her words, erasing her scowl with a kiss that made her blood hum. "Come now, Skylark. May we not work together as a team?" he said against her mouth. He pulled back, leaving her breathless and want-ing, and righted his own mask. Then he pointed down an alley. "Shall we, my dear?"

Robin blinked stupidly, hating how smug he sounded, how easily he had been able to rattle her senses, and grumpily pulled her scarf back into position. "Fine. Lead the way. But don't think that I'm not going to give Rosa the what for when we get home," she grumbled. Velph let out a breathy laugh, and turned toward the alley he had indicated. They made their way down it silently, and together, and met a brightly lit building at the end.

"Too many lights on this side," Velph observed. "We shall go around to the west entrance. It should be less well-lit there, and I can shoot out some of the lamps. *If* I am strong enough."

Robin just glared in response.

Velph took them back up the alley and around the block, skirting a narrow river trapped between stone gutters, and back to the building.

"What does that word say?" Robin asked, pointing at the letters carved into an elaborate stone lintel, the shadows and lighting making them hard to discern.

"Hospital."

"We're stealing from a hospital?" Robin gasped, momentarily aghast. She rubbed the base of one thumb with her hand, tried to shake off the phantom press of a curfew soldier's boot knife.

"Only medicines and surgery supplies. I am afraid my convalescence used rather a lot of our hostess's stores. We must replenish them for her."

"Yes, but a civilian hospital? I don't know how I feel about this."

"Do not worry, my dear. They can requisition more," Velph said. He leaned down and kissed Robin's cheek, placating and sweet. The nose of his mask was cold against her eyebrow.

Lucky, Robin thought bitterly. In Pyria, they can't.

Velph unholstered his gun. He reached into one of the many deep pockets that adorned his dark coat and withdrew a small black cylinder. He fitted it over the mouth of the gun's barrel, and then, with absolute and perfect precision, he shot out the lamps. The lights died with tiny popping sounds, the usual bark of a gun completely muffled.

"What's that?" Robin asked, staring in wonder as he put the cylinder away.

"Something the Klonnish military has been devising," Velph said with a youthful grin. "Useful, no?"

Before Robin could respond, a voice called out in Klonnish. Robin caught the words for *lights, alert*, and *Night Watch*.

"Hells!" she swore, and brushed her shoulder with crossed fingers. Velph muttered a curse of his own as he tugged her back into the shadows and they retreated down the alley.

"Now what?" she asked, voice hushed to a mere whisper. "There's no way we're getting inside that building now."

"I did not expect the Night Watch to be so vigilant," Velph replied, lips twisted in distaste, or irritation, or both. "Still, we should try."

"And risk you getting shot up again?" Robin hissed, crossing her arms over her chest. "No, thanks. I don't think so."

"Skylark," Velph said warningly. His eyes, when he turned the nose of the helmet toward her, were narrowed. Robin lifted her chin, meeting his glare with one of her own.

"No. I've made up my mind. We'll try another night."

"This is not your mission. It is mine," Velph said evenly. He tilted his head to the side, musing, or regarding, or whatever the hells the gesture meant. Not for the first time, Robin hated how difficult he was to read with his godsdamned helmet on. "And I will complete it with or without your help." He started to stride out of the shadows, but Robin planted her hand against his sternum and held him back. He flinched, and she was sorry for it, but it also proved her point.

"I thought you said you were on my side, here."

"I am on your side, but I am also a man indebted to our hostess, and I will not renege on my promise." He pried her fingers off his elbow and stuck his head around the corner to survey the street.

Robin bit her tongue as a watchman walked the length of the hospital and vanished around the side. "I'm not asking you to never go in there," Robin whispered when he was gone. "Just not tonight."

Velph had apparently decided to ignore her, though. He ducked around the corner without another word, moving swiftly toward the shadows of the hospital.

"Omens," Robin swore. "Bloody rudding omens." She wasn't about to let him do this alone; the whole point of her being here was that he couldn't do it alone. "Scrubbed-up, stubborn coal-bag," she muttered. Then she brushed crossed fingers over her shoulder to ward against ill-luck, and shot across the street in Velph's wake. He had made it to his destination, and was pressed flat against the hospital's wall, where the eaves of the roof would hide him from any watchmen peering down from above.

"That window, there," he said as Robin sidled up beside him. "That is the one meant to be the dispensary."

"You're not strong enough to climb that, and WINGS can't carry us both."

"Then I suppose you will have to push me up it, my dear," he said cheekily.

Robin was about to argue, but Velph boosted himself onto the lower ledge of a window, and was already reaching his long arms up for the decorative scallops along the top. The sound of boot steps around the corner removed any further chance of hesitation—they needed to get in that window, quickly, quietly, and unseen.

Keeping the thrust low on WINGS, Robin rose slowly, grabbed a handful of Velph's belt, and helped propel him up the wall. He clung to the sill, grimacing, as she picked the lock, and they both scrambled inside just as a pair of watchmen played the directed light from their lanterns along the wall. Velph shut the window behind them, and drew the curtains so their silhouettes wouldn't give them away.

"That, my dear," Velph said as he turned to her, "is an incredibly useful skill. And explains just how it was you were able to so effectively escape my palace. Wherever did you learn it?" His tone was intimate, teasing, voice low and rough with exertion and lust. It made the hairs on Robin's arms stand up and shiver in pleasure.

"Lock picking? Scavenging in the factory fields of Pyria."

"And you still have both your thumbs?" he chuckled.

Robin pressed said digits against his bottom in answer, and he huffed out a muffled laugh, skittering sideways and away from her reach. Fishing through another deep pocket, Velph produced a candle and a book of matches, lighting it with practiced ease. In the light of the tiny flame, he inspected the shelves, moving quickly but calmly, while Robin scooped everything he indicated into a satchel she'd found hung up on the back of the door. When it was full, Velph accepted the satchel, leaving Robin's hands free to control WINGS.

Task complete, they waited until the sounds of the Night Watch had moved inside—the slam of doors and the pound of boots echoing through the hallways indicated their arrival, while the shouts of startled patients and upset medics marked their progress. The path outside clear, Robin helped Velph scramble back out the window and made a controlled fall to the ground.

"*Loa! Loa!* The Skylark!" someone shouted from

above, and Robin and Velph gave up sneaking, pelting as fast as they could for the first alleyway they could reach.

Not so clear, after all, Robin thought with disgust.

"I told you this would happen!" she snarled at Velph. "Go. Get out of here. I'll lead them away." Before he could argue with her, Robin peeled off in the opposite direction, making sure to cross the street, cutting through a pool of lamplight so the watchmen would see her and follow.

"Stop!" screeched a watchman from the hospital roof, and pieces of stone shot up into the air around her, filling the alley with powder as bullets whizzed by her head and slammed into the ground. Robin ran straight at the side of a townhouse, kicked off against the wall, and used the momentum to propel herself into the air. She slapped on the pack's thrust and buzzed showily over the heads of the watchmen, trying purposefully to draw their attention, to ensure that they would follow her instead of Velph.

More bullets peppered the air. Robin flew higher, out of their range, and circled the chimney pots, keeping the bricks between her and the guns. The low drone of an aeroship crept toward her from the direction of the mid-town airfield.

"That's my cue," she said to herself, and dove low to weave amid the streets, startling the people rising early to go off to their jobs as bakers or maids.

When she was satisfied that she had lost the Night Watch, she landed and made her stealthy way back to Rosa's. Around the back of the house was a door to a small mudroom, with two more locked doors that led, on one side, to the salon, and on the other, the kitchen. She rapped a quiet pattern on the entrance to the salon, and a few moments later, Rosa poked her head through a crack in the door. She wore a flimsy little dressing gown that was more for show than warmth, so Robin didn't blame her for not swinging the door wide.

"Something the matter?" she asked conversationally. Behind her, Robin could hear the raucous laughter of a crowd of people. Business had picked up again since it had stopped snowing every godsdamned day, and Robin felt a brief flash of guilt for intruding. It was quickly burned away by the flames of her anger, however.

"Where is he?" Robin snarled.

"In the kitchen," Rosa said with a smile. "He asked for privacy to better inventory your spoils." She withdrew, and Robin stomped through the opposite door. She found Velph stacking bandages in a cupboard, his helmet off and resting on the table—which was awfully cavalier of him with the rest of the *zentapi* a mere door away—and his coat thrown over the back of a chair. In just his shirt, waistcoat, and trousers, with his scarf lying open on his shoulders, he was sweaty and vulnerable-looking. The muscles in his back flexed as he piled boxes at the back of the pantry, his shirtsleeves rolled up to reveal a delicious amount of forearm.

"Welcome back, my dear," he said without turning around.

"Do you know how bloody condescending that sounds when you say it like that?" Robin snarled, slamming the door shut behind her.

"Like what, my dear?" Velph asked breezily.

"Like that! Gods, you are impossible! You nearly got shot again," Robin snapped, fumbling with the buckles of WINGS's straps, hands shaking in a rage that was sudden and consuming. "*I* nearly got shot. That was a monumentally irresponsible thing you did out there. We should have left. You should have listened to me. Now they know the Skylark has a compatriot."

"Do they?" he asked, still not turning to look at her. "Are you certain? Did anyone see me?"

"How in the hells am I supposed to know!" she said, and shrugged out of WINGS. She set the pack on the table next to his helmet. "But your stupid helmet shines like a star and is twice as recognizable! It wouldn't surprise me at all if they did."

"Why, Skylark, I do believe you are genuinely angry with me," Velph said and turned at last to face her. His expression was wide-eyed, and slightly hurt.

"Of course I'm godsdamned angry with you!" Robin shouted. "You rudding scrubbed-up snob! You could have died!"

Velph laughed, and Robin punched him in the mouth.

CHAPTER FOURTEEN

Velph reeled back against the counter, hand flying up to his lips. His fingers came away bloody, and he blinked dumbly at the red stains on his skin. "You . . . hit me."

"I told you, you weren't healed enough!" Robin snarled, cradling her throbbing knuckles. "I told you it was a bad idea. I told you!"

She glared at him, biting down on her bottom lip to keep from sobbing as tears welled fast and hard. She hiccoughed, shoulders tensing as she fought against the flood of emotions threatening to drown her.

"I was *terrified* I was going to lose you!" she confessed in a rush of words. She didn't even realize that that was what had her so worked up until she'd said it.

Velph looked up at her in shock, gray eyes wide and honest. Gone was the self-assured smirk, the shrewd, calculating gaze. This was his naked self, the one he so rarely showed, and it was like adding fuel to the fire of Robin's rage. Something new flickered across Velph's face, something that softened the harsh planes and angles, something that curled in the corner of that kissable mouth, something that dusted an emotion akin to happiness into the edges of his features. He sprang forward and wrapped his arms around her, cradling her firmly against his own chest.

"Shhh, shhh," he whispered in her ear. "I did not die. I am here."

"I just *got* you," Robin choked, and as swiftly as the rage had come, it was doused in a fear so profound that Robin could no longer hold back her sobs. "I can't watch you die again."

"Oh, my poor dear," he said softly, laying his cheek against her neck. His beard was soft at this length, springy, and smelled of the fragrant oil Rosa had given him to keep it well kempt. His lips were gentle on the shell of her ear as Robin clung to him, desperate and sniffling. "How cruel of me," he murmured. "I am sorry, Skylark. I promise, you will never be rid of me. I am yours, and you are mine, and I promise, nothing will ever come between us again."

"You can't promise that. You *can't.*" Robin shook her head in vehement denial, fingers digging into the flesh of his shoulders, and Velph grunted as the buckle of her goggles smacked against his jaw. "The gods only know what might happen next time! You've already been shot once, you rudding great moron! Don't make promises you can't keep."

He pulled back, just enough that he could look down upon her face, then gently pushed up her goggles and kissed the tear tracks on each of her cheeks. The calluses on his thumbs were rough against her jaw, his own scars a bizarre and comforting texture against her neck that told her he was *alive.* She'd thought he died in the fire that created those scars, but he'd escaped, survived, and he was here now—kissing her.

"Then I will promise to take better precautions," he whispered against her temple, where goggles and flesh touched. "And I promise to do everything in my power to keep us together."

Robin nodded, sniffing, and turned up her face for a kiss. Velph was happy to give one, his long fingers spreading across her shoulder blades, possessive and comforting. His mouth tasted like blood.

"We should get ice for your face," Robin said between humid breaths.

"I will keep," he said, pulling away to tilt his head the other way, to find a better way for them to slot together. "I would much rather be doing this."

"You'll be sore in the morning."

"I am sore now." He tilted his hips against her stomach and something hot and hard pressed against Robin's belly. Even through her leather jacket, it seemed as warm as the sun.

"Oh," Robin said, jerking away, startled by the frankness of his touch. She stared down at the placket of his trousers. "That's . . ."

"For you," he said gently.

Robin stepped out of the warm circle of his arms, and he let her. She turned her back, unsure if she could handle the naked emotion on his face, and ran her hands over WINGS, slowly, reverently. Buying time. Her head was spinning. Her mouth was watering. Her lungs had somehow shrunk up into little balls under her ribs.

"Skylark?" Velph asked gently. "My dear?"

"I . . . upstairs, please," she said. "I don't . . . not in Rosa's kitchen."

Silently, the air heavy with the things Velph wanted to do and that Robin was too afraid to say, they piled up their gear. Velph donned his helmet, and Robin fetched a cloth, soaking it in cool water from the hand pump. Then they made their way up to the attic by way of the back stairs, so neither of them would be seen by the *zentapi's* patrons.

Once there, they laid aside their uniforms and masks. Robin stripped off her jacket, and Velph removed his scarf and waistcoat, leaving them both to stand in just their trousers, socks, suspenders, and shirts. Robin's breasts were bound in one of the strange cloth bustiers that were more forgiving than a corset, but other than that, and the color of their trousers, they were dressed the same. Velph had undone a few more buttons at his throat, and an intriguing smattering of dark hair teased Robin through the gap.

Intimate, that's what this is, Robin realized. *I've never been so undressed with a man before. You've lost your mind, Captain, bringing him up here like this.*

Entirely too conscious of the fact that she'd unwittingly pulled them into strange new territory, Robin led Velph over to the vanity stool and gently pushed him down. Blood had already begun to dry in the bristles on his chin, and he watched with wide, cautious eyes as she used the damp cloth to gently scrub at the cut her knuckles had left. She deliberately did not look at his lap. When she was finished, she stood, wringing the pink-stained cloth between her hands, twisting and twisting it while she tried to figure out how to say what it was she was feeling.

Torn, was one word for it.

She wanted it. She wanted Velph. She wanted to give him everything his body was wordlessly asking for. More than that, she wanted to take it. She wanted to claim him, to make him hers, to show the world that she loved him. She wanted to know what it felt like to lay with a lover. She wanted to learn what it meant to be a worshiper of these particular Arts. She wanted that sleepy, content smile that Rosa wore in the mornings for herself, wanted the love bites she'd seen on Grier's neck scattered across her own, and to scatter them across Velph's. She *wanted* it.

She just had no idea how to say so.

And she feared it, too, because this was not how it was supposed to be done. The Klonn way made it just another form of exercise, pleasurable but ultimately meaningless, and Robin didn't know if she could do that. The gods saw everything, and if she . . .

She wasn't naïve. She knew that there were Sealies out there who took joy in their bodies before marriage and were not shunned, were not hated, were not struck down by the gods of ill-luck. The woodland gods would even celebrate, she was sure. But Robin didn't know if she could be one of them.

She wanted to be. She did. But what if she was . . . well, what if she was awful at it?

Velph broke her from her thoughts by prying the cloth from her hands and setting it on the vanity table.

"Why do you fret, my dear?" he asked softly, cupping both of her hands between his, kissing gently the backs of the knuckles that had split his skin. His grip was warm.

"I don't . . . I-I haven't . . ." Robin stuttered, and she could feel the heat of embarrassment rising in her cheeks.

"Ah," Velph whispered, pulling himself to his feet. He drew her into him, dropping his head to nip and nibble at her neck, to whisper in her ear with that low, gravelly rasp. "You have never before been a patron of the Art of Pleasure."

Robin couldn't help the giggle that bubbled up from behind her sternum. "That is an extremely Klonnish way of saying I'm a virgin."

"Mm," Velph agreed, leaning in for a proper kiss, but pausing just shy of her lips to ask: "Would you like to learn?"

Without waiting for her answer, he kissed her, softly at first, brushing against one side of her mouth, then the other, pressing her bottom lip between his own. He parted her lips with more insistence, let his tongue trace around the back of her teeth, as if searching for whatever flavor her laughter might have left.

Robin sagged into him, gave herself over to the kiss, and surprised herself by making a noise that could only be called a moan. Shyness swelled back up in an instant, and Robin ducked her head against Velph's collarbone, cheeks blazing.

"Oh, my dear," Velph panted roughly into the skin beneath her ear, chuckling softly. It made her shiver all over. "Do not be embarrassed by any noises. Let us show the professionals around us what it *really* means to be a devotee."

Robin scrinched up her nose, kept her forehead pressed into Velph's collarbone. "I . . . I can't."

Velph exhaled, long and slow—not quite a sigh; more an attempt to regain his composure. He wrapped his arms around her and buried his face in her hair.

"I will not be disappointed if you choose not to tonight," he whispered, his hands sweeping up and down her back, comforting. "No, that is a lie. I will be very disappointed. But I will *understand.* And—you must believe me in this, Skylark—never again will I seek to hurt you, or rush you. Especially in this."

Robin fisted her hands into his shirtsleeves to keep herself from letting them wander. "How did this happen?" she whispered. "What a sick sense of humor the gods must have, putting us on opposite sides like this."

She pulled back then, pressed her palm against the place on his sternum where the bullet had gone in. It was padded still, just slightly, with bandages, and the reminder of his mortality, of what she had almost lost, made her go still.

"Skylark?" Velph asked, sensing the shift in her mood. He leaned forward gently and pressed a warm, damp kiss on the triangle of skin exposed by her own open collar. "What is it that yet troubles you?" His voice buzzed against her skin, the echoing vibrations in his chest relayed through her hand.

Robin pushed him back a little, far enough that he raised his head to meet her eyes. She studied him, studied the patient, slightly fearful expression he wore as he waited for her to speak. Twice now, she'd almost lost him. And every time, the thought of that loss had filled her with choking fear and rage. Despite everything, he was still the one she wanted, the one she *loved*. She didn't want to lose him—*couldn't* lose him again. And if she did this with him now, made this wordless commitment, losing him later would be even worse. There was no way she could bear it.

And yet, what choice would she have? He was a fugitive, already. What if he was declared a war criminal? What if one of them was captured? What if all of this worked, and the war ended, and Robin went home . . . then what? Could he even come with her?

There was no part of this that ended with them retiring in a cute little cottage by the sea, sitting side by side on matching rocking chairs, enjoying their hives and their freedom.

Velph searched her face, his expression closing off now, unreadable in response to what Robin could only guess he was seeing in her own. Only the smallest twitch of the muscle along his jaw betrayed any sense of the turmoil that must be going on inside his head. Then, unexpectedly, he gathered her hands between his own, brushing his finger in a diagonal line along her palm, from the base of her pinkie finger to the mound of her thumb.

Robin's lungs stuttered, and her heart suddenly beat out of sync as she dropped her gaze to the path he had drawn across her palm. Did he . . . had he meant to . . . ?

Robin had given up on the thought of ever having a Marriage Line for herself when she'd been made a pilot. But as she stared at the phantom trail bisecting her scars, her throat felt too full to breathe, larynx burning, brain racing so far ahead of her mouth that the words jumbled up on her tongue.

"Marry me," she blurted. It came out in a breathless rush.

Velph went still, surprise stiffening his posture. "Skylark, I—"

"Marry me," Robin said again, sure now. Because yes, *yes*, this felt so *right*. She took his left hand in hers, and ran one fingernail across his palm, just like he had to hers. She scratched hard enough to leave a light red mark behind along the shiny white scar tissue, and it made Robin's insides quiver.

"If you have a Marriage Line, then you're Sealie. That's all there is to it. The marriage scars would get you over the front lines. They'd never let you into the country as a Klonn, but as a Sealie, as one of my people . . . we could go back to Saskwya, together."

"Skylark," he said again, and then, "my love." Robin shivered in delight, hearing that word fall from his lips. He licked his bottom lip, blinking, thinking rapidly, cheeks flushing a delectable shade of pink. A grin curled at the corners of his mouth until he was beaming a full-faced smile so open and free, so unlike any Robin had ever seen on him before, that Robin felt her own expression gleefully pulling wide to match.

"Well?" she prompted.

"Having you bound to me, making you my wife, it is the answer to concerns you did not even know I possess." He pulled her palm up to his face, kissed her right in the center, lips lingering and warm. "How strange that you should ask me now, when I had already resolved to ask you. But there are . . . truths that we must . . . that I must—"

Velph choked off his own words, looking chagrined, and ducked his head so she couldn't catch his next expression clearly. The glimpse she had managed to catch had turned his eyes to watery silver, filled them with . . . was that guilt?

"Oh," Robin said, pulling her hands from his, stomach plummeting. "I see."

She turned away from him and retreated to the bed,

dropping slowly down to sit on the edge of it, mortification warring with the pain of rejection. She couldn't look up at him, didn't want to see whatever excuse he was weaving written on his face. She wanted to curl up and cry. Wanted, all told, to punch him again. Which was probably not something she should be considering about the man she'd just asked to marry her.

Violence was not the way she should be handling her disappointments.

"Oh, oh no, Skylark," Velph said, moving to sit beside her. He used one long finger to lift her chin, pulling her eyes up to look at him, to meet his earnest, serious gaze. "My dear, that is not a no."

And then he kissed her, hard and searching and wonderful. But distracting.

Robin startled back, hands sliding up to cup his chin, holding him at bay. "Wait, what? What does that mean?" She searched his face, looking for signs of betrayal, or amusement, or anything that would indicate subterfuge. When she found none, she breathed, "You're serious."

A wry smile lifted one corner of his mouth. "Of course. I could never refuse you, my dear. Surely you must know that by now. But I . . . there is something I must confess to you. Before, ah . . . before we proceed. I . . ." Velph pulled back, untangled himself from her and stood by the side of the bed, heels together, hands clasped behind the small of his back, as if standing at attention, as if she were his commanding officer. "I . . ." His voice cracked, his face flushed, and he turned away to pour them both a glass of water.

Robin accepted hers and sipped slowly, anticipation and worry churning in her gut. What was so important that her normally eloquent Velph had lost his words?

"I am—" he started again, and Robin realized all at once that whatever it was he was about to say, it was going to change things, and the honest truth of it was that she didn't want anything to change. She didn't want to know.

"No. I don't care," Robin said, pushing to her feet. She set her glass on the bedside table and closed the distance between them. "You don't have to tell me. Whatever it is, I don't care."

His eyes blazed silver as they searched her face. For what? Fury? Disgust? Calmly, she reached out, took his glass, and set it beside her own. When she turned back to face him, his eyes were closed, one hand threading through his hair as pain arced through his features.

"You do not understand," Velph said softly. "And I am uncertain as to how to . . . I do not . . ."

"Hey," she said, gathering his hands in her own. Her heart blazed within her, all the anger and hurt burned away, her mind made up. "Look at me. Whatever it is, it doesn't matter. I told you before—we're the same, you and I. We're just us, no matter what other titles or orders are imposed on us. We're just us, a pair of nothings—"

"A pair of nothings," Velph interrupted, burying what Robin thought was a hint of a flinch, a flicker of sadness, behind a small half-smile. "You certainly do have a way with words, my dear."

Robin swatted him on the arm with a playful scowl. "The point is, we can start over, be just Skylark and Velph. It doesn't matter for a Sealie wedding."

"We can?" he asked, clearly surprised as he gazed deep into her eyes. "We could . . . but would your gods not . . . ?"

"The gods already know our sins, our names, our hearts," Robin said. "It doesn't matter to them."

He looked down for a moment, expression studiously blank, and Robin's heart stuttered again. She felt her face and fingers go cold. Then he glanced back up at her through the fine black lace of his eyelashes, and the mischievous, boyish smile she liked so much curled into the corner of his mouth. "Well. The solution does seem obvious, then."

"Oh?" Robin asked, breath whooshing out of her as he pulled her roughly against him. "Does it now?"

"Mm," he said, leaning down for a kiss. "You shall have to make me into a Sealie."

Robin spluttered against his mouth, and Velph pulled back to glare at her and wipe his mustache clean. "Skylark. Yuck."

"Sorry!" Robin said, hands flying to her lips to stifle a mortified giggle. "Sorry, I just . . . do you know what that sounds like?"

Velph flashed her a grin as he leaned in to growl against her mouth, that lovely deep grumble that he used when he was at his most serious—and most seductive. "I know exactly what it sounds like."

Then, abruptly, he lifted her off her feet and deposited her back on the bed. Robin gave an undignified and surprised squeak, but didn't have time to protest. His hands were in her hair, his lips against her mouth, and Robin grinned. She opened her arms and her thighs to him, so he could press against her, could cover her in heat and love. He was hard again, she could feel it, separated by only a few layers of cloth.

I can have it, Robin realized. *I can have that, and I can have this. I can have him, his Arts of Pleasure, and a husband in the Sealie way, too.*

"Let us start over. Let us be only ourselves, and not as others would shape us," Velph said between the kisses he peppered on her eyelids, her cheeks, the tip of her nose.

"Then one of us better find some white silk before we get too carried away," Robin laughed.

CHAPTER
FIFTEEN

Velph pulled back to sit on his heels, mouth swollen red and stretched into a wide smile. "My scarf is silk. Is it white enough?" Using one of Robin's knees for support, he leaned down, rooted through the pile of his discarded clothes, and held it up for inspection. Two small drops of blood from his split lip were drying to rust near one end, and he frowned when he saw them.

Robin propped herself up on her elbows and arched an eyebrow. "Why, by all the gods, do you have a silk scarf?"

Velph grinned and gave her that boyish, one-shouldered shrug that was so incongruous with his normally poised and perfect nature. "Rosa provided it. Silk is quite warm, my dear."

"Not so warm as wool," Robin lobbed back.

He smirked and waved the scarf in front of her face. "Will this do, or must I venture out into the *zentapi* in all my proud indecency?"

Robin swallowed hard and did not let her eyes drop to where the pride in question stretched tight against his trousers. "That'll do," she said, blushing at the crackled huskiness of her own voice. "Now, turn out the lamps and c'mere."

He did, and then sat on the bed opposite Robin, smoothing the scarf along the rumpled coverlet between them. Moonlight spilled through the room's large window, bathing them both where they sat. It traced his features in silver, turned his tumble of dark hair to a night sky burnished with streaks of stars. His eyes were shadowed, deep pools of mercury, pupils wide and hungry as he touched her sweaty, messy white hair and murmured, *"Beautiful."*

Robin reached for where she'd left her boots by the side of the bed, and pulled the knife out of the tongue of the left one. Her replacement boot knife was slim and wickedly sharp, with a discrete, low-profile leather handle in the same shade of brown as her boots. It was nothing like the ornately carved and richly etched blade the Wise Women would have used to bind their marriage, but it was good enough. The knife wasn't what was important here. The cut was.

She placed the blade on the scarf, and reached for the candle and book of matches she kept in the bedside table drawer, as well as the roll of bandages and bottle of antiseptic she had on hand in case she nicked herself while working on WINGS. She handed these to Velph, and then fetched one of the half full glasses of water and the tray that the decanter and glasses had been brought in upon. The last thing she retrieved—hidden behind the oil lamp and used only when Rosa or Thorne brought her a tea tray—was the little pot of honey she'd procured from the market. She poured a small amount into the lid, and put the pot back on the side table.

Arranging the items on the tray between them, Robin retook her position on the bed and folded her legs under her, mirroring the way Velph sat, facing her across the varied accouterments.

"What happens now?" he asked, voice reverential and hushed, eyes skimming the tray's contents.

"Well, first we clean our hands, and the knife," Robin said, handing him the antiseptic and cutting a length off the roll of bandages. "Nothing worse than an infected Marriage Line."

"Oh, nothing at all worse," Velph teased gently. He

wiped down the blade of the knife, and balanced it on the lid of the honey jar, laying it carefully so it would touch neither tray nor honey. Then, per Robin's instruction, he cleaned his own left hand thoroughly, but perfunctory. Robin moved to take the liquid-soaked bandage from him, but he chose not to relinquish it. Instead, he took her left hand in his own, and gently spread the antiseptic over her already scarred palm, tender and thorough. *Meaningful.* A promise. A vow.

The intimacy and warmth of his care wrapped around Robin like a cozy blanket. It made her face flush, and her heart stutter, and tingling heat started to pool behind her navel. "How, uh, how do the Klonn get married?" she asked, voice a whisper in the thick silence as Velph worked.

"There is a certificate from the government," Velph said as he finished her hand and set the used bandage on the side table. "Each of the trothed signs it. The certificate is stamped by an official, and filed by a clerk, and the families of the married pair celebrate with a ball, or, if they are of, ah, less influential means, head to a tavern for a night of practicing the great Arts of music, and dance, and, eventually, lovemaking."

"Sounds a bit sterile," Robin said, lighting the candle.

"Not at all."

"What does the government have to do with marriage, though? Something like that, well, it should be between you and the gods."

Velph chuckled. "Spouses must be registered to ensure the social benefits go to the right person. Pensions, medicine allowances, and, in the event of a death, to whom the estate falls. How do you handle such things in Saskwya?"

"Well, everyone just knows who is married to whom." Robin handed Velph the knife, careful not to touch the blade. "It's not a big community. Both of you showing up together with bandaged hands is enough."

"But the Saskwyan government, how would they ensure you receive the right social care?" The distress in his voice was touching.

Robin finished arranging everything and looked up, shrugging. "We're Sealie. We're not eligible for any."

"*Nothing?*" Velph asked, horrified. "You mean to say that you fight their war, but they give you no . . . no aid?"

"I get paid," Robin said, failing to see why this revelation would be so shocking. The Benne considered the Sealie to be parasites on their society. Leeches who drained their resources and burdened their economy by sheer force of number. Driven from their homes by the Great Sickness, the Sealie had been forced to turn to the Benne for aid, and while it had been given—grudgingly—they had been labeled as second-class citizens, ticks, in return.

"Well," Velph huffed, and his face was a thundercloud. "That is certainly unacceptable. Perhaps it is a good thing that I made a point to procure this before our mission tonight." He reached back for his coat, tossed haphazardly over the foot of the bed, beside his helmet, and rifled through one of its many pockets. Robin started to object, as he would have to reclean his hand, but then closed her mouth before the words left her tongue. The damage was already done, and she didn't want to argue—anymore, at least—on her wedding day.

Velph pulled a folded bit of paper from an inside pocket and set the coat aside, turning back to her with a shy, almost sheepish smile.

"Is that . . . ?" she breathed, startled.

"A Certificate of Marriage, yes," Velph said ruefully. "Did I not mention that I had already resolved to ask for your hand? Not tonight, of course, but eventually, when the time was right." The look he gave her as he unfolded the paper was tender, and rueful, and hungry, and filled with all manner of things Robin couldn't define. "I never expected that you would ask me first," he said softly, turning the paper so she could read it in the small flicker of candlelight. "Do me the honor, my dear Skylark, of becoming my wife in the Klonnish tradition as well?"

Robin stared at the parchment, mouth dry and heart racing. It was large, crisp, and bordered with an intricate design in blue. The ink looked new, and there was some sort of wax seal in the bottom corner, embossed with the flourishing crest of King Eloy. Robin's understanding of written Klonnish had improved immensely in the last year, but her ability to take in the meaning of the words before her vanished in a haze of delight when the word "marriage" bubbled up off the paper. Fear quickly followed it, and she swallowed hard.

As much as sharing a Marriage Line with her would make Velph a Sealie, signing this would make her Klonn—in the eyes of the Klonnish government, at least. What would happen to the part of her that was still Sealie? Would signing this be a betrayal of her people? Would the gods shun her?

She looked up at Velph, sitting there, expression unshuttered and hopeful, and then dropped her gaze to the array of items laid out, in true Sealie tradition, upon the tray. Velph had agreed to become Sealie, had been ready to marry her through the traditions of her people. Did she not owe him the same?

Setting the paper against the coverlet, she turned her hands palm up and sent a quick prayer into the heavens. *Forgive me*, she thought. Then, out loud, she said, "What do I have to do?"

Velph grinned wide and pulled her to her feet. Snatching up the paper, he laid it against the vanity table—the only surface wide enough in her small room to allow it to lie flat.

"Your name goes here," he said, indicating the first of

two blank signature lines. "And mine goes here."

"That's it?" Robin asked, slightly disappointed. For a culture that boasted reverence to the Art of Pleasure and the Art of Love, this was decidedly . . . unromantic.

Velph's lips rose in a smirk, and he leaned in to nip a quick kiss. "No, dearest heart. After this, we finish the marriage ceremony by your traditions. And *then* we become devotees to the Arts."

Robin couldn't hold back her grin as her heart soared. Some part of her, she realized, had feared that, having once again gotten his way, Velph would no longer see the use of her silly Sealie ceremony. She thought back to the many conversations they'd had in his forest palace, where he'd insisted that the Klonn way was the only way, and marveled at how he had changed. Perhaps there was truth to the idea that love altered a person for the better, after all.

Robin retrieved a quill and an ink pot from the vanity drawer, and leaned down to affix her name where Velph had indicated. She hesitated, though. They'd never exchanged their full names. Would signing her proper name now defeat the purpose of hiding her identity? Worse, would it put her family in jeopardy?

If she signed Skylark instead of Robin, would it somehow lead the Klonn government here? She was a wanted fugitive, a terrorist in their eyes. Would they even grant her a legal marriage under that name?

She glanced up at Velph in the vanity mirror, unsure. He met her gaze, laying one warm, long-fingered hand across the small of her back. "I don't know which name to sign," she said softly.

"Ah, yes, of course," Velph said. "It must be your true name, as it shall be mine, but I will not look, if you prefer."

Robin nodded, and, true to his word, Velph turned away. Then, steeling herself, she hurriedly signed: Robin

Arianhod. She stepped back and handed Velph the quill. He bent over the certificate and, using his free hand to keep his face averted from her side of the paper, scrawled his own name on the other line, so swiftly and messily that Robin couldn't actually read what it said. Then he laid down the quill and gathered her hands in his own. "Thank you," he whispered, kissing her knuckles.

"Ready?" Robin asked, with a pointed glance at the waiting tray.

"From the moment you kicked my aeroship."

Robin laughed, and pulled him back over to the bed. Quickly, she went through the process of recleaning their hands, applying a fresh coat of antiseptic to both their skin and the blade. Then they settled back on opposite sides of the tray.

"Hold out your left hand, like this," Robin said, her own hand out and palm up already. "No, move yours toward me more, so the knuckles of our pinkies are side by—yes, like that. This way, it's all one clean slash, across both our hands at the same time." With his help, she bound their wrists together with the white scarf, so neither of them could accidentally jerk away when the cut was made. "Okay, your other hand—pinkie finger out."

He followed suit, making a fist with his free hand, finger out. "Now what, my heart? Are there words to speak? Gods to invoke? Vows to promise?"

"No. The gods'll be paying attention as soon as we finish the next part." Robin took a shaky breath, heart pattering behind her ribs like a caged bird. Her hands shook, and she knew Velph could see it, could *feel* it, but he didn't tease her, didn't ask her if she was all right. Likely because his hands were shaking, too. He swallowed heavily, as if parched. "Do what I do," she said, "same time as I do it, right?"

Together, they slowly dipped their pinkies in the glass of water. "This is to call for the attention of the gods of water," Robin said softly, voice croaking as she held his gaze. "They watch over sailors, and travelers, farmers and merchants. As mutable as liquid poured into a different vessel, and as unchanging as the hardest glacial ice, they're the gods of kisses and, er . . . fluids."

Velph chuckled, and Robin arched an eyebrow at him. He stopped, but couldn't seem to force his mouth into any expression but a wide, almost goofy smile. That was okay, though. Robin couldn't stop smiling, either.

Next, they held their pinkies over the small candle flame, careful not to drop water on it as their skin gently dried. "This is to call for the attention of the gods of the air and fire," Robin explained, and Velph smiled kindly, drinking in every word. "They watch over soldiers and pilots, smiths and musicians, storytellers and bakers, political speakers with fire in their hearts, and those who fight to have their voices heard. They're the gods of things passionately blazing and quietly banked, of gales and gentle breezes, of hearts and caresses."

When their fingers were dry, they dipped their pinkies in the honey and held them there. "This is to call for the attention of the gods of earth and lives," she said at last. "These are the gods that care for the ground, and the animals, the plants, and us. They watch over animals of burden and livestock, over the wild things that flit between forest shadows and the pets that share your home, the strays you must show kindness to, for you never know which god is looking through their eyes and judging you for your cruelty. They're the gods of fertility, of budding and growth, of harvest and, eventually, death, of a return to the earth to give life to the next round of lives. They're the gods of things reaching for the sun and burrowing under the ground, of fruit and meat, of death to nourish, and of birth to replenish. Open your mouth."

Velph complied, and she placed the dab of honey on her finger on his tongue. She opened her own mouth, and

Velph followed suit. Robin closed her lips over his sweet finger, sucking and tonguing gently at the thick honey, kissing it away. Encouraged, Velph did the same, drawing a groan from Robin that surprised and embarrassed her.

Velph burst out laughing at her mortification, her hand falling away. Robin pulled back, dropping his finger from her mouth so she could use it to scowl at him.

"Oh dear, have I ruined the mood?" Velph chuckled into the tremulous darkness. Between them, the golden flame of the candle flickered warmly.

"It's fine. Like I said, it doesn't matter what we say. Hand me the knife."

Velph startled and stopped laughing, expression sober. He lifted the blade from where it still rested against the lid of the honey pot, but didn't offer it to her. Robin raised a brow.

"I . . . I think I would like to do it," Velph said gently. "I want to be an . . . active participant. I want your gods to know that I desire this. I wish to prove it to them, if you will allow it."

Robin was warmed by the conviction and determination in his voice. The only other times she'd heard him use that tone were moments where he'd professed his affection for her. It made her breath shake in her lungs, and her face flush.

"Okay," she said, turning the knife over with a fancy flip she'd learned from one of the other mid-flights, offering it to Velph hilt first.

He took it slowly, reverently. "Show me what to do," he said, and that husky growl to his voice, the one that made her knees go weak and her insides shiver, was back.

"Like this," Robin said, placing the blade so it would first pierce the mound of her thumb. "Then draw it toward you. Clean, but not so fast that you lose control of the depth of the cut. And not so shallow that it won't scar."

"Skylark, are you . . . are you certain—?"

"I trust you," Robin said simply.

Eyes darting across her face, he licked his lips, swallowed hard, and then bent his head to his task. Robin tensed up, anticipating the pain, but refused to let the fingers of her left hand curl into a protective fist. Blood welled in the wake of the blade, streaming down her wrist to soak into the white scarf, falling in small spatters into the glass of water, onto the candle, through the smoke, and into the honey.

"Good," Robin said softly, teeth clenched against the pain. "Keep going."

Steady, and with near surgical precision, Velph drew the knife across her palm, making sure that where it left her skin, by her pinkie, it immediately began to slice into his. Their scars would line up beautifully. Robin reached up, placed her free hand on his neck to steady him as he sucked in a breath and forced himself to cut his own flesh. As soon as he lifted the bloody knife away, the Marriage Line complete, Robin used her grip on him to pull him down into an absolutely filthy kiss.

Now, it was Velph who was groaning. There was a clatter as he dropped the knife on the tray. He fisted his own free hand into her shirt and hauled her closer, jostling the tray between them.

"Are we married, Skylark? Are you now my wife?" he asked, words mashed against her lips.

Robin giggled into his mustache. "As much as you're my husband, Velph."

Velph groaned again, gravelly and low. He rose to his knees to arch over their wedding accouterments and pushed her head back, plundering her mouth with his honey-coated tongue.

"Wait, wait," Robin panted. "Gods, let's get this stuff off the bed, and bandage our hands. Hold on."

Velph snarled and let her go very, very reluctantly. Their mouths parted like molasses, his fingers releasing her shirt as though they were freezing and stiff. Robin quickly used the knife to cut the knot in the wedding binding, as she'd seen the Wise Women do, making two even halves. She washed away the excess blood on Velph's hand with half of the glass of water, and bound his cut with half the scarf. Catching on quick, he did the same for her. Then he moved the tray off the bed and onto the bedside table.

And then, apparently finished with being patient, he bore her back onto the mattress with his body, sliding between her legs, tangling his fingers in her hair, and licking his way up her throat, aggressive and taking control and *perfect*. Robin didn't even have time to worry about not being good enough, or practiced enough, because he was doing all the work. All she had to do was lay back and enjoy. And take mental notes, determined to be the one who took him apart next time.

His long, clever fingers plucked each button on her shirt from its hole, and he followed the line of bared flesh with his mouth. Robin moaned, and then giggled, surprised at the volume with which the sound had emerged.

Velph lifted his head just enough that she could see his wide, hungry grin. "Well now," he murmured against her skin, leaning so close that his breath tickled her navel as his long fingers plucked at the buttons of her trousers. "Ready to become a studious patron of the Art of Pleasure?"

His mouth closed on the jut of bone above her hip, sucking a bruise into her naked flesh, and all Robin—feeling absolutely *wrecked*—could say was, "Oh, gods, *yes.*"

CHAPTER SIXTEEN

Robin could tell when she awoke that it was daylight on the other side of her curtains, but she wasn't quite ready yet to face it. The market bell tower was chiming seven o'clock, and Robin winced against the echoing pound. Then memories of the night before slid through her mind, rousing phantom tingles under her skin, and Robin's eyes popped open. She peered down at her body, startled to see that she was naked, and that a pair of arms lightly furred with black hair were wrapped around her like a particularly amorous octopus.

Oh.

A soft breath against the back of her neck sent shivers down her spine.

Oh, gods! she giggled to herself. *I'm married!*

She waited to see if dread would settle in, if regret would dampen her golden joy. But it didn't. She wanted to check her new Marriage Line, but Velph had her left hand pinned under her side, his arm warm and heavy against her waist. She craned her head around to stare at her lover—her *husband*—instead.

"Why do you glare at me, my dear?" Velph asked, without even opening his eyes. A laugh was startled out of Robin before she could hold it in, and she had to admit, it felt good. Freeing. Joyful. She rolled back, clambering over top of Velph to get out of the bed, and he grumbled as they swapped positions, burrowing back under the blankets, eyes still closed.

"I'll go fetch us some breakfast," she said, and gave

him a quick peck on the tip of his nose. He muttered something inarticulate, face scrunching up, and pulled the blankets higher. Robin brought a hand to her mouth to stifle her laughter. She'd never seen him be so . . . innocent, so vulnerable and child-like. So *human*. It made her heart swell with affection.

Groaning at the chill of the boards beneath her feet, the nip of the cool air against her bare skin, Robin pulled herself out of bed and toward the door. Spring was on its way, but not fast enough. She wrapped herself in one of the ridiculously frilly dressing gowns that Rosa had left for her upon her arrival—but that she had never had cause to use before now—as she went.

Fumbling with the knob with her off-hand, she opened the door and made her careful way downstairs. She hesitated at the bottom of the back stairs, trying to gauge the mood of the house before she made her way inside the kitchen. All was silent. Peering around the corner, Robin saw that Rosa sat in the plush red chair by the hearth, curled over a cup of tea. The pot was under its scraggly knitted cap on the chopping block, but Robin wondered if it would be warm enough still, even with the cozy; Rosa didn't look like she had slept a wink. Dark shadows piled up under her eyes, and a crease pulled at the skin between her brows.

She looked up as Robin padded quietly into the kitchen, though she was not, as Robin had thought, alone. Thorne was seated at the table, out of view from the angle Robin had viewed the kitchen's interior, frowning over the odds and ends of some sort of gizmo with which he was tinkering.

"G'morning, Skylark," he muttered, but didn't raise his gaze from the assortment spread out across the table before him.

"Oh, thank the Arts," Rosa said from her perch, a sultry, knowing smirk twisting her full lips. "The tension between the two of you was beginning to grow so inflated I wondered if I would have to pop it like a zeppelin bag."

Robin felt her cheeks color and went to the cupboard so she could prepare tea for herself and her new husband, fetching down a tray and two cups.

"Skylark," Rosa cried, hopping to her feet. She set aside her cup to grab for Robin's wrist. "Whatever has happened to your hand?"

"Huh?" Robin looked at her left hand, held gently in the other woman's grip, confused. Then she realized that Rosa wouldn't understand what the bloodstained white silk meant. "Oh. Uh. This is, um, a Sealie thing."

Thorne set aside a screwdriver, frowning as he looked up. "Self-harm?"

"No!" Robin said, mortified. "No, it's, um . . . I just . . . oh, gods, maybe Velph should be here for this."

"Why would—?" Rosa started, but Thorne interrupted her.

"Is it a *sex* thing?"

"No!" Robin blurted. Her whole face was going red now, the blush spreading like wildfire across her skin. "Well, yes. Kind of! It's a . . . it's just a Sealie thing, all right? I don't want to talk about it right now."

"Well, glory to the Arts, then," Rosa said with a saucy whistle as she moved over to the stove to boil a kettle. Fresh rolls sat in the middle of the harvest table, and Rosa shuttled a few little pots of nut butters and sweet sticky jams to Robin's tray, along with a plateful of the rolls. "Tell me, does your dear archnemesis now have a matching bandage?"

Robin leaned hard on the counter, arms locked, face down and blazing. She knew if she looked up, Rosa's shrewd gaze would pounce on her, carefully studying every twitch, every blush, parsing the truth even without the aid of words. "I . . . uh . . ." she stuttered, mouth suddenly dry, joy pulling her lips up in a smile that bordered on hysterical glee. "Yeah, he does."

"Must be a very *interesting* sex thing," Thorne said, grinning lazily at her.

"Oh, gods! Please, please, *please* just stop talking," Robin said, snatching up the tray the second Rosa set the full teapot upon it.

"Have fun!" Rosa called after her as Robin fled the kitchen, her face still burning. Delighted laughter followed her up the stairs, and Robin decided, after a moment, that she didn't actually mind at all.

When Robin returned to the attic room, she found Velph awake and sitting up. He had shuffled up against the headboard, legs akimbo beneath the blankets, hair a ridiculous, tousled mess. He was rubbing grit out of his eyes, but he offered up a lazy, contented smile when he saw her.

"Good morning, dearest wife," he said, voice thick and gravelly with sleep—among other things. His eyes were hooded, but Robin was fairly certain they gleamed with lust more than with the remnants of slumber.

"Good morning, my dear husband," she answered, setting down the tray on the bedside table. "I've brought breakfast."

"Mm," he said, and the grin he wore became downright lascivious. "While I appreciate the gesture, that is not quite the breakfast I have in mind." And, lightning quick, he tugged her back into the bed.

"Velph!" she squealed, but it was half-hearted and devolved into a wicked fit of giggles as he rolled them over. After, Robin flopped back onto the fluffy pillows and sucked in a slow lungful of the stuffy air. The room was warm and close, and smelled of sex. Her eyelids dragged closed, and she held herself still, debating over the merits of allowing herself to just drift off into the siren's song of sleep. Robin turned her trembling hands over on the blankets and raised her palms.

Whichever god of luck, or good fortune, or love you are—thank you. That's twice I owe you now.

"You brought bread rolls?" Velph said, rising from the bed to inspect the contents of the tray.

"Mmhm. They're not going to be warm anymore, though."

"Yes, but is that adequate? For your tribute, I mean, my dear."

Robin's eyes snapped open. Relaxation twisted into a sort of restless alertness that she would have paced off if she'd been able to.

"Uh, yeah, that's adequate," Robin said, suddenly self-conscious. "How did you . . . ?

Velph huffed. "Come now, my dear. Did you think I had not noticed? Every morning, some of your breakfast goes to your ritual. Your Sealie practices are unfamiliar to me, but they do not go unnoticed." He broke off the heel of a small roll and held it out to her. "Is this enough? For your gods?"

Robin blinked. "Our gods. And yes," she admitted. "That's enough. You . . . you're sure you don't mind if I . . . ?"

Velph sighed, and pressed the bit of bread into her hand. "I do not. Though it is perhaps unwise to practice openly anywhere in Klonn, even within the relative safety of this *zentapi*. And I will admit I have a powerful curiosity about it."

Robin tried not to be hurt by that. She knew he didn't mean anything by it, not really. He was a product of his culture, just as she was of hers. So instead, she wrapped herself in the frilly dressing gown again and knelt by the fire, placing the bread against a coal.

"Is it . . . is it acceptable if I am here?" Velph asked.

Robin frowned and looked over her shoulder to

where he sat perched on the edge of the bed, a blanket wrapped loosely around his waist. "Why wouldn't it be?"

"I assumed it would be done in private, this sort of thing."

Robin grinned, and shrugged. "It is, a little, I suppose. But not between spouses."

His shoulders dropped, the tension draining away, and for the first time, Robin got a good look at the scar on his chest in broad daylight. It was small and angry, about the width and length of her thumb, a deep pock that even now was still more red than white. Thorne had regrettably needed to cut the wound wider to dig out the bullet.

"Then I suppose it is good that you are my wife," he said, pleased.

Robin felt the prickle of a blush on the back of her neck, felt it creep along her cheeks and nose, and thought that that was probably answer enough. She turned her attention back to the fire, broke up the bread, and turned up her palms. She whispered out the prayers of thanks, bargained for a renewal of her good luck.

When she was finished and just brushing off the crumbs, Velph sat forward on the edge of the bed and said, "I heard no names. Do your gods not have names?"

Robin snorted, pulling herself upright with the mantel and brushing ash off her knees. Velph continued to watch her, nude save for the curl of blanket, expectant. Robin stopped short.

"Wait, you're serious?"

"Yes." He gave a lopsided shrug.

Robin paused, unsure of how to answer. "I thought you . . . you mean, you don't . . . huh. Well, you, uh . . . you don't name things that are intangible."

"Whyever not?"

"I don't know. You just don't."

Velph mulled this answer over. "What about happiness?"

"Happiness is tangible." Robin splayed her fingers over her heart. "I feel that. Here."

"I see," he said. "As do I."

"Besides," Robin added, leaning down to peck a kiss against his lips, "the gods have never told me their names. It would be awfully impertinent of me to give them one."

"If they do not speak to you, then how do you know they are there? What if it is all just plain, boring luck?"

Robin sighed. *Oh, the Klonn.* "Faith."

"Seems a flimsy reason," Velph huffed, brows drawn down, lips twisted into a scowl. He was like a toddler who knew there were rules, but didn't understand them and therefore didn't like them. It was funny, and endearing.

Robin held up her scarred palms. "I'm alive, and I'm free," she said. "I was guided to WINGS. I was guided to you, and now, you're my husband. I have to believe that I was also guided here, to the only safe haven I might find in Lylon. If that isn't proof that bargaining with the gods works, then I don't know what is."

"And do you do that every time?" Velph asked, pulling off a piece of the loaf for himself. "The bargaining?"

"Yes," Robin admitted. "You can't get something for nothing."

"Seems tedious," Velph said, placing the bread delicately between his lips.

Robin puffed up her chest, ready for a good drag-out fight, but then quickly decided against it. She wasn't going to waste the morning of her wedding fighting with her husband over something she suspected he would never really understand, even if he claimed he wanted to. This would just have to be one of those things they politely disagreed upon and didn't talk about. Mama and Papa had things like that.

For a moment, Robin let herself think about it. About the promises they had made. About the small bed in their small attic bedroom. She let herself think about white silk and a red cut that was on its way to becoming a white scar; about crossing the front lines with their left palms on display; about a small brown house in Pyria, down the street from her parents; about a hive and a flower garden; about small children with Sealie-brown skin and Klonn-blue eyes.

Robin sat down beside him and picked at the other roll.

"What happens to the bread?" Velph asked softly, and Robin smiled, accepting his question for what it was—a white flag. It seemed as if he didn't want to fight about things that wouldn't change, either. "What is the point of burning it?"

"The gods inhale its smoke," Robin said, and it felt strange to articulate it. No one in Saskwya had ever asked about why such sacrifices to the gods were made; it was just understood. "They like the taste, and the smell."

"And you bribe them with this ephemera?"

Robin shrugged a little. "It seems to work." Velph turned back to the fire, watched the crackling flames in silence for a while.

Out of place again, she thought to herself. *Tarnished pot of honey on a paper doily. But not alone for once. Not alone.*

Things fell into a comfortable sort of rhythm after that. Robin and Velph spent ample amounts of time—according to Rosa and her staff—exploring the many facets of matrimony, sharing weighted looks over morning meals, and suggestive barbs over evening games of chess. The *zentapi* buzzed with life as business increased, and Rosa's network of spies started to bring in more and more leads.

"Why not the harbor?" Rosa asked over tea one afternoon, taking a delicate sip from her cup. They had taken to having their daily chats in the kitchen, now that Velph was often to be found in Robin's room.

"The harbor?" Robin prompted, knowing that there would be more. Rosa never dropped such blatant hints unless she had a specific plan in mind.

"Mm," Rosa agreed vaguely. "Ships are said to have arrived from the dry dock, and are awaiting their commissions in the harbor. The loss of these would be a crippling blow to Klonn's already depleted navy, no?"

Which was how, several nights later, Robin found herself circling on the air currents above the harbor to the west of the city, trying to get enough space around the bullets whizzing up at her from the watchmen's station along the roofs of the buildings to drop down and plant her incendiaries.

The rigging of the ships loomed into the night like skeleton trees after a fire, and made it hard to be sure of clear passage through the ropes. Something flew past her head, close enough that she heard it zip through the air, and Robin screeched, startled. Her heart rabbited against her ribs as she cut a hard left in midair, getting the masts of a naval ship between her and what she presumed was the Night Watch. Wood splintered around her as more bullets flew, and Robin cut the power to WINGS, dropping down onto the deck.

It was barren of sailors, being nearly three in the morning, but the warning bell was clanging loud in the harbor. If anyone was on board, they'd be topside in moments. Robin ducked down behind a cannon, hoping the pocket of shadow would hide her long enough for her to catch her breath. The air stank of rotting fish, of salt, of wood and canvas, metal and gunpowder, hemp rope and sweat. It smelled a lot like a glider, if she ignored the odors of the sea, and Robin closed her eyes against a painful welling of homesickness.

"Omens, this is a rudding mess," she hissed, wiping the edge of her scarf across the amber-colored glass of her goggles, making sure that none of the debris had scratched the lenses or lodged in the frames, that nothing would obscure her vision. "Why not the harbor?" she asked the night air, mimicking Rosa's clipped tones. "Crippling blow, my arse."

"And a lovely arse it is," growled a voice to her left. Robin whirled, her knife in her hand as though it had jumped there of its own accord.

"Omens! Velph!" Robin scolded quietly, sliding the knife back into its small leather scabbard. "That's a good way to get yourself killed."

"And talking to yourself is a good way to be found, my dear," Velph countered with a grin. "But now that we are both on board the ship we're meant to blow up, what, pray tell, is your plan?"

"Um . . . don't get shot?" Robin said, peering out from behind the cannon. The ship's deck was still empty of life, but she didn't know how much longer that would be the case.

"And beyond that?"

Robin shrugged. "An explosion is an explosion, right? Doesn't matter if it's the one we planned."

Velph huffed a small laugh. "Fair enough, I suppose. Light it and drop it down the hatch, perhaps?" He held up one of their backup blasting sticks, his free hand dipping back into the leather satchel looped over his shoulders. The incendiary in her satchel didn't have a long enough fuse for them to light the bomb and flee to safety, but the blasting stick did.

Robin shook her head. "It'll cause more damage if we do it near the waterline. The ship will catch fire and sink."

Velph grimaced. "Seems a bit much, does it not?"

Robin grabbed him hard by the front of his black coat and tilted her head to get under the mask for a kiss. "That's sorta the point, husband."

"Very well," Velph conceded and gestured with the

blasting stick toward the darkened gangplank. "After you, *wife*."

Bullets followed them, peppering the path with small bursts of flying wood and debris, but luckily, the deck was filled with so much *stuff* that it almost seemed a ludicrous waste of ammunition. None of the projectiles came any-where close to finding their mark.

"It's almost like they're not even trying," Robin mur-mured as they crouched together behind a coil of rope so new, it was practically still green, and so large, it was easily thicker than her calf.

"Perhaps they are not," Velph ventured. "I cannot imagine that the king would want WINGS harmed."

"Oh, thanks. That certainly makes me feel special," Robin grumped, rolling her eyes though she knew Velph wouldn't be able to see it behind her mirrored lenses. A slither of memory cut beneath her flippant dismissal, and Robin shivered; his comment rang uncomfortably famil-iar. He'd said much the same the night he'd been shot.

The boards under them creaked suddenly.

"They are on deck," Velph hissed. "We are out of time."

"Maybe we can—"

"Skylark!" he snarled. "Stop prevaricating and go!"

"Go where?" Robin asked, but he was already clam-bering over the side, long limbs attractively competent at scaling the ropes attaching the warship to the docks. "Ah, good answer."

With a pop of her engine, and careful attention to keeping any sustained burns from showing off their po-sition like a flare, Robin joined him, crouching down into the shadows cast by a pile of crates. Given the direction her luck had run tonight, she feared they'd be labeled with munitions seals, and that one stray bullet would blow them into their next lives, but for once, the gods were on her side. Just foodstuffs. Still, she brushed crossed fingers across her shoulder, just to be sure.

"Blasting stick," she said, holding out one gloved hand. Velph slapped the stick into her palm, and then rooted through his satchel to add two more when she wiggled her fingers impatiently. "I'll do this ship. You do that one."

"And the third?"

"Forget the third. We're hemmed in. Two will have to do for tonight."

Velph nodded, and brushed his knuckles across her cheek and jaw tenderly. "Maybe we will be lucky, and the third will catch, too," he said. Then, with a quick kiss, and a promise to see her back at Rosa's, he eeled into the shadows of the crates and was gone.

Robin propelled herself to the side of the ship with a quick, short burst from WINGS, sticking her fingers into the woodwork and setting the toes of her boots against the top ledge of a porthole. It was still a few feet above the waterline, but it would have to do. She could hear the Night Watch getting closer, shouting reconnaissance to one another. Soon, someone would think to look over the side.

Robin lit the first stick with her exhaust, kicked in the window, and threw it inside. She chucked the other two sticks in after it, figuring they'd go up nicely when the first did. But just as she'd expected, the sound of shattering glass had drawn unwanted attention, and Robin had just enough time to kick off before her perch was discovered. She shot straight up, hard and fast, hoping that distance and the darkness of night would make her invisible. Or at least hard to hit.

Below, the pop and whizz of bullets gave way to a bone-shuddering *fwump* as the blasting sticks detonated. Robin slapped her hands over her ears and let the shockwave tumble her back, out over the water. She flipped over and over, heels over head, until the horizon swayed and something dark and glittering rushed toward her. At first, she thought it was the stars. Then she realized she was plunging toward the night-black oil slick of the ocean.

She slapped her hand on the control box and WINGS's blades snapped open, trilling their haunting tune as they stabilized her fall. Robin strained upward, throwing her hands above her head to toss her weight in the direction she wanted to go, and finally managed to fling herself back toward the clouds.

"Holy rudding hells," she panted, taking a moment to shove her goggles up and mop away the cold sweat that had sprung up on her face. A second, distant *fwoosh* sounded from the direction of the harbor, and another fireball danced into the sky. The smoke puffed and drifted, mingling with the low clouds, heavy with snow.

Sparing a small thought for the icy water below her— if Robin had fallen in, she would have frozen to death long before she drowned, she was certain—she raced back toward land. She skidded to a stop on the end of the dock where she had last seen Velph.

She couldn't spot him, though, and hoped that meant he'd already headed out.

I better do the same, she told herself, *before anyone thinks to look over here.*

Pressing down on the control box, Robin jumped back into the sky and aimed herself for the center of town.

Down on the pavement, men and women were shouting to one another, calling the alarm and clanging warning bells. In the distance, the rumbling trundle of the fire brigade carts rattled along the paving stones, familiar to Robin from the long nights of bombshells and explosions she'd endured in Pyria. A line of people with buckets paraded down to the water, and Robin spared a thought for the fishmongers and merchants whose livelihoods were now in danger of burning, and—not for the first time, nor likely for the last—she cursed King Eloy and his war roundly to her gods. At least nobody would be looking up now, not with two of the three new ships on fire and threatening to drift or drop onto the rest of the harbor.

Deciding to spare her fuel reserve, Robin found a blind alley to descend in, near one of the quiet market streets that was always dead at night, the shops shut up and deserted until morning. WINGS whispered a quiet song as she folded away the blades, clear and sad in the quiet of the street, a soft sigh of sound in tune with the faraway clang and roar of the harbor.

Before she could head the short distance back to Rosa's, a shout rose from a neighboring street, shattering the stillness and freezing her limbs with fear. "Loa! There! He's cornered!"

A wave of watchmen surged down the street in front of her, and Robin pressed herself into the shadows of the alley, barely breathing, adrenaline making her blood whoosh loud in her ears.

Instead of slinking the other way, as a wise vigilante ought, Robin threw herself into the air after them. There was only one "he" she knew of who would garner that kind of enthusiasm in the watchmen, and she wasn't about to lose him to them again. Above the rooftops, she could clearly see where they were headed, and her stomach plummeted to her feet—the distinctive silver glint of Velph's helmet shone bright in the center of a wide thoroughfare, trapped between eight approaching watchmen. And the other dozen or so were not far behind. The gods of ill-luck clearly hadn't had their fill of them, it seemed.

Giving no warning, and zero second thought to her decision, Robin dropped out of the sky and landed beside Velph. The surrounding soldiers gasped in surprise, wrong-footed by her silent, sudden arrival, and Velph immediately leapt into action, taking advantage of their shock.

He whirled, fists and feet a blur of wicked precision. In the span of a blink, he had possession of someone's knife and another's truncheon. Robin grinned at one of the men dancing back and forth before her, his own truncheon raised, a gun in his other hand. He looked very, very uncertain.

"If you shoot that, you might hit one of your colleagues," Robin cautioned him.

"We-we are prepared to d-die for the Art of W-War," the man said, and Robin amended her estimated age of him from mid-twenties to about fifteen. Not that much younger than she herself was, though it was clear from his inexperience that the Klonn didn't draft them young.

"You don't sound convinced," Robin pointed out, and godsdammit, was he really so wet behind the ears that he—yes, apparently he was. He swung wide, telegraphing every move, and Robin had the gun out of his hand, and his wrist broken with a swift and well-placed kick, before he had even finished his punch.

Let it never be said that hand-to-hand lessons at the Air Patrol had been useless.

The boy screeched and fell back, dropping his truncheon to clutch at his wrist, and two more surged toward Robin. She danced away, avoiding blows, and then ducked under Velph's arm to snap her fist into the nose of a man who'd been trying to come up on his flank.

Velph laughed, delighted, and aimed his stolen gun at the ground. *Pop, pop, pop,* and three more watchmen were left rolling on the paving stones, clutching at their bloody feet as they howled.

And then their luck ran out. Reinforcements arrived, fanning out until Robin and Velph stood, back to back, in the center of a circle of gun barrels. Trapped, knowing that one wrong move might very well prompt their deaths, Robin slowly raised her hands and dropped her stolen weapon to the ground. Behind her, Velph snarled, but did the same.

"Steady!" called a voice, and Robin's eyes snapped to a man wearing the leaves of a general on his epaulets. He moved confidently through the ranks, stopping just behind the firing line, and regarded them with hands tucked behind his back. "Well now," he said. "The Skylark and the Wolf, both. What a pleasant, fortuitous surprise." He raised one hand in a fist, and, voice pitched to carry, ordered: "Kill them both."

CHAPTER
SEVENTEEN

"Wait!" Velph cried, lunging forward, arms spread as though he could shield Robin with his own form. Robin struggled to follow along with their clipped Klonnish. "You cannot. I . . . the king wants the Skylark alive, does he not?"

The general arched an imperious eyebrow, head cocked just a bit to the side. His eyes narrowed. "The broadsheets now say *dead* or alive. Forgive me if I do not wish to take chances."

"The broadsheets are wrong," Velph snarled, and he turned slowly in place, silver helmet focused on each man in turn. When he was turned mostly away from the general, his back blocked from view to most of the surrounding watchmen, he dipped his hand into the satchel at his hip and deftly and subtly fished free a blasting stick. Robin understood at once, and stepped forward to take it from his hand, careful to keep it as hidden from view as she could.

"The *king* wants the Skylark and the pack *both*, and *unharmed*," Velph said, voice clear and authoritative, the way he'd once sounded with the soldiers in the forest, the day he murdered Al.

Robin shuddered at the unbidden memory. She didn't want to think of him like that, not now. Not anymore.

"Do you surrender?" the general asked placidly.

"Up yours!" Robin snarled, dipping the blasting stick into WINGS's exhaust and holding it aloft. A chorus of horrified gasps sounded as the lit fuse burned into view, and then, like rats before a flood of light, everyone scattered. Weapons were dropped, people stumbled and scrambled to get away, and Velph locked eyes with her and smiled.

With seconds to spare, Robin hit the button to deploy WINGS's blades and sheared the burning fuse from the stick. It fell to the paving stones, hissing softly in the moisture pooled between the stones, and fizzled out.

Robin sighed, sagging in relief. It had, she realized in hindsight, perhaps been foolish to risk a gambit like that, but she would rather see WINGS destroyed than see it fallen back into the hands of the king.

"Well done, my dear," Velph said quietly, gathering her up into a comforting, yet careful, embrace. His long fingers pried the now useless blasting stick from her grip, stashing it away again inside his satchel.

"Why didn't you run?" Robin asked, voice muffled against the fabric of his coat. "If that hadn't worked, I could have killed you."

"You would have me leave my wife to die alone? How ignoble do you think me to be?" he answered, chuckling. Robin pulled back, arching until she could look him in the eye.

"You really want me to answer that?"

She'd meant it to be teasing, but instead of laughter, sadness flickered through Velph's gaze and curled tiredly into his smile. He stepped back and let her go, hands dropping to hang at his sides, helmet nose pointed down and away. "No, perhaps not."

Guilt squirmed through Robin's gut, punctuated by the metallic snick of WINGS's blades as they retracted. She hadn't meant to sour their success. Powering WINGS down completely, she reached out to lay a gentle hand on Velph's arm.

"Come on," she said. "Let's go home before they realize we haven't been blown to smithereens."

The following morning was a somber affair. Neither Robin nor Velph had said much, and had parted ways once the dishes from their morning meal were cleared away, each chewing on thoughts and worries that they weren't quite ready to share. Robin found herself in the kitchen, curled up in the plush red chair, while Velph had retreated to the attic to sulk, or brood, or whatever it was he did when he decided to act like an entitled, scrubbed-up coal-bag. He was being churlish for reasons that Robin couldn't fathom, upset over something he refused to share with her, and Robin was more than happy to let him alone. She had plenty to occupy her thoughts with; she didn't need his sullen temper rubbing off on her own.

While things had most assuredly not gone to plan, Robin was determined to count the harbor mission a success. They had destroyed two of their three targets, and had managed to escape capture—though they'd come uncomfortably close to failing at that part.

Still, there was something about the evening that tugged at her intuition, that whispered that maybe all was not right. She didn't have long to dwell on it, however, as the kitchen door flew open with an abrupt gust of frig-id air and Rosa swept inside, late-spring snow flying off her cloak and hood in a delightful flurry, eyes bright with excitement as she waved a small cloth packet.

"For you, Skylark!" she announced, brandishing the packet like a war prize.

"Okay . . ." Robin said, uncurling just enough to take it from Rosa's outstretched hand. She opened the drawstring to find even smaller packets, each filled with—"Gods, this smells like my mother's fish stew," she said, sticking her entire nose inside the bag. "Where did you get this?"

"There was a new spice merchant at the market,"

Rosa said, shaking off her cloak and handing it to one of the young fellows who seemed to act as both her valet and general dogsbody for the entire house. He vanished with it, taking Rosa's scarf and gloves with him.

"Wait, there are Sealies in Klonn?" Robin asked, startled. An embarrassed flush burned through her cheeks as she realized how foolish that sounded. Of course, there would be Sealies in Klonn. Refugees never fled in just one direction, after all. "What were they like?"

"Kind," Rosa said, shaking her dark-red ringlets down from her elaborately befeathered cap. Her hair, Robin had learned, was tinted weekly by Grier, by means of the same mix of pigments they had once offered to color Robin's. "A bit timid. They sold from a table at the back of a wagon."

"A *wagon*," Robin breathed, setting her feet against the cold floor to sit up straight. "I've never seen one in person."

Rosa bustled one of her many kettles onto the hob, looking back at Robin over her shoulder. "But are you not . . . ?"

"My grandmother owned a wagon, and a nice hive, too. But when the Great Sickness drove them into the cities, they used what was on it to build their first house. The boards became floors; the wheels, a table—nothing was saved. It's all . . . it's all gone now." She picked at the frayed edge of one of the ribbons that held the spice sachet closed, unwilling to examine the squirmy, angry feeling in her gut, or the bizarre, secondhand nostalgia she held for a way of life she'd never actually known.

"Ah. I see," Rosa said, continuing to poke around the pantry and dig through the cupboards for . . . what, Robin didn't know. It looked like she was pulling out vegetables: bright orange carrots, potatoes, something vibrantly green and fluffy, like the tops of celery.

"What are you doing?" Robin asked, looking around

at the food that now littered the countertops. Rosa didn't answer, struggling as she was to pull a massive cooking pot out of a cupboard beside the sink.

Robin set down the sachet and jumped up to help her.

"Thank you," Rosa said, grinning down at Robin as they heaved it over to the side of the kitchen where a big old brick hearth lay quiet and gray. There was an articulated iron pole across the mouth of the fireplace, installed on a pivot so that whatever was hung on the pole could be positioned over different parts of what Robin assumed would be a cook fire. It was on this pole that Robin and Rosa hung the pot.

There was also a small door in the wall that had revealed itself to be a bread oven when Robin had gone poking around—an oven, it seemed, the zentapi never used; all the bread was bought fresh, every day, from a nearby baker. It was a luxury that Robin still worked hard to not resent, that the wealthy citizens of Lylon still had access to bakeries, and afternoon markets, and all the other daily little joys that the people of Pyria did not.

"Are you planning on cooking something?" Robin asked, hands on her hips as she watched Rosa walk back to the vegetable-littered table, muttering to herself. "Rosa?"

"Hm?" Rosa replied, looking up at Robin as though she'd not heard a word Robin said. She lobbed the spice sachet at Robin and grinned. "Fish stew, you said?"

"Yeah."

"Lovely. I thought that you might show us, Skylark. Bring the food of your people to our table. Let us find a way to bridge some of the chasm our peoples have dug between our cultures."

Robin gaped at her. "Are you . . . are you sure?"

"Ai. I wish to learn more of these fascinating spices. Who better to teach me than someone who knows them intimately?" The smile that pulled at her painted lips was wide and genuine, and Robin felt something new worm its way through her chest—the warmth of acceptance.

"Is this not allowed?" Rosa asked, smile fading as concern crowded into her features.

"Oh, oh no. I mean, yes. I'd be happy to show you," Robin rushed to reassure. Rosa's smile returned. "Thank you," Robin whispered, voice choked and wet with the tears that burned at the backs of her eyes.

"Of course, love," Rosa said.

Which was how, an hour later, Robin found herself fussing over her former archnemesis and current husband as he sat curled up in the ridiculously plush, red brocade chair while she showed him how to use the potato peeler. He'd been fetched down from his brood in the attic by the sound of Robin and Rosa's laughter, and was told to help or stay out of the way. He'd elected to help, and so the chair had been pushed up under the little bread oven, where he would be out of Robin's path as she bustled around the kitchen.

"This is absurd," Velph complained, his earlier brown mood at least mostly dissipated as he tried to peer at the potato through the eye slits of his helmet. "I cannot see it. And it hurts my hands."

"Oh, so you can see fine when you need to pilot an aeroship, but the holes are too small when you have to work for your dinner? I see how it is," Robin teased, dropping a kiss on the helmet's forehead. All the same, she took both potato and peeler from him and handed him a long iron poker instead. "You get to mind the fire, then. Coals are better than flames. We don't want to scald the pot. Or . . . you know, you could take off your helmet."

"No," Velph said, grimly poking at the little pile of kindling that spread fire to the wood in the hearth. It would be an hour, at least, before the fire was ready to cook on, but that was fine with Robin. It would be about the same time before she had everything chopped up, anyway. "That, I shall not do."

Robin rolled her eyes and bit the inside of her lip to keep from commenting. If he wanted to keep his sullen mood, she supposed that was his right. "All right," she said. "Fire duty it is, then."

She was glad she hadn't pressed him to take the helmet off when Thorne and Rosa walked into the kitchen a few minutes later, the latter toting a large package of paper-wrapped fish.

"I don't know if it's the kind your mother used, but we found something, at least," Rosa announced, triumphant. "I have not been to the fishmongers myself since—dear me!" She stopped, whatever revelation she'd just come to clearly more shocking than she'd anticipated. "There is a nobleman in my kitchen, tending to a fire. That is certainly something I have never seen before," she said with a rueful smile, peeling herself out of her outerwear for the second time that day.

Velph made a sarcastic noise at her.

"Is it fileted already?" Robin asked.

"No," Thorne said, putting the fish down on the counter, next to where Robin was making short work of the root vegetables.

"That's fine. I can do it," Robin said, keeping her eyes on the rise and fall of her blade.

"Well now, you are just quite full of surprises, my dear," Velph said, and Robin blushed at the admiring tone beneath that velvety growl.

Good, she thought. *Maybe his tantrum is nearly at an end. Omens, who knew that marriage would be so exhausting?*

"What I am," Robin countered, wiping her hands on her borrowed apron before she unwrapped the fish, "is the only child of a house that was barely scraping by. We had no frivolous money for servants, or premade anything, and what we couldn't make, I stole—oh, this fish looks nice. Good choice."

Awkward silence answered Robin's flippant confession. When she turned around, she found each of the three Klonn fussing with something superfluous. Not one of them would meet her eye, and Robin huffed.

"Right, okay, so when I said that war is hardest on the poor, did you think that I was making light?" she asked.

"Of course not," Velph murmured at length, when no one else answered.

"Then stop being so godsdamned sheepish about my honesty. We're all here for the same thing, right? To stop it. To make the lives of people like me better. To make the lives of people like you safer, so let's just . . . let's just skip to the deboning, okay? Gods."

The four of them worked in charged silence for a few moments. Thorne ferried water into the cook pot, Velph unearthed the old bellows to encourage the fire, bottom lip held firmly between his teeth, while Rosa resolutely chopped the vegetables Robin had abandoned to look after the fish. It was . . . well, it was bloody *aggravating*.

"It is Eliam's fault," Velph said softly, breaking the tension.

It was quiet enough that Robin wasn't sure she'd heard him properly, but Thorne and Rosa both blanched and turned to stare at him. He gave a soft, bitter chuckle. "Oh, what. We all know it. He was a selfish warmonger who used the excuse of the Great Sickness to grasp at land he had always coveted, and when Auden pushed back—"

"Land that shouldn't have been either of theirs to claim," Robin pointed out. The Wild Woods had belonged to the Sealies, or rather, to the gods, before the Great Sickness had allowed the Benne to "absorb" it under the guise of alliance and friendship. A deception they later used to indenture those Sealies who survived into aiding Saskwya's defense against the invading Klonn.

"That's the excuse our glorious King Eloy uses to keep the war going," Thorne said. "That the Benne stole land belonging to Klonn."

Robin slapped her knife down on the block. "But it shouldn't—"

"I agree with you," Thorne said, hands thrust outward, empty. "But Eloy is a fickle, feeble tyrant who loves the crown more than he ever loved his father—"

"You cannot know that!" Velph interrupted. "You cannot just proclaim that he held no love for the king."

"I think that fact has been made more than apparent by the events that followed King Eliam's death, do you not?" Thorne challenged.

"It was a heart attack!" Velph said.

"It was a convenient one! Eloy was crowned sovereign of the Empire, and within the week, all talk of loss had vanished from the upper ranks," Thorne said, and Robin gawped, startled by their rage and frustration, confused by this mention of loss. As far as she knew, Klonn had always fared better than Saskwya. Why would they have ever feared losing?

"Six years ago, there was talk of surrender," Rosa said quietly, leaning over to explain when she noted Robin's look of consternation. "The government had begun to prepare for the reality that this was a war they could not win. And then King Eliam died. And the surrender was off."

"I never heard that," Robin said, and Rosa nodded.

"I am sure it was not made public. It was never reported widely here, either."

"The only thing the newspapers reported was that dear King Eliam had died, and that his noble mission to save the heathens in the neighboring lands from their own exotic ignorance would live on," Thorne supplied, and Robin was surprised to hear the bitter venom in his voice. Near the fire, Velph twitched, shoulders tense, spine stiff, and expression—what little she could see of it, anyway—closed off.

"Their pages were clearly bought out, and made to become the mouthpiece of the monarchy," Thorne continued. "And now, King Eloy chooses to ignore the advice of the nobility and his generals both, all while the coffers of Klonn slowly dwindle, and the press upon the people grows ever harder to bear."

"That is not how it happened!" Velph bellowed, heaving himself from his seat, fists clenched, iron poker raised in threat.

"And how would you know?" Thorne challenged, unafraid. "I have family at court, and this is how they reported it. Do you?"

Velph hesitated. His eyes darted between each of them, assessing, weighing his response. Robin waited. Quiet. Pressing down on the desire to fidget, to grab his arm, to demand. She realized, suddenly, that he was withholding something, and begged him silently to explain. But he didn't. He took a step back, and dropped the arm holding the poker aloft to his side.

"No," he said softly, pressing his free hand over the scar on his chest, curling back down into his chair. His jaw clenched, a single muscle popping with strain beneath his skin. He moved like an old man, like his wound had reopened and his heart's blood was gushing out. "Not anymore."

CHAPTER EIGHTEEN

Despite the heated opinions and tense conversation that had overshadowed its preparation, Robin's stew was a smashing success. Companionable silence returned, and after, everyone retired to their respective chambers, content with the warm fullness of a good meal well served.

Robin and Velph were quiet as they made their way up to the attic bedroom they now shared, fingers locked together. Once inside, they shed their alter egos, Velph's silver helmet set aside to rest on the chair alongside WINGS. It was comfortable, intimate. Domestic, Robin let herself think. Papa had wanted this for her, had tried over and over to convince her to marry, to settle down and leave the Air Patrol behind.

Maybe I should have listened, she thought sadly. If she had, Al would still be alive, and she would be home, in Saskwya. But neither would she have met Velph, or Rosa, or Thorne; neither would she have found WINGS.

When Velph was seated on the end of the bed, working off his socks, Robin stepped between his knees. He let his socks go, and laid his ear against her sternum, listening to her heartbeat with his eyes closed, black-lace lashes fanned against his pale cheeks. Robin ran her right hand through the thick, raven-dark mess of his hair, soothing. His arms clutched at her waist, and he was warm, and alive, and *hers*.

Still, as they curled up beneath the bed sheets that night, Robin felt a profound, undefined sense of dread.

If not even the rebellion could be unified, bickering and squabbling amongst themselves like hens, then would the fighting ever truly end?

"Do this for me," Rosa pleaded. She was standing in Robin's attic room, holding up one of those terrible Klonn dresses with all the buttons and the bustier, and a hem so long that no woman could ever possibly run away in them. They were like straitjackets with frills, and Robin hated them.

"The others have been wishing to meet you for months. I have had letters upon letters, some more desperate-sounding than others. Please, Skylark," Rosa said. The *zentapi's* madam, clearly having just finished and afternoon at own worship of the Art of Pleasure,brandished a creamy envelope with swirling Klonnish writing.

When Robin, pulled from her deep study of a map of the streets of the city, had asked after its contents, Rosa had announced that it was an invitation to a dinner party for *zentapi* managers, to be held that very night. On the outside—to the Night Watch—it would appear a luxurious frivolity. But for those in the know, it was the best way to hide a network-wide meeting.

"I don't see how a dinner party is going to—" Robin protested, but was simply interrupted and overruled by Grier pushing their way into Robin's haven with an overflowing tool kits of feminine torture devices that they immediately set to work brandishing upon Robin.

As Robin was scrubbed and polished within an inch of her life, Rosa held up the dress and petted the copper-coloured silk to make it shimmer prettily. As if Robin were a magpie who could be lured into complacent by shiny things.

"Tonight is meant to create solidarity among the network," Rosa cooed, sweeping the avalanche of fabric on the bed when it's beauty failed to sway Robin. "The others need proof that you believe in our cause. That the Skylark is—and you must forgive me for this, my dear—biddable to the will of the democracy."

"You mean, you need me to prove that I'm a good little puppet," Robin sneered as Grier turned her this way and that to get a barely-warm-enough washcloth in all sorts of places Robin would prefer Grier left alone. But when she tried to take it from Grier's hand, he own were slapped away.

The refrain of *Sealies do as their told* floated up through her memories, echoing sharp in Renge's cadence. So, too, did Ripka's words of warning, when she'd been turned away from continued use of Recine's *zentapi*, all those many weeks ago. Rosa was right, the network was fractured. Not all who participated in it were willing to align themselves to the Skylark's image.

While the raids and the bombing runs were effective demoralization tactics, and had put a dent in the supplies of Klonn's military, there were still too many places outside of Lylon that could take up the slack in manufacturing. The requisitions for the needed ammunition, ships, and weaponry were simply shuffled off to the next available facility, which meant that Robin's attacks were actually doing very little. The only way the network could pose a real threat was if Robin could travel between the cities—and for that, they would need the aid of the other *zentapi*. Which, in turn, meant that Rosa had to convince the lot of them that not only was it a good idea to stand up to their king, but that they should also give succor and sanctuary to the Skylark.

Robin was well aware that the money funding the rebellion couldn't last forever, and that, if they truly were to end this war, the Skylark would need refuge in every major city from Lylon to the coast. But she still didn't appreciate the insinuation that she needed to prove herself, that she needed to be pliant and biddable and submissive in order to achieve that.

"Show to them that you are dedicated to our cause, that you are serious, and they will expand our network fivefold. Some come even from as far away as the Frankin border. This is an important occasion, Skylark. Beyond assuring their assistance, it will afford us the opportunity to evaluate those who come, to watch what they do. If anyone truly wished you harm, they would not be able to resist when you are within arms' reach, no?"

Robin's scowl deepened. "I'm sorry, are you saying that this is a trap, and I am the godsdamned bait?"

Leaning against the doorjamb, arms folded across his chest, silver helmet cocked nonchalantly to the side as he watched this nonsense unfold, Velph snorted hard. Robin flicked her gaze up to him, and resisted the urge to send a rude gesture along the same path. He snorted again, clearly amused by her predicament.

"Yes. Exactly so." Rosa held up the dress, smiling and hopeful. She looked between Velph and Robin, evidently pleased with the scheme she had concocted, and proudly displayed the atrocity of feminine fashion. There were . . . *frills.*

"You could have just said you needed me to help vet some new contacts," Robin grumbled, chafing still at the insinuation she needed to prove her allegiance to the rest of Rosa's cohorts. "I still don't see how an evening gown is necessary, though. Why can't I wear my Skylark getup?"

"If we are putting it to a vote, I prefer the gown," Velph said from the doorway.

"With that neckline? You would," Robin spat, but not unkindly. Velph's eyes sparkled through the eye slits of his helmet, lips curled up in that oh-so-familiar smirk.

"Take the dress, my dear," he said. "Show them you are civilized."

Robin's mock-glare turned real. "You mean, not a

Sealie?"

"I did not," Velph said hastily, pushing off the door-frame to hold up his hands, placating. "I meant only that the Skylark has been portrayed deliberately nationless. They will all, therefore, assume that you *must* be Klonn."

"Well, I'm not," Robin said, glaring all the harder when Rosa nodded her agreement.

"Their allegiance is more important than the truth in that respect," Velph pointed out gently. "And while they all wish to see an end to the war, I suspect many would still take issue with trusting that end to come from the hands of the enemy. You must impress upon them that you are the best choice, my dear."

"Let us give them something to be impressed with," Rosa added. "So they may see you as we do."

Resistance crumbling under the emerald plea in Rosa's eyes, Robin reached out and grabbed the frothing creation that was all pumpkin-orange ribbon, chocolate velvet, and coppery silk out of Rosa's hands. It would flatter her Sealie complexion and match her eyes, she had no doubt, but it looked simultaneously too small for her to fit into and composed of far too much material to be practical. She would never be able to use WINGS without setting her own arse on fire.

"I don't understand you people," Robin said. "But fine, if flagrant displays of wealth is what'll do it for them, I concede." She rose and started to undo her robe.

Velph settled back into the doorway, getting comfortable.

"Perhaps a little privacy?" Rosa said, flicking her gaze down the stairway with pointed meaning.

"Oh, I am not embarrassed," he parried back, smiling. "Pray continue, my dear. I shall keep any others from entering."

Robin rolled her eyes and crossed the room. Pushing him out the door, she closed it firmly in his face. His laughter echoed back through the wood as his footsteps retreated down the stairs.

Then, turning back to the center of the room, Robin hung her head in submission, arms out. "Have at it."

Rosa pounced.

Between Rosa and Grier, who appeared shortly after Velph left, Robin was manhandled into the stays and bloomers, the cream-colored stockings and the wooden-heeled shoes. Satisfied that the process was now begun to her liking, Rosa flitted off downstairs to attend to her duties as the evening's hostess, leaving Grier to wrestle the dress into shape around Robin's decidedly non-Klonnish frame. Feat more or less accomplished, Grier bade her sit at the vanity mirror and smoothed a hand over her unbound hair. They twisted a few chunks up, testing the arrangement, and frowned.

"Needs a hairpin or two," they murmured, more to themself than to Robin. Still, Robin reached for one of the various drawers in the vanity, careful not to pull too far away.

"Will these do?" she asked, holding up the assortment of hairpins she'd secreted away upon her arrival. In the mirror, Grier's eyes grew saucer-big, and a shocked little gasp escaped their lips.

"Where . . . wh-wherever did you get that?" Grier stuttered, letting go of Robin's hair to reach a tentative finger toward the hairpin Velph had given her. Robin paused, a strange sort of protectiveness flaring against something in Grier's tone, in the awed and reverential way they trailed the barest tip of their finger along the edge of the wolf-shaped cameo.

"It was . . . a gift," she said carefully, eyes narrowing. "Why? Does it mean something?"

Grier gave a small little nod and met Robin's eyes in the mirror. "This . . . the wolf, it belongs to the royal family."

Robin exhaled, the knot of concern that had been balling up at the base of her throat dissipating. She'd already known as much. Velph had told her he was nobility, and there had been enough resemblance between him and the portrait of King Eloy that hung in Rosa's parlor that she had already guessed he was at least somewhat related to the Nutvig family line. That was the way of the nobles, though. They all shared at least some of the same blood.

"Ah, right," she said softly. "Let's not use that one, then."

Grier nodded, color returning to their cheeks, and Robin quickly stashed the hairpin back inside the drawer. Grier's deft fingers made quick work of styling her white locks into an artful arrangement pinned back with several of Rosa's rose-shaped hairpins, even with its shortened state. But their eyes remained wary, almost shell-shocked, and they said not a word. When they were done, Grier helped Robin don the Skylark's goggles, so they nestled perfectly against her scalp like a tiara, and then quickly shuffled from the room.

Robin pinned her lone rank pin into place at the corner of her neckline; it seemed lopsided without its mate, the brass feathers tarnished and bent. Then, with one last look in the mirror, and a deep breath to steel her nerves, she pushed to her feet and made her way down to the party forming below.

She was met at the bottom of the stairs by Velph, who grinned like a besotted fool before he quickly composed his face into perfect blandness once more. He'd shaved, she noticed, his beard once more trimmed into an artful, youthful scruff. His dark suit and thin black gloves set off the silver of his mask, making it glitter like a star in the firmament, and Robin was desperately glad he hadn't found one of those ice-blue pilot uniforms to wear. It was bad enough that he looked so godsdamned comfortable when compared to her own clothing. She wouldn't have been able to stand the evening at all with him dressed again as her enemy. It would have been too much like being back in the forest palace.

Robin pulled at the fitted bodice of her dress, wishing she hadn't let Rosa bind her corset so tightly, and tried not to be bitter. Her entrance caught the attention of the people standing nearby, and slowly, all the dark heads in the room turned. She felt nothing so much as like a doll on display.

Bait. But also rallying point, she reminded herself. *You're an icon. You're a godsdamned folk hero with your own song. Omens. It's just one night. You can do this, Captain.*

"You look beautiful, my dear," Velph whispered in her ear, the cool metal of his helmet's nose brushing against the small hairs at the nape of her neck. Robin couldn't help but shiver, tingles of pleasure and memory both sliding down her spine.

"Thank you," she said, and allowed him to lead her to the first of what Robin was sure would be an inane series of conversations. Thank the gods that Velph was there to talk for her, because she didn't feel up to chattering. Her accent would give her away, she was sure, no matter what Rosa had said about the network using Saskwyan as a code.

The salon had been closed to clients earlier in the afternoon and cleared out. The large harvest table had been moved out of the kitchen and now sat covered with an expensive damask cloth, elaborately set with thin china, and laden with a dozen candelabras. The gauzy red draperies that were used, under normal circumstances, to partition the room into private little nooks, had all been pulled back, held by brass hooks that left them billowing out from the walls in an artful cascade of fabric. The fireplace smelled heavily of Rosa's exotic incense, and it mingled with the scent of the thick, fortified wine the Klonn liked, pungent and grapey. The greenish, sweet plum liquor Velph had preferred danced in cut crystal decanters that spotted the tabletop like confetti.

People of all genders drifted through the room, dressed in silks and velvets, fabrics whose worth Robin didn't even want to try to calculate. They scattered in clusters, as if they were gems that had come loose from their fittings and gone tumbling off a fine necklace, assessing, judging . . . just waiting to cut her up with their tongues. It was like walking into a room full of Renges.

Thorne stood by the door, in shirtsleeves and a vest that matched the emerald tone of Rosa's dress, opening the door for yet another woman swathed in vibrant colors and crisp white lace. Rosa smiled and pressed a glass of thick wine into Robin's hand as she went to greet this newest arrival. Robin hid her disdain for the drink in a bland smile of her own. She didn't sip, but appreciated the wine as a social prop, all the same.

The room filled quickly after that, guests arriving in twos and threes until the salon was packed full of women in their finery and gentlemen wearing swords that Robin was certain were only meant to be useful in ceremony, and would shatter at the first parry.

She felt distinctly uncomfortable with so many people in the room, her identity made plain by her goggles and hair. She kept herself in the corner as much as possible, hand over her untouched glass so no one could slip poison inside, back to the wall so neither sword nor knife could slip between her shoulder blades or underneath her ribs. She felt naked without the comforting weight of WINGS tugging at her waist.

Robin tried to excuse herself when the dinner bell was rung, but was instead shown to the place of honor on Rosa's left. As hostess, Rosa was at the head of the table, far opposite to a stately older woman with a scary amount of product in her hair. Velph, at least, was seated at Robin's other side, so she wasn't totally abandoned to try to cope alone.

Robin squirmed in her seat, feeling strangely guilty as Rosa's smiling employees—dressed conservatively, for once—served out the soup course. It was a thin beef broth, with green onions that floated about the surface in rings. Robin tried not to be disappointed. She was in Klonn, at a Klonnish dinner, wearing Klonn garb—of course, the cuisine would be Klonnish, too. Had she really expected Rosa to serve her mother's fish stew?

No matter what had happened previously within the privacy of these walls, when neither client nor guest was about, Rosa and Velph had both made their positions on the matter clear. Tonight, she was to comport as though she were Klonn. She tried to shove down her homesickness and the nauseous needles of familiarity, the ghosts of her imprisonment, and, with the polite, small gestures of a formal dining table, did her best to copy Velph and mince her way through the meal.

Rosa stood as the soup bowls were being cleared, and Robin felt her face flush with embarrassment as she proceeded to give a flowery and flattering speech about the Skylark and her fight for the freedom of the common Klonn—in Saskwyan, of course, because that's how the rebels kept their conversations secret. Robin had to bite her tongue hard to keep from correcting Rosa—the Skylark didn't fight for just their own people's sake—so that, when she at last sipped her wine at the end of the speech, the tooth marks stung.

The next course was a bitter, sour salad with so many different vegetables that Robin felt a keen sense of shame. Not even the officers in Saskwya had produce that was this fresh. Everything they'd been served in the Officers' Lounge had been small, tough, wrinkly, or dried. The dressing tasted of unfamiliar spices and burned Robin's mouth, making her choke. She used more wine to wash away the taste, and when she next took a deep breath, she realized that her head was trying to float off her shoulders. She switched to water, but there was another toast—this time, from the cranky Klonn matron on the far end of the table. It spoke of promises to aid, if possible, and to shelter, if needed. "If, if, if," was all Robin heard of the speech. It was a tactful and evasive reply that gave Rosa nothing.

Robin saw the determined disappointment flash through Rosa's emerald eyes, and was forced to hold her glass aloft again as Rosa rebutted by making a second toast, referencing the harsh penalties faced by Saskwyan sympathizers, the rigidity of the luxury taxes, the strain on a *zentapi's* business when soldiers of all genders were called away to the front lines.

Robin gulped desperately at her ice water as the world started to swirl in circles. She had no head for wine, and was quickly losing her bearings.

Next was a course of sliced, undercooked meat and gloopy potatoes, and the matron rebutted with thinly veiled accusations that Rosa's business seemed to be flourishing as Robin tried not to gag on the smell of cooked beef blood. She ate the potatoes only because her stomach felt simultaneously too empty and too filled with the slosh of alcohol.

Rosa toasted again, and Robin groaned, finally catching the measure of the political back and forth she was engaged in and wishing dearly that she could crawl under the table and sleep. She had no head for politics, either, it seemed.

Robin leaned across the arm of her chair and hissed in Velph's ear: "Why can't she just ask these people to support us? Why all of this bugaboo?"

"Cannot," Velph corrected absently, sounding so like the cruel version of himself, the version that had been her captor, that she reared back and blinked at him. "That is not how things are done here in Klonn. One does not simply disagree—one discusses until a compromise is met."

"But we're not discussing," Robin protested. "We're getting drunk."

"That is part of it, too," Velph admitted, one side of his mouth pulling up into an amused curl. "In a few hours, no one will remember what they were arguing about, and a consensus will be reached."

"So discuss!" Robin said, turning to her other side to whisper to Rosa. "Just, no more toasts. I beg you."

Rosa looked at Robin's flushed cheeks, and shook her head. "Apologies," she said, but Robin had the distinct impression that it was a platitude only, hollow and weak and ineffective.

They're not rebels, she realized suddenly. *They're pretending at dissension and organization, at purpose. But they're gadflies. All of them. Biting, annoying, but ultimately easy to swat and ignore. They've been playing this game of underground chess for years, and the only thing it's ever done is inconvenience our mutual enemy. They're ineffective. This is not how you end a war.*

And Rosa rudding knows it.

CHAPTER NINETEEN

The soft clink of a teacup being set before her pulled Robin's wine-fuzzed attention to the table. Dessert had been brought—an iced concoction of early spring strawberries and frothed cream—and the gentleman across from her had taken it upon himself to pour her a spot of tea, probably hoping that he might actually succeed in engaging her in the frivolous small talk he'd been attempting all evening, and which Robin had ignored as tactfully as she could.

Robin stared at the milk swirling at the bottom of the cup, curdling slightly in the heat of the tea, and gagged.

She thought of the tarnished honey pot on the stained doily in the Officers' Lounge. Of the starving children in Pyria and Klonn, alike. Of the absurdity of all of this. Of how *offensive* it was that she was only good enough to be among them if she pretended to be *of* them.

And wasn't that what had caused the war in the first place? Refusing to understand, or accept, that your fellow humans were just as human as you? That they had a right to live, to the land they had cultivated for generations, to their beliefs and traditions and *culture*?

Frustrated, and sick, and exhausted with the rudding uselessness of it all, Robin pushed the teacup away. Then she stood. The matron at the far end of the table, who had been making yet another speech full of empty promises and insults that weren't even brave enough to be presented as such, stuttered to a stop. Scandalized gasps ran the length of the table.

Beside her, Rosa gestured furiously for her to sit. Robin did not.

"I'm sorry," she said, and more gasps followed, whether at her use of contractions or her accent, Robin wasn't sure. Nor, at this point, did she care. "I'm sorry, but this is rudding ridiculous. Will you, or won't you support us?"

Rosa flinched at each one of Robin's contractions, as if they were each as loud as a gunshot. Beside her, Velph's mouth was a thin line, his eyes narrowed and hard through the eye slits of his helmet. But there was a glitter in them that almost made her think he was . . . pleased? Maybe even *proud*?

"I . . ." the matron said, and every head turned to her. She flushed purple with rage, but took a deep breath and said, in strained but civil tones, "A Saskwyan. I might have known."

"My heritage isn't the issue on the table," Robin snapped, banging a fist on the surface in question. The candelabras rattled, and the teaspoons quaked on their saucers, creating a discordant jangle. "Your allegiance is. So choose. Are you gonna join the network, or are you gonna tell the Night Watch that Madam Rosa is abetting a pair of wanted fugitives?"

"You cannot—"

Robin held up her palm to forestall the protest already growing on the woman's lips, and another murmur ran the length of the table at the sight of her scars.

"No. Those are your only choices," Robin interrupted. "Because, if you tell me you're gonna go home and do nothing, say nothing, give nothing away, then you're a godsdamned liar. So, choose a side, and choose it *now*."

She swept her gaze along the table, including the rest of the assembled people in her decree. The drink made Robin's head light, but she also felt heady with triumph.

She had finally taken her own fate into her own

hands, just as she'd promised herself, the gods, and WINGS, all those many months ago. Her decisions, this decision, would be her own. It was time to seize what had been waiting for her, and she had. It felt rudding fantastic.

This is one Sealie who's done doing what she's told.

The shouting that followed Robin's proclamation was impressively restrained. More like hissed whispers that raced up and down the table. At last, Robin sat, slumping back in her chair as she crossed her arms, watching those around the table with as careful an eye as she could manage in her wine-muddled state. Nobody stood, or pointed angrily, or seemed to really do more than gossip and whisper. Not even the matron, who was stony-faced and tight-lipped, glaring up the table's length to where Rosa remained at its head.

This is pointless, Robin decided. *More useless wheel-spinning, and for what?*

"There, saved you the trouble—" Robin began.

Rosa turned her face away. Her fists, though, were bunched in the emerald silk of her frothy dress, and her jaw was tight and clenched. Robin should have known better. In Saskwya, her ultimatum would have been met with rousing cheers and strained shouts, people declaring in the heated moment that they were either for, or against. In Klonn, a place where it seemed no one was who they pretended to be, and where every conversation had seventeen layers at least—in Klonn, of course no one would stand up and say, "Me!"

Robin sighed and, deciding there was little left to lose in this situation, raised her palms to the gods, thanking them for the dinner. Then she pushed back her chair, and left Rosa to do damage control. Robin wanted tea, she wanted it with honey, and she wanted it now. Rucking up her skirts so she could walk in a proper infuriated stomp, she made her way over to the tea cart that sat against the wall. Aware that every Klonn eye was following her, Robin prepared herself a new cup.

"Oh," she said, when she realized that her honey jar wasn't present. "Omens, of course." She'd moved it to the kitchen cabinets for easy access, having taken Rosa's gesture of the spice sachet as tacit acceptance, if not approval, of her culinary choices, and while they had talked about Robin being passed off as nationless, the omission felt more like a deliberate insult now. It didn't feel like culture-blindness anymore—it felt like her Klonn conspirators were trying to erase her entirely, to "fix" her, and "make her better," the way Velph had once tried to do in the forest palace. Only subtler. More quiet. Insidious.

The dress, the honey, the silly dinner party . . . it was colonization—of a single person, true, but no less abhorrent. Despite Rosa's proclaimed interest in her way of life, the purported acceptance and even encouragement of Sealie traditions and culture behind closed doors, she never truly believed in cultural equality. All the tiny actions and aggressions were adding up. Robin was, she realized with sudden clarity, only a fascination to Rosa.

Worse than a prisoner, Robin was rudding *curio*.

"I thought only the Benne could be pilots," said a well-endowed woman with a big nose. She had come to stand between the tea cart and the doorway to the kitchen, which Robin had been about to escape into. She fought against the urge to roll her eyes. She doubted the woman was intentionally trying to intercept her—likely she was doing the Klonn equivalent of shouting out her support for Robin's declaration by coming to stand beside her—but it was inconvenient, all the same. The woman's own eyes narrowed, appraising Robin as she swept them up and down her figure. "You do not speak with the same poise as the Benne operatives who seek shelter within my walls."

The woman's voice was as well-endowed as her

bosom and nose, loud enough to carry over the hissing whispers that still buzzed about the table like angry bees. Within moments, though, the whole room had sputtered into silence, every eye on Robin as they waited for her response.

"If only the Benne can be pilots, then I guess I must be Benne, hey?" Robin said, shocked by her own callousness and impatient for the woman to go away; she wanted her to flitter back like the overgrown butterfly she resembled and spend her attention elsewhere. "If you'll excuse me, they left my honey in the kitchen."

"Honey," the woman said, affronted, lips twisted in disgust. She made it sound like a bad word.

"Yes, *honey*," Robin said, reveling in the pointed dig as she tried to sidestep the woman. She, however, remained in Robin's way, scowling down at her as she snapped open a fan and twitched it below her ample chin.

But then Rosa was there, pressing a fragile teacup into Robin's hands and dropping a daub of whiskey into it, smiling and playing at the perfect hostess even as her eyes glowered at her.

"That is only because you have not tried it like this— it is perfectly traditional at meetings where business is to be discussed."

"I don't want whiskey," Robin said. "I don't like whiskey. And I've had enough to drink."

"Nonsense," the fat woman scoffed. "Of course you do. Every young lady does." She turned to Rosa. "Your pet bird's wings want clipping."

Robin flinched, curling in on herself. It hurt more than she expected to hear her own thoughts voiced out loud by someone else.

Out of the corner of her eye, she saw Velph rise from his seat, slow and deliberate. He didn't step forward, didn't come between them, but it was clear he was ready to, if the need arose. She almost wished he was wearing his sword, so he could at least lay his hand upon its hilt threateningly. But unlike the other men in the room—and likely specifically *because* he was a fugitive who was meant to be asking for their help and mercy—he was unarmed. Robin forced herself to flex her free hand, to release the fist that had curled involuntarily, to take a step back. She couldn't punch every problem. Especially if she wanted these people on her side.

Instead, she took a deep breath and forced her voice to remain steady. "I am no one's pet. And I want honey," she insisted, and something inside her twisted up sharply, so tightly that she thought it could snap at any second. Every eye in the room was on her now, the air gone sharply cold despite the crackling fire, the silence turning expectant.

"The whiskey is much finer, and is more proper. You will like it once you try it," the big-nosed woman said with a dismissive air of finality, and it was like a blow, the sheer, entitled arrogance of that statement.

The way it resonated along Robin's spine reminded her of every single time the Coyote had insinuated the same, before he'd become her Velph; the way that Renge had been just as imperious; the way that every commanding officer in the Saskwyan Air Patrol had dismissed and commanded at the same time; the way that everyone spoke as though they were doing her a favor when they pointed out that the way she did things, the way she liked things, the way she ate, and prayed, and thought, and spoke, was *wrong*.

"And stand up straight, Miss Skylark," the woman admonished. "You are ruining the line of your dress and making wrinkles."

"Enough!" Robin shouted, slamming the teacup back onto the tea cart. It cracked, and hot whiskey-tea rushed out of one side to puddle on the floor. "*Enough.* I can speak my own mind. I can make my own choices!

And I will!"

The woman reared back, the fan held above her breast as though Robin had physically accosted her, features slack with shock. At the table, the other Klonn glanced around at one another, scandalized. Velph was statuary still, his head tilted at an angle that suggested curiosity, like an actual wolf perking an ear. Rosa seized her arm, and made as if to drag Robin into the kitchen so she could have her temper tantrum in secret. Like a *child.*

"That's all you Klonn do!" Robin snarled, yanking her arm out of Rosa's grip and stepping back, out of grabbing range; she ignored the tearing sound of her petticoats as they snarled in her stupid heels. Robin pointed one sharp finger at the fat madam's expansive nose. "That's all anyone does when they see one of us! You take, and you tell us where to go, and how to live! You push us around! You bully! You tell me how I'm supposed to dress, and talk, and think, and how to drink my godsdamned tea, and you know what? I like honey in my tea! I choose to take my tea with honey, and I choose to hold on to my ways, and I choose to use contractions, and you know what else? I choose to end this rudding war. Now. And without all of you!"

Her oath rang through the otherwise silent salon like the ring of a bell in a god's temple, and Robin felt a frisson of something crawl up her spine. Destiny? Fate? A divine promise? Upstairs, from her little attic room, Robin could swear she heard WINGS chime a response, the pack's cyclical chord fading into the quiet along with the rolling echo of Robin's voice.

Righteous anger spent, Robin sat down abruptly on one of the sofas that had been shoved against the wall to make room for the dining table. She was trembling, and she wasn't exactly sure why.

Rosa stalked over, Thorne protectively at her heels.

Robin felt curiously detached, though, unafraid of her hostess's ire, unconcerned that she'd probably just made herself—and her husband—homeless again. That she'd likely also just signed their death warrants. It wouldn't be hard for someone, *anyone*, including Rosa, to blab their hiding place to the Night Watch. That had always been a risk, true, but now, after that flagrant display, in front of a room full of strangers, Robin felt sure it was inevitable.

"You are a fool and an ingrate," Rosa hissed at Robin, and then swung one of the curtain panels that usually framed the private nook around the small area, closing Robin off from the rest of the salon.

That was . . . not what Robin had been expecting.

"Oh," she heard herself say, and then pulled up her knees so she could hide her face in her skirts as she shook. She pushed her goggles further up her head to keep them from fogging over as she heaved sucking breaths into the silk.

Panic, she thought distantly. *I'm panicking. Pretty badly, too. How 'bout that?*

On the other side of the curtain, Thorne was politely thanking their guests for coming, asking them to remember that the success of their endeavors relied upon their discretion—ha!—and apologizing for the Skylark's impatient outburst. "Saskwyans, you know," he murmured as they left. "Uncomfortably passionate."

Which is an awfully Klonn way of saying I'm hot-headed, stubborn, uncouth, and uncivilized, Robin seethed to herself.

Low murmurs filled the room, racing past Robin's ears too fast for her to pick apart the words in the Klonnish sentences. They had switched languages so she couldn't understand, and it was even more condescending to realize it. Her comprehension was good enough for codes, but not good enough for *communication*. As much as the words escaped her, though, the tone was easy enough to read—dismissive, pitying, condescending. Each one made Robin curl into her skirts a little harder, as though she could somehow bury herself in their silky billows, safe and invisible.

Eventually, the last guest was seen out, and the employees were ushered up to their beds with assurances that the cleanup could wait until morning. The curtain was whisked back, but Robin didn't look up. She knew who it was. Even on the room's thick carpet, she could recognize the sound of her husband's footfalls. Without looking up, she held up her left hand, and wasn't at all surprised to feel him press a tickly kiss against her Marriage Line.

"Well now," Velph said softly. "That was . . . an entertaining turn of events."

Robin puffed morosely.

"Do you regret the outbu—?"

"No, I don't," Robin said, turning her head to look up at him, cheek still pressed against the silk covering her knees. His expression was unreadable, guarded behind the mask of his helmet. Velph sighed and took a seat beside her, stripping off his gloves. As had become his habit, he pulled her hand into his lap, running his finger back and forth across the sensitized skin beside her Marriage Line, comforting and absentminded, sending a delicious shiver through Robin's insides. The nose of his helmet was turned down, his gaze on the mostly healed scar that matched his own.

"Would it not, perhaps, be better to give all of this up?" he asked softly, and Robin's brows pulled together in confusion.

"All of what?" she answered, wishing that she could see him properly.

"This—the fighting, the sabotaging, the missions." He looked up at her then, eyes narrowed and unreadable. Robin pulled her hand back, the embers of anger starting to flare once more. Velph leaned in close, voice low and husky as he said, "We spoke once of running away, of creating a new home, together . . . what if we took WINGS, and ourselves, and just went somewhere. If I said I knew a place, a place where we could be together, unchallenged, would you come?"

Robin closed her eyes as he nuzzled against her neck, brushing small kisses to the sensitive flesh, blurring together with the wine to leave her feeling confused, distracted—pliable. For a second, she gave in to it, let the warmth and the swirling shiver of the room sweep her up in its embrace, and let go of her frustration and anger. She thought again of her fantasy, of a small brown house, and a beehive, and the laughter of children with her brown skin and blue eyes. But then, bombs fell upon the home of her dream, rubble and debris flying, and her nonexistent children screamed, covered in dust and terror, their clothes tattered and their flesh too close to their bones with hunger. It was unsustainable, even as a fantasy.

Tears welled, burning against her eyelids, and Robin shook her head. "No. It's a pretty dream. But nowhere like that actually exists. And even if it did, my answer is still no," she said, pushing Velph back to look him in the eye, serious and determined in a way she hadn't felt since the day she'd fled with WINGS. "I'm ready for this to end, and I'm ready to take whatever drastic measures are necessary to see it done."

Velph's gaze searched her own, and he opened his mouth to speak, his shoulders hunched and head dipped as if he was about to make a confession. Robin sat up straighter, wondering if this was the moment he was finally going to tell her what had been eating at him since that close call at the harbor. But whatever he was about to say was lost as Rosa swept into view.

"I had plans!" Rosa snapped, lashing out as she knelt down to wipe at the puddle of tea by the cart. Picking up the broken teacup, she dashed the porcelain violently against the wall, shattering it into a terrible spray of tiny shards. "You agreed to listen to me. To follow me!"

Robin firmed her chin, not cowed, and straightened, setting her feet down on the floor, knees together. "I don't want to take the long road anymore."

"We do not need ultimatums! If we keep on as we are, chipping away—"

Robin stood. "And how long would that take? How many more people will die while your plan slowly unfolds? How many children will starve to death in a Sealie slum? How many more Klonn will lose their spouses? What about those soldiers you embrace, the ones who die in the mud? Hasn't this gone on long enough? Ten years, Rosa! *Ten*!"

Rosa looked away, eyes boring holes into the wall beside the door, jaw clenched so tight that the veins in her neck stood out grotesquely, her hands balled into trembling fists at her sides. Thorne stood behind her, rigid, and unmoving, staring at Robin as if he dared her to make him feel ashamed of all the dithering and uselessness of their little plans. And Velph, beside her, sat once more still as statuary.

"I've been doing this wrong. I've been doing it wrong this whole time," Robin said softly. She moved to the middle of the room, between the three of them, arms out like a peace offering. "You understand that, right? I've been . . . waiting. Taking orders. From my generals, from my pilot—from my parents, even. Every single person I've met has told me how to live my life. Velph ordered me around when we were prisoners together, and now, you all direct me like I'm of no more mind than a . . . than a gun. And I was passive. I let it happen. I've never thought about how to use the opportunities I had. But that's not right. That's not what I'm for, that's not what WINGS is for. I can fix this. I can end the war."

"And how do you propose to do that?" Rosa snapped,

skin flushed high with her fury. "Stand at the front lines and wave your arms about, proclaim the peace begun? Fly around Klonn like a dizzy honeybee and blow up every aircraft factory on the same day?"

On the sofa, Velph winced.

Above him, the exaggerated portrait of King Eloy glared out at them with obnoxious smugness. Robin matched him with a glower, annoyed at the haughty way he held himself, the arrogant tilt of his head, the exaggerated heroicness of his painted likeness, and, with sudden clarity . . . she understood.

The solution—the final solution—appeared from the foggy haze of her wine-filled thoughts like a revelation.

"Oh," Robin breathed. A terrifying calm settled on her shoulders, even as she felt her heart thunder against her ribcage and her eyes drop wide. It felt right. Obvious. The answer had been staring at her, literally, all along. Robin crossed her fingers and brushed at her shoulder. For the first time in gods knew how long, she was going to make a proactive decision about her own destiny. For the first time, she wouldn't just react to the situation thrown at her. She would be in control. Robin's throat seemed to open up, all the cool air in the room whooshing into her lungs, filling her with determination and a fierce, violent joy. "Yes."

"*Ai?*" Rosa asked, eyes twitching from face to confused face. "*Ai*, what?"

"No more of this gutter warfare," Robin said, and her heart throbbed in her chest, keeping time with her idea, chanting, *yes now, yes now.* "No more scurrying like a rat through the alleys, striking where I can. No more harassment campaign. No more rudding toasts! Just . . . no more." She raised her arm and pointed straight between the eyes of the portrait, challenging the smug smirk with a toothy, narrow grin. "I'm going to kill King Eloy of Klonn."

CHAPTER
TWENTY

"You . . . you *what?*" Velph said, and when Robin dropped her gaze to where he still sat perched upon the sofa, she realized that he was shaking, too. No. No, not shaking. Laughing. His helmet was thrown back, and his mouth was stretched into a wide rictus of a grin, his whole body shaking with terrifying mirth. But it was pitchy, and wrong-sounding. "Skylark, my dear—"

Robin dropped her arm, letting it fall back to rest by her side. Doubt slithered into her certainty as she listened to her husband laugh. Maybe it was foolish . . . she wasn't exactly clear-headed at the moment . . . but no. No.

Robin shook her head. *It's the only way, she told herself. Believe in yourself, Captain. You know this is the only way to end the war.*

"*Kill the king,*" Rosa repeated, aghast, and her outburst made Velph bend double, holding his stomach as he guffawed.

"You cannot be serious," Thorne said, closing the space between him and Rosa with a few quick strides. He wrapped an arm around her shoulders, possessive and protective.

Holding her up? Robin wondered. *Or holding her back?*

"I . . ." Robin began, but wasn't sure how to continue, because Velph was howling, brushing at his cheeks under his mask with the back of his hand, and she was starting to get concerned. "Velph, why are you—?"

"Kill the king!" he chortled, shaking his head. "My dear, you are absurd."

"But it makes sense. This is the best way to do it," Robin said, hugging herself, trying to stave off the desire to curl under the unexpected ridicule. She forced herself to take a deep breath, to straighten her arms by her sides, to make herself feel taller, more sure. "You all told me that it's Eloy prolonging the war, that Eliam wanted to surrender. Cut off the head of the monster, and the rest of the body will flail. Long enough, at least, for it to all fall apart."

Velph sobered in an instant.

"Monster," he repeated in breathless horror. The cool, formal mask of indifference he always used to hide his thoughts and emotions from the world when they were in turmoil slammed into place. It stung to see him use it when it was just the four of them, though. She'd thought he trusted her more.

"Oh, and you would like that, would you?" Rosa scoffed. "Who do you think would win, then? Ha! Saskwya as master of Klonn. Tell me, Skylark, what becomes of me, then? You do not have *zentapi* in Saskwya. I would be shut down. I would starve on the streets. Or," she snarled, taking a step toward Robin, even as Thorne's grip held her back by the elbows, "or is that the point? Will you make the people of Klonn suffer as the people of Saskwya do?"

Robin couldn't deny that the vindictive future Rosa painted was, on some small, extremely selfish level, at least a tiny bit attractive. But she also knew that she would never wish that kind of suffering on anyone, least of all the people who had protected her here in Lylon.

"I don't want anyone to win! I just want it to be over!" Robin said, feeling small, and alone, and vulnerable, realizing that her wish wasn't as easy to achieve as she'd hope. Somebody would have to win, wouldn't they? There was no way King Auden would call a ceasefire if Eloy was dead and he could just flood his troops into Klonn while the empire was in chaos.

But an end was an end, and she had dithered and delayed and tried to find another way long enough. It had to be this. And it had to be her.

Something hot was building in her throat, churning in her stomach, and she wasn't sure if it was determination, or sorrow that her friends refused to see what she did, that they were at last showing their true selves and were not the allies she had once thought, or if it was the wine and the horrible Klonnish food, or some other deep sort of worry. All she knew was that she felt ill.

And at the same time, more certain of herself, her decision, than she'd felt since she'd looked the drafting officer in the face at age eleven and chosen the Air Patrol.

"*Monster,*" Velph repeated again, voice strained and husky.

"Isn't he?" Robin challenged. "He held you prisoner in your own home. He had his servants beat you. He made you fly for him against your will, made you kill. He's drawn out the war, and for what? Glory? Vanity? You can't actually tell me, can you?"

"You do not know . . . you cannot possibly—" Velph said, but his grin had faded, gray eyes flicking back and forth behind the eye slits as he cataloged her expression. Her determination. Realization made his head jerk back, as if she'd aimed another blow at his mask. "You—you are *serious.*"

Lifting her chin, Robin whispered: "Yes. I am."

"No!" Velph growled, shoving to his feet and lunging forward. His right hand circled her throat, forcing her to look at him as he snarled down at her, though he was careful, she noted, not to squeeze. She glared up at him, meeting his gaze as defiantly as she had the day they met, a similarity that echoed uncomfortably in her memory. "You do not know . . . do not understand what you are saying."

"Skylark?" Thorne said, reaching a hand in her direction, clearly torn between holding Rosa in place and helping Robin.

"I'm fine," Robin said, waving him off. "Velph, we need to talk about this seriously—"

"We do not!" Velph yelped, letting her go as if her skin had burned him. Robin stumbled, knocked off balance by his abrupt release. Velph backed away, stopping only when his legs hit the sofa. His hands were shaking now, too. "This is a terrible farce, and I will not play this game with you. It is . . ." His mouth was trembling, features fighting against something that looked almost like betrayal. Then he firmed his chin, gray eyes hardening as he straightened to his full height. "It is in *very poor taste* indeed, my dear."

Robin righted herself and took stock of the emotional stalemate in the salon.

Velph refused to believe she meant what she'd said, Rosa seemed horrified by the idea of outright murdering a tyrant king, and Thorne looked thoughtful, maybe even, Robin thought, convinced.

One out of three is better than zero, she thought glumly, returning to her abandoned place at the table in search of a glass of water. *I may have misjudged this. How long does wine affect the senses?*

Silence followed her, but it was tense, strained, far from the companionable atmosphere she had come to expect from the people gathered in the room. She found the water decanter, refilled her glass, and lifted it to her lips, taking great gulps in the hopes it would clear the fuzz that still blurred the edges of her perception.

"Why not *your* king?" Rosa spat, finally, cracking the brittle hush. "Why not throw Saskwya into turmoil, and not Klonn?"

Robin resisted the urge to roll her eyes—it was a legitimate question, and they deserved her seriousness right now. She set her glass back amongst the detritus of the evening's meal. "Aside from the fact that I couldn't get across the front, even if I wanted to, we both know that Auden and Eloy will never choose a ceasefire. If they had their way, they'd fight until the last man standing. Eliminating one of them would expedite the process. And I am here. Not there."

Velph made a wounded heaving sound, pressing a fist to his heart. "I do not . . . Skylark, *why?*" he asked, and it was nearly a whine. He crossed the room swiftly, closing the distance between them. Robin half-expected him to wrap his fingers around her neck again, but instead, he took her face between his palms, gentle and desperate. His Marriage Line pressed like a brand against her skin. The pain that flickered through his gaze was raw agony, and Robin felt her own heart pinch with confusion.

Why was he taking this so personally?

"Do you hate me so much?" he asked softly, voice thick with gravel and emotions she couldn't parse. His thumbs drew small circles against her cheeks. "Is what we have so vile?"

"Of course not," she said, reaching up to wrap her own fingers gently around his wrists, trying to steady him, calm him. His pulse was thready and wild under her thumbs.

"Then *why?*" he growled, eyes shifting back and forth between her own, searching desperately for something she didn't understand.

"Because it has to stop, Velph. It all has to *stop!* We have the power to do that. To end the war, just as we said. To be free. Please, I don't—"

"Do not make it sound like a *gift!*" he snarled, and just like that, he shoved her away from him again, as swift and as unpredictable as he'd been when they'd danced in the sky. He swung into a full-body clench, and Robin backed up quickly. Would this be the time where she got decked, instead of being the one to do the decking? "Foolish girl. This plan will get you killed! Even if you could get to him, killing one man will not make an army stop fighting, or an officer stop commanding. The generals have standing orders in the event the Domed Palace is ever bombed. There is contingency upon contingency. What you propose makes no sense."

"There is no other way," Robin said flatly. Velph gave an inarticulate roar of frustration and turned away. Distress etched sharp into every line of his body, into the way his hands scrabbled at the sides of his helmet, as though he wanted to tear at his hair.

"There is," Rosa said, her own tone laced with cool venom. "She could go home, kill Auden instead of Eloy."

"Think, Madeira," Thorne said softly. "What would they do if a pilot who had been captured and tortured, for all they know, suddenly returned with tales of escape and a fantastical weapon, only to then assassinate their ruler? Auden's daughters would cry brainwash, and the war would get worse. What revenges would they perpetuate, then? If it is Eloy, and perpetrated by his own citizens—it is *political*, a coup. Not an act of war."

Rosa buried her face in her hands, groaning softly. "It is . . . by all the great Seven Arts, it is terrible," she hiccoughed. Pregnant silence jammed the room, and Robin held her breath as Rosa sighed, shoulders slumping. "But it . . . is a good plan."

"*No!*" Velph bellowed, whirling back around. "And that is my final word on it! I am your husband, Skylark, and you must—"

The words felt like a physical blow, like the punch Robin had braced herself for, and she drew herself up, facing the man who had made himself her opponent once more. Who was, she told herself, not the man she'd married. This was the version of him she thought he'd left behind in the forest palace, the overbearing, domineering coal-bag, the enemy soldier in the metal, wolf-shaped mask. The man who held her heart in his hands, and had chosen to squeeze.

"Pick your next words very, *very* carefully, my dear," Robin hissed, and Velph stopped short, startled. "I'm your wife, not your chattel."

"I-I . . ." he stuttered, and like an updraft dying out from under her, he switched tack again. His body slumped, the rage ebbing. His hands loosened. He reached out with his left, and she took it. His palm was clammy with sweat, and the anger in his gaze had burned down into a molten slag of fear and sorrow and grief. He brushed the knuckles of his right hand against her cheek, tender, and then dipped his hand into a pocket sewn to the inside of his jacket. From it, he withdrew a folded, and familiar, piece of paper.

"Velph," Robin said softly. "I know you hate this, but what else is there to do?"

"You say you do not hate me," Velph said softly, "but if you go through with this ridiculous course of action, if our life together means so little to you, then you may as well rip this up now. It will be destroyed all the same."

Velph pressed the piece of paper firmly into her hand, and then turned away, crossing to stand before the hearth, shoulders bowed in defeat. Or resignation. Maybe both. Robin looked down at the paper, but she didn't need to open it to know what it was.

"Skylark, what—?" Thorne asked.

"It's our marriage certificate," Robin answered, handing it off to him as she started toward her husband. "Velph, I don't understand. What does—?"

A startled gasp and a low oath cut her off, and Robin paused, looking back at Rosa and Thorne. Thorne had unfolded the certificate, and they were both bent over it, gaping. "Is something wrong?" she asked, and Rosa's head snapped up, her eyes not on Robin, but on Velph.

"This . . . it cannot be . . ." Rosa sputtered, shaking her head. Thorne looked as though he might faint. Concern and uncertainty flared hard within Robin, and she looked from Rosa to Velph, and back again.

"Okay, what in all the hells is going on?" she demanded, glaring at Rosa and Thorne.

"Your marriage certificate, it says—" Rosa started, but the soft *thunk* of Velph's helmet hitting the carpet made all of them jump. Robin looked over at him, the dread she'd felt the past few weeks rising stronger than ever, sending her heart racing, choking her breath inside her throat.

"Velph?" she whispered. "What are you doing—?"

"There is no point in hiding now," Velph said, shoulders rounded with misery, the lines of his face creased with betrayal. He looked impossibly weighted, and terribly defeated.

"What have you done?" Robin demanded. "What does the certificate *say*?"

Velph ran a hand through his sweaty hair and made a derisive noise. "It says, my dear, that you have married Elias Chanlis Nutvig." He raised his eyes to hers, meeting them unflinchingly, like a man prepared to face a firing squad. "The Crown Prince of Klonn."

CHAPTER TWENTY-ONE

Robin's body moved without conscious thought. One moment, she was standing in front of Velph—no, in front of Elias, prince, *enemy*—and the next, she was plunked on her arse on the carpet, staring up at the man she thought she knew, the man she had—*oh omens, married, I married him, oh gods*—in horror-laced alarm. Before she could even so much as blink, though, a streak of bright green silk flashed across her vision. It resolved itself into Rosa, who'd crossed the room to press what looked to be an unopened fan to the base of Velph's throat. He had his hands up, leaning away from her as much as he was able with the fire at his back. Robin couldn't tell what was so threatening about a few flimsy scraps of—

There was a sharp *click*, and Rosa moved in a swirl of emerald. Her fan sprang open, a spread of deadly little blades popping out of the spines. "I knew it," she hissed, painted lips curled back in a ferocious snarl. "I knew we never should have trusted you. Did he send you? Have you been feeding him information about us, about the network, all this time?"

"Come now, Madam," Velph said softly to Rosa, though his eyes stayed locked on Robin's. "There is no need for violence. I assure you, there is no love lost between myself and my brother. I am not here on his behalf, nor acting in his interests."

"He's right, Madeira, my love," Thorne said, stepping forward. Rosa turned her head to look at him, eyes narrowed. "The crown prince has been missing from the royal palace for years."

Robin jerked at that, coming back to herself as though waking from a dream.

She heard herself gasp, felt her lungs burn and her throat ache, and pressed one scarred palm against her heart. It fluttered like a caged bird under her hand, and every fear that had kept her awake at night in the forest palace, every horror she had entertained and tried to dismiss, every tale she had been told and second-guessed, surged against her brain, swollen and shrieking..

"No, no," Robin heard herself whimpering, like a kicked dog, like a wailing spirit. Her voice shook, and her hands shook, her whole body was a trembling, breathless mess, and she swallowed, swallowed, swallowed so she wouldn't *scream*.

"Skylark," Velph—Elias—he said softly, reaching down for her, and Robin scuttled backward, putting Rosa between them, slapping his hand away—his left hand, his *Marriage Line*—with a yelp.

"Don't touch me!"

He recoiled, heel knocking into his helmet, making it wobble and roll. Robin stared at it, unable to look away, and though there was no blood, it seemed just like a decapitated head, the husband executed and replaced by this nightmare prince. Son to the murderous monster responsible for it all, for the pain, the suffering, the death. Brother to the King who redoubled the atrocities of his father when Eliam had died and passed the crown to Eloy.

Stupid, stupid, stupid little girl! Robin scolded herself, curling in, hiding, because the truth was so sharp, so painful, it was like crashing in the forest again, like watching Al die, like being betrayed by a colleague and shot out of the sky all in one nausea-inducing second. *So desperate, so lonely, so ready to play the game of love! Look at you now, you little fool! You should have known!*

Her fingernails scraped at her scalp as she hid her face in her knees out of shame at her gullibility. Memories swirled inside her head, images, snippets of dialogue, as though her mind was desperate to find the pieces she had missed, to find the ammunition that would let her hate him. He had to have given it away, had to have given vital information . . . or spied on them . . . or secretly hated Robin this whole time. He was a liar, his feelings couldn't be true, and he was her enemy.

Her *enemy.*

And yet . . . and yet . . .

There was nothing.

She sucked hard at the close, stuffy air of the salon, tasting leftover smoke, and food, and the silk of the dress obscuring her face.

There was nothing.

The man—her husband—Coyote, Elias, Velph—he was born of a king who had declared war over land that was never his to take, was brother to another king who refused to stop that war because of pride and ego, but he himself had done everything to avoid it, to end it. He'd run away, he'd given her WINGS, he'd watched her flank, he gave her his Marriage Line, and had kept the horrible filth of his true name from her not to trick, or deceive, or lie, but because that was *not who he was.*

What crime had he committed, but the very same one she had herself—hiding her name? He had asked her once, back in the lumber room all those weeks ago, what he had done, personally, to ever be named her personal enemy? He'd told her he was nobility, told her he had a brother, told her of their fractured relationship, told her that he had flown under duress because of a brother and a king, told her he resented being the killer of Saskwyan pilots and captor of Sealie mid-flights.

Robin had assumed that he'd been the older boy in the portrait in that hateful parlor. That the younger son, the chubby-cheeked beatific one, was the one the king was threatening to control Velph.

She'd had it the wrong way around.

Velph had been the babe, who'd grown up under the malignant thumb of first his father, King Eliam, and then been turned into a weapon for love of his country and on the orders of his brother King Eloy.

Velph had never told her he was the crown prince, but it wasn't an outright lie, so much as a glider-sized omission. It didn't mean that what he'd told her in the palace, what he'd shown her of his own imprisonment, his own disdain for the war—it didn't mean that all of that was insincere. Did it?

"What do you mean?" she asked, squeezing the words out of a throat that felt shredded, from lungs that refused to hold enough breath, and forced herself to look up at Thorne. "What do you mean, he's been missing?"

"I told you, I have family at court," Thorne reminded her. "Close enough to the Nutvigs to know that the crown prince was not just shy of crowds, or conveniently elsewhere when it came time for appearances, as the people of Klonn are told." Thorne looked up at Velph, then, his dark eyes filled with questions. "He's been gone."

Robin let herself turn, let herself look at him, really look at him, the man who shared her Marriage Line. He was gaunt and wrecked-looking, eyes red-rimmed, left hand cradled to his chest as if Robin's slap had broken his fingers.

"I fled," Velph corrected, throat bobbing as he swallowed, eyeing Rosa's fan blades warily. "I did not— do not—agree with my brother's war. But I could find no way to convince him to end it. So I ran away. Like a coward. In shame. Instead of convincing him, instead of trying harder, I ran. Like the disgrace I am."

Part of Robin wanted to jump to his defense, to admonish him for being too hard on herself, to tease him into a better mood. But the impulse shriveled as fast as it had grown.

"Fled," Rosa repeated, gaze narrowing further, suspicious. Over her shoulder, Velph met Robin's gaze. The mask of indifference was gone, and for a second, she saw again the man she fell in love with. Heard once more the various, loving conversations they'd had. Felt the gentle caresses and impassioned kisses. His gray eyes pleaded with her above the cascade of Rosa's dark-red curls, asked her for her forgiveness, her understanding, her faith that, though he may have kept his identity a secret, she knew his heart to be true.

"And was recaptured," Robin finished for him, pushing herself awkwardly to her feet, knees knocking, hands sweaty, mind racing. "Recaptured, and locked away in the forest palace."

"I am sorry," Rosa snarled, renewing her grip on Velph's shirt, the fan blades still held dangerously close to the skin of his throat. "This is all just too convenient. What makes you think that he is not a traitor? Prince or no, it seems to me that, of all of us here, he has the most to protect, and the most to lose. The most reason to sabotage each mission."

Velph scoffed. "Why would I want to harm the Skylark? What possible reason would I have for asking her to be shot at? She is my wife!"

No matter where he comes from, no matter his name, the most important title to him is "husband," Robin realized, heart swooping and sore from all the sudden wrenching and awakenings. *And no matter my name, or where I come from, I'm his wife. I love him. Gods, I'm in love with the Crown Prince of Klonn.*

"He wouldn't," Robin insisted, raising her chin, daring Rosa to test the depth of her stubbornness.

"How can you know that? Can you vouch for it?" Rosa seethed. "You do not know him, not as well as you—" she began, her voice going low, dripping in condescension, and no, Robin was not having any of that.

"I know him a damn sight better than you do," she snarled, stepping forward. "I've danced with him, and there's no better way of knowing a man than that!"

"Silly, romantic pilot nonsense!" Rosa spat. "You can't—"

"I beg your pardon, Madam!"

"Hold on, now—" Thorne started.

"Well, what else do you want me to do?" Robin roared, shutting everyone else up in an instant. "Huh? Tell me! What am I supposed to do here? Trust you?" Robin jabbed a finger at Rosa. "Trust *him*?" A second jab at Velph. "Trust no one, turn tail and run back home? I *can't*. I have to, *have* to believe that—" To her own mortification, her voice wobbled to a stop as her throat closed up, and she sniffed hard, blinking back the tears that suddenly threatened. She pressed the heels of her hands against her eyes, sucked in heaving breaths that she refused to admit were sobs, catching any tears in her cuffs before they could embarrass her and fall. Her compatriots, her colleagues—her friends?—waited her out. "This changes nothing."

"Skylark—" Rosa chided.

"*This changes nothing*!" Robin screeched.

More silence from the salon. And from the top of the building, the eerie, echoing chime of WINGS could be heard, almost as if in agreement.

"In fact," Robin said slowly, pausing to take another steadying, deep breath. "In fact, this is even better."

Rosa stared at her, mouth a firm line, eyes assessing and shrewd. Finally, she pulled back, releasing Velph and putting away her fan slowly—it had been hidden underneath her bustle, the decorative tassels she always had hanging out from underneath the ruching of her swag attaching firmly to the fan's handle.

Clever, Robin thought. Out loud, she said, "Thank you."

"Well?" Rosa asked after a moment of strained silence. "Better how?"

"It's better," Robin said, and moved to stand before Velph; he was tense, watching her carefully as she came to a stop before him, expression blank. "Because now, when we kill the king, we can be sure that the one who replaces him will be on our side."

CHAPTER
TWENTY-TWO

"*Rudding hells*," Velph snarled, face blanching. "You really mean to . . . you want me to be . . ."

His words ended on a strangled, choking sound, and Robin was reminded, suddenly, that he wasn't that much older than she was. That he wasn't some great, terrible archnemesis or hobgob, or even her thoughtful, mature husband. He was a young man still, in the way that she was still just a young woman. It wasn't his fault that Robin's childhood had been swallowed up in forges and gliders; his own had been stripped away from him, as well. She squeezed his arms, reassuring, tried to press her confidence and forgiveness through their flesh and into his blood, so she wouldn't have to struggle with inadequate words.

Velph pulled free with a violent jerk. He covered his face and turned away to go stand by the fire, shoulders hunched as though trying to get his breath back from a gut-punch. Every twitch of his back screamed, "don't follow me!" So Robin stayed where she was.

"We are doing this, then?" Rosa asked softly. "We are going to assassinate King Eloy and place Prince Elias on the throne?"

Velph's posture stiffened, but otherwise, there was no indication that he either agreed or disagreed with Rosa's statement. Robin couldn't even tell if he was reacting to the thought of murdering his brother, the thought of being king, or the sound of his real name being said out loud.

Sighing, Robin turned to where Rosa waited, a few steps away, Thorne placid and thoughtful by her side. "I don't see that we have any other choice. If we want the war to end, then this is the only way to do it."

"Then . . . then I will fetch the maps," Rosa said, lifting her chin with resolve, even as her voice betrayed what Robin was sure was probably dread. "I would rather we had found a different route, but I . . . I will do no less than I asked of you, Skylark, and I will follow where you lead."

Thorne nodded once in agreement with Rosa's announcement, and then, together, they made for the stairs. They paused at the bottom for a moment, whispering intensely to one another. Robin wondered what secrets they were making, what plots of their own they might be hatching, but stopped when Rosa shook her head viciously, and Thorne reached out to brush a tear from her cheek. He leaned down to give her a tender, meaningful kiss, and Robin looked away, suddenly embarrassed to be watching such intimacy.

She longed for her own version of that comfort, and her heart ached, bereft of her husband's touch. But the man beside her was more than her husband now, and it felt somehow wrong to reach for his hand when she'd so recently slapped it away.

She moved to stand beside him, and he turned to her, just barely. His expression was shuttered, back once more to the cold formality he had worn to protect himself in the forest palace. It shattered something inside Robin to see him like this again, to see him regress to hiding behind a cruel shield. But she couldn't tell him how to mourn, or how to prepare himself for the task ahead. That was for him to handle, and when it was done, it would be her job to help him forgive himself—*and me*, she realized, the truth of it hitting her like a shock of cold water thrown in her face.

A sudden vision of a future where Velph had banished her from his palace, from his life, loomed large in her imagination. He might despise her for this. He might want her gone. Exiled. Reviled. And, as king, he could do it. He could claim their marriage meaningless, and send her packing back across the front.

He could *hate* her.

Robin swallowed hard and pressed her hands to her temples, tried to alleviate the headache that suddenly pounded there, a pulsing agony to match the one blooming in her heart.

Robin could very easily win this war, but lose everything else.

"Vel—uh, Eli—" she said, mouth dry, but her husband drew back with a full-body flinch when she reached for his hand. "I . . . I'm sorry?"

"Are you?" he rasped. "Do you understand what you ask of me? Honestly?"

"What's the other option? If you can think of a better one, tell me." She paused, and when he didn't reply, she said, "Should I just give up? Hand WINGS over, then?"

"Trust me, wife, if the Skylark and WINGS were ever to be captured, the crown would be certain to make a horrific example out of her," Velph choked. "The pack has proven to be repairable by anyone who understands it well enough. But the pilot? The pilot would be made a gory spectacle."

"And you don't think that's grounds enough to dethrone him?" Robin gasped.

"You did not say *dethrone*, my dear," Velph said, voice low and dark. "You said *kill*."

For the first time, in the face of what she'd asked the man she'd married to do, Robin's resolved wavered. "Well, I mean, we could—" Robin waffled.

"No," Thorne interrupted, coming down the stairs with an armful of rolled papers, Rosa on his heels. "Even if you did manage to usurp Eloy, there would be infighting as long as he's alive. A civil war would tear Klonn apart. Before it could ever be resolved, we would be overrun."

The four conspirators watched each other, cataloging body language and expressions carefully, gauging intent.

"Fine," Velph finally croaked, and something in his body language, in his face, crumbled. "Fine. Yes. Just . . . may your gods forgive me, my dear. Yes."

Robin reached up, then, slowly. She cupped his face in her hands, ran her thumbs across his cheeks, sweeping away the honest, rolling tears that he didn't seem to know he was shedding. She stretched onto her toes, and kissed him. It was a gentle kiss, nearly chaste, lips pressed against his like a seal in wax, like a promise imprinted on his skin.

Thorne pulled a low table over to one of the sofa nooks, and Rosa laid down what turned out to be a carefully preserved hoard of antique architectural drawings.

"What?" she asked at Robin's raised eyebrow, pretending—poorly—to be in a better humor than she'd been in before she left. "A girl can have her hobbies, ai?"

"Of course," Robin said, drifting over to the table, her fingers entwined with Velph's so that he followed along in her wake, small and slightly broken, but hers. She had decided that since Velph was the name he had given her, Velph was the name she'd use, regardless of what it said on a slip of paper. She brushed crossed fingers over her shoulder, lifted her free palm skyward to pray to the gods of clarity, and wisdom, and strength for guidance in this thing they were about to do. "Thank you, Rosa," she said when she was finished.

"Do not thank me," Rosa answered, laying a hand on Robin's arm. Robin chose not to comment on how it shook. "Everything that is Klonn in me curdles at the idea. But I will admit that it is the most logical choice, and I must commend you for choosing to take a route we

Klonn would never have considered."

"I guess there's something worthwhile about being Sealie, after all," Robin teased, trying to lighten the mood. But it felt forced. They were plotting murder; laughter only cheapened the life they were about to take. Rosa gave her a sad smile and patted her arm once, withdrawing her hand as she turned her attention to the maps.

"Thorne, dear, pour us some drinks before we sit, would you? If we must plan to kill a king, then at least we shall do it with the aid of fortification."

"Those who would kill a king," Thorne muttered as he disappeared into the kitchen to retrieve the required libations. "Sounds like a bloody folk song."

Behind her, Velph made a shaky, gasping noise and gripped her fingers tight.

Robin surrendered her cup with a wistful sigh. She had been hoping someone would pour out a little more, just to soothe her nerves, even if it did taste foul. Her calm assurance of a few hours ago was beginning to wear away under the rough pressure of the reality of what she'd proposed.

"I cannot think anymore. I am full to the teeth with planning," Rosa said softly, rising to collect their empty glasses and place them on the tea tray Thorne had brought with the decanter of that horrible green liquor Velph had always favored. "Tad, darling, care to retire with me?"

"Yes, coming," he said, standing and taking the tea tray from her. He plucked the decanter off the tray and put it back on the table in front of Velph. Then, together, they retreated into the kitchen with a soft swish of fabric and the scuff of house slippers against the lush carpet.

Velph refilled his own glass and offered it to Robin. She nodded, reaching out to accept. She took a sip, and then passed it back.

"You've been quiet," Robin said softly, when he finally sipped for himself. "Are you making plans?"

"No."

"We can—"

"No," Velph said softly. "Just . . . silence for a while, please. I need time with my thoughts."

"Yeah, sure, of course," Robin said, chagrined. Of course, he wouldn't want to talk about it.

She considered going upstairs to sleep, but her head was too full of diagrams and plans to let her drop off. And she wasn't sure she wanted to leave things so fractured between them. She couldn't force him to speak, though. So she waited and, as Velph sipped in silence, reread the maps of the palace interior, committing each twist, each turn, each door and staircase to memory, burning it into her mind with the fire of her conviction.

The plan was simple: Elias Nutvig, Crown Prince of Klonn, would walk in the front door. With him would go his cousin, Taddeus Thorne—whom they would confess had found Elias and had talked him back around to the king's cause—and, as Thorne was her patron, Madeira Rosa, Thorne's lover, would accompany them. Elias, having been absent from the court for so long, would be welcomed by the servants and attending courtiers, and his brother, knowing the truth of Elias's defection, would in all probability ask to speak to his brother alone. Elias would do his utmost to not be separated from Rosa and Thorne, which would require the king to take him to one of a handful of places: the king's study, the war room, Elias's childhood chambers, one of the private negotiation-slash-dining rooms, or down to the prison cells.

The Skylark could not go with them, because no matter how they dressed her up, there was just no disguising WINGS. And Robin had to have WINGS when she assassinated the king, because she clearly had to be the

Skylark. Neither Velph, nor Thorne, nor Rosa could kill Eloy Nutvig, as it would then be an act of secession and treason, and not an act of politics and war.

And she had to kill him with an audience.

To do so, she had to get inside the palace, fully armed and dressed in the guise of the Skylark. And she had to do so unseen.

Without warning, Velph slammed down his glass, startling Robin so bad she jumped, and bumped the table, which sloshed his drink all over the floor—though, thankfully, it missed any of the maps. She had a feeling Rosa would never forgive her if she ruined her fine collection of ill-gotten gains.

"Velph?" she asked as he folded double, fingers threaded on the back of his neck. He made a hoarse, choking sound. "Oh, gods, how much did you have? You're really drunk," she said, fearing he was about to be sick. "Need a bucket?"

"No." He looked up, and his eyes were red and sparkling. "I am sorry," he choked, his lashes spiking, tears falling fat and quick into his beard. Robin scooted her chair closer to him.

"It's all right," she said, reaching out to take his hand in her own. "It's okay."

"No," he said, shaking his head. His eyes, when he looked up to meet hers, were a turbulent storm of emotion. "No, please allow me to . . . I owe you an explanation."

"You really don't," Robin started, but he placed the tips of his fingers against her lips, silencing her gently.

"I should have told you my name—my true name. But when I first showed my face to you and you did not know me, I thought . . . I thought, 'here is my opportunity. Here is my chance to court her as I am, and not for who I am related to.' In time, though, not telling you has become . . . well, *cowardice*. I am a coward." He heaved a dark sigh, the hand over her mouth sliding down, curling loosely against her collarbone. "I could not risk losing you if you knew the truth. I cannot, my dear, my heart, my wife."

And then he was kissing her, powerful and passionate. Desperate. His hands slid up her arms and over her neck, tugging until she was half-sprawled across his lap, one strong thigh between her own. "Forgive me, Skylark," he breathed.

"Robin," she caught herself whispering before she meant to. She pressed her mouth to his, making sure he felt the shape of every single, vital word: "Robin Arianhod."

"I do not—" he started, and then realized what he'd been offered.

"It . . . um, seemed only fair," she added when he pulled away, questioning. "I know your name now."

"Robin," he repeated, a wide, nearly goofy grin reminding her again of just how young, how handsome, he really was.

Dazzled, that's what he looks like, Robin decided.

"Not one bird, but another," Velph said, hands clutching her hips, face tilted up toward her as if he were a sunflower and she a goddess of summer light. "Come, kiss me again, Robin Arianhod, of the robin-nosed glider."

"Oh, wow," Robin breathed when they parted enough to allow for it. "I . . . uh . . . wow."

Velph laughed sinfully, and it rolled through Robin like a thunderclap, igniting the underside of her skin.

"There is more where that came from, wife," he whispered in her ear, nibbling along the side of her neck. His long fingers circled her waist, pressing her down as he lifted his pelvis off the sofa and ground up against her.

"Oh, rudding hells, *yes*," Robin said, and then crashed back against him, trying to crawl into his mouth with lips and teeth and tongue.

Velph slid his hands down the outsides of her thighs, pulling her tight against his waist. "Hold on," he said against her mouth, wicked glee shining in his eyes, and then stood. Robin whooped in surprise, laughing and flinging her arms around his neck to do just that as he carried her up the stairs to their small attic room.

The great glittering dome of the aptly named Domed Palace glittered precisely because, as it turned out, it was made up of millions of octagonal panes, and each of those of gold-flecked, mullioned glass. Finding which panes opened, however, now that was the tricky part, especially in the murky darkness of night. Fittingly, the moon seemed nervous to show its face, offering only a few cool glimpses of light through the thick cloud cover.

Robin didn't dare risk the light of a lamp, so she had to run her gloved hands over the lead seams until a handle poked her fingers. There was no lock on the window— why would there be? The thought that anyone would be able to both scale the palace walls and climb down inside without being seen by the palace guard was preposterous. Still, just to be sure, Robin brushed crossed fingers over her shoulder to scatter any ill-luck that might be clinging to her and worked at the latch.

It may have been unlocked, but that didn't mean it was easy to open.

She hadn't wanted her hearing impaired, so she'd forgone the Skylark's normal cap and instead had pulled her white hair back in a simple twist, held this time by the wolf-cameo ivory hairpin she'd dug back out of the vanity drawer after being reminded so thoroughly of her husband's continued affection the evening before. It had felt more appropriate, somehow, than one of the rose-shaped ones. Rather than take the time to remove her gloves and use her lock picking tools, Robin pulled out the hairpin, loosening the plain black scarf that covered her head, and used the tip to dig at the seam of the pane until it opened a sliver. She quickly wrapped her hair back up, then squirmed her fingers into the opening in the frame.

The window was only just big enough to fit both Robin and WINGS, and she had to wriggle a bit to keep the fuel casing from scraping against the edge. She lay flat on the narrow dome ledge and maneuvered her head, shoulders, and most of her waist through the gap, hinging down, toes hooked over the lip of the ledge. Then, before gravity could take over, she turned on the pack, let go with her toes, and flipped midfall.

Using only the barest amount of thrust—just enough to keep her airborne, but not enough that the light from the exhaust pipes would reflect off the glass and gain attention—Robin hovered, her head now even with the open window, and peered down into the shadows of the throne and reception room. Just as Velph had said it would be, the throne room was quiet, the doors closed and the lights off when the court was adjourned to their suppers and private entertainments. Nothing stirred in the darkness.

The quiet roar of the pack jammed against her ears, so listening for anything else was out of the question. But there was, at least, nothing loud enough to mean that people were coming her way—no shouts, or gunshots.

The closer she got to the floor, and as her eyes adjusted to the deeper darkness, the more detail she could make out. The room was cavernous, easily the size of the canteen at the Air Patrol base in Pyria, but done all in a marble so pale, it seemed to glow even in the meager light of the moon. Dark veins ambled through the stone, like giant mouths with craggy jaws just waiting to surge out of the floors and walls and snap her up. Golden speckles amid the blackness sparked like muted stars in the soft glow of WINGS's exhaust, and Robin tried not to think about the excess of wealth that must have been wasted on a room like this.

Everything not covered in marble was swathed in ice-blue velvet, sumptuous and opulent; the entire back wall behind the throne was hung with the stuff. The throne itself, framed between two empty flag stands and set upon a four-step dais, was huge—wide enough for two to sit side by side, at least. Robin could tell that there were engravings on the back and arms, but couldn't make them out. Not in this light.

There was no companion throne, for King Eloy had no spouse. No heirs. No lust, the Sealie rumors said, for anything but blood.

That couldn't be true. Every king was human. Perhaps it was that no fine Klonnish lady would have him. Either way—*one less widow to worry about.*

She landed and crouched on the vast, pale marble floor, counting the blonde-wood doors on the eastern wall, and pushed her goggles up onto her forehead so she could see better in the low light of the room. Then she scuttled through the darkness to crouch in front of a small servants' door, fifth from the throne. Velph had drilled blueprints and passageways into her head from the moment they'd awoken at noon, and Robin was thankful that she still had her pilot's mind for coordinates and maps. Certain of her choice, she stripped off her gloves, folding them over her belt, and went to work on the lock with her picks.

It was stiff, but gave easily enough after a wrench, and she carefully pulled it inward. If she'd been at home, she would have pressed down to keep the hinges from squeaking, but these were well-oiled and clean.

The hallway that opened before her was utterly black, with neither lamps nor windows to allow even a small bit of moonlight into the passage. The faint glow from

WINGS's banked pilot light, spilling out the bottom of the exhaust pipes, was thankfully enough to keep her from stumbling as she made her way through the corridor, hand sliding along the wall so she could count the steps between the next set of doorways. "One, two, and then a left," she whispered to herself, charting her progress on the map in her head. "Three more doors, and a right, and then down three—oomph, four steps. Across the room, and . . . aha! Door."

She pressed her ear against the jamb, listening. This was the negotiation room, the first of three places Velph had thought his brother might take him. But there were no noises inside, no guards outside, no light spilling out from the threshold. There was nobody here.

On to the next, Robin thought, backtracking to the start of the servants' hall and aiming next for the king's private study. The creeping and the half-lit gloom, the way her heart pounded in her throat, reminded Robin all too sharply of a similar excursion through a palace in the forest, half a year ago. The night she'd escaped. The night she'd first kissed the man who now shared her Marriage Line. Shoving the memories back, she focused as she peered down this next corridor. No guards, and, when she pressed her ear to this door as well, no sound. Next, was Velph's childhood bedroom—nothing. Darkness. And though she wanted to stay, to rifle through his books, see if he had a small stuffed toy tucked up on a shelf somewhere, to learn more of him now that she knew the real him, she forced herself to leave.

Her friends had already been in the palace for over an hour; she had to find them. Finish the mission. The next location on Velph's list of probabilities was the war room. After that was the place Rosa had called a prison, and Thorne a dungeon. The war room and prison cells were equidistant from where Robin now was. Which was the better bet, though? And, more importantly, which was more likely to have people who would catch her before she could turn and flee. Prisons had, well, prisoners who might raise a cry. But the war room might be filled with officers who knew Robin on sight and would not hesitate to shoot.

Might as well stay above ground, if I can, Robin decided. *Don't want to waste my time sneaking around the stairs if I can avoid it.*

She brushed her shoulder with crossed fingers and headed for the war room, but this, too, was empty. The room was vacant of both life and light, the door open and unguarded. Any other time, she would have greedily soaked in the maps, snatched as many documents as she could have carried, and destroyed what she couldn't. Now, she stared at the topographical map on the massive planning table with uncomprehending, apprehensive eyes. She ground her teeth together to keep from growling out loud and slapped a fist into her own palm rather than punch the wall in her frustration.

With a sinking feeling, Robin made her way to the prison, no longer bothering to creep. Having not yet found a single soul—not even a servant—it was likely that the commotion, if it was happening at all, would be happening underground. But when Robin crept down those final stairs, it was only to reach a darkened pit at the bottom. The torches of the guards' antechamber were doused. Robin could see, in the dull orange glow from her tailpipe, that the tables and chairs were abandoned, covered with a thick layer of undisturbed dust, and the heavy door to the cells had been left very slightly ajar, as if someone had wanted it to look locked, but had had no key themselves.

Robin pulled it open, just a bit, and peered into the hallway. The cells themselves, the ones Robin could make out from the doorway, at least—she didn't dare go inside and have someone lock the door behind her—

were empty.

A frisson clambered up her spine, and what little flesh was exposed on her wrists and neck goose pimpled in the damp, cool air of the antechamber. Klonn was at war; there should be prisoners. Guards. The king's flag had been flying from the apex of the Dome, indicating that he was in residence. Velph, Rosa, and Thorne had gone to the palace, and had not returned to tell her it was closed up. There had been *lights* on when she had flown up from the outside. There should be *somebody*; the whole palace should not be absolutely barren.

Something wasn't right.

CHAPTER TWENTY-THREE

Robin paused in the threshold of the door, debating. The hall was eerily quiet, but just in case her friends were locked up at the end of it, in one of the cells she couldn't see, just in case they were tied up, gagged, maybe even hurt or unconscious, left to bleed out alone in the darkness . . . she had to check. She could return then to her search of the upper floors with the assurance that they were not locked away down here, waiting for her to save them.

Robin took a moment to steady her nerves, gulping in the musty air and preparing herself to walk, willingly, into her greatest fear—a lightless cage with no view of the sky. Then she lit the candle she kept in one of her belt pouches, jammed one of her lock picks into the inside of the heavy door's lock to keep it from trapping her inside, unsheathed her boot knife, and stepped carefully into the total blackness of the hall.

The first of the cells were down a small set of steps, which were crumbled with age, small flakes of stone and pebbles breaking away from the mortar to plink against the bumpy flagstones of the floor. Robin stood at the bars of the first cell on her left. She pushed her arm through to shed as much feeble candlelight as possible into the space. Empty. The cell itself was small—no larger than her little attic room, with a sloped floor that led to a drain in the center, and scuffed iron rings drilled into the walls. Two narrow, ill-used cots were pushed against the side walls, stripped of all linens and comfort, and a single hand pump tap protruded from the wall in the back, presumably so prisoners could access fresh water and wash out the pocked, rusting chamberpot shoved into the back corner.

Everything was covered in a thick, grimy layer of dust; it stuck to Robin's finger when she reached out to gauge how recent it was. No one had been in this cell in a long time, and no one had cleaned it in even longer. The drain gave off a faint reek of unwashed flesh and human excrement, and Robin wrinkled her nose and moved on. Each of the cells she checked were the same—barren, and dirty, and increasingly foul-smelling the further from the door she got. Coughing, Robin pulled part of her scarf over her mouth and nose, and pressed on.

The only sound was that of her footfalls on the gritty flagstones, crunching so loud in her straining ears that it felt like she made as much noise as a faulty aeroship engine. A rat scuttled away from her light in the second-to-last cell, and Robin barely caught her shout of surprise before it made it past her lips, startled as she was by the sudden burst of life.

Omens, she cursed, listening to the vermin scuttle back the way she'd come, dislodging its own chunks of flaking mortar on the stairs. *I'm too rudding jumpy. One cell left. You can do this, Captain. You have to.*

Robin turned to face the last cell, and had so expected to find it empty that it took her a moment to register that she was instead staring at a strange wooden box. It lay there, on the ground, unvarnished and hastily, inexpertly cobbled together from what looked to be scrap lumber. It wasn't much larger than one of the cots, and had probably been used to transport a stack of them at some point, judging by what little she could understand of the stenciled Klonnish written on the side. The lid was bizarrely weighted down, though, with several flagstones that had been prised up from the floor around the drain placed haphazardly on top, and when Robin got close to the bars to cast light into the shadowed corners of the cell, she could see a thin trickle of ichor leaking from the lower corner of the box into the sinkhole of the drain.

The smell here was atrocious, and Robin realized that what she'd assumed was the reek of terrible plumbing had been instead the sweet, disgusting, oily odor of rot. It clung to the back of her throat and made her gag. The feeling of *not right* got worse, and Robin was half-turned down the hall to flee before she realized that she had to know what was inside. Had to see, because what if it was one of her friends in there, being tortured, or hurt, or . . . no, no. She just needed to know.

The door to the cell slid to the side easily enough, incongruously well-oiled and in good repair, and every hair Robin had shivered upright. In the distance, the scuff and scuttle of the rat scrabbling on the stonework caught again in her ears, but she blocked it out, focused solely on the box. She set the candle on the floor, far enough away that it wouldn't light the box aflame if it was knocked over, and started to remove the flagstones on the lid. It was heavy, slow work, and each second it took made her nerves scrape and twist. Pausing to take a deep breath set her to retching, and she had to pause to empty her stomach in a back corner of the cell when she'd removed the final stone.

Wiping her mouth with her cuffs, Robin approached the box, cautious, and feeling foolish for being afraid, for being unable to shake the feeling that something awful might yet jump out at her.

The phantom of *not right* loomed large, and Robin glanced around quickly. Nothing moved in the darkness. She was alone still. Only the rat and the sound of her own heartbeat rushing beneath her skin were detectable. Still, she unsheathed her knife, just to be safe. Dread filling her guts, Robin reached for the lid, lifting it just enough to peer inside.

Don't be Velph, she prayed. *Don't be any of them. Please.*

The smell that greeted her was overpowering.

The sight, moreso.

She'd been right—something was indeed rotting inside this box. Or rather, someone.

Whoever this was, they'd been dead for a while. And despite whatever form of embalming the body might have been subjected to, it was starting to collapse. The skin, once pale, was now a bloated, ruddy color that gave way to a sickening blueish-green around its hairline. Bodies, if they were preserved in dry air, and not burned, as was proper, could last years. It was impossible to tell how long the body had been here, how long this person had been dead. It could have been days, or it could have months. Why would someone hide a corpse down here, though?

Squinting against the tears that blurred her vision as her eyes watered, she traced the lines of the corpse's face in the air. They were hard to make out in the dim light, but were just familiar enough that she recognized the man inside.

Robin gasped in shock, and dropped the lid with an echoing bang as she stumbled, backing away from the coffin, swallowing hard against the oily stink that coated her tongue and biting her cheek to keep from vomiting on the spot. She knocked over the candle in her scramble to retreat, plunging the prison into a close, suffocating darkness that matched the terror in her mind.

Robin backed all the way out of the cell, horror rippling under her skin, the pilot light of WINGS the only thing left to light her way. She gasped for the fresher air, desperate and confused and wishing her eyes would adjust faster.

"It can't . . . no, it can't be . . ." she muttered, turning in a circle, tugging at her hair in distraught confusion. "He's been dead too long."

The rat scuffled at the steps leading to the guard's antechamber, and even through her spinning turmoil, Robin realized why the sound had kept pinging for her—it was too big to be a rat. Too large.

Knife brandished, Robin spun to face the doorway.

And there, silhouetted against the soft glow of the lanterns at the top of the stairs, stood the seneschal.

"You!" Robin snarled, lunging for him. But before her foot had made it to the first step, the seneschal had backed away, pushing the door to the prison shut with a sinister grin.

"No!" she cried, shouldering at the wood. Luckily, the lock pick she'd wedged into the mechanism did the trick, and the door couldn't close all the way. Robin threw her entire weight into it, and the heavy door crashed outward, throwing the seneschal back.

How is he alive? How did he survive the explosion, too? Robin thought, scrambling to get around the doorjamb and at the imperious coal-bag before he could cry the alarm. He was already up and scrambling for the stairs, though, and all she could do was sprint after him as her boots slipped and slid against the uneven ground. The passage was too narrow to attempt to use WINGS, and he had longer legs.

Robin paused when she made it to the top of the stairs, head whipping back and forth, trying to find his trail. The slam of a door off to the right had her hurtling in that direction, hand on the control box, ready to fly over the heads of guards or soldiers if they tried to stand in her way. The seneschal's flight took them back down familiar corridors—still eerily empty of people—and Robin realized just before she slammed through the last door that he'd led her back to the throne room. Jamming the button on the control box hard, Robin took to the air halfway through the threshold, circling the dome to dodge any bullets that might be aimed in her direction. She had enough space for a controlled turn, and skimmed the inside of the dome, glass rattling in her wake.

It was only on her second pass that she realized there'd been no gunshots. No one was shooting at her. No one was in the moonlight-flooded room, save for the seneschal. He stood rigid by the throne, thrown into shadow by the slant of the light. She couldn't see both of his hands in silhouette, but she took the chance to land gently, far enough away that she could take off again if she heard a gun.

"You lived," she snarled at him.

"Barely," the seneschal snarled back, and his voice was reedy and small. Not quite the menacing timbre she remembered. The explosion must have done a great deal of damage to his torso and neck, where he would have been hit by the brunt of it. "Do not fear, I had the best care."

"Royal care?" Robin challenged, and adjusted the grip of her knife to keep it from getting sweaty. "Not from the king, it would seem."

The seneschal's laugh was wet and tight.

"That *was* who was down in that box, wasn't it?" Robin asked, still tasting the phantom stink of rot on her tongue. "King Eloy?"

The outline of the seneschal's head dipped toward the throne, as though leaning close to hear someone speak . . . or nodding in deference.

A discreet cough sounded from the throne itself. Drowned entirely in shadow, Robin had been unaware that anyone was sitting there. Had they been there the whole time? Had they watched her break in, and sneak out, and said nothing? Why? If Eloy was dead, then who . . . ?

Robin brandished the knife at the newcomer and rocked her weight back, ready to lunge or take flight as necessary. But the shadow, as it stood and stepped forward, resolved itself into the one person she'd been most desperate to discover was safe.

"Velph!" she cried. "Get away from him."

Standing now on the bottom step, Velph paused to fold his hands at the small of his back. He tilted his head, amused. Amused. "Hello, my dear," he said. "I see you have found my final secret. You have always been far too clever for your own good. Though, I regret how it was revealed to you. This is not the way I had planned for it to be shared."

"The seneschal!" Robin gasped, gesturing wildly with the knife.

"He is of no threat to me," Velph said casually, taking another step forward before casting a narrow-eyed glare over his shoulder. "Though he himself is in a great deal of trouble for failing to lock the throne room door, as instructed."

"I—I don't understand. Velph?" Robin asked, lowering the knife. "What are you . . . ? I don't . . . Eloy . . . your brother, he's . . . is he already dead?"

"Indeed," Velph said, and Robin wished that she could understand what she was seeing in his face. She wanted to run to him, to hug him and find her own comfort inside his embrace, but something held her back. Her instincts screamed at her, her mind spun, and her heart cried, and then, with a sharpness of clarity that pierced her like an arrow, the pieces clicked into place.

"You . . . you can't . . ." Robin protested, but it was automatic, and a stupid thing to say in the face of her entire world collapsing so perfectly. Like someone had neatly swept in and poked the exact wrong card in the foundation of her card-house world, and the entire thing had just slumped to the table with a papery sigh of defeat. "If he's . . . then you . . . then you're . . ." She looked up at him, lost in the shadows of the dais, and couldn't bring herself to say the words, to make it real.

He said it for her: "Yes. I am already the king."

CHAPTER TWENTY-FOUR

For the second time in as many days, Robin felt keenly her own stupid, willful naivety. Rosa had been right; Wolf, Coyote, Velph, Elias—whoever he was, Robin didn't know this man in front of her at all.

Confusion oscillated with hurt, cries of, *How could he?* mixed with, *It's not true!* and *I love him—oh gods, I love him, oh gods, I married him,* and *The enemy? No, he can't be, he can't have kept this secret from me, not me, not all this time, but he's been the king, and he set the Night Watch on me, oh gods, he has been the king this whole time, and he has not stopped the war when he could have, he could have,* drowning in the repeated, thumping refrain of *please, I love him, I love him, I love him.*

But he was the enemy.

And had clearly been the enemy for months. And she had refused to see it. She had just trusted that he was on their side, like a naive little idiot. Because, no matter their plans to install him upon the throne, no matter the promises and the romance, the declarations of love and the sweet, stolen kisses, the truth of the matter was that he'd lied.

Again.

The body in that box had been there for far longer than they had been within these palace walls. As much as her heart still wished to give him the benefit of the doubt, to believe that he had simply done the grisly deed for her, the evidence was irrefutable.

"How long?" Robin asked, staring up at the unreadable, mockingly tender expression of her husband. Was he actually proud of the way he'd fooled her? "How long have you been king?"

"Come now, my dear," he said softly, sweetly, as if he hadn't just pulled her entire world out from under her like a trick rug. He stepped forward, reached out to cup her face, and Robin flinched back hard, stumbling back out of range. He paused, and hurt flashed through his eyes before it was replaced by that careful blankness she knew so well. "You are far too clever for a question such as that."

"Oh, Velph, no," Robin said, stomach sinking as denial flooded in. She sucked in more air, would not let herself tremble, would not let herself collapse. This isn't fair! Robin thought, tongue dry against the roof of her mouth. She swallowed hard, but she couldn't seem to get a godsdamned breath. "This wasn't how it was supposed to go," she hissed, and hated the way it sounded like air being squeezed from a zeppelin, hated the desperation of it. That she sounded like a spoiled child, instead of like a soldier of Saskwya.

Instead of like the Skylark.

"And how was it supposed to go, then?" Velph asked, soft and sweet.

"You godsdamned know," Robin snarled, suddenly and completely unable to hold on to the rage and the pain, the betrayal for even a second longer. "How could you lie like that? To me!"

Moving as though of its own volition, Robin's right hand reached out and snatched the pistol that was holstered at his side. The move was too fast and too uncalculated for him to have been able to predict it, and Robin had the hammer cocked, the sights aimed between his eyes, before he had even really registered it. He blinked at the business end of the gun, and then slowly, as if it was only just now sinking in that she was upset with him, how betrayed Robin felt, his placid mask melted into a glower.

"Come now," Velph hissed. The sound carried across the room with an eerie, hollow echo, and every hair Robin possessed shivered upright. It reminded her of the way his voice sounded when he wore that infernal helmet, of the stress and fear and hatefulness of those early days in the forest. "I had to. Do you not see?"

A hot, thorny spike of pain exploded to life around her heart. She clenched her jaw against the desire to scream, to weep, and focused on sucking in air through her nose—in, in, in. Focus. *Aim.*

She flexed her fingers around the butt of the pistol. "Did you ever actually love me?"

"Yes," he said quietly, voice low and ragged, emphatic. "Of course. From the moment you walked across that wing." He wasn't foolish enough to take a step toward her, but he spread his hands out to the sides, scarred palms where she could see them. Though the details were lost to the shadows that shrouded him, she knew what the gesture meant. Could see what he'd done for her—the burn marks, the gun calluses. The Marriage Line, what he'd vowed to do *with* her. "Robin, I had to. Would you have trusted me if you had known I was king? Would you have loved me?"

"Of course not!" Robin blurted. She knew from the way he drew himself up that he had drawn that *hated* cloak of false indifference and superiority around himself, but his voice, when he spoke, betrayed a depth of emotion he didn't normally allow free.

"There, you see?" he said miserably. "I am not proud of how I have behaved, what I have kept from you. It has eaten at me every moment of every day from the moment we were wed. I . . . I married you under false pretenses, and I cannot—"

"You what!" the seneschal yelped from the dais. "Sire!"

"Silence!" Velph roared back. "This is the one thing in

which I will not be ruled, Hortensin!"

There was a huff and a loud click, and lamplight flooded the room. Holding her free hand up to shade her night-blind eyes from the sudden glare, Robin came face to face with the second corpse she'd seen today. Or, at least, a man who looked as if he should be a corpse. The seneschal, standing still beside the throne, was gruesome. His face was like a half-melted wax figure, garish in the glow of the gas lamps he'd lit along the back of the dias, his sleeve pinned at the shoulder and clearly empty.

"Your Majesty—" the seneschal tried again, stepping toward them, and Robin swallowed a scream and scurried back, the pistol now trained on the specter before her.

She screamed out loud when a pair of arms encircled her unexpectedly, cutting the power to WINGS with familiar, sickening dexterity. And then they began to pluck at the wrist strap.

The fears she had thought laid to rest reared back to life with the ferocity of a wildfire in a windstorm. Was it not enough that he had torn out her heart with his lies? Did he really have to prove her worst nightmare to be true—that all of it, everything he had done, from the forest palace to the privacy of their attic bedroom, had been solely for the sake of taking WINGS for himself?

"No," she said, struggling against his hold. "Don't touch me. Let me go!"

"Hush, love," he said against her ear. "Do not be unreasonable. I do not seek to hurt you." His fingers curled along the barrel of the gun she still held pointed vaguely at the seneschal, twisting, twisting until her own finger made a popping sound and the pain forced her to drop the pistol into his waiting hand.

"I . . ." Robin breathed, sagging back into his embrace.

She was tired—gods, she was tired. She was sick of fighting, sick of being scared, sick of looking over her shoulder all the time. Sick of being hungry, and cold, and filled with hate.

The hollow in her chest had filled with something bright and hot, a realization. She could give up.

If she wanted to, right here, right now, she could just . . . *stop*.

Give up. Give in. Give him what he wanted. And get what she wanted in return. She could have him, and it would be so, so easy. Because despite everything, his touch still made her skin rise in goose bumps, his scent filled her with the yearning to bury her face in his neck, to let him fold her into his embrace and stay there. The sound of his voice, like a purring cat, still lulled her, still called to the fire in her blood the way no one else's ever had.

She *wanted* it, all of it, everything he was saying with his words and his fingers as they curled between hers, the warmth of his chest through his jacket, the prickle of his hair along the shell of her ear, the soft puff of breath against her skin. She wanted the promises, the futures they could have together. She wanted all the little moments that would add up to a lifetime of loving and being loved.

She'd spent the last two days arguing with people about morals and ethics, about war-time crime. She'd spent the last ten years of her life fighting this fight, and she was done. She wanted to stop.

And she could.

Right now.

Robin dropped her knife and swiped at her face. She was not crying. She was not.

Only, she couldn't seem to get her gaze to stop swimming, to get her breathing under control. Her cheeks burned, and she ignored the fact that they were also wet, that they stung with salt and anger and a sorrow so deep that Robin had never, ever felt anything so gut-wrenchingly awful. Had never felt so hopeless, so helpless, so useless.

"I waited six years for you, Robin Arianhod," Velph said in that gravelly, intimate growl she had always loved. "I waited six years for Saskwya to give me the mid-flight who could repair the pack. Who could set me *free*."

"If that's all you wanted, then why did you marry me?" Robin sobbed, but even to her own ears, the words, the accusation, sounded low and tired. Weary in a way that all her many arguments with her parents about her safety never had.

Gods, they'd been right, though. She should have quit the Air Patrol the moment she'd finished her apprentice-ship.

"Because I fell in love," Velph said simply. Gently. Honestly. He turned her around to face him, cupping his hands behind her neck, fingers threading through her hair, gentle and affectionate. His thumbs brushed her cheeks dry. "Because you never feared me. Because you met me face to face. Because you were strong, and clever behind that yoke, more so with a wrench in your hand. Because you believe in the kindness of people, and that the hate our countries hold for one another can be quenched with the right leader. Because you are good. Because you pitied me when I deserved none, when I had let myself be controlled. Because . . ."

"Be-because?" Robin choked out.

Velph rested his forehead against hers and smiled—an attempt at levity and a desperate plea for forgiveness: "Because you kicked my aeroship."

Robin closed her eyes, and a single sob clawed its way out of her throat, low, like the sound of a wounded ani-mal. "I . . . I can't. The man I love—Velph isn't real."

"Your Majesty," the seneschal said warningly, but Velph waved the man off. He didn't move, gaze locked on hers.

"Velph . . ." he said gently, sadly. "The name and the life are a construct, yes. But the man, I am here, Skylark. Robin. Wife. This is me. I am still the man with whom you have shared so much. Is this not what you wanted, my dear? You said you would have me be king. Well, a king I am."

"Deh," the seneschal said forcefully, and Velph snarled and pulled away, scowling over at the man. He was careful, she noticed, to keep one hand curled with gentle firmness around her wrist.

"*What*, Hortensin?" he snapped.

The seneschal's eyes narrowed, and though he swept a little bow of apology, it was mocking and furious. What followed was a volley of Klonnish too quick for Robin's overtaxed mind to follow.

They were arguing, shouts building, anger flung at one another in harsh, guttural Klonnish, and Robin wondered vaguely at the seneschal's gall, to screech at his king like this.

The king.

Fool, Robin cursed herself, all the scattered bits of memory that were now lit with new and brilliant clarity replaying in her mind. The clues had all been there. Velph had tried, several times, to confess something to her, and she had been too stupid, too stubborn to let him. She had assumed, when his identity was at last revealed, that that had been the secret with which he'd been burdened, but now, she understood. He'd been trying to tell her this. But why, she wondered, had he played along? Why had he toed his brother's line?

Why in the hells hadn't the war ended, if he'd been king?

If he really loved her, as he said he did, then he knew how badly she wanted that. And he'd had the power to do it this whole time, and he hadn't, and it didn't make sense.

The shouting abruptly stopped, and Robin realized

that Velph had gone ash-pale.

"Do not forget our other guests, Your Majesty," the seneschal said, in clipped and accented Saskwyan, drawing Robin's attention from the quagmire of her thoughts. His eyes were on her, she realized, and a smug smile lay curled into the good corner of his mouth. He'd wanted to make sure she heard, then.

"What have you done?" Velph snarled at his subordinate. "I gave express instructions—"

"And they have been followed, Sire," the seneschal sneered. "To the letter."

"Velph!" Robin gasped, tugging back on her arm, trying to free herself from his grip. "What's happened to Rosa and Thorne?"

He pulled harder, pulled her to him as he leaned in, lips brushing close to her ear in that way that had always made her shiver.

"Trust me," he growled. Then, to the seneschal, he said, "Bring them in. And turn up *all* the lamps, would you? I grow tired of standing in darkness." He flicked an imperious hand at the seneschal, who ground his teeth, gave a somber, tight bow, and retreated.

Using the grip he still had on Robin's wrist, Velph pulled her toward the dais as more lamps flared to life, controlled, she supposed, from somewhere outside the throne room. Robin stumbled up the stairs, ungainly and awkward compared to Velph's confident strides, and resisted only when he dragged her over to the throne. The carvings were visible now—wolves, just like her hairpin.

It was his mother's, she remembered suddenly, and Robin's stomach curdled. He'd told her who he was ages ago; only, she hadn't realized what it meant. *Godsdamned Klonn,* and *their ridiculous, stupid hairpins.*

Velph sat, looking every bit the regal noble, and patted the seat beside him. "Come, take off WINGS and sit with me. Let us hold our first audience as king and queen," he said softly, and Robin startled, that word slamming into her like a baton between the eyes

"What? No! *Queen?* I'm not . . . I can't . . . *no*," She struggled against his hold, but he refused to let go, his features pulling down into a scowl.

"Foolish girl, what did you think would happen when your husband became king?" he said, fingers tightening on her sleeve. "Of course you—"

"No," she said again, firm. "I . . . it's not my place."

"You are my wife," he growled. "Your place is by my side."

"Don't you dare," she snarled back. "And let *go*, you rudding coal-bag." Robin tore her wrist free and rubbed at the reddened skin, glaring at him from the safety of a few good steps back. "I am not a pet, or a thing you can own. I am a person. I am a Sealie, and I am proud to be a Sealie, and you can't take that away from me!"

"Take that away from you?" Velph repeated, startled. "Robin, why would I want to—?"

"I don't want this," she said. Hurt, sudden and raw, flashed across Velph's face, and he pushed slowly to his feet, anger ticking the muscle in his jaw as he stared at her. "I don't want anything to do with any of this."

"And you think I do?" he shot back. He gestured vaguely at the room around them. "I have never wanted what Eloy had. My brother was a vain, foolish man who preferred that history record King Eloy as extremely handsome, rather than as extremely just. But *this* is what I was given. And I must do with it what I can."

"How did he die?" Robin asked, and she couldn't seem to get her voice above a strained whisper. "Did you—?"

"No!" Velph cut her off, genuine shock widening his eyes. "Robin, how could you—?"

"We were planning to assassinate him. Don't pretend like you didn't already agree to kill him," Robin said, holding up a finger to forestall his offense. She suddenly wished she hadn't let go of her knife.

"It was an illness of the heart," Velph protested. "The same as my father. The sudden onset of the body wasting, and the pooling of blood, and then he was just gone."

"When?" Robin asked.

"After the explosion," Velph said, and he seemed in earnest, everything about his body language screaming that he believed what he was saying, but he was a liar, and he had lied to her already for *months*. "Hortensin, my seneschal, was brought back here for his recovery, and when I broke in to steal medicines for myself, he caught me and—"

"*Your* seneschal," Robin interrupted. "I thought he was an agent of the king."

"And now I am the king," Velph said, as if he didn't believe her to be very bright in that exact moment.

"Wait, wait," Robin said. "Something isn't adding up. He was your jailer, and now he's what, just obedient to you? What was that shouting match just now, then?"

"He serves the crown," Velph said, dismissive, impatient. "And I wear that crown." He grabbed her shoulders, fingers digging in, desperation crawling into his eyes. "Why this preoccupation with insignificant details? Why do you defy me, Robin? Am I not offering you everything you have ever asked of me?"

"I never asked to be a queen," Robin protested, horrified.

"You asked *me* to be a king!" Velph shouted back. "What else is a king's wife?"

"I didn't—I didn't think that you'd . . . it didn't *occur* to me!" Robin spluttered, ashamed to realize that she had been so keen on using her husband's title to end the war that she hadn't realized it would also mean she'd be saddled with a title, too.

Velph let her go roughly, face contorted with raw, naked rage as he turned from her. His long fingers clawed at his hair, tugging spikes into its messy length. "Foolish, stubborn, impetuous woman," he snarled, turning back around. "How can someone as clever as you be so rudding stupid? What did you think would happen, then, when your scheme was done and I took the place of my brother?"

Sobs crawled up the back of Robin's throat, but she swallowed them down, squinching her eyes for a moment to keep it all in, to keep it together. She took a breath and ignored how it shook when she pressed it out through her mouth.

Across from her, Velph huffed a bitter laugh. Robin licked her lips, screwing up her gall, and said the thing she didn't want to, the thing she truly feared. "I didn't think you would want me. You'd be king, there'd be princesses, you'd have your pick—and I'd go home."

He stilled. For a moment, he was utterly still, like statuary, like a god had struck him with an invisible hand, turning his bones and blood to stone. And then, with a great heaving, sucking breath, tears welled in his eyes as he stared at her.

Suddenly, the space between them felt like a chasm they'd never be able to cross.

"You thought—*you* thought that *I* . . ." His voice crackled, and he took another heaving breath. "If you regret our marriage, Robin, there are other ways to have it annulled than to abandon me to a throne I never wanted! There are far less cruel ways to leave me behind!"

His words were sharp, but his posture was curled in on itself—he hugged his elbows, arms over his heart, head turned to the side as he fought for control. To pull that mask she so hated back into place.

"Leave you . . . abandon . . ." she stuttered, guilt mixing with confusion and hurt and anger. "I can't abandon you to something you clearly wanted. You say you don't, but I'm not as dumb as you think. Your brother's been dead for a while, Velph. Don't tell me you didn't want to be king, when you . . ." *Just say it, you coward*, Robin snarled at herself. "When you obviously murdered him *long* before you came to find me in the city. Murdered him and hid it from everyone."

"I did not!" he snarled. "Hortensin said he had been ailing for weeks, that it was good that I had survived, that it would be best if I stepped in without fanfare, for the war effort. That it would keep the troops from being demoralized, and Auden from taking advantage—"

"There's his name again!" Robin said. "If you're the king, why are you taking orders from your *secretary*?"

He looked up at her, lost, and reached out a hand. "Robin. My dear. I had . . . I had no guidance. I never expected to take the . . . I never trained for the throne, and I had only him to show me. . . and you didn't want me, I thought. You didn't come back for me."

"Velph, I was convinced that you were *dead*," Robin pleaded, fighting between wanting to wrap him up in her arms, to protect him from the world, from the terrible, terrible truth that she was starting to understand, and staying as far out of grabbing range as possible. "Why would I—?"

He turned from her, wiping subtly at his cheeks with the back of his hand, and sank wearily down onto the throne, leaning forward with his elbows on his knees, head low. "After you left me to burn in that forest"—Robin flinched, but didn't respond. He was being purposefully hurtful, lashing out at her for what she'd said—"after I had recovered enough to travel, I returned here, thinking I might beg my way into a pardon for my absence, that I might earn back some familial collateral to spend on helping you, on finding you. Only, I arrived to find Eloy dying and only Hortensin aware of the full depth of my attempted treachery. When he vowed allegiance and silence, so long as I accepted the crown and kept him on as seneschal, to take his advice, I . . ."

Velph looked up at her. His gaze pleaded with her to understand, to forgive him, and Robin was struck with the reminder, again, that they were both so *young*. Herself just eighteen, her husband twenty.

Children, really, in the middle of a war started by his grandfather and her king. Scared, biddable, following orders. Trained from a young age—eleven, for the gods' sakes—to do what they were told, to listen to the adults, to fight, and hate, and shoot, and for what?

"I didn't know what to do," Velph said softly. "He was so sure. Hide the body, empty the prison, keep the palace running as if . . . I was back and forth, all the time, as soon as I was well enough for Rosa to trust me. I did . . . I-I—" He broke off, eyes going wide with some sort of inner revelation that Robin wasn't privy to, hands trembling where he covered his mouth.

"He was just . . . mysterious dying," Robin said, folding her arms over her chest. "And no one at court knew? You honestly expect me to believe that? That he just conveniently grew ill right when your seneschal knew you had survived after all? When he knew that he had leverage against you, could control you? You do hear how that sounds, right?" Robin threw up her hands. "And even if I did decide to believe you, why hide the illness? Why this farce? Why play dress up in a freedom fighter's clothes? What was it all for? To stay close to WINGS?"

Velph smiled, a little shamefaced curl of the lip. "To stay close to you, Robin," he said. "WINGS was a bonus."

"Then why not *tell me*?" Robin screeched, tired of the back and forth, the circling without ever firing a volley, the midair dance that never *began*, never *concluded*.

"Because I was scared," he said softly, eyes downcast, shame curled into the lines of his body. "I found myself with a crown I never wanted, and I . . . I am not proud of it, but I balked. I ran. And then I found you, and I knew that, if I was ever to have a chance to win you on my own merits, you could never know. But then you concocted this ridiculous scheme to assassinate, well, me, and now . . ." He made a sad little hiccuping sound. "Here we are."

Robin took a deep breath, stalling to let her mind catch up with all these revelations. Her brain felt like she'd been doing barrel rolls in a glider without a safety harness.

"And now?" Robin asked, trying to buy time. "What happens now?" She'd wanted to sound confident, angry, but it came out small, and hurt, because she felt so . . . so used. So worthless, and tiny, and so godsdamned stupid she could just scream, except she couldn't seem to get her lungs to expand for it. She could exhale, she could talk, she could beg, but she couldn't breathe.

He had torn out her ability to exist along with her heart. He had taken his logic, and his explanations, and had spun them into a web of guilt that tangled around her more than any web of lies he'd ever spun. Everything he'd said made sense, tracked against the person she knew him to be, but it didn't absolve him of the betrayal, of the obliteration of her trust. Her heart begged her to believe him, to set aside her doubts and her fear and have faith. But could she?

He's right. This is what I wanted. I could have exactly what I want. I could have Velph. And I could have Elias. I could be queen. The granite walls of her resolve began to shiver and rumble, the mortar of her defiance flaking away. A husband who loves me, the power to end the war, he's promised that . . . but at what cost? I could have everything, but at the cost of everything that makes me Sealie. Is that a price I'm willing to pay?

Velph touched his chest, as if to prove that it was still where it should be, and Robin resisted the inane urge to touch her own, to see if the gaping hole she felt there was actually gushing blood.

With a single, eloquent shrug, he whispered: "Now, I

will do as you have asked. For love of you, my wife, I will end the war."

CHAPTER
TWENTY-FIVE

Before Robin could answer, the wide double doors on the far side of the room banged open, and an outraged scream filled the hall outside. It was accompanied by the sound of heels trying to dig into carpets, the grapple of leather gloves on cloth and skin, the grunts of people being made to go where they didn't want to.

"Your goggles," Velph hissed as he turned to face the door, and Robin had just enough time to push them down over her eyes, preserving her identity.

The seneschal appeared first, followed by a contingent of guards in impeccable cobalt-blue uniforms. Rosa and Thorne were among them, marched into the room by a pair of burly guards, pistols to the backs of their heads. Rosa was disheveled, her usually impeccable hair in disarray, making it clear who had been screaming and resisting out in the hall just moments before.

Robin's stomach swooped, and then dropped, thrilled to see her friends alive and well, but suddenly very aware of the peril they were all in—Velph included. Robin had the inane urge to grab for his hand, squeeze his fingers, ground herself in his touch the way she had before. Maybe even tug him down the stairs, out the door, and be gone and away, away, away.

When the group reached the dais, the guards forced Rosa and Thorne to their knees before the throne. The fine wine-red dress Rosa had been wearing was crushed, the sleeves ripped where she had obviously struggled to get away, her bustle askew. Robin tried, subtly, to see if the tassels still dangled out the back, if Rosa was still armed with her wicked fans, but she couldn't tell. Thorne had a bruise forming on his face in the shape of a fist, his own knuckles scraped and bleeding. One dripped blood sluggishly onto the marble floors, proving that he had at least given as good as he got. His fine embroidered jacket was missing, and he was in just his waistcoat and shirtsleeves—they were rolled up, though, which made Robin think he'd shed the jacket himself in order to have a better range of movement. The holster that had hid a gun at the dip of his waist was missing, however. Thorne grinned up at Robin, his teeth bloody, and Robin tensed, nodding once, slowly.

They weren't beaten yet.

Robin flicked her eyes to where her knife lay at the bottom of the dais, and Thorne's eyelids flickered in response. He'd seen it.

"For the love of the *Arts*!" Rosa gasped, glaring back at the man who'd pushed her. "What is the meaning of . . . ?" She trailed off as she turned her gaze to the man sitting on the throne. Elias, King of the Klonn Empire, had taken a slow and deliberate seat, head high and shoulders down. But Robin saw what Rosa had clocked in that moment, the things that only friends and intimates would notice—he looked wrecked. The rims of his eyes and the sides of his nostrils were swollen and red, his hair a spiky tangle from where he'd pulled at it, the skin of his cheeks tight and pale, tear tracks still drying.

He looked broken, and scared, and used, and like he was only just realizing it. Just as Robin was.

Robin, unsure what was about to happen, but having decided that holding the higher ground was always the best option, took three deliberate steps back toward the throne.

"Skylark," someone gasped from the back of the crowd, and Robin lifted her own chin, making the amber lenses of her goggles flash. With deliberate slowness, Robin set her palm on Velph's wrist, where it rested on the arm of the chair. A clear show of allegiance.

The Skylark, for right now, was the king's to command. And until they had found a way to settle this whole mess and call the ceasefire, as he'd promised, the king would be the Skylark's to protect. He was *Robin's*, and she'd be damned if she was going to let anything happen to him, or their friends. Let the rudding guards interpret that as they liked.

"Your Majesty?" asked the seneschal, stepping forward in concern. Velph waved him off, pushing wearily to his feet. Robin stepped aside as he came forward, stopping at the edge of the platform, but hovered close to his shoulder.

"Madam Rosa," Velph said gravely, meeting Rosa's gaze. "It is done."

Rosa pressed her lips together in a tight line. Beside her, Thorne bowed his head and then intoned, low, and in precise Klonnish that Robin was just barely able to understand: "The king is dead. Long live the king."

Robin winced, trying hard to keep her grimace to herself. It wasn't, she supposed, a complete lie, but it wasn't exactly the truth, either.

Around them, the guards echoed him, cautious and confused, throwing looks at one another, hands going to pistols but not drawing them, shifting and hissing under their breath. So even they hadn't known what Velph and his seneschal had been hiding.

The man in question, standing now just to the side of Rosa, grimacing and grinding his teeth, bowed to Velph, his one remaining fist clenched hard.

He's angry, Robin thought, shuddering. *He knows something's changed. That he's not in control anymore. This is dangerous. Watch him.*

For a moment, no one spoke, the air heavy with

uncertainty. When they'd left the zentapi earlier that night, Robin had experienced a wild fear that she might never see her friends again—not alive, at least. That Velph and Thorne's ruse to get the king away from the body of his court and guard would be unsuccessful, that Robin would come upon them with Velph, and Rosa, and Thorne's lifeless bodies at his feet. Seeing Rosa and Thorne on their knees brought that fear galloping back, choking her breath in her throat.

The seneschal said something meaningful in Klonnish that Robin couldn't parse, and a frisson of surprise crested among the guards and lapped around the room. Velph drew himself up, his misery making way for affront, and he snapped his eyes over to Rosa and Thorne.

No, Robin thought, feeling the situation starting to slip away, the mood of the room becoming frazzled and fractious. *What did he say? What's happening?* Several of the guards drew their weapons, but thus far, no one had yet aimed them at anyone.

Velph wouldn't kill them, would he? No. Despite everything, she knew him well enough to be certain of that—

Robin realized, though, just a fraction of a second too late, that while Velph was now indeed king, he was not the one the guards obeyed. He was not the one in control.

She snapped her eyes to the seneschal, stepped around Velph, and reached for the control box to deploy the blades, to use them as a shield, to get between him and a room full of high nerves and twitching trigger fingers.

"Skylark, what are you—?"

"*Ina!*" the seneschal snarled, hate burning behind his eyes and a smug smile curled grotesquely against his ruined face. *Now.*

The guards surged forward, pushing past Rosa and Thorne to rush up the stairs of the dais. Velph cried out, clearly surprised, but Robin didn't have time to focus on that.

Thorne dove for the knife, getting his hands around the hilt, and tossed it to her. Robin snatched it out of the air, pushed Velph back against the throne where no one could sneak up on them, and slashed at the first guard who came at her. He had his arms out to grab, to grapple, and Robin arced the blade up under his elbow, severing tendon and spraying blood. The guard cried out and collapsed to the side, taking two of his comrades down with him as he tumbled down the steps. In the gap of bodies their fall left, Robin caught sight of Thorne and Rosa, standing back-to-back, fans and fists brandished, holding off a second contingent of guards who were clearly under orders to capture, not kill.

More hands came at her, and Velph ducked to the side, shouting orders that were being ignored, letting his own fists fly when words weren't enough. He wrenched a sword off one of the guards who wore more gold braid than the others, and though it was too bejeweled to be anything but ceremonial, the metal cracking against wrists and skulls was painful enough to drive his attackers back.

A hand closed on her scarf, threatening to pull it tight and throttle her, but Robin sliced away the fabric, revealing her hair in it's messy, pin-held knot. Several of the guards blurted something at the sight of the pin, hesitating just long enough for Robin to smash her boot into their knees and ankles, forcing them down, and away. One unexpectedly fell toward her, mouth agape in surprise, and Robin stumbled back, fetching up against the throne. She ducked as hands reached for her, spinning around the ornate back of the throne, scrabbling to get away.

Velph was on the far side of another wave of guards, and Robin's heart seized as she realized she'd let them separate her from her husband.

"Velph!" she shouted, pushing her way through,

trying to get back to him. He called something back, lips moving, but she couldn't hear him. Confused calls between the guards created a ringing cacophony of painfully sharp white noise, but beneath it all, the seneschal laughed—a low, mean sound that chilled Robin to her core.

A hand landed on the back of her neck, fingers curling into her collar, and Robin swung around, aimed a punch at the guard's face. He blocked, and Robin swung with her other fist, hoping to catch him off guard with the knife, but he had recovered too quickly, using the momentum of his block to turn about and come back up under her arm. He snatched her hand and yanked her forward; she crashed into his chest. He grabbed a handful of her hair and pulled her sideways, keeping her feet splayed awkwardly and off balance, her arm twisted up behind her. Pain radiated up her shoulder, and Robin cried out, fingers spasming, making her drop the knife.

"Skylark!" Rosa screeched in warning.

Robin stomped on the guard's foot, but the man held her firm as someone stooped down in front of her to scoop up her knife.

Robin had been hated in many ways, by many people, her entire life. Benne pedestrians who'd sneered at her for daring to take up space on the streets and in the shops when she was a child; fellow apprentices envious of her natural skill or hard-earned promotions; captains who'd despised sharing their glory with a dirty tick; the Klonn she'd shot down in her robin-nosed glider; the *zentapi* masters and madams who couldn't bring her to heel.

But no one had ever looked at her with such undisguised *loathing* as the seneschal did, Robin's knife clasped in his remaining hand as he straightened. He skimmed the tip of the wickedly sharp blade up her front, scoring her jacket lining and pinging the metal off of each brass button. Robin bit her tongue, determined not to cry out, not to give him the *satisfaction* of hearing her blubber and plead, if—*when* he plunged her own knife into her. The muscles of her stomach quivered and contracted, followed by those in her chest, as if she could prevent the blade from slipping into the soft flesh of her belly or between her ribs if she could only clench hard enough.

She struggled against the excruciating hold of the guard, but he held her too firmly. She was trapped. The upward skim of the blade stopped, finally, directly over her heart. The terrible mess of the seneschal's face wrinkled and heaved, like the ground cracking apart during an earthquake, more emotion on his face than Robin had ever seen. He was *gleeful.*

Rosa screamed again, pinned now under two guards with their knees on her back, struggling to keep her eyes on Robin even as they pushed her face-first into the floor, the grip on her wrists cruel. Thorne was snarling, writhing against the hands that held him back, kept him on his knees, two guards on each arm, and another with a foot grinding down against his ankle.

And Velph. Velph was trapped behind a wall of cobalt, weaponless and scrabbling, grabbing and shoving at guards who didn't fight back, whose only job was to keep them apart. Robin met his desperate eyes over their heads, could see him mouthing "no, no, no" over and over again—"*Nema, nema, nema!*"

Robin took a deep breath, clenched her jaw, thought *I love you, I love you, I'm sorry, I'm so sorry, I screwed up, I got it wrong, I'm sorry, I love you* as hard as she could, and waited. Velph's desperate denials gained voice, became a hiss, a wail, and then, suddenly, a roar.

"You will not!" he commanded, his voice booming through the hall, clapping back at them from the marble, dancing in the shivering glass of the dome. "Enough!"

A rage unlike any Robin had ever seen in him before radiated from his features, from the lines of his body. The guards trying to block him froze, confused looks darting between them, suddenly unsure of their choice of who to follow. The seneschal straightened, a matching fury twisting his face, and the guard behind Robin shifted enough for feeling to flood back into her pinned arm, making it tingle agonizingly.

"Enough of this!" Velph thundered again, and the guards around him actually took a step back en masse, as if fearing he really was a wolf who would rake out and claw at them in his anger. "I am your king, not him. And you will obey me, or you will be shot for traitors!"

Another murmur swept the room, and the hold on Robin relaxed even further.

"Release them. All of them," Velph growled. It was the voice, the timbre that Robin liked best, but like this, it was authoritative and frightening. "Now."

"These people are traitors, Your Majesty," the seneschal said calmly, with equal gravitas, if not authority. "They broke into the palace with the express intent of taking your life. The penalty for such treason is death. They must be executed, *deh*."

"Not if I pardon them," Velph snarled.

The seneschal reacted as if scalded. "You cannot!"

"I am king—"

"*Ai*," the seneschal said, haughty disdain curling his lip. "Shame, that."

The guards standing between the two of them parted like a flock of startled birds, suddenly not wanting to be in the middle anymore. Velph stalked forward, closing the distance between him and the seneschal until he stood just off to Robin's right.

"*Insolent*," Velph growled, and the seneschal backed down, offering up a courtly, apologetic bow of submission that fooled no one. All the same, the guards followed suit, letting go of their respective prisoners. Thorne rushed forward, pulling Rosa up off the floor and into a desperate embrace.

Robin shook out her arms, fisting her hands to try to speed up the process of getting feeling back, bouncing on her toes and readjusting the lay of WINGS against her back. The seneschal was up to something, and she was going to be ready to stop him.

When the seneschal straightened, he said: "Apologies, Majesty. Insolent, ai. But not incorrect. The Skylark is a threat, a symbol of the rebellion. You cannot simply let her go."

"The Skylark is my wife," Velph said simply.

Gasps of shock and angry whispers filled the hall. Robin didn't know all the words, but she'd bet even money that none of them were flattering. The beginnings of betrayal started to fill the guards' gazes, and Robin felt a sad moment of vindication.

This is exactly what she'd been trying to tell Velph. She didn't belong here. She wasn't a queen. She was a tarnished pot of honey on a lace doily, dented and broken, out of place among the posh superiority of the Klonn, just as she'd been among the Benne. She could see this to its end, and she would, but she couldn't *stay*.

"Careful, my lord," the seneschal warned. He followed it up with a string of Klonnish that Robin couldn't parse, but ended it with a sneered, "*Ai, deh*," and a mocking tilt of his head.

"You dare use such vile language to speak of your queen—" Thorne shouted, starting forward, and Rosa, no less furious, but at least more sensible about whatever insult had been leveled against Robin, grabbed at his sleeve to pull him back.

"So what?" Robin challenged, when no one else moved to do or say anything. Her question crackled in the air. "So *what* if we're married? Who cares? How does that affect you, or your quality of life, or the things that keep your own people happy and prosperous? What business is it of yours if we're married? Who rudding *cares*?"

"I care . . ." the seneschal snarled, eyes dropping to Velph's hands, "when it corrupts the crown."

"Sod off, you rudding frozen coal-bag," Robin hissed.

"Sealie filth," he snarled back, hatred flashing in his eyes. More murmurs swept through the guards, and the uneasy tension grew thicker.

Velph balled his fists, but wisely didn't step into the insult. "She is your queen, Hortensin—"

The seneschal gave a full-body shudder, as if the very idea of Robin wearing any sort of crown filled him with such revulsion that he couldn't keep still. "She will never be queen! You cannot mean to marry—"

"He already did," Rosa said suddenly, stepping forward to press a folded-up, cream-colored paper into the seneschal's chest. The man stumbled back a step from the force, surprise leaving him open-mouthed and gawping like a fish. Everyone waited, the room itself seeming to hold its breath in anticipation, as the seneschal struggled to unfold the marriage certificate one-handed, still stubbornly clutching the knife, and read its contents. Velph drew himself up, looking smug, satisfied—proud, even. Despite her misgivings and turbulent emotions, Robin couldn't help but feel flattered, and the heat of a blush rose in her cheeks.

"You . . . signed it with your real name," the seneschal said finally, and it sounded like he was speaking through gravel, like the truth of it was clinging to his molars, and refused to be dislodged by his tongue.

Velph raised an eyebrow and leveled a genuinely confused look at the man, arms crossed loosely over his chest. "Why would I not?"

"Then . . . you are serious," he choked. "You *mean* this."

"I do. Did you have cause to doubt?"

Robin felt her face go redder, this time with embarrassment. Was it so hard to think that someone like Velph might love someone like her? Or was it just that she was Sealie, a foreigner and second-class to even the working Klonn. "I . . . I thought maybe it was a ploy, or . . . or that you . . ."

"I did not do this for a ruse," Velph said.

"Married!" the seneschal howled, eyes shining and breath wheezing from his nose as he tore his eyes away from the certificate, whirling to glare fire at Robin. "To that headstrong, vulgar *bitch*. Your Majesty, no. You cannot. She will destroy us all, destroy Klonn, tarnish the glory of your family name—bring vile filth into the royal bed. You cannot, you *cannot*—"

"She will save us all," Velph said firmly. "As she saved me."

"Stop talking about me like I'm not even here," Robin snapped, scowling.

The seneschal clutched at this head, crumpling the certificate. "You have let poison in through your ears, and it has traveled your veins, curdled your mind. You are not fit to be king. Your brother would be so disappointed."

"My brother was a fool," Velph snarled, and the seneschal reeled back as if struck, blanching under his scars. "And my father before him for starting this rudding war to begin with!"

"*Nema!*" the seneschal gasped, melted face tight with shock. The marriage certificate slipped from his fingers to flutter forgotten to the floor. Rage twisted his features, and the guards nearest to him drew their pistols. They hesitated, though, unsure of just who they were meant to support. For the first time, real fear leapt up in Robin's throat. The situation was rapidly getting out of hand, the tension ratcheting higher and higher, like a bomb ticking ever closer to detonation.

"Your brother was more a king than you will ever be!" the seneschal moaned, staggering to the side as if about to swoon. "He understood! He was doing civilization a favor, wiping ridiculous little beliefs off the face of the world!" More than one guard gave a small nod of agreement.

Everything Sealie in Robin bristled.

"The world would have been better for it," the seneschal pressed, a manic sort of gleam in his eye. "The Benne, the Sealie, they all would have been *saved*."

"Saved?" Robin choked, stepping forward, unable to hold her own ire in check. Velph held out his arm in warning, entreating her with a quick look over the seneschal's head that silently begged for her to stay back. "Is that what you think? That the war is meant to save us? Your people suffer, too! Soldiers at the front, pilots in the air—the sailors drowned, the orphans and widows starving in your slums—"

The seneschal gave a frustrated cry, tearing again at his hair, at the scars on his face. He dropped the knife in his distress, and it clattered under the soles of his boots.

"Klonn has no slums!" he corrected. Forcefully. With all the blind belief of a man who had likely been told so over and over again, and who had believed it wholeheartedly simply because he was told he should. "Good, law-abiding, natural Klonn citizens are taken care of by the government. If you see skivvying wretches in the streets, it is because they are thieves, illegal sneaks and terrorists, like you!"

"Just because I am Saskwyan and a vigilante does not make every person who suffers in your kingdom an outsider who—"

"Skylark!" Thorne barked in warning, at the same time Velph hissed, "My dear."

Robin snapped her mouth shut, jutting her chin out, angry at being silenced. The seneschal was clearly mad and unstable. Why weren't the guards stepping in? Was the prejudice and hatred so rampant, so deep-seated in the Klonn, that it overrode even their loyalty to the crown?

"We have no legitimate quarrel with the Saskwyans," Velph said, calm and measured. "We never have."

The seneschal gave an inarticulate cry of rage and spun, drawing a pistol from the nearest guard's holster. Robin was not surprised when he leveled it squarely at her head.

"*Nema!*" Velph yelped, but Robin simply moved her hands out to her sides, cautious and watching.

"You are a disgrace to the throne, Elias," the seneschal seethed, spittle flying from his lips. "I have been running this kingdom in your absence for months. And this is how you repay me for my loyalty? *Nema!* This will not be borne! If you will not do what needs to be done, then I will."

"Robin!" Velph cried, the same time Rosa and Thorne screamed, "Skylark!"

The shot rang out, loud in the cavernous room, and Robin exhaled.

CHAPTER TWENTY-SIX

Something solid but soft smashed into her, knocking Robin to the side. She hit the ground with her shoulder first, the weight of the thing—a body?—on her back keeping her from crunching into WINGS, her head smacking hard against the ground. Stars exploded behind her eyes, the world tilted, and then it all . . . *stopped.*

A harsh buzz filled Robin's ears, her brain, her veins. Because everything was *wrong,* absolutely, all at once, wrong. Screams echoed in the distance, drowned out by the buzzing sound, and Robin turned her head toward the noise. Chaos met her gaze, and she struggled to make sense of the blur. There was a spray of blood, a black fan tipped with knives, the flash of dark-skinned fists and cobalt uniforms, boots on the ground, but it was all wrong because it was all somehow in the *way.*

Distracting.

Superfluous and inconsequential.

In the way.

It pulled her away from the hand that she couldn't seem to reach.

The hand was pale-skinned, lying palm up on the marble of the dais, the strong pilot's fingers curled gently inward, like they were cupping something infinitely, *intimately* fragile. There was a single spot of red, glinting wetly in the light of the sconces that lit the room, ruby and enticing on the heel of the thumb. Raised scars were silver-white from where the skin had once been terribly burned, a constellation of adoration that she knew intimately.

The hand was close to her. So close. Right in front of her face.

All she had to do was reach out, and touch it.

And then everything would be okay. She knew it, in her soul, in her heart. If she could just touch the hand, if she could just make it move, if it would just *move, godsdammit*, everything would be okay. The world would stop being wrong.

But her arms were like heavy weights, and her lungs had stopped working. Black fuzzed at the edges of her vision, and her head throbbed. She wanted to close her eyes. She wanted to swallow. To scream. To reach. She couldn't do any of it, though. She was stuck. Trapped. Frozen.

And the hand wasn't moving.

The hand wasn't moving.

It wasn't until something—someone?—pushed the weight pinning her to the floor off of her side and yanked at the strap over her shoulder that Robin managed to suck in a breath.

And then she was being hauled to her feet, and the hand was getting further away.

"No!" she cried out, reaching for it, but the man, a great hulking mountain of a man beside her, he was strong. Robin would not be separated from that hand, though, or the pool of glittering red that was spreading slowly, so slowly across the marble to pool underneath it.

Robin didn't care. All she wanted was to make that hand move.

"By all the Arts, Skylark!" another voice called, and Robin remembered that this was Rosa. This was her friend. Her friend held at bay by guards who—no, that wasn't right, she'd seen the flash of the fans dancing in the air, twirling and twining like a glider and an aeroship. Like a bird and it's chosen mate amid the tree canopy above a glider crash. "Skylark! Snap out of it!"

Hands scrabbled at the straps, at the clasp at her waist, clumsy in their desperation, and no, no, that wouldn't do. She had been given this pack by . . . by *him* . . . it was a gift from a queen to him, and from him to her, and she would not let, she would not—she snapped her elbow up, jabbing her attacker square in the throat. He stumbled back with a gurgling cry, hands going to his neck, freeing her.

"Votch," he muttered, in a voice that Robin knew but that wasn't the one she wanted to hear. The one she needed to hear.

Robin took one step away. Two. The room went still. She blinked.

Before her was the throne, and behind her, the door swarmed with startled, horrified guards who must have come running when they heard the shot. To the left, the seneschal was backed against the wall, weaponless now, Rosa's deadly blades up against his throat. Thorne stood to her right, holding his throat and gurgling as he sucked in air, as if someone had punched him in the neck.

And there, on the ground, face up and . . . and legs sprawled was . . . *was . . .*

"No," Robin moaned, and felt her knees give way, numb as they hit the marble dais, splashing into the blood by his shoulder. "Don't . . . no . . . don't you *dare . . .*"

The wound was like nothing Robin had ever seen. The hole was tiny, but the flesh and cloth around it was burned, the powder scattered out like the points of a gruesome star. His chest was half-collapsed, blood soaking up through the cloth of his shirt in pinpricks that bloomed outward as she watched. She pushed her hand down on it, hard. He didn't wince, didn't jerk away. There was no movement. No growling curse. No up and down. No shaking away.

No . . . *no . . .*

His face was . . . he was . . . there were little constellations of ruby stars in his scruff, red stars in the nighttime of his hair. Mouth open, lips slack, cheeks losing color, eyes . . . beautiful, silver eyes . . . they were open and . . . empty.

"No," Robin moaned again, and a soldier stepped forward, approached the stairs of the dais to block her. Thorne moved to stand between Robin and the person, warding them off. She didn't care, went around, wouldn't be separated. She had let herself get separated in the heat of the fight, and she refused to do it again, to let some-one in on his flank, to lose the ability to . . . to lose him to . . .

She touched those lips. They didn't move. No breath fluttered from them. She leaned forward, kissed them like a maiden from a tale and whispered, "Wake up. Don't do this to me. Please. Don't make me do this again. You promised . . . you *promised* me you wouldn't, and I . . ." She pushed hard on the wound, but he didn't stir, didn't inhale, didn't respond. "Come on, you rudding coal-bag! You stupid, lying arsehole! Get up! Get up!"

"Skylark," Rosa said softly, pityingly, and no, no, absolutely not. There was nothing to pity her for, because he was going to blink, and smirk at her, and kiss her back, and tell her that of course he loved her, *my dear*—

Robin sucked in a stuttering breath. She kissed him again, harder, and he didn't—he *didn't*—

"You promised," Robin sobbed. She pressed her face against his neck, and wound her arms around his shoul-ders, lifting him into her lap. She threaded her fingers through his bloody hair and squeezed him close, and she'd lost her breath again, couldn't seem to get any air around the horrible, harsh sobs that made her whole body shudder, made her stomach heave and her throat burn. "Please, please, please—"

And then, in the midst of it all, the seneschal screamed: "Do not simply dally there! Kill the Skylark!

Kill her!"

"*You*," Robin snarled, glaring up at the man who had threatened them both, tormented them both. The man who had . . . had *killed*—

But then a guard shoved through the crowd, scattering the ones who had apparently decided to side with their king, rather than with the seneschal, determined to follow the order. Thorne tried to block him, but the guard got a hand on one of the straps for WINGS and tugged, and no, no, he was falling out of her arms, he was going to hit his head on the ground, and hadn't he been hurt enough, hadn't he been tortured—

Grief surged up, chill and weighted, and Robin realized as she was yanked away, as she scrambled to get her feet under her in the slick of his blood…

Velph was dead.

He couldn't be hurt. He couldn't wince, and smirk, and tease her. He couldn't kiss her fingers when she touched his lips, and call her "my dear." He would never kiss her again.

He was *dead.*

Robin screamed. Screamed like the thunder. Screamed like rage personified. screamed like a god of vengeance, like the wind of a hurricane and the hobgobs in the fairy tales who railed against unfairness and deceit. She screamed and whirled around, clocked the guard with a fist covered in Velph's blood. He fell back, stumbling and slipping, and Robin got her feet under her.

Undeterred, the seneschal used the distraction to lever himself free, shoving Rosa off and scrambling for the safety of the brace of palace guards who had defected, or who had only ever been loyal to him.

"Give me the pack," he demanded, his scarred features twisted, his mouth filled with blood, looking every bit the monster he was, cowering behind his traitors.

"You want it?" Robin snarled between clenched teeth,

scowling brows, and tight jaw. "Come and get it, you un-believable *bastard*."

Then she slammed her hand down on the ignition button on the control box. WINGS flared to life, and Robin shot into the air. She circled the dome once, twice, as the guards below turned against each other. Some fought to chase after her, to heed the seneschal's order, while others fought to prevent them. Infighting, just as Thorne had warned. Civil war on a small scale, just waiting to spill out into the streets, to become nationwide, until it swallowed Klonn whole in its destructive maw.

The window at the top of the dome was still open. She could escape. Fly out into the night like a shooting star, and keep going. Down to Frankin, like Velph had once suggested. Or back to Saskwya, anti-aircraft cannons be damned.

What did she care now if they shot her down? What did it matter?

There was nothing left for her in Klonn, nothing important—the war, the mission to end it, it was all meaningless. Her chest was hollow, her extremities numb, her head buzzing like a hive of livid bees.

There was nothing at all she cared about—

And then Rosa screamed.

I can't leave them here, Robin thought. *Not like this. I can't be that selfish. They've risked everything for me. They're here because of me. I can't. I have to go back, have to—*

But she didn't need to finish that plan, because the seneschal had Rosa by the hair, and was dragging her into the center of the throne room behind his guards. Thorne struggled to reach her, firmly the captive of several more. They stopped in the dead center of the room, the seneschal straddling Rosa's body as she yanked ineffectually at his wrist, her legs tangled in her skirts, her torso pulled at an awkward angle that left her no leverage to kick back with, to use that lithe elegance that Robin had seen her employ on the roof where they met.

"Get down here, little birdie, and do as I say," the seneschal bellowed, his voice ringing and rolling like a winter storm across the marble and glass. "Or the next bullet is for her!" He cocked the pistol and pressed it against Rosa's temple. Rosa went still.

Little birdie—that's what Mama used to call me, Robin thought, and then closed her eyes against the sudden spark of pain. Against a backdrop that was already full of so much loss, so much agonizing heartache, this last blow, the corruption of this small, tiny little part of her life, was so blazingly unfair that it threatened to make the numbing safety of the shock she was hiding in shatter.

She sucked in a sharp, stuttering, shuddering breath, and waited for her body to break apart, to rain down in irreparable shards. Maybe, if she was lucky, some particularly sharp piece—the jagged edge of her shattered heart, perhaps—would bury itself in the seneschal's hideous eye.

Rosa was watching her when Robin opened her eyes again, staring up at Robin with a grim, resigned look in her emerald eyes. Eyes that could so easily be dimmed, filled with a life that could so easily be extinguished. And this death would be Robin's fault, too.

"Fly, Skylark," was all she said. Robin didn't hear the words so much as saw them form against Rosa's painted lips, saw the permission, the sad acceptance of her fate light her friend's face.

"No," Robin said, and then again, firmer, "No."

Her mind raced, trying to find a way out of this, a way around this, but she didn't have a tactical mind like Velph, or even Wade. She had always been the brawn, never the brains. All she had was her fists, and the strength of her arms, her ability to sneak, and her sheer cussed stubbornness. The only thing she knew how to do was *fight*.

So fight she would.

Robin straightened, descending slowly from the ceiling, hovering just above the slick marble floor for a moment to see if she could taunt the seneschal into aiming the gun at her. He didn't waver, so she touched down and killed the thrust. WINGS purred and ticked as the casing cooled.

"Now, take it off," the seneschal demanded. "You have tainted it enough with your Sealie filth. The pack belongs to Klonn, to me, and I shall see it returned."

Robin just grinned at him and spread her arms in invitation. "I've already told you. You want WINGS? You have to come and get her."

The seneschal roared and swung the pistol up to aim at Robin, but she'd been expecting that and quickly dove to the side. WINGS was quick to flare back to life, and she skimmed the floor of the throne room, bowling into the guards surrounding Thorne and knocking them away. The seneschal's shot pinged off the back wall, ricocheting once into one of the swags of ice-blue fabric, where its trajectory ended.

The few guards who had sided with the seneschal tried firing on her, but Robin dodged them too, dropping quick to let the bullets sail up and smash through the glass panes of the dome, showering the people below with shards. She swept low again, smirking at the seneschal, daring him to shoot. He obliged, and this time, the bullet whizzed past Robin's leg to sink into the wooden doors on the far side of the room.

Thorne, free now, tackled the seneschal from behind, and the gun went skittering across the marble. They tumbled over Rosa, who leapt to her feet and pushed up her skirts, hooking them under her bustle and out of the way. One of the guards grabbed the pistol, but Rosa kicked it out of his hand, sending it flying. Robin wasn't fast enough to snatch it out of the air, and it landed with a coughing kick, discharging a bullet straight up at the sky.

The seneschal dove for it, but Thorne was between

them in a flash, knuckles flying at the man's face. The seneschal reeled back from the punch, blood trailing in a grisly arc from his nose. Rosa, on her feet and unencumbered, fans flashing, kept the remaining guards busy, joining the fray against the turncoats. Robin landed, skipping to a stop as she reached for the gun, and the seneschal lunged for her, grabbing hold of WINGS's straps. Robin twisted in his grip, smashing into his ribs with the pack. He let out a whuff and stumbled back, slamming into Thorne.

Robin got her hand around the butt of the pistol, but the seneschal was back, his one arm snaking around her neck from behind, fingers digging in. A childhood spent in the slums of Pyria had taught her how to fight dirty in ways the Air Patrol's combat training never had, and she snapped her elbow up at his face, aiming for his nose. He saw it coming and jerked his head to the side. Her elbow bashed into his cheek, and he yelped, pain slackening his grip. Thorne yanked at him, but he wasn't letting go.

"Give it to me! It is mine, you thieving bitch!" the seneschal screamed in her ear, and if she could just get to the damned gun, she could end this. "You wear the queen's hairpin?" the seneschal screamed above her, clearly having gotten his first good look at the back of her head. "How dare you flaunt it so, you brazen whore!"

Robin rocked forward, trying to rip away, but he got his hand in the back of her collar and tugged. Stars danced in her vision, and she gasped against the choke hold.

"Checkmate," he hissed directly into her ear.

Robin's heart lurched. *Chess, Velph, the afternoons in the forest palace, desperately pretending that they were not prisoners, that they could enjoy their leisure time—*

Robin shouldered him in the chest, driving the hard edge of the exhaust pipe against his thigh, the leading edge of the fuel canister under his chin. He winced and cursed under his breath, but only tightened his grip.

He managed to wrap his body around WINGS from the side, pressing down on her with all his superior height and weight, trying to drive her into the ground. He *laughed*, and it was an ugly, bitter sound.

Cold fury at her own inability to hit the target surged through Robin. She was a failure. Even at murder. She needed to end this, before the chaos and the infighting spread outside this room. Before Thorne's prediction of a Klonn torn apart by civil unrest and rebellion turned true. She'd wanted to end the war, not shift its direction.

"Shut up!" Robin snarled, casing the room, gasping for breath. She had no knife, no gun. Her friends were surrounded. She was out of options. She was losing.

If Velph were here, he'd know what to do, know exactly how to push and what strategy to take. He would have planned for this eventuality. There would have been other options. Other strategies. Other ways to move the pieces around the chessboard to get the checkmate.

But Velph was dead.

"Give it up, little birdie," the seneschal whispered obscenely in her ear, "or I will be forced to cut the pack off your corpse." A thin, vicious smile sliced his already gruesome face in half.

Rage flared, and Robin's lip curled back, teeth bared in a feral snarl. No, he didn't get to use that phrase. He didn't get to call her that, didn't get to take something that meant so much, and make it cruel and demeaning.

Think, Captain, think. You're good at this—the plan has changed. Taste the wind, find the updraft, calculate a new angle of approach.

"Surrender!" the seneschal bellowed. His fingers dug in hard around her larynx and Robin gasped.

A weapon, Skylark. You need a weapon, and all you have is WINGS . . . Realization struck, and Robin had the absurd urge to smack her own forehead at her stupidity.

Deliberately, calmly, she let go. She spared one small prayer to the gods of forgiveness for what she was about to do. She released the hand that was pulling at his wrist, laid it over the control box, waited until the seneschal had curled over her shoulder, yanking at her straps, until he was pressed tight against WINGS—and depressed the button that deployed the blades. They sprang upright like a switchblade, filling the air with that cyclical, clear note of music unique to the pack.

Against her, the seneschal gagged and jerked, con-vulsed once. And then he went terribly, terribly still.

CHAPTER
TWENTY-SEVEN

There were a few, small seconds of utter, dread quiet and stillness. Like the gods had stopped time, made the whole world freeze in place. All sound ceased. All air stopped moving. Robin's heart skipped a beat.

And then time resumed. The seneschal was dead weight, legs gone out from under him, and Robin yelped as the sudden change in direction hauled her around, and she toppled over to land hard on top of him, her stomach driven up against her ribs, breath wuffing out of her lungs. The seneschal's arm was still clamped around her shoulders.

"Let go, you rudding coal-bag!" she snarled. Her goggles had shifted. She couldn't see. But she heard the gasps that powdered the air.

"Skylark," Rosa shouted. "Be still! And you," she added, voice aimed in the direction of the scuffling sound of boots on marble. "The rest of you stay where you are. Do not touch her!"

"Rosa!" Robin called, flailing blindly. Her voice was unnaturally loud amid the horrified quiet. It crashed against the silence, echoed along the patchwork glass of the dome. "You rudding arse, let me go! Rosa! Are you okay? Is Thorne?"

"Hold still," Rosa said tightly. The clip of her heels as she pounded across the marble was sharp in Robin's ears, too harsh, threatening suddenly. Thorne's heavy boots echoed in counterpoint. Rosa knelt beside them, her bladed fan slicing through the hopelessly twisted straps of the harness, freeing Robin's arm from the control box. Her hands were shaking, and her face, the sliver that Robin could see of it, was pale, her lips thin.

The seneschal's grip tugged hard at the back of her head, mashing the padded nosepiece uncomfortably against her eyebrow, and she jerked her upper body away from his.

Air slapped against the sweat that had collected under Robin's eyes, and she blinked hard against the sudden brightness of the throne room before she managed to get her hands around the rims and hold the mask in place, preserving her secret and turning the world to amber again. The goggles were cracked, fragmenting her vision nauseatingly.

A sudden and inexplicable surge of fear rushed up Robin's throat, and she gulped down on the air. Turning her head slowly, Robin looked down over her shoulder. What was left of the seneschal's face stared back.

"Oh, gods!" she whispered, and felt foolish for doing so. Disrespectful, even. She sprang to her feet, stumbling back away from . . . from it. She bashed into Rosa, and her knees went out from under her, dumping her onto the floor. Anguish flooded every fiber of her being, washed the underside of her flesh. She felt nothing, and she felt everything. Every extremity, every nerve was awash with pricking numbness, cold and empty and, gods, she had—

Thorne grabbed her, hauled her backward, pressed her against his shirtfront to keep her eyes off of what was on the floor. But it was too late. It was already burned into her memory.

WINGS's uppermost blade had sliced clean through the seneschal's jaw, cleaving his head from chin to eyes. The second blade was embedded in his clavicle, and the third and smallest stuck out obscenely from his gut.

The seneschal was very, very dead.

Just like Velph.

Robin refused to look, refused to see again the lifeless stare in her husband's gaze, the unnatural ash to his skin. Instead, she turned her face into Thorne's chest and screamed.

"Skylark," Thorne whispered against her head, tender and filled with pity.

And then she was crying, face hot and wet and itching, and it was horrible, horrible. "It took him, Thorne! It took him, too! This war, this godsdamned war, it's taken everyone. Al, and Wade, and Mama and Papa, and . . . everything! My home, my family . . . my love!"

"So get your revenge," Rosa hissed, crowding in close. "End the war. Seize it, Skylark. Do it now! While you have the chance."

"I . . . I c-can't . . . I don't understand."

"Stand up!" Rosa tugged at Robin's shoulders, urgent, desperate. "Damn your gods, stand up, Skylark!"

"What are you——?" Robin said.

Rosa snatched Robin's left wrist and turned her hand to the guards crowded around the bottom of the dais, palm out, holding it aloft like a battle flag. Behind them, other people had begun to flood the throne room. Some wore the serviceable linen and cream-colored uniform of the serving staff, but some were in grand nightdresses and caps, robes and slippers—courtiers and nobles aroused from slumber. Apparently the palace hadn't been quite so empty of hangers-on as Velph had ordered. Likely all of these folk were loyal to the seneschal.

Were loyal to the seneschal. But no longer.

"There!" Rosa called to the people who were slowly hemming them in. "There, you see? The Skylark wed Elias! She wears the Nutvig family wolf." Rosa gestured to Robin's head, where the knot of her hair had come loose, but where the hairpin was still woven through a few frizzing locks. "And I hold their Certificate of Marriage."

Shock lined every pair of eyes, horror rounded every

mouth. A roar of objection crashed through the crowd, echoing in Robin's ears and smashing against her chest. Guards gestured and shouted at each other furiously. Rosa let go, fishing through a pocket in her skirts for a crumpled and blood-stained, cream-colored piece of paper.

"When did you . . . ?" Robin asked, but her sluggish mind couldn't form the words. The last time she'd seen the marriage certificate, it had been falling from the seneschal's hand, left and forgotten, trampled beneath the chaos. Robin wondered how, and when, and *why* Rosa had had the presence of mind to save it.

Velph was gone. What was the point of keeping it? It was just a stupid piece of paper. It didn't *matter* . . . it didn't matter. Robin was a widow now.

Her whole world seemed to take a confusing, disorienting shift into the wrong as she realized what that paper meant. She stumbled and stared down at her knees, vacantly bemused by the fact they seemed to be shaking.

Another pair of boots echoed in the quiet. Robin looked up and around, hands raised, ready to fend off a new attacker, ready to beat back the first person who would come at her for this deed. The man who approached was one of the guards; his rank pins, she noted absently, identified him as a captain. Robin didn't understand, didn't know why the officious man approached them with an ashen face, until he reached out and accepted the marriage certificate from Rosa.

"Elias . . ." he whispered, voice filled with damp horror. And then he turned a gaze filled with fire and a promise of pain on Robin.

He lunged for her, but Thorne was faster. He had the man flattened to the marble in a trice, big enough that it only took a single arm in the small of the man's back to immobilize him.

"I support her claim!" Thorne thundered at the

crowd. The furious muttering died out, though Robin had no idea why the support of a tinker would mean anything to them.

No other guard dared approach, dared object. Silence fell, shocked and subservient. Rosa's lips curved into a sneer as she once more picked up the paper.

"Brave Skylark," Rosa whispered in her ear. "What an amazing thing you have done. Be brave just a little longer. Just do as I say, and all will be well. Retrieve WINGS."

Robin stared into Rosa's earnest green eyes, then down at the marriage certificate Rosa had pressed against the only clean spot left on her tattered, grimy jacket. Numbly, she accepted the paper and nodded. Fingers shaking, she folded it and placed it in the pouch attached to her belt. Then she turned to face the monstrosity of the seneschal's remains.

Screwing up her courage, Robin put one boot against the seneschal's shoulder. She yanked on the pack, and the corpse shivered with the motion, a mimicry enough of life that Robin had to let go of the straps and let them fall into the pool of blood forming beside the body.

She forced herself to look at him, to really look at the clay of the man's face, to prove to herself that he was really, truly dead. She wanted to kick it until it turned into strawberry jam and raw sausage.

Instead, she turned aside, and kept her face as still as she could, tucking her fists under arms as she said, "I think I might be sick."

Robin swallowed hard to keep her stomach down where it was supposed to be. The world smelled of loosened bowels and raw meat, and Robin clamped her palm over her mouth. Then she forced herself to try again. She had to do it. She had to. Another cry of protest went up as Robin put a boot on the seneschal's corpse and tugged.

WINGS came free, and Robin, slow, aching, feeling like she'd aged a hundred years in as many minutes, redonned the pack, tying the cut straps awkwardly across her chest.

Wasn't air-worthy. Didn't matter.

It was only symbolic anyway.

Only to keep it with her. Then, loudly, over the din of the protests, Rosa whistled sharply. The room went quiet again, its occupants staring with expressions that ranged somewhere between confusion and hatred.

"Rosa? What are you doing?" Robin asked. She was interrupted by Rosa plucking the hairpin out of her chignon and holding it aloft.

"The king is dead!" Rosa shouted, and her voice rang clear and triumphant over the crowd.

Half a heartbeat behind her, Thorne echoed: "The king is dead."

Then, slowly and one by one, the weary, angry, obedient guards, with their cobalt uniforms and resentful expressions, kneeled—reluctantly, but kneeled all the same.

"No, no! I will not allow this!" the captain howled from the ground. He wriggled and snarled, but Thorne did not let him up.

"Oh, no. No," Robin said, because she suddenly understood. She knew what Rosa was about to do, and she didn't want it. "There's another way. There has to be," Robin hissed desperately, voice low because this was a sham, and an argument that Robin didn't want to be having here.

Rosa smiled at her once, sadly. "My kind, daft friend," she said, voice full of fond affection. "What any individual wants matters very little in cases such as these."

"You can't be serious!" Robin said, shifting uncomfortably. The blood and brains splattered on her coat smelled horrendous, and she desperately wanted to wipe them away, to erase the horror and the gore of these past few hours, of this moment. Instead, she folded her hands behind her back, at parade rest, in an attempt to keep her composure despite the wild beating of her heart, the roiling turmoil in her mind as she began to understand what Rosa meant.

"Think of it, Skylark!" Rosa said hastily. "Victory not only over your enemy, but against the war that has plagued your entire life. You can end it. With one word, you can end it. If you do this, if you say *ai*, this will be in your power."

Realization landed in Robin's gut like a swift and burning fist. Getting what she wanted, going home—that was the one thing that Robin Arianhod could never do. Not because she was a Sealie. Not because everyone ordered her about, and trapped her into things she didn't want, or even because she was the keeper of WINGS. It was, pure and simple, because she'd made a choice that she couldn't take back; that, even now, she didn't want to take back. Robin was who she was.

And the Skylark was the king's widow.

Cold shock splashed up Robin's spine, and she shivered all over. For the first time, she felt it, she was sure—the touch of a god. She didn't like it. But if this was what it took, then she, good soldier that she was, would fall on that wire.

Sealies do as they're told, she reminded herself.

Rosa hoisted Robin's left arm above her head again, Marriage Line on display. Robin took a deep breath, leveled her gaze at the kneeling soldiers, and thrust out her chin.

"The king is dead!" Rosa shouted one last time, her voice strong and unwavering as it bounced along the marble and glass of the second palace that was to be Robin's prison. Rosa's other hand was pressed hard over her heart, and she smiled as she looked at Robin and cried, "Long live the queen! Long live the queen! Long live the queen!"

Rosa pressed the wolf-cameo hairpin into Robin's

hand and gently nudged her toward the throne. Head high and her whole soul numb with grief, Robin crossed unchallenged to the throne. She moved on legs she thought would be shaking, but were instead firm with resolve and acceptance of the awful, strange destiny the gods had thrust upon her. She removed WINGS as she forced herself to climb the dias. Then, meaningfully, pointedly, she placed the pack on the seat of the throne. She turned to face the crowd of guards. Her guards. Her subjects. Her *people.*

She looked down at the ivory hairpin she held in one hand, bloody fingerprints marring the white shaft, cameo of the wolf facing the crowd. Once, what felt like a lifetime ago, she had wondered if hairpins held some sort of special meaning in Klonn—if they were status symbols, or held some sort of secret language. Now, she understood that Velph had marked her as his from the moment he'd put the pin in her hair back in the forest palace. That he had told the world—told everyone but her—of his intention to join with her, to add her to the royal family. That he had, in essence, already considered her his wife.

At the time, it would have infuriated her. Now, she felt . . . acceptance.

Understanding.

Nothing.

She knelt. From the murmurs of the soldiers, Robin could tell that the previous ruler would never have gone down on his knees before his people. But Robin was not Eloy. Robin was not Eliam. Robin was not, though it pained her, was not even Elias.

Rulers, kings, queens—they should serve their people. Protect them. Not the other way around.

Robin folded her hands before her, making sure the cameo of the wolf was visible. She bowed her head. She swallowed once, weary and hurting, and then, on her knees, she looked up and said: "I am the Skylark, widow of King Elias Chanlis Nutvig and, with no surviving heirs to challenge me, Queen of Klonn."

A murmur ran through the room, but nobody stepped forward to challenge her. Several people looked to Thorne, and the guard captain who silently seethed in his hold, but Rosa and Thorne, her friends, they were beaming up at Robin.

"And as my first act as . . . as queen," Robin added, voice raised and—by some gods-given miracle—not shaking, "I declare a ceasefire. Klonn surrenders. The war is over."

CHAPTER
TWENTY-EIGHT

Every funeral Robin had ever attended had been for a
colleague, or an officer or diplomat she didn't know.
She'd never had to bury someone she loved before. Al
hadn't been given a proper burial, and she wouldn't have
been allowed to attend, even if he had; she wasn't close
family. She had thought that a terrible way to grieve such
a loss, but this . . . this was somehow worse.

The night of her accidental accession to the Klonnish
throne, Robin had been kept under heavy guard in Velph's
childhood apartments. Rosa had urged her into his ridiculously luxurious bathtub, and had scrubbed her fingers
through Robin's hair, soaping, soothing, washing away the
blood that left a pink stain behind. Thorne, with the support of his sister Pulmira, who, just as Thorne had said,
turned out to be quite high-ranking in the court, spent the
night dealing with the details of cleaning up, briefing the
guards, liaising with the rest of the court, informing the
media, and—*gods, bloody omens*—drafting the articles of
surrender to send to Saskwya in the morning.

Robin had wanted to be there, had wanted to help,
but she couldn't stop staring at the blood on her hands,
on her trousers, so Rosa had sent a runner to her *zentapi*
for clothes and had bullied her into the bath. Robin knew
it was pathetic that she couldn't even wash herself, but the
glass bottles of soaps kept shaking right out of her hands.

It felt like she hadn't stopped shaking in the full week
since.

The courtyard where Elias's casket—glass-topped,

so the people could see their beloved Crown Prince one last time—and Eloy's—closed and made of an expensive, shiny wood that would hide his decayed state—had been placed had been filled with mourners for a week. Robin had cried herself to sleep beside it, out in the open air, every night, when the last of the well-wishers had departed.

Right up until the moment Robin had had to stand at the mouth of the ornate mausoleum on the far side of the square, off to the side of the main courtyard, Robin had thought it was some kind of temple or concert hall. Now, she knew it was where the bodies of the royal family were kept, forever. A museum of remains that had swallowed up all of Velph's kin before him, and was about to swallow him down its gullet, too, never to return him to her.

The mausoleum was made of the same white-and-blue marble as the throne room. It matched nicely with the bright gold silk of Robin's gown, all embossed and patterned with subtly woven larks, the same shade of gold as her circlet—which had been made swiftly for this occasion.

Doeskin gloves and her feathered goggles, the amber lenses still cracked, finished the ensemble. Robin—stuffed into a tight corset, long and hindering skirts, and the ridiculous Klonnish neckline—felt like a doll. Like a mocking representation of a widow. She was a *symbol* more now than when she was fighting for the freedom of the people and soaring across a propaganda poster.

For the Klonn did not wear black to funerals.

At a Sealie funeral, she would have worn black, and the corpse would have been burned, the ashes preserved in a box and kept among their ancestors on the family wagon, or on a mantel in the house, or scattered into the flowers of a meadow that had once been a favorite in life, to feed the flowers that feed the bees. But the Klonn preserved the bodies, as if they believed the spirit was still trapped inside them, and was not already out seeking its next life, its next flesh.

They laid out Elias's body, and Eloy's with him, inside the royal tomb, placing each on the far sides of the family wall, as though the feud that had been between them in life still carried on in death. And Robin sprinkled the entrance with honey and mead, and set a letter with her final farewells to her husband on fire. The letters were meant to convey one's last thoughts to the dearly departed, to find them on the wind, to let them leave this life happily, and resolved.

Robin—the Vigilante Queen—was the only one to burn a letter on that day. And she did so only when the rest of the service was complete, the crowd of mourning citizens had dispersed, and the rest of her royal "guests" had moved inside. Only then did she make her farewells, sprinkle the threshold, and burn the letter. Sick with grief, she held onto the corner, standing alone on the white-and-blue marble steps of the tomb, until the flames licked her fingers, the last remaining ashes of paper scattered, and it was time to go inside for the wake.

Rosa found her, hours later, in the curtained-off enclave beside the ballroom. It was a small, private space for the members of royalty to rest and recover when the rigors of being the center of attention became momentarily overwhelming. Or, as in Robin's case, where one could go if they needed to escape even one more person's exclamations over how sorry they were for Robin's loss, how stricken they were over the death of her husband, and the terrible tragedy of it being paired with the death of his brother. It had all made her want to scream.

Robin was sitting on one of the damask lounge chairs when Rosa sniffed her out, utterly crushing her new dress, and clutching a preserves jar filled with mead as though she feared it would wander off if she let it go. Considering the number of strings she'd had to pull to even convince the head cook to brew the stuff, the begging that'd had to happen, the bribes that had accompanied the copy of her mother's recipe that Robin had written out for the woman, it was entirely possible that someone might walk off with it if she were to set the jar down. Though it was three weeks too young to drink, really, and utterly vile for that very reason, it was precious. And she would be damned if she was going to see it lost.

She'd *needed* it for her own funerary rites. And now, she needed the leftovers to get her through the wake. It was the only taste of home she would get in . . . well, maybe for the rest of her life.

"So," Rosa said, swooshing over to flop onto an elaborate chaise beside Robin. "Rumor has it that the Vigilante Queen has been telling the palace servants that she wants a *zentapi* madam as her Mistress of the Glass." She arranged her skirts so they overlapped artfully with Robin's. Swathed in a dark, glimmering emerald that shaded to magenta in different light, Rosa looked nothing so much like the throat of a hummingbird. "Can I take this to mean you have forgiven me for forcing your hand?"

"Maybe." Robin offered Rosa the mead. "If, by that Glass thing, you mean that I want you as my . . . um, official best friend, or whatever they call it, then yeah. If I have to be cooped up in this palace and suffer for it, then so do you. You're the one who got me into this rudding mess. And I need . . . I need someone on my side. Someone to watch my back."

"Oh my, how they will talk. First a Saskwyan queen, and then a Mistress of the Glass who trained as a madam? How scandalous. I approve." Rosa took a sip of the mead and wrinkled her pert nose. "But not of this. This, my friend, is revolting." She handed the jar back.

"It gets better with age. But now you know how I felt

with all that milk in my tea. And it's not like any of this has been proper so far." She gestured with her free hand, encompassing the wake, the palace, their private nook, all of it into their understanding of "this." She grimaced as the motion sloshed her mead, threatening to spill its precious contents over the side.

"This?"

"I've got a dozen scrubbed-up Benne snobs out there, along with their full retinues, all trying to parlay a surrender into a full capitulation. You know, King Auden wants WINGS as part of the treaty? Not rudding likely." Robin took a sip of the mead for herself. She sucked in air through her teeth to keep from wincing at the, ah, freshness of it in front of Rosa, after having just defended it. "And they can't even wait until Velph is . . . until he . . . he's been in his tomb for two hours, Rosa. He's not even reborn yet! It's crude. I already feel like my brain is going to explode. The expense of the . . . of all of this, alone. We should be spending this money on rebuilding hospitals, or helping farmers to replant their crops, or . . . or giving the poor something to eat. Not on balls and gowns and frippery and . . . and a c-coffin made of glass and si-sil—"

"Hush," Rosa said softly, taking the jar to set the mead aside and pull Robin's hands into her lap. "Your dear Velph was beloved of the people. And once they learned what he had suffered, once they had heard your story, there was no question that this had to be an extravagant state affair."

"I miss him!" Robin croaked. "I . . . I can't . . . Rosa, I can't do this. I said I didn't want it, said I'd leave, and it broke his heart. Gods, he died thinking that I didn't want him, that I was trying to escape him. But maybe if he was here, I could have been queen with him, maybe then I could have . . . now, I can't—"

"He died loving you and knowing that you loved him, too. I know he did. Never worry on that account."

"But I can't be queen for him."

"Yes, you can, Skylark," Rosa said softly, and kissed her cheek. Then she shook her head ruefully and thumbed away the lipstick she had left behind. "You can, because you must. Because he gave you the hairpin, and his Marriage Line, and he trusted you with his people, knowing that it may have been at his side, or not."

Robin sniffled and nodded, and tried to dab at her eyes without ruining the cosmetics Rosa had insisted she wear, even knowing that her fractured lenses would make her eyes impossible to see.

"Still doesn't mean I like it."

Rosa squeezed Robin's fingers. "You may not like it, and you may not approve, but there are expectations that come with your office, and you must fulfill them. Some of those expectations might seem like excess, but believe me when I say—more even than in spying or whoring—appearances are everything when it comes to being convincing as royalty. When this is over, when the truce is negotiated, then you may turn your attention to aid and restoration. Until then, you must play the Vigilante Queen."

"But not without you."

Rosa huffed out a little laugh. "No, I dare say not. But Skylark . . . Robin . . ." Rosa wrapped her arm around Robin's shoulders, warm, supportive, comforting. "Saskwya will send you a Mistress of the Glass if you asked for one. Would you not prefer a Saskwyan?"

"A scrubbed-up Benne snob? No, thanks!"

"Then a Sealie?"

Robin snorted. "The Saskwyan war cabinet will accept that I am a former glider pilot from the Air Patrol—one look at my palms, and you can't say otherwise. But a Sealie? No way. As far as they know, their only Sealie pilot was shot down by the Coyote, and that was that. My hair is light enough now to be Benne, and my goggles hide my eyes. Nobody but you, Thorne and I know that the Skylark is Robin, and it's going to stay that way. If I ask for a Sealie, they'll know what I am, and that's worse. They'll think they can just run over the entire process and tell me what to do."

"For Sealies do as they're told?"

"Exactly. And I can't let that happen."

"Do you not see?" Rosa said warmly. "Velph chose well. You fight for your people, though you have been their queen for so short a time."

"It's the right thing to do," Robin protested.

"But you will remain the Skylark forever? For the rest of your reign?" Rosa pressed.

Robin took a breath before answering. "I don't know. Maybe forever? Maybe just until the treaties are signed? Or, I mean . . . who's next in line? Would I be leaving the country in good hands? Or would it all just happen all over again—a new seneschal whispering new poison, a new war, a new conflict?"

"You could marry," Rosa suggested haltingly. "Find a lord or lady you trust to take the mantle from you."

"No," Robin snapped. "I'm never, ever going to fall in love, ever again."

Rosa patted her hand. "I did not say that you should fall in love."

"Well, I'm not marrying, either," Robin said. "No one else is going to tell me what to do. This is one Sealie who doesn't follow orders anymore."

Rosa leaned her forehead against Robin's shoulder and laughed, trying to lighten the melancholic mood. "You are every bit the stubborn rudding idiot I would expect a Sealie to be. And believe it or not, I do, in my heart, feel that you are our best hope. A Saskwy-an queen? And the Skylark, to boot? I could not have scripted the propaganda better myself. I could not have hoped for better an arranged marriage."

"But it *wasn't*," Robin protested.

"Which is what makes it even better," Rosa assured her. "For love of the sky, you became a pilot; for love of your people, you became the Skylark; for love of your archnemesis, you joined the cause; and because he loved his people, you will love them for him. You will take up his crown and rule in his stead as the Vigilante Queen. It is the ideal fairytale."

"It's my *life*," Robin protested, and then the tears were coming again, and Robin should be ashamed that she was hiding in what essentially amounted to a back closet with a woman she'd only really known for a few short months, sobbing like a child. "I don't want to be Captain Arianhod, or the Skylark, or . . . what did you call me? Or the Vigilante Queen. I just want to be me. I want to go home and be my mama's little birdie, and my papa's pride, and . . . and my husband's widow. That's all I want."

"I know, my dear," Rosa said softly. "But your gods have other ideas for you. You can save us all. Does not matter if you are Skylark. Or Robin. You already have."

Robin thought it would be far too selfish to say, *but I don't want to*, so she just pressed her face against Rosa's breast, and wept.

When she'd cried herself out, she felt shaky and weak, and the room spun around her head. Her thoughts kept oscillating between Velph, and pity for herself, and remembering what she'd done to the seneschal. Robin had killed in the line of duty before, but never had it been so personal. Never with purpose, and, worse still, never without a void of regret, never with actual joy. Robin didn't feel guilty for what she'd done, which made her feel even worse.

The air grew heavy with a sudden sadness, with the welling of utter grief. It had been creeping up on her, every so often, when she wasn't prepared for it. Mostly, whenever she caught sight of the scar on her left palm.

She rubbed it now, tracing the cut of her Marriage Line under the leather of her glove.

"Do you wish to talk about it?" Rosa said gently. She handed Robin the jar of mead, and Robin sipped obligingly.

"I just . . . miss him so much," Robin admitted.

"It will get better," Rosa whispered. "Every day, you will miss him less. Every day, you will cherish what you had more. And you will learn to perform your new role to the best of your ability."

Robin snorted and looked away.

Rosa reached out and turned Robin's face so their eyes could meet. "You can do good here. You know that. You can win your war against war. You can do the one thing that the rest of us have fought so hard for, the thing you have yearned for."

"Ceasefire?"

"Yes."

"I could. I am. I will." She looked away again, looked at the ice-blue curtain that separated this small enclave from the rest of the ballroom. Then, after a moment, she reached out and patted Rosa's shoulder. "I'm in way over my head."

"Yes, I suspect you are," Rosa said gently.

"At least I'll have you here to kick my shins when I use the wrong soup spoon."

Rosa laughed. "Yes, you will."

"So, you'll be my Mistress of the Glass?"

"I would be honored."

"This is a stupid idea, isn't it?"

"Most likely, *ai*," Rosa agreed. "But, in honor of a stupid idea, a slightly stupid gift." Rosa reached into her seemingly magical bustle-pocket and retrieved a pair of goggles. To call them just goggles, though, was nearly an insult.

They were heavier, more ornamental than the goggles Robin currently wore, and significantly less practical than the mask they had been patterned after. Delicate copper feathers mimicked the drab brown ones Robin had glued to Al's duty goggles. They winged outward from mirrored gold lenses, which would keep Robin's eyes from being visible at all. Robin could watch without being watched in return. The buckle was heavy brass, and the fawn-colored leather surrounding the lenses was well-padded and stamped with larks. The small studs holding the goggles together were also copper, and were embedded with small chips of a precious yellow stone whose cost Robin avoided trying to calculate.

In short, they were breathtaking.

"Oh, Rosa," Robin said softly, awed. "They're perfectly . . . imposing."

"Impractical for flight, I know," Rosa admitted. "But for court . . . well, every queen needs her crown."

"Thank you," Robin said, and meant it. She turned in the settee, pulling off her Skylark goggles so Rosa could repair her ruined cosmetics with a gentle and deft hand. Then, carefully, and with as much dignified solemnity as when Pulmira had placed the small gold circlet on her for the first time, Rosa helped Robin fit the new goggles on her face. Rosa's fingers worked gently against the back of her head, and when she was done, Robin pulled back. She handed over her regular goggles, and Rosa secreted them away inside her bustle.

"I still want to keep those. They were Al's," Robin whispered.

"I will keep them safe," Rosa promised. "As your Mistress of the Glass, it is my duty. And as your friend, my privilege. *Your Majesty.*"

Robin pulled a face. "Oh, gods, don't you *dare* start calling me that."

Mama and Papa;

I am sorry to have made you worry.

I wish I could have written to you earlier, but please be reassured that I survived the crash. I'm alive. I'm well.

Well, no, I am not well. But I will be soon. I hope.

You will have received this letter and package from the hand of Captain Wade Perwink, my former pilot and the new Saskwyan ambassador in Klonn. Please don't press him for too many details, as he is sworn to secrecy about my location for all of our sakes.

Things have happened that were beyond my control. I was captured, but I won free, and have worked with the rebels in support of the woman they now call the Vigilante Queen. I wanted to come home straight away, but things have gotten complicated.

The things keeping me here are not something I can really say no to. I was hoping that once this was over, and the war was finally done, I'd be able to hang up my wings and come home to Pyria. Come home as, and be your daughter again. Just that and nothing, or no one else.

But I'm not sure if I can come back now. Maybe not ever.

All the same, I couldn't bear the thought of you not knowing.

I miss you, and I love you. I can't wait to stand in a park and stare at the sky with you, unflinching, and un-afraid. Free. Or maybe here in Klonn, if that's how it has to be. There are Sealies here, did you know? And they still roam.

The Vigilante Queen has declared that the ancestral lands of the Sealies will be returned to them, wholly, so long as they fall within the borders of Klonn. She is push-ing King Auden to do the same, to release the Sealies of Saskwya from their financial bondage and servitude, to rescind the segregation laws. It is not a perfect solution, but it is the first step toward a reconciliation—we hope.

Please keep me in your hearts, and in your prayers, and please keep my secret. Don't tell the Air Patrol that I lived—don't tell anyone. My survival must stay a secret, at least until the Vigilante Queen is firmly established, or perhaps replaced with a more suitable person of the royal blood. She hears tell that there is a man by the name of Thorne who may have connections to the throne. I think he might be a good candidate.

One day, I know, the bees will lead you to me. Wherever that is.

Your little birdie.

Postscript—I can't send you Klonnish coin to spend, but I'm told this necklace is worth twenty times what Papa makes in a year. Break it up and sell the jewels slowly. It is a gift from the Vigilante Queen. I'd say it's likely more than enough to do anything you like. Perhaps even to build a wagon and a roving hive? If you do, you would be very welcome in Klonn.

EPILOGUE

R obin coughed and shoved her work goggles up onto her forehead, only faintly amused by the curl of dark smoke that puffed by her face. The edges of the black cloud swirled into nothingness, stirred by a second violent exhale.

"Gee, thanks, WINGS," she sighed once she had her breath back. She smeared the back of her thick work glove along her cheek. It came away black with soot and mechanical grease, burnished with oily rainbows under her amber work lamp.

Her skin was hot, but it didn't feel like she'd been burnt. The faint acrid scent of singed hair lingered in the air, and she wondered how much eyebrow she had left. If that wasn't where the smell was coming from, then she must have shortened the wisps of hair that always clung to her ears when she tried to put her hair back in a messy bun.

Gently, soothingly, she patted the casing of the rocket pack splayed open on the workbench like a flayed bird.

"Look, I don't like taking you to pieces like this any more than you like being taken to pieces," Robin crooned. "But you are full up with rust and other, uh, *stuff*, and . . . just . . . I want you to be healthy, you understand? So no more spitting up on me."

The casing made the soft pinging sound she liked so much as it cooled down.

"Please?" she added, for good measure, because WINGS was the type of machine that sometimes needed a bit of sweet-talking, as well. She brushed her fingers gently across the lines of script stamped into the casing's side—Frankinese, Saskwyan, and Klonnish—digging her fingernail into one of the grooves. Velph would have teased her for talking to the pack, for calling it a "her," and for asking nicely. It would have been annoying, and haughty, and a little bit snide. And she would have given anything for him to be needling her right now.

"Keep nattering to that thing, and it might just talk back," said a voice from the doorway. Robin's heart leapt into her throat, and she whirled around, hope building against grief and—

The entire frame was blocked by Taddeus Thorne.

Not Velph.

Never again Velph.

Robin swallowed what was left of her heart and offered Thorne a shaky smile, blinking hard, forcing herself to see the person in front of her, and not the one she'd been hoping for. Not the one she would never see again.

Thorne had voted himself Robin's bodyguard, and had made her security measures his personal mission ever since . . . well, just since. He followed in her footsteps exactly like a big, mountain-sized shadow. And now he was throwing said mountain-sized shadow from the hallway onto Robin's worktop.

"Wouldn't mind if she did speak to me," Robin admitted, pulling the gas lamp closer to the worktable to dispel the shadows. She leaned over WINGS to peer at the fuel hose. It was still intact, so the small backfire hadn't happened inside the casing—ah, the output ports, then.

Robin grabbed the lamp's flexible neck and yanked it after her as she crouched at the end of the bench, staring up into WINGS's belly. "At least then she could tell me what was wrong. She's rattling something awful when I climb to cruising altitude, and that pretty song she makes when the blades are deployed is a bit strained. I'm afraid that . . . some, uh . . . you know . . . when I . . . I think some, uh . . . got into the casing, and it's all gummed up with . . ." *blood*, she wanted to say, but couldn't. *Brains. Flesh.* "You don't normally bother coming inside, though. Were you worried about the backfire? Or did you—?"

Robin turned to Thorne, and the rest of her words jammed up behind her teeth. Thorne's expression was completely poleaxed. His pale eyes rounded comically at the sight of her face, and he doubled over, wheezing with surprised mirth. He laughed like a mountain, too—rumbling, and gravelly, and shaking all over like an earthquake in the foothills.

Robin stared at the thatch of his dark, ashy hair and pursed her lips. "Har, har. I suppose I'm all-over soot?"

"Rosa will be unhappy," Thorne chortled. "You have walked out halfway through dressing again."

"No, I didn't. I—" Robin looked down at her attire to prove him wrong—and couldn't.

Her heavy oilcloth work apron had taken the brunt of the messy blast, but he was right: she was wearing her good silk stockings and bloomers, her white silk chemise, and her corset—the blue one covered in feathered embroidery that Rosa insisted she wear when she was to be squeezed into one of those Klonn dresses built to emphasize the curves Robin didn't have.

"You did."

"Apparently. But I had a thought, you know? The intake manifold could be tweaked to—oh, and of course, there's the rattling, which I think can be solved by scouring the—" Robin said. She turned back to WINGS, pushing her goggles back down over her eyes, and then paused, oilcloth gloves hovering over the pack's innards. Another thought had occurred to her, like a god had reached into her head and flicked a propeller into motion, and she clicked her teeth closed on the rest of what she'd been about to say. Instead, she added: "You didn't come in here because of the backfire."

"No, Your Majesty."

"I've forgotten something again."

"Yes."

"Something important?" Robin asked, dread knotting underneath her sternum. She pushed her gloves down her wrists and yanked them off her fingers.

"Something important."

"Hells." Robin stripped off her work apron and goggles, and laid them over WINGS's exposed innards like one would tuck a child into bed. "What?"

"The new Saskwyan ambassador arrived today. You have a carriage ride through the gardens to attend," a second, feminine and unmistakably annoyed voice sounded from behind Thorne. He gave Robin an exaggerated wink, and then stepped aside and abandoned Robin to her fate.

Madeira Rosa stood seething in the doorway, hands on her ample hips, lipstick an angry red slash across her face. "Your Majesty," she added, which was really—when coming from Rosa—just another way of saying, "*You idiot.*"

"Oh, buggering Omens," Robin said. "I'm sorry."

"You are always sorry," Rosa rejoined. She held out her hand, finger flickering at Robin in her patented *Come along, now, dear* gesture. "And yet you continue to wander off to your workshop mid-task. Robin, I swear, as your Mistress of the Glass, I will chain you to your throne if you do not begin to take this seriously. It has been *months* now—"

"I do take it seriously," Robin said, crossing the room and squeezing between Rosa's ample frame and the door-jamb. The hallway beyond was rife with stabbing yellow sunlight, and Robin winced as her eyes adjusted from the dimmer glow of her private workshop's concentrated lamplight. "And you would never chain me."

"Try my patience, and you will soon see, Your Majesty," Rosa said. "I will walk you around the palace with a golden chain attached to your wrist, like a pet bird." Rosa reached into one of the seemingly endless array of pockets she secreted into her bustles and pulled out a comb. "Now, march."

"That would be undignified," Robin said, walking down the hallway, as ordered, all the same. If there was one thing that Rosa had discovered—to Rosa's distinct advantage and Robin's disadvantage—it was that Robin had been a soldier in the Air Patrol long enough that an order barked in just the right tone would always make her body leap into motion before logical thought caught up.

Rosa reached out as Robin passed her and, with great practice, pulled on the leather thong tying back Robin's hair. The bun tumbled out. Rosa matched her pace to Robin's, and set about trying to tame the tangle of white locks into a smoothly hanging sheet, feet moving in perfect tandem to Robin's own.

Thorne followed after them like a rowboat caught in the jetty of a first-rate ship of the line, as helpless to resist Rosa's nagging as Robin was, bemusement in the lines of his eyes.

"*This* is undignified, Your Majesty," Rosa corrected. "I am sure that no other Queen of Klonn has ever had to be chased all over the palace to properly complete her toilette. Uhg! Soot! Black soot in your white hair." Is it singed from WINGS?

Rosa attacked the locks beside Robin's ears with plenty of vigor, and a handkerchief that had materialized from her bodice.

Hair smoothed, Rosa moved around to Robin's front, walking backward in her voluminous skirts and simultaneously, it seemed, putting away the comb to retrieve a damp, rose-scented cloth from her bustle (*Where was she hiding that, that it didn't leave a wet stain on the brocade?*). She used it to wipe clean Robin's face and neck, and then swapped it out for the contents of another pocket, pulling forth a fabric roll filled with what sparing cosmetics Robin would suffer. The brushes had already been dabbed in the various powders and creams and primed for immediate use, so all Rosa had to do was slip them out of their slots and attack Robin's face.

"Hey! You're getting really good at that," Robin said, eyes on Rosa's hem as she moved smoothly down the hall, hands flying across Robin's cheeks. "You used to trip all the time."

"I have had a lot of practice of late, Your Majesty," Rosa said with a smirk. The former *zentapi* madam always wore her hair pinned back in a pile of red-tinted corkscrew curls coiled at the nape of her neck. One of them had come loose and was dangling right along her nose. She kept trying to blow it aside, but it stubbornly refused to yield. Robin laughed, and pushed it back behind Rosa's ear for her. "Thank you. And do not smile. You will ruin the lipstick line."

Robin bit the insides of her cheeks and kept her mouth still as Rosa painted on the glossy, golden color that she claimed complemented Robin's bronze skin. Then, finished and apparently satisfied—for now—Rosa secreted away the cosmetics and held out Robin's court goggles.

Right, about to be seen by the rest of the hullabaloo, then, Robin thought. She paused to don them, and they resumed walking.

At the first turn in the hall, they were ambushed by a pack of companions-in-waiting, armed with underpinnings and a dress.

"Traitors!" Robin teased as a pair of sharp fingers dove in to finish the half-completed task of lacing up the wretched corset. She thought they belonged to Drienna, but there were so many companions-in-waiting, and they seemed to be kept in such constant rotation, that she couldn't be sure.

"Squeeze me all you like," Robin wheezed, "you'll never force me to have a waist."

"Careful. She may take that as a personal challenge, Your Majesty," Grier replied with a cheeky wink. They were standing to the side, Robin's belt in hand, waiting for their turn. Grier was one of the few people who had known Robin as the Skylark back in the zentapi, before she had become the Vigilante Queen. They were also one of the few who was comfortable enough to make sport with her like this.

"Just you wait," Rosa assured Robin as she helped Drienna sweep a sea of gold brocade over Robin's head. "One day, we will feed you up enough that you will lose all that desperate, wartime skinniness, and all that muscle in your stomach will turn soft and sweetly rolled."

"And then, without the upper-body strength to pilot WINGS, I'll fall right out of the sky," Robin countered, just as gently.

As Rosa had made her opinion on the queen's flittering about amid the clouds on a solo, weaponized rocket pack perfectly clear on a number of earlier occasions (that opinion being an emphatic, "stop it," to which Robin had answered, "no"), neither said anything more on the subject.

The whole cadre of companions surged back into motion, a tightly run ship at full mast, and sailed toward the reception hall. With each footstep, the pile of glimmering fabric swirling around Robin's shoulders and tripping up her feet somehow transformed into fluttering, elbow-length slit sleeves, an uncannily folded poof of a bustle, and a fitted bodice that showed off her narrow torso to great advantage, despite Rosa's attempts to fatten her up.

The toilette convoy finished just as they reached the

great white doors that separated them from the gardens. Coming into harbor now, Robin the flight mechanic had somehow been transformed into Robin the royal, resplendent in a suffocating corset and delicate, dainty shoes that pinched ever so slightly at the toes.

Robin missed her Skylark goggles, which were softer and didn't tug at her hair if it was up in an elaborate style. She missed her leather trousers and her solid, practical boots. She missed being able to roll out of bed and be ready for the day in mere minutes, instead of having to sit in front of a vanity for hours as Rosa primped and polished and positioned. She missed being treated like a soldier, instead of like a woman.

But she wasn't a soldier anymore. She was a queen, however reluctant. She had responsibilities, and expectations, and as much as it galled, Robin understood why this farce of fashion was necessary. To be taken seriously, she had to look serious. And there was nothing more serious than intimidating luxury.

That didn't stop her from paring back the spending in the palace, however, rerouting it toward better causes—charities, assistance programs, infrastructure repair, hospitals, relief aid. Over the past months, it had become something of a fashion among the court to dress in something simpler, to re-wear or re-make a gown rather than buy a new one, to boast of how many ways one had helped the needy that week. It was shallow, and effacing, nothing more than courtiers copying the trend that Robin had set, but she didn't care.

It was *working*, it was *helping*, and that's all that mattered.

The retinue paused at the door, and though Robin would have preferred to open them herself, she waited for the footman to swing it wide. *Expectations. Bah.*

Sunlight stabbed into the hall, blinding her for just a brief moment, despite the goggles. And then she was swept down the stairs toward the middle carriage in a line of three. Thorne murmured in her ear as she went, reminding her that the first carriage would hold her honor guard; the second, the ambassador and herself, with Thorne riding in the rear guard position behind the open-air cab; and the third would hold Rosa, and the ambassador's bodyguard.

Robin lingered at the bottom of the steps. The Saskwyan ambassador had his back to them, speaking in hushed tones with another Benne noble—likely his bodyguard—whom Robin couldn't see clearly. Nerves wriggled in her stomach and she resisted the urge to fiddle with tassels at the end of her fluttered sleeves. She was absolutely *dreading* this.

She'd spent her whole life being talked down to by the nobles of Benne, and now that she had finally managed to gain control of the yoke—inasmuch as a queen ever really had control—she was faced with someone who would, the moment they realized she was Sealie, do everything they could to take it away from her.

This is one Sealie who will not do as she's told. Not anymore, Robin reminded herself, gathering up her courage. The fact of her heritage had to come out, eventually. If not now, if not the moment the ambassador heard her speak, then likely when she pushed back on the allocation of the Wild Woods, or when the apiary expert she had invited to take employment at the Domed Palace arrived, or—gods of luck be on her side—when she managed to convince her parents to be among the first Saskwyan Sealies to move to Klonn with the promise of wagons and hives of their very own. One way or another, it wouldit would it would be discovered that the Vigilante Queen was Sealie; that she was Robin Arianhod, former pilot of the Saskwyan Air Patrol, thought to have been shot down over a year ago by the now deceased Coyote. And the instant he heard of it, King Auden would assume that he'd had suddenly had the good fortune, by the blessing of his All Mother, to become ruler of both nations; that Robin was a puppet who'd put herself onto the Klonnish throne for him.

I am Klonn, Robin reminded herself. I *am of these people and for these people, as much as I am Sealie. As much as Velph was Sealie. And I will do right by his home, the people, and the duty he entrusted to me. She pressed her lips together hard in an effort to disguise their trembling. But by all the gods of all my ancestors, how I wish he was here to do this beside me.*

The Saskwyan ambassador wore the flame-colored, formal uniform of a highly decorated Benne officer, rather than the bottle-green and fawn-brown she had worn during her time in the Air Patrol, and she wondered if he had ever actually served in combat. She'd requested that Auden send a veteran as liaison to help them parlay a treaty. But she realized now that she had no way to verify if her request had even been considered, let alone honored. Even if it had, this man could have been veteran of riding a desk, instead of a glider or a warhorse, and it would still technically count.

"Your Majesty?" Rosa prompted gently when Robin had hesitated too long on the final step.

"Right. Yes. Of course," Robin said, sucking in as deep a breath as the corset would allow, throwing back her shoulders, and marching toward the waiting Benne.

Behind her, Rosa muttered something about needing another comportment lesson, but she followed dutifully nevertheless. One of the footmen blasted a soft note on a silly little copper trumpet, catching the attention of the mingling crowd of coachmen, gardeners, guards, and grooms.

The ambassador waved off the other Benne noble at its sound, sending them toward the third carriage. He then took a moment to adjust the lay of his clothes, seeming to self-consciously check himself over before he turned to face her, which was far more respectful than that Robin had expected. He cared to make a good first impression, and she appreciated that. Closer up, she could see that his hair shone blond under his brimless cap, and his shoulders were broad, his figure trim—a former pilot, she decided, pleasantly surprised. Probably the son of a wealthy noble who'd never danced with the enemy—

The ambassador turned, cornflower-blue eyes shaded against the sun by his hand.

His *only* hand.

"Omens!" Robin breathed. She came to a halt so abrupt that Thorne bumped into her shoulder. "Oh, by all the gods of luck and all the omens of delight, they sent Wade."

"Who?" Rosa asked, leaning in close to whisper, flicking open a fan to hide their words from prying lip readers who might be hiding in the verge. "Wait, Wade Perwink, as in your—?"

"My pilot!" Robin said, and threw herself across the courtyard, rucking up her skirts to run straight at him.

"Your Majesty!" Thorne called as she barreled into Wade, but it was too late.

The ambassador was stunned, too afraid to do anything more than grab the Klonnish queen by the shoulder to keep her from ricocheting off his broad chest.

"I, uh, beg your pardon, Your Majesty. I don't—"

"Wade!" Robin whispered, hissing up at him, filled with fizzing delight. *A friend.* The King of Saskwya had sent to bargain on his behalf one of Robin's only Saskwyan allies, and he never even knew it. *Oh, the fool isn't going to get anything now.* "It's me!"

Wade's jaw dropped open, and his eyes popped wide. "Robin!" he gasped, though he had enough sense to keep his voice down. "*What—how . . . ?*"

Robin stepped back and grinned, grasping his hand between hers. Her own pilot's scars were hidden by her gloves, but she could still feel his through them. "I told you once, in the air—make me king and I will find a way to end the war, didn't I?"

Wade, stunned and pleased, just threw back his head and laughed.

Around them, Robin's companions scuffled and whispered behind their sleeves, confused and gossiping. The grooms were too well-trained to react, while the guards were subtly wary, glancing to one another for reassurance or their cue. Rosa, exasperated, snapped her fan shut and stepped up so she could shield this private moment from view with her body, and Thorne moved in so close—in case he was needed—that Robin felt him tread on her train.

There was a confused noise from the third carriage, the sound of someone slamming shut a door, and then the crunch of boots on the gravel path as Wade's body-guard decided it was time to actually do their job.

"Captain Perwink!" they shouted, and this voice grated up Robin's spine. "Are you okay? What is the queen—?"

Fury, clean and clear, flooded Robin's head, filling it with the angry buzz of bees. She jerked back, head whipping around, vision dark and red at the edges at the sound of that *hated*, hated voice.

"Your Maj—"

"Move!" Robin shoved her friend to the side. It was rough, and she would have to apologize later, but right now, Rosa was between her and justice. Thorne caught Rosa around the waist, and they both stumbled back a step.

"Traitor!" Robin snarled, one hand balled in her skirts so she could stalk toward the approaching Benne noble, other hand pointed, accusatory, right between their eyes.

Utterly taken aback by this wrathful accusation, Captain Catherine Renge stumbled to a stop, skidding in the gravel. Her face immediately drained of all color.

"Murderer!" Robin screeched, the dark ball of hate that had calcified in her gut when she realized she was trapped in Klonn forever cracking open and flooding her insides, crawling out of her mouth—vile, and hot, and *wonderful* in this exact moment.

"What?" Renge said, falling back a step, looking startled and confused, empty hands up in a plea of understanding. Around them, the queen's honor guard, in their ice-blue uniforms trimmed in queen's copper, closed ranks. "Me?"

"You!" Robin confirmed, and shoved her so hard Renge toppled over, still too surprised to understand exactly why the Queen of Klonn was attacking her. "Guards, hold her!"

Renge tried to scramble away, but two of the guards grabbed her arms and hauled her back to her feet. Robin was viciously pleased to see that her palms were flecked with blood from where she'd scraped them on the gravel, her hair coming loose from its perfect bun.

"What have I done?" she squealed in horror. "Your Majesty, I've just arrived. I don't—Ambassador!" She turned to Wade for help, but he remained where he was, face pointedly turned away.

This was between Robin and Renge. He wasn't going to intervene. Whether because Robin was queen, or because he already knew what Renge had done, Robin wasn't sure. She had no doubt, though, that when they'd heard report of Robin's glider going down, the heartless cow would not have been able to resist her brag.

Robin took another step forward, getting right in Renge's face. Rosa wound her arm around Robin's, trying to hold her back in as dignified a manner as possible.

"Your Majesty, peace," Rosa urged.

"Stay out of this," Robin snapped.

"Think of the implications—"

"This woman is Captain Catherine Renge," Robin said.

The name shattered against the air like crystal thrown against marble. Robin's throat burned to have uttered it. Tears, scalding and thick, choked her voice, gathered at the bottom of her court glasses, made her chin tremble.

Rosa gasped, her grip going lax in shock. Wade's eyes bounced between Renge and Robin, pity for one and spite for the other clear in his gaze. Thorne rolled onto the balls of his feet, preparing for whatever order Robin might decide to give next. And Renge, the wretched bitch, sneered at this foreign queen and her quivering hatred the same way she had once sneered at Robin as she dumped out a pot of perfectly good honey in sheer spite.

"Who?" Grier whispered, when it seemed that the horrified silence would drag on forever.

Robin swallowed hard, lifted her chin, and reminded herself that she was a queen now. She took no orders, and she was not one to be sneered at. "Catherine Renge sabotaged the glider of Robin Arianhod and Alistair Brigid, the last two Saskwyans to ever be shot down by the Coyote."

Grier gasped, and Rosa let go of Robin's arm and took a theatrical step out of the way.

"Your Majesty, please—" Renge babbled, face draining again of all color as guilt and realization set in. "You can't know that!"

"But I do," Wade growled.

"That was—I told you that in confidence!"

"In *pride*, you mean," Wade corrected her coldly. "You were drunk, and you were pleased. You were *celebrating*."

"Wade!"

"That's Captain Perwink to you!" Wade snapped. "I never wanted you in this entourage, and now I have the perfect reason to send you back."

"You can't!" Renge wailed. "I'll be shamed! I can't

show my face—"

"Not until after it's healed, at least," Wade agreed.

"Wha-what?" Renge said, words tumbling to a halt.

But it was Robin who answered. She released her skirts. She balled her fists. She pulled back an elbow.

And then, with a snarled, "This is for Al," the Vigilante Queen punched the Saskwyan ambassador's former bodyguard straight in the mouth.

Those Who Would Kill a King
(by an anonymous Klonnish poet)

In dead of night, in dead of war,
Conspirators met who numbered four.
They were those who would kill a king.

In order to force a peaceful ceasefire,
The four did meet and did conspire,
To go forth and kill a king.

The shape of the moon, and the shape of the knife,
Matched the shape of the palace, and of the life,
Taken by those who would kill a king.

They stalked the darkness, desperate and bold,
To douse his vanity, greedy and cold.
Beware, oh selfish and tyrannical king.

But alas, among the number, was one,
Who of the king's mother, was also a son.
Pity to those who would kill a king.

The fight it raged, and blood it drew,
The people's will snuffed love, it is true.
Take heed of those who would kill a king.

A Vigilante Queen prevailed,
And ended the war, and all this entailed,
And wept at night, for her love did fail.
Never provoke those who would kill a king.

Peace we were given, peace their sin earned,
And woe to those who have not this lesson learned:
For it is the people whose will may not be spurned.
Do not provoke those who would kill a king.

Acknowledgements

And here we are, for the final time in this series, at the thank-yous.

I'm going to start with the biggest, which goes to my original editor Kisa. Votch, I cannot even express in words how profoundly impressed and grateful I am to have you with me on this book. You are a jenga master, and I'm wowed at how you took scenes, paragraphs, even individual lines from previous drafts and cobbled together a working outline for the rewrites. This story is a thousand times stronger for your hard work, your input, and your thoughtful, mindful conversations with me. Your love for Velph outshines mine, and he and I are both indebted to you for attentive shepherding of his new character growth and narrative arc. Thank you for all your hard work.

Thank you to Leigh Ripka, who donated a nice chunk of change to the Snakes & Lattes annual Cantanathon Against Cancer for the right to name a character.

Thanks to Adrienne Kress, who has been my guide in this new territory that is Young Adult fiction, and to my mom, who finds typos like a heat-seeking missile.

I also want to give a massive, massive shout-out to author and animator Elizabeth Hirst (https://elizabeth-hirstblog.wordpress.com/) for the absolutely incredible work she did on the hand-animated book trailer for The Skylark's Saga. Elizabeth and I were speaking several years ago at a SF/F convention, and she mentioned how she'd like to put together a tentpole for her new animation demo reel, and said something about a music video. I mentioned that I'd been debating filming a book trailer using Victor Sierra's The Skylark's Song (http://victorsierra.net/) which was inspired by these books, and bam, suddenly we were making an animated book trailer. Elizabeth is an incredible talent, who is also generous, gregarious, and kind, and so, so hardworking. I hope you are all as thrilled and astounded by the trailer as I am.

And of course, an equally massive thanks has to go to Elize Morgan, Courtney Wolfson, and Alpaca vs. Llama, for their keen interest in an animated future for The Skylark's Saga. Fingers crossed.

And finally, thank you to you, my dears, for going on this adventure with my hero—soaring with her, laughing with her, crying with her, loving with her, and, ultimately, changing the world for the better with her. May you be inspired to save your world in your own ways in return.

"Everything that is done in this world is done by hope."
—Martin Luther King, Jr.

"It is through disobedience that progress has been made; disobedience, and rebellion."
—Oscar Wilde

Also by J.M. Frey

(Back)
Triptych
City By Night
The Dark Lord and the Seamstress, a coloring storybook
Hero Is A Four Letter Word, short story collection
"Whose Doctor?" in *Doctor Who In Time And Space: Essays on Themes, Characters, History and Fandom, 1963–2012*
"How Fanfiction Made Me Gay," in *The Secret Loves of Geek Girls*
"Time to Move," in *The Secret Loves of Geek Girls Redux*
"Bloodsuckers" and "Toronto the Rude" in *The Toronto Comic Anthology vol 2*
"The Promise" in *Valor 2*
"TTC Gothic" in *Amazing Stories vols 1-4*
Lips Like Ice, as Peggy Barnett
Time and Tide

The Accidental Turn Series
The Untold Tale
The Forgotten Tale
The Silenced Tale
The Accidental Tales, more stories from the Accidental Turn series

The Skylark's Saga
The Skylark's Song
The Skylark's Sacrifice

About the Author

Photo by Marion Voysey

J.M. Frey is an author, actor, and professional smartypants. She's appeared in podcasts, documentaries, radio programs, and on television to discuss all things geeky through the lens of academia. J.M. lives near Toronto, surrounded by houseplants because she is allergic to fur. She's a tea and wine nerd, and her life's ambition is to one day set foot on every continent (3 left!)

Her debut novel *Triptych* was nominated for two Lambda Literary Awards, nominated for the CBC Bookie Award, was named one of *Publishers Weekly's* Best Books of 2011, was on *The Advocate's* Best Overlooked Books of 2011 list, received an honorable mention at the London Book Festival in Science Fiction, and won the San Francisco Book Festival for Science Fiction.

www.jmfrey.net

www.ingramcontent.com/pod-product-compliance
Lightning Source LLC
Chambersburg PA
CBHW072044190726
48294CB00005B/1399